THE SCARLET LETTER

NATHANIEL HAWTHORNE was born in 1804 in Salem, Massachusetts, a descendant of the William Hathorne who had emigrated to New England with the first generation of Puritan settlers in 1630. Hawthorne's interest in the history and legend of his region was revealed in his early stories, which began to appear in print in the 1830s. New England Puritanism and its legacy provided Hawthorne with the means of exploring many of the themes that concerned him deeply, among them the conflict between patriarchal authority and the impulse to a variety of freedoms, including the freedom of the artist. Though he immersed himself in the early literature of New England, Hawthorne's own writings are peculiarly modern in some of their leading characteristics. One is the self-reflexiveness of narratives which make the telling a part of the tale. Another is the concern with signifying practices, with the relationships between objects (a Red Cross, a Black Veil, a Scarlet Letter) and what they come to signify.

Never willing to submit to the conventions of the realist novel, when he abandoned the short story and the sketch for longer works, Hawthorne claimed the imaginative freedom of the romance. His first—*The Scarlet Letter*—was published in 1850 and brought him immediate critical recognition, if not financial success. In quick succession he completed two more romances—*The House of the Seven Gables* (1851) and *The Blithedale Romance* (1852)—and consolidated his position as a major writer of his day. After his appointment as consul at Liverpool and Manchester in 1853 Hawthorne produced no more fiction until 1860, when *The Marble Faun* was published. Returning to Massachusetts in that year after travels in France and Italy, he struggled to finish other romances but left them uncompleted at his death in 1864.

BRIAN HARDING is a Senior Lecturer in the English Department of the University of Birmingham. He is the author of *American Literature in Context II, 1830–1865* (1982), and the editor of Hawthorne's *Young Goodman Brown and Other Tales* for the World's Classics.

NATHANIEL HAWTHORNE

The
Scarlet Letter

Edited with an Introduction by
BRIAN HARDING

Oxford   New York
OXFORD UNIVERSITY PRESS

Oxford University Press, Walton Street, Oxford OX2 6DP

Oxford New York Toronto
Delhi Bombay Calcutta Madras Karachi
Kuala Lumpur Singapore Hong Kong Tokyo
Nairobi Dar es Salaam Cape Town
Melbourne Auckland Madrid

and associated companies in
Berlin Ibadan

Oxford is a trade mark of Oxford University Press

Text © Ohio State University Press 1962
Introduction, Note on the Text, Chronology, Explanatory Notes, and Select Bibliography
© Brian Harding 1990

First published as a World's Classics paperback 1990

This Borders Books edition first published 1993

British Library Cataloguing in Publication Data

Data available

Library of Congress Cataloging in Publication Data

Data available

ISBN 0 19 251055 X

Printed in Great Britain by
BPCC Paperbacks Ltd
Aylesbury, Bucks

CONTENTS

THE SCARLET LETTER

CONTENTS

INTRODUCTION

Stigmata and Stigma in History and Fiction

WHEN public punishment was common in monarchial Europe, torture and execution had a political as well as a juridical function; they were ceremonials by means of which the power of the sovereign, injured in the commission of any crime, was seen to be reconstituted. Thus, in Michel Foucault's formulation, the body of the criminal—'displayed, exhibited in procession, tortured'—served as public support for a procedure that had begun in the obscurity of the legal process. In and on the body of the criminal, the sentence had to be 'legible for all'.[1] Foucault's theory of the legibility of the publicly affirmed sentence applies exactly to the punishment inflicted on William Prynne in the year 1637, when the Puritan polemicist had his ears completely cropped and his cheeks branded with the letters 'S' and 'L' in the palace yard at Westminster. According to Lord Finch, one of Prynne's judges in the Court of the Star Chamber, the letters branded on his cheeks signified 'Seditious Libeller'.[2] Since Prynne had written repeated attacks on what he considered the abuses of the episcopacy, some even while a prisoner in the Tower of London, it must have been self-evident to such a defender of the monarchy as Finch that Prynne was 'seditious' because in England, as in New England, at that time the term was beginning to be applied to any act that was likely to cause discontent with the government and threaten its stability.[3] In

[1] Michel Foucault, *Discipline and Punish: the Birth of the Prison*, tr. A. Sheridan (London, 1977), pp. 43; 48–9.

[2] Finch's statement is recorded in vol. 4 (1809) of *The Harleian Miscellany: Or, a Collection of Scarce, Curious and Entertaining Tracts*, p. 228. Hawthorne withdrew the 1793 edition of this work from the Salem Athenaeum in 1828 and on 6 November 1849. See Kesselring (1949). For a useful discussion of the relevance of Prynne's punishment to *The Scarlet Letter* see Isani (1972), though he draws some unconvincing parallels between Archbishop Laud and Arthur Dimmesdale.

[3] See Battis (1962), p. 216, who quotes Zechariah Chafee Jr's article 'Sedition' in the *Encyclopedia of the Social Sciences*, vol. 12 (1934).

attacking the bishops, Prynne was challenging the authority of the king, for Charles I depended on the support of the lords of the Church to maintain his position. Yet the 'criminal' quickly demonstrated that there were problems in making any public sentence legible. When he was about to undergo the branding, Prynne said to his executioner, 'Come, sear me, sear me, I shall bear in my body the marks of the Lord Jesus.' After being branded he claimed that the letters stood for 'Stigmata Laudis', punning on the name of his chief persecutor, Archbishop Laud, and the Latin *laus* (praise) so that the marks intended as badges of shame became—in the minds of Prynne and his Puritan supporters—signs of the Lord's favour.[4]

In calling his story of Hester Prynne 'The Scarlet Letter' rather than 'The Scarlet Woman', Hawthorne distinguished it from the many novels already published in the United States dealing with conflicts between young women and the rigid laws of seventeenth-century Puritan society in Massachusetts. By 1850 such fictions were numerous enough to form a novelistic sub-genre.[5] The originality of Hawthorne's narrative lies in its association between power, or authority, and signification. In chapter one—'The Market-Place'—we are told that, since men of dignity such as the Governor of Massachusetts, his counsellors, a judge, a general, and ministers of the Church were present at Hester's public punishment, 'it was safely to be inferred that the infliction of a legal sentence would have an earnest and effectual *meaning*' (emphasis added). The sentence will have the meaning intended by the judges if the spectators 'read' Hester as a letter and understand her passionate act as the signified of that signifier. But the story of the letter will prove to be a story of the difficulty of reading both letter and sentence when the authority that imposed the meaning is problematized.[6]

The Scarlet Letter is essentially a story of crime/sin and punishment. It tells of the 'ignominy' (literally, the loss of

---

[4] *Harleian Miscellany*, 4 (1809), 232–3.

[5] See McElroy (1968) and M. D. Bell (1971).

[6] Millicent Bell (1982) has an excellent discussion of 'the obliquity of signs' in *The Scarlet Letter*.

name) of a woman who has broken scriptural and statutory law
in a community dedicated to the maintenance of the authority
of the law. Since the central and overarching concern of the
narrative is with authority—with the ultimate source of all
authority and the relationship between that source and the
men who are empowered to act as its mediators—the
characters of those mediators (and the fact that they are men,
not women) must be significant. In *The Scarlet Letter* the
magistrates and ministers named are historical figures, for the
narrator of the fictional story of Hester Prynne acts the part of
an historian, setting the account of her punishment in the
context of the history of England as well as New England. The
allusion to the death of Governor Winthrop in the second
scaffold scene, which takes place seven years after the opening
events, sets the date of Hester's appearance in the market-place
at 1642, little more than a decade after the beginning of the
Great Migration that peopled the Massachusetts Bay colony
with settlers. Yet the narrator's strategy in telling his story is to
conceal as much as to reveal. He makes historical allusions
that seem significant, but he declines the role of authoritative
commentator or interpreter, leaving the reader to speculate on
their meaning.

Richard Bellingham, for example, is an important figure in
this story of Puritan justice, for he is said to be the chief
magistrate when Hester Prynne is sentenced to wear her badge
of shame. Among his professional associates before he left
England to become a major figure of authority in the
Massachusetts Bay colony, the narrator names Bacon, Coke,
Finch, and Noye. This naming could appear to be nothing
more than historical documentation, included to give the
weight of history to the fictional Bellingham, but it cannot
surely be mere chance that leads the narrator to name two
merciless persecutors of William Prynne among the English
lawyers Bellingham knew. Finch and Noye not only particip-
ated prominently in the trials and punishment of Prynne, they
were also eminent men of law who used their expertise and
their position to interpret the laws of England in favour of King
Charles I in his struggle with parliament, thereby earning the

detestation of the parliamentarians. Coke, in contrast, was a champion of the rights of the people against royal prerogative, but his personal rivalry with Bacon, and his persecution of Sir Walter Raleigh, blemished even his record of impartiality.[7] Judgements, and the judges who make them, are repeatedly foregrounded in *The Scarlet Letter*. Roger Chillingworth, we are told, began his investigation of Arthur Dimmesdale 'as he imagined, with the severe and equal integrity of a judge' only to become the victim of a 'terrible fascination' with his quest for 'mortality and corruption' (p. 129). This apparently simple and self-evident antithesis between integrity and corruption is offered to the reader in 'the Leech and His Patient' (chapter 10) but by this time the text has subverted the moral scheme that sets judge and criminal clearly apart. In fact, the text has problematized the very notion of justice.

In the text Richard Bellingham is named as the Governor of Massachusetts in the year when Hester Prynne is judged and sentenced, but in 1642 the historical Bellingham was not governor, as Hawthorne certainly knew, since a major source of his knowledge about the early history of the colony was Governor John Winthrop's *Journal*.[8] In his *Journal*, Winthrop told the story of Bellingham's marriage, in the previous year, to a woman who was already promised to a friend of his. Obtaining her consent, Bellingham had performed the marriage ceremony himself, and had done so with unseemly haste, for he had ignored the publishment law. This flagrant disregard for the niceties of the law when they interfered with his will and his pleasure was also demonstrated in his refusal to leave the bench when 'the great inquest presented him for

[7] See below, note to p. 106. Alfred S. Reid (1955) believes that the significance of the judges named lies in the fact that each was involved with the infamous Overbury murder case, a sexual scandal that revealed the corruption of the Jacobean court. For further comment on Reid's theory, see below, note to p. 127.

[8] Governor John Winthrop's journal has been published in an annotated edition under the title *Winthrop's Journal: 'History of New England 1630–1649'*, ed. J. K. Hosmer (1906; 1959), hereafter abbreviated to JHNE. It was available to Hawthorne in an 1825–6 edition with the title *The History of New England from 1630 to 1649*.

breach of the order of the court'. In a bizarre way, Bellingham's behaviour is a mirror image of that of the Lords Bishop at Prynne's trial before the Court of the Star Chamber. As Prynne and his co-defendants claimed, the bishops were both accusors and judges. Bellingham was both accused and judge; or rather, he used his presence on the bench to prevent the other magistrates from proceeding. His defence against the charges that he had acted against the practice of the country in marrying himself and against the order of the court, in not publishing the contract where he lived, was that he had acted from the strength of his affections. For this, and *not* because of the 'chances of a popular election', as the narrator of *The Scarlet Letter* would have us believe, Bellingham was excluded from office in the year 1642.

The narrator stresses the representative character of Bellingham. He is, we are told, a fit leader of the Puritan community because in him 'the stern and tempered energies of manhood, and the sombre sagacity of age' have triumphed over the 'impulses of youth' (p. 64). With the other eminent characters who look down on Hester from the balcony above the scaffold, Bellingham is described as 'wise and virtuous' but quite incapable of 'sitting in judgment on an erring woman's heart'. The Puritan dignitaries are 'doubtless, good men, just, and sage', but it is to the 'warmer heart of the multitude' that Hester feels she must look for sympathy. Since sagacity and justice are twin themes here, Hawthorne's deliberate historical mistake[9] in making Bellingham governor at the time of Hester's sentencing must call into question the *narrator*'s stated belief that both qualities belong with age and belong to the male sex.

The governor and the eminent men who surround him on the balcony in the market-place are 'distinguished by a dignity of mien, belonging to a period when the forms of authority were felt to possess the sacredness of divine institutions'. Later

[9] The phrase—and the theory—are derived from Colacurcio (1985). In this indispensable article he argues that the deliberate suppression of the historical fact of Bellingham's disgrace is an index of Hawthorne's concern with Puritan attitudes to sexuality.

in the story we are told that the 'fathers and founders of the commonwealth' considered it their duty to assume the 'outward state and majesty' (p. 230) appropriate to public office in Massachusetts. In fact, the early leaders of the colony felt the need to insist on the dignity of their offices, and felt it acutely, precisely because they could not rely on a respectful, subservient attitude in the colonists. Since authority was not hereditary in early Massachusetts, the men in positions of authority—the magistrates—found that they could not assume deference in those over whom they ruled; they had to demand it and even punish those who asserted their equality with their judges.[10] Governor Winthrop was particularly insistent that the magistrates should behave solemnly in public. Dignity, then, was part of the political strategy of those patriarchs who, like Winthrop, resisted the democratizing forces within New England society. Yet these were men who, if they had stayed in England in the 1640s, would almost certainly have played their part in challenging the 'forms of authority' associated with the king and with his bishops. They were, in fact, allies of the very men who challenged the prerogative courts in the years of intensifying struggle between the king and parliament.[11] In his historical essay 'Main-Street', which was first published in 1849 and was to have been republished as a companion piece to *The Scarlet Letter*, Hawthorne told his readers that, in its early years, New England was 'the essential spirit and flower of that which was about to become uppermost in the mother country'.[12] In the 1640s that spirit was the spirit of revolution, which was about to manifest itself in the English Civil War. In the same passage in 'Main-Street' the martial spirit of the New England train-bands is linked with the military prowess of Cromwell's Ironsides. The association clearly identifies the independent spirit that led some English Puritans to emigrate with the anti-authoritarianism of those Puritans who remained in England and temporarily brought down the institution of monarchy.

[10] See Breen (1970) for a discussion of attitudes to authority in the Massachusetts Bay colony. [11] See Haskins (1960).
[12] See below, note to p. 30, for further discussion of 'Main-Street'.

INTRODUCTION

Yet the independent spirit of Puritan leaders did not necessarily imply a belief in toleration. To most of them, toleration was a weakness, not a virtue, for they considered it subversive of morals. In the words of Richard Baxter, one of the English Puritan theorists, 'the more Theocratical, or truly Divine any Government is, the better it is'.[13] As a consequence, so he argued in his A *Holy Commonwealth* (1659), 'in a true Theocracy, or Divine Common-wealth, the Matter of the Church and Common-wealth should be altogether or almost the same'. In England, even under Cromwell, this was not a realizable prospect, but in Massachusetts, where government was in the hands of 'Visible Saints',[14] it did seem to the early colonists that—as the narrator of *The Scarlet Letter* puts it—'religion and law were almost identical' (p. 50). Both were 'so thoroughly interfused' in the character of the people that 'acts of public discipline' such as Hester's punishment became 'venerable and awful'.

The 'righteous colony of the Massachusetts', as the beadle calls it, was actually established by a royal charter which granted land in the New World to a joint-stock company, to be managed by men chosen annually by the freeman of that company. Technically, a plantation governed by an elected General Court could not be called a theocracy, but in a more profound sense it could, because the governor (Winthrop) believed that his authority was 'from God' although he was chosen by the people. In this Winthrop was representative of his generation of Puritan leaders. They believed, as he did, that 'my charge is of the Lord' who 'hath called me to this work', and consequently that they were 'Gods upon earthe'.[15] As Christopher Hill says, this was an age when authority was being challenged, yet the forces challenging it maintained their belief in the sacredness of authority.[16]

If authority was 'from God' then any attempt to undermine

[13] Quoted in Schneider (1930; 1958), p. 15.
[14] Schneider (1930; 1958), pp. 16–17.
[15] For the Puritan belief that authority was 'from God', see Battis (1962), p. 71. Winthrop's words on magistrates are quoted in Haskins (1960), p. 120.
[16] Hill (1961; 1964), p. 3.

it—or the structure of the society on which it depended—was regarded as criminal. In the 'Bodie of Liberties' drawn up in 1641 to protect the citizens of the colony from the arbitrary exercise of power and, in particular, to limit the discretionary powers of the magistrates, death was prescribed not only for such crimes as adultery, idolatry, and witchcraft, but also for 'the treacherously or perfidiously attempting the alteration or subversion' of the fundamental frame of polity adopted by the colony.[17] Had Hester's radical opinions been known to the authorities, to them she would have been guilty of precisely such subversion.

An apparently casual, or even jocular, allusion to a dispute concerning 'the right of property in a pig'[18] clearly indicates the narrator's awareness that the rule of the godly in the Puritan colony had economic and social implications. In 1642, when a certain Mrs Sherman accused the wealthy and influential Captain Keayne of stealing her pig, most of the elected members of the General Court (deputies) sided with her, while the governor and the *ex officio* members (assistants) supported the captain, regarding the charge against him as a stirring of socially subversive forces. As Hawthorne was well aware, the history of New England could be read as the story of the emergent democratic spirit in its struggle against traditional authority within the colonies as well as outside them; against privilege in Massachusetts as well as pretensions to authority exercised from England.[19]

An even briefer historical allusion—this time to the Pequod War in which Bellingham is said to have played a part—suggests that the narrator perceives the relevance of that example of the brutal exercise of Puritan power to the story of

[17] Quoted in Hildreth (1849), p. 278. Hildreth gives a detailed account of the Bodie of Liberties.

[18] See below, note to p. 101, for Hawthorne's sources on this subject.

[19] George Bancroft, the American historian whose account of the development of freedom in early Massachusetts is recommended to young readers in Hawthorne's *True Stories from History and Biography* (1841; 1852), stressed the importance of the idea that all authority resides in the people. Hawthorne would have found this emphasis in vol. 1 (1837) of Bancroft's *History of the United States, from the Discovery of the American Continent*.

Hester Prynne's punishment. In 1637 the white settlers massacred numbers of the Pequod tribe in the conviction that they were carrying out God's purpose by ridding the land of the heathen. There are various estimates of the number of old men, women, and children butchered in the Pequod fort on the site of the present Mystic, Conecticut. Winthrop put the total at one hundred and fifty. Neither he, nor any of the men who recounted the incident in the histories written at the time or soon after, expressed any regret or remorse for the slaughter. A striking feature of the violence—to modern readers—is likely to be its specifically anti-female implication. In the words of one recent commentator, the genocide at Mystic enacted an image of 'prohibited and profane' female sexuality.[20] Significantly, it occurred in the very year in which the Puritan authorities moved to crush the Antinomians, who—like the Pequods—were seen to represent a threat to the purity of Puritan religion.

Male Judges and Female Outlaws

The Antinomian controversy brought to a head the question of spiritual authority in Massachusetts. In the unsympathetic opinion of Governor Winthrop, the Antinomians, as the name suggests, felt themselves not 'bound to the law'; they did not consider it a sin to break the law because, in their view, 'our sinnes they are inward, and spirituall, and only are against Christ' (JHNE, I 246). In other words, the Antinomians distinguished categorically between the laws on the statute book, which they considered man-made, and the inner, or spiritual, laws which the individual alone could recognize as God's. Winthrop's account of the Antinomians, both in his journal and in his *Short Story of the Rise, Reign, and Ruin of the Antinomians* (1644), is concerned mainly with Ann Hutchinson, the figure who is twice associated with Hester Prynne in *The Scarlet Letter*, where she is described as 'sainted' by the narrator. To Governor Winthrop, Mrs Hutchinson was

[20] Kibbey (1986), p. 110.

INTRODUCTION

no saint; she was a dangerous and 'seditious' woman whose
pride was such that she dared to judge the ministers of the
Church by her own spiritual standards. Winthrop was
particularly concerned because her followers, who included—
he admitted—some of the wisest and most godly members of
the community, 'looked at her as a Prophetesse' (JHNE I, 252)
and consequently considered her doctrines to be inspired. Her
two most dangerous ideas, according to Winthrop, were: that
the person of the Holy Ghost dwells in the justified person; and
that sanctification is no evidence of justification. If the second
doctrine now seems too technical to affect public order, it did
not seem so in 1637, for it meant, in effect, that outward
behaviour (good works) provided no evidence concerning the
condition of the soul and no proof of the soul's salvation. The
only proof Mrs Hutchinson acknowledged was that provided
by the presence of the Holy Ghost within, but what to her was
evidence of God's presence was proof of her offence according
to her judges. At her trial she had almost cleared herself of the
charges brought against her when she threw away her case by
claiming immediate revelation. She believed, so she said, that
she could hear the voice of God speaking directly to her soul.
To the men who represented spiritual authority in Massachusetts, the mediation of clergy and scriptures was essential.

So great was Ann Hutchinson's confidence in her inner
light that she believed she could tell which of the ministers of
the Church were 'elect' and which of them merely performing
their duties under the convenant of works. Actually, in Mrs
Hutchinson's opinion, few of the ministers were 'sealed with
the spirit'. John Cotton had the seal of the spirit, but the Revd
Mr Wilson—as she told her followers—did not. To Winthrop,
such judgments were clear indications of her arrogance. He
was not prepared to take any cognizance of this 'inner light'
and he was outraged by the lack of respect towards those who
'went not her way'. Worse still, Mrs Hutchinson made public
her views on the clergy, for she had the effrontery to evaluate
as well as interpret the sermons of the ministers when she held
her own meetings and addressed her audiences on spiritual
matters.

In November 1637 Winthrop told Ann that the magistrates were bound to restrain her because she had arrogated to herself powers that rightfully belonged to the ministers. She replied: 'If you have a rule for it from God's word you may.' This brought the angry retort: 'We are *your* judges, not you *ours* and we must compel you to it.' The issue could not have been clearer. To Governor Winthrop, who conceived true (civil) liberty on the analogy with a wife's willing submission to the authority of her husband,[21] Mrs Hutchinson's self-reliance was a challenge to the whole frame of Puritan polity. The commandment she had broken, he told her, was the fifth, which commands us to obey and honour father and mother, by which is meant all in authority. Emphasis on parental authority was so strong in seventeenth-century Massachusetts that many condemned criminals attributed their wickedness to a lack of proper family discipline earlier in their lives,[22] so Winthrop was here merely expressing a common assumption about the relationship between disrespect and sinfulness; but Ann made her position plain when she declared, on leaving the Assembly that had been called to pass judgment on her, 'The Lord judgeth not as man judgeth, better to be cast out of the church than to deny Christ' (JHNE, I, 251).

Hester Prynne is not, of course, to be equated with Ann Hutchinson, although she is associated with the 'sainted' outlaw by the narrator of *The Scarlet Letter*. One obvious difference between the historical and the fictional women is that the former's 'crime' was not sexual. Ann was not accused of adultery; the commandment she had broken was, Winthrop asserted, the fifth. Yet this distinction is less definite than it at first seems, for—to the Puritan mind—there were sexual implications to Ann's Antinomianism. Edward Johnson, for example, in his *Wonder Working Providence*, wrote of 'silly

---

[21] The exchange quoted comes from Winthrop's *Journal*, vol. 1, p. 194. His speech on liberty, with the wife's willing submission to her husband's authority as the model of civil—as opposed to natural—liberty, was made in 1645. It is recorded in vol. 2 of the *Journal*, pp. 237–9. The fullest account of the Antinomian crisis is to be found in Battis (1962).

[22] On parental authority see Faber (1977–8).

women laden with diverse lusts' who claimed higher esteem
than those (men, of course) 'indued with power and authority'
from God to preach his word.[23] To the Puritan leaders,
evidently, a proper submissiveness in matters of belief was the
only acceptable behaviour for women; to reject authority in
spiritual matters could only indicate a lack of order in one's
emotional life.

A more obvious difference between Hester and Ann is that
the former makes no overt, or public, challenge to the moral
and spiritual authority of her judges. Instead, she seems to
accept their verdict on her passionate act, regarding it as evil
and herself as guilty. She determines to stay in Boston because,
we are told, she recognizes it as 'the scene of her guilt' (p. 80)
as well as her punishment. There is no suggestion here that she
believes her adulterous love is justified by its intensity or
spontaneity. Moreover, Hester's anxieties about Pearl obviously
derive from her own guilt. She fears the wildness she sees in
Pearl's resistance to all rules because she attributes the
'disorder' in her offspring to the fact that 'in giving her
existence, a great law had been broken'. (p. 91) Noting that
Hester refers to her passionate act as a sin no less than nine
times in the story, John McWilliams has argued that too much
has been made of Hester the romantic rebel, the Lawrentian
dark lady.[24] In the text, according to this argument, she is only
intermittently resentful of the power of the community, nor is
she consistent in her rejection of its moral judgement. Her
Puritan upbringing in England and her resultant conventional
piety (she teaches Pearl the Westminster Catechism, with its
uncompromisingly dogmatic Calvinism) are obviously at odds
with her passionate nature, but it is only when she is in the
forest that the wildness in Hester triumphs over her conventional and submissive self.

McWilliams's argument is convincing if Hester Prynne is
read as a character in the conventional sense, one whose
motives can be adequately decoded and whose behaviour has
sufficient consistency for the reader to recuperate a convincing

[23] Johnson (1959 edition), p. 28.
[24] McWilliams (1984), pp. 65–6.

fictional personality from the text. But there are two sets of
problems involved in responding to Hester as a character. One
is the ambivalence of her comments. When, for example, she
rejects the Revd Wilson's offer to take the scarlet letter from
her breast in exchange for her revelation of her lover's name,
she exclaims 'Never! . . . It is too deeply branded. Ye cannot
take it off' (p. 68). Her comment can be taken as evidence of
her submission to the judgement of the ministers and
magistrates, since they determined her sentence, but it can just
as well be interpreted as a declaration of her indifference to all
laws except those of the heart. No mere minister of the church
can remove a mark that is 'branded' on her by her own
suffering. She might intend to say that, once her sacred
passion has been vilified by public and external moral
judgement, the psychic wound cannot be healed by any
merely public gesture.

Equally problematic for Hester's 'character' is the inconsistency which makes it difficult for the reader to know what her
views are. We shall return to this when we consider her
association with the heathen wilderness, but a deeper cause of
uncertainty about Hester's significance in the text of *The
Scarlet Letter* is the elusiveness of the narrator's own moral
position and his equivocation on the subject of Hester's sin.
Presumably, it is the narrator who comments on the inscrut-
ability of a providence that produces a 'lovely and immortal
flower' (Pearl) from the 'rank luxuriance of a guilty passion'
(p. 89), but we cannot be sure; possibly he is merely reporting
Hester's feelings.

In the opening pages of the romance the description of
Hester Prynne stresses her monumental dignity. In presenting
her thus the narrator distances Hester from any suggestion of
sexual promiscuity, even though it is clear that she has 'fallen'.
What is more, the apparently inappropriate, or at least
gratuitous, association of Hester with the Virgin Mary—in
'The Market-Place'—clearly adds to her significance and
stature even though the narrator states that the hypothetical
(and, in historical terms, improbable) Papist in the Puritan
crowd would have been reminded of the divine mother by

contrast with the human sinner. In whatever way the reader responds to this allusion, an association has been made with the most sacred female figure in western culture. What is more, a letter which was intended to stand for one word—the letter 'A'—has been momentarily replaced by an icon.[25] It is consistent with this narrative strategy that when Hester and Pearl visit the governor's house the bond-servant who opens the door to them should 'perhaps' deduce from 'the glittering symbol in her bosom, that she was a great lady in the land'. The account of the servant's awe at the sight of the letter reminds us that the 'A' is a signifier whose signified is determined by and for the Massachusetts Puritan community in the 1640s. The bond-servant is a free-born Englishman and a newcomer to Boston. If he can read, he will *not* read the letter as the Puritan system assigns meaning to it. His response must remind the reader of the narrator's own reaction when he discovered the rag of scarlet cloth in the attic of the Custom House. Convinced that there was 'some deep meaning' in the mystic symbol, he at once decided that the letter had signified 'rank, honor, and dignity' in past times, though he was unsure what that rank had been. When he read Pue's manuscript, he quickly discovered that—to those who imposed the sentence on Hester—the letter 'A' signified *dis*honour. In the text, therefore, that system of signification is problematized, and with it the whole system of moral certainty that produced it.

To Bellingham, Hester Prynne is a 'scarlet woman, and a worthy type of her of Babylon' (p. 110). The allusion is to Revelation 17: 3–5. There, the woman dressed in scarlet is—according to the words written on her head—the 'mother of harlots and of earth's abominations'. The text on which Bellingham is drawing was a text used by Protestants to defame the Roman Catholic Church. In alluding to it, Governor Bellingham is reducing Hester to the status of a type rather than an individual. As the narrator tells us, in wearing the letter Hester Prynne will lose her individuality and will become 'the general symbol at which the preacher and

[25] Gervais (1979), and see below, note to p. 56.

moralist might point, and in which they might vivify and embody their images of woman's frailty and sinful passion' (p. 79). This happens graphically at the governor's hall, when Hester's image in the polished breastplate is so distorted by the convex surface that 'the scarlet letter was represented in exaggerated and gigantic proportions, so as to be greatly the most prominent feature of her appearance' (p. 106). The explicit theme in this episode is the moral state of the infant Pearl, which is linked by the Puritan minister to her knowledge of the catechism. In refusing to make the proper response to the orthodox Mr Wilson's question concerning her maker, Pearl is refusing to acknowledge the heavenly father from whom governor and magistrates derive their authority. On that authority depends the effectiveness of Hester's sentence.

The sentence will have an effectual meaning for the Puritan community if the signifier (the letter) and the signified (the never-written word 'Adulteress') remain in fixed relationship. If this remains constant, Hester will be the 'text of the discourse' whenever there is a minister present to read the letter. But 'many people refused to interpret the scarlet A by its original signification. They said that it meant Able; so strong was Hester Prynne, with a woman's strength' (p. 161). The people who refuse to read the letter as the judges intended do so because they respond to Hester as a woman rather than as a 'type', as a sign, or as a text. In thus 'misreading' the letter they are subverting the system of law based on the belief that the authority of the lawmaker is 'of God'. The people of Boston do so spontaneously and unselfconsciously, for they act, as the narrator tells us, from the heart. So, too, does Arthur Dimmesdale when he allows the suppressed wildness in his nature to speak out and calls Hester his 'better angel' (p. 201). The strategy of subversion, however, is the narrator's, for it is the narrative itself that undermines the stability of the system of signs by which the values of the Puritan theocracy are maintained.

Hester herself, as we have seen, appears to submit to the judgement of the Puritan patriarchs and to acknowledge her 'sin', but her claim—made seven years after the sentencing—

that what she and her lover did 'had a consecration of its own'
(p. 195) reverses all that has gone before and leaves no doubt
that she appeals from the level of the iron laws of the Puritans
to the 'higher' law of her own heart. Appropriately, Hester's
declaration of faith in the Holy Spirit within—in the erotic as
the manifestation of the true self—[26] is made in the forest, or
wilderness, that is the antithesis of Puritan Boston throughout
the story. Hester's years of outlawry—of existence outside the
Puritan system of values—have taught her to look with a
critical eye at 'the clerical band, the judicial robe, the pillory,
the gallows, the fireside, or the church' (p. 199). Her lack of
reverence for the whole interlocking structure of 'god-given'
authority and social conventions (customs) is such that the
narrator links her with the very epitome of wild lawlessness—
the Indian.[27] In this she contrasts vividly with Dimmesdale,
who is both by temperament and profession 'trammelled' by
the 'regulations, [the] principles and even [the] prejudices' of
the system to which he belongs. Arthur's sin—his act of
adultery—was not, in the words of the narrator, a 'sin of
principle': it was a 'sin of passion'. Chillingworth rightly
suspects that Dimmesdale has 'done a wild thing' in 'the hot
passion of his heart' (p. 137), but there is never any doubt that
intellectually Arthur Dimmesdale is a thoroughly submissive
member of the Puritan community and depends on 'generally
received laws' (p. 200).

In 'Another View of Hester' (chapter 13), the scarlet woman
is credited with a 'freedom of speculation' that, to the
seventeenth-century Puritan patriarchs ('our forefathers' is the
narrator's term for them), would have been 'a deadlier crime
than that stigmatized by the scarlet letter', had they been aware
of it. The word 'crime' makes the point unequivocally: as we
have seen, such speculation was an offence against the civil
powers. At this stage of his narrative, the elusive and

[26] See Baym (1973), p. 22, for a clear statement of the opposition between
the erotic and the institutional.

[27] On the links between Hester's passion and the wildness of the
Indians—and generally on the association between women and repressed races
in nineteenth-century American fiction—see Herzog (1983).

sometimes equivocal narrator speaks plainly. He gives more weight to the association between Hester Prynne and Ann Hutchinson than he did at the beginning of his tale. Hester's Antinomianism is made explicit: 'The world's law was no law for her mind' (p.164). Though fulfilment in motherhood means that she will not become the foundress of a religious sect as Ann Hutchinson did—a 'prophetess' whose words would 'undermine the foundations of the Puritan establishment'—Hester's speculations are radical enough, for she imagines the destruction of the 'whole system of society' and its building up anew. At issue here is the relationship between God's law and man's systems of authority. Her speculations involve an essential modification of 'the very nature of the opposite sex, or its long hereditary habit, which has become like nature'. In other words, they concern the relationship between principle and prejudice, or custom.

The narrator's comment on Hester Prynne's 'freedom of speculation' links it with the intellectual emancipation taking place in Europe in the years in which the story is set. The brief, and tantalizing, comment on the spirit of the age reminds us that the years between 1642 and 1649 (between the opening and closing scaffold scenes in *The Scarlet Letter*) were those in which the institution of monarchy was challenged and temporarily overthrown in England. To read the letter in the context of English history is to keep in mind that the first battle of the Civil War (Edgehill) took place in 1642, when Hester mounted the scaffold, and that Charles I was beheaded in 1649, the year in which Arthur Dimmesdale made his public confession from the scaffold in the Boston market place. One implicit (or veiled) theme of Hawthorn's story is revolution—a topical theme in 1849, the year in which *The Scarlet Letter* was begun, for the previous year was the Year of Revolutions in Europe: revolutions against monarchy whose progress was followed with keen interest in the United States. The narrator's anachronistic use of the term 'scaffold'[28] links the story of Hester with events in France at the end of the eighteenth

[28] See Reynolds (1985), pp. 58; 63, for the importance of the term 'scaffold'.

century for he tells us that the Puritan scaffold was part of a penal machine considered to be 'as effectual an agent in the promotion of good citizenship, as ever was the guillotine among the terrorists of France' (p. 55). The irony of the collocation lies in the difference between the Puritan conception of citizenship (membership of a holy commonwealth) and the atheistic philosophy that informed the revolutionary French republic.

Historical allusions or references provoke the reader to speculate, but again the narrator does not offer guidance for those speculations. The scholar who has done most to alert us to the importance of 'revolutions abroad' in the text of *The Scarlet Letter* and who has most thoroughly discussed Hawthorne's readings in European history comes to the conclusion that the narrator disapproves of Hester when she challenges the social order of the community and the spiritual order of the universe. In this reading the narrator rejects Hester (and Dimmesdale when he is affected by Hester's ideas) because he sees himself as a member of an *ancien régime* toppled by revolutionary violence. Reading from the allusions to the guillotine in 'The Custom-House' to the account of Dimmesdale's suffering on the scaffold in *The Scarlet Letter*, Larry Reynolds not only argues that Hester loses the narrator's sympathy when she becomes a radical thinker but also asserts that the narrator's biases closely resemble those of Nathaniel Hawthorne.[29] Reynolds's royalist reading of the text owes something to his knowledge that Hawthorne read Alphonse de Lamartine's *History of the Girondists* (translated from the French in 1847) and found in it a sympathetic treatment of the doomed Louis XVI, with a particularly moving account of his execution. Very probably Hawthorne did sympathize with the royal victim, and quite possibly Hawthorne's use of the 'guillotine' jibe at the Whigs (not his own invention) gains added point from his knowledge of Lamartine; but the text of *History of the Girondists* relates to the text of *The Scarlet Letter* more directly, for Lamartine interpreted the French Revolution

[29] Reynolds (1985). Forceful 'conservative' readings are also offered by Ziff (1964) and Lang (1987).

as a rebellion of the spirit of philosophy against the traditional authority vested in kingship—a rejection of the mysteries of monarchy. According to Lamartine, the throne was not challenged by sedition but by philosophy itself. Royalty fell because 'institutions grown old and exhausted' were challenged by 'fresh institutions full of sap'. What is more, Lamartine traces the impulse of rebellion back to 'Guttemberg' (sic) who, without knowing it, was the 'mechanist' (*mécanicien*) of a new world because he made the independence of reason inevitable. 'Every letter of this alphabet which left his fingers, contained in it more power than the armies of kings and the thunders of pontiffs.'[30] If Hawthorne had wanted an epigraph for *The Scarlet Letter*, he could hardly have found a better one, for his story demonstrates vividly the power of a letter of the alphabet.

But our understanding of Hester Prynne's significance does not depend solely on her claim for the consecrating power of her passion or on her association with an unspecified intellectual emancipation. In the 'Conclusion' we are told that, earlier in her life, Hester had believed herself to be the prophetess of a 'new truth'. Characteristically, the narrator does not tell us what that new truth was, or was to be, though—if it was to establish the whole relation between men and women 'on a surer ground of mutual happiness'—it must obviously have had something to do with sexual equality. Hester has come to recognize that she cannot be the destined prophetess because she is 'stained with sin'. In her belief that the prophetess must be above moral reproach, as in her

[30] Lamartine (1847), pp. 13–14. Lamartine's tribute to Gutenberg's importance was anticipated by Andrew Marvell in *The Rehearsal Transpros'd* (1672), a work written in defence of dissent against absolute power in religion: 'O *Printing*! how hast thou disturb'd the Peace of Mankind! that Lead, when moulded into Bullets, is not so mortal as when founded into Letters! . . . The first Essay that was made towards this Art, was in single Characters upon Iron, wherewith of old they stigmatized Slaves and remarkable Offenders; and it was of good use sometimes to brand a Schismatick. But a *bulky* Dutchman diverted it quite from its first Institution, and contriving those innumerable *Syntagmes* of Alphabets, hath pestered the World ever since with the *gross Bodies of their German Divinity*.' Hawthorne read *The Rehearsal* in 1831 (see Kesselring, 1949). I am grateful to my colleague Tony Davies for calling my attention to the relevance of Marvell's work.

conviction that such a prophetess will come, Hester anticipates a contemporary of Hawthorne, and an acquaintance of his, who was considered to be a prophetess of a new order by those (mainly women) who listened to her ideas. This was Margaret Fuller, who had held inspirational 'Conversations' for classes of women in Boston from 1839 to 1843 and who had published a major statement on the relationship between the sexes in the transcendentalist *Dial* magazine in 1843, when she edited that periodical of immense ideals and small circulation.[31] In 'The Great Lawsuit: Man *versus* Men; Woman *versus* Women', as the article was called, Fuller stated that 'those who would reform the world must show that they do not speak in the heat of wild impulse; their lives must be unstained by passionate error; they must be severe lawgivers to themselves' (*Dial*, IV, 29). The idea that women reformers could be lawgivers to themselves puts Fuller clearly in the Antinomian tradition, and she had no doubt that women could be prophetesses, for she cited as evidence the respect with which great and holy women had been treated in Israel.

Fuller's major thesis in her article, as in the book that it became in 1845—*Woman in the Nineteenth Century*—was that women would not be able to achieve their full potential as human beings until they were liberated from the demeaning ideas that men had of them. In her view, women did not want flattery or money ('gifts' that confirmed the superiority of the male giver); rather they wanted 'the religious, the intelligent freedom of the universe, to use its means, to learn its secret as far as nature had enabled them, *with God alone for their guide and their judge*' (*Dial*, IV, 23; emphasis added). The insistence that God, not man, should be judge—that God's law should be unmediated by any human and hence (given the prejudice of the age) male interpreter—plainly links Fuller with Ann Hutchinson. If there is to be an interpreter of Divine law, he must come—Fuller insists—'not as man, or son of man . . . but as Son of God' (*Dial*, IV, 14). Unable to escape the prejudicial implications of gender in the language she uses,

[31] See Capper (1987) for a succinct account of Fuller's efforts to educate women by means of her inspirational 'Conversations'.

Fuller is clearly attempting to find an alternative to patriarchal authority in the idea of the Divine Son.[32]

In expounding her belief that women could fulfil themselves once liberated from male bigotry and prejudice, Fuller drew on a concept of self-culture she found in the writings of William Ellery Channing, the great Unitarian preacher, who regarded women as 'souls . . . each of which had a destiny of its own . . . whose leading it must follow, guided by the light of a private conscience' (*Dial*, IV, 41). Channing's language here is close to that of the Quakers when they spoke of the 'Inner Light' that was to be trusted above any external authority. It is not surprising, then, that Fuller adduces examples of Quaker prophetesses, as well as Hebrew, when she wishes to counter male prejudice against women's ability to speak effectively in public. The Quaker faith in the individual soul left no room for prejudicial distinction between male and female in the spiritual realm.

In *The Scarlet Letter*, too, a blatantly anachronistic reference to a Quaker victim of Puritan intolerance (on p. 49) can only mean that the narrator wants to suggest a continuity from the Antinomianism of Ann Hutchinson in 1637 to the prophecies of the Quaker victims of Puritan law in Massachusetts in the late 1650s. In Hawthorne's 'The Gentle Boy' (1832), Quaker fanaticism equals Puritan bigotry in its dehumanizing effect, yet in 'Main-Street' (1849) the narrator-showman who takes his audience through a pictorial history of Salem unequivocally endorses the Quaker sense of calling. They 'have received from heaven a gift that, in all epochs of the world, has brought with it the penalties of moral suffering and persecution, scorn, enmity, and death itself . . . the gift of a new idea'. The gift is dangerous, the showman says, because it threatens tradition, which has been built up by the 'toilsome ages'. Quaker inspiration challenges *custom*, in other words. Having stated this, the showman adopts the tone and attitude

---

[32] Swann (1987) argues that—when decoded—Hester's ideas are more extreme than those of Ann Hutchinson, Margaret Fuller, or even the Shaker Mother Ann Lee. Hester looks forward, Swann believes, to the Second Coming of Christ—this time as a woman.

of a member of the establishment who can understand why the solid citizens found the Quakers intolerable. They 'trample on our wise and well-established laws in the person of the chief magistrate'. Here, as so often in Hawthorne's works, the narrator adopts (or is it mimics?) a moral stance that he does not consistently maintain, if he maintains it at all.

The possibility that Margaret Fuller may have served as a model for Hester Prynne,[33] like the association between Hester and the Antinomian Ann Hutchinson and (less emphatically) the Quakers, suggests that gender is the key to the thematic opposition between inspiration and custom-tradition, or between the spirit and the letter of the law, in the text of *The Scarlet Letter*. Looking beyond the text to other Hawthorne romances, Nina Baym has argued that woman is regularly opposed to society in them, and stands for a core of energy in self and world that predates patriarchal religion altogether.[34] But to identify a theme is not to resolve the problem of interpretation, for the judgement on those women who are associated with the freedom of the spirit is notoriously elusive. Even the narrator's reference to the 'sainted Ann Hutchinson' in *The Scarlet Letter* can be read ironically. In Hawthorne's historical sketch 'Mrs Hutchinson' (1830), the Antinomian is treated unsympathetically as a threat to the very survival of the Massachusetts Bay colony. Here the narrator identifies with the orthodox Puritans even to the extent of accusing Ann of 'carnal pride'. What is more, the sketch is informed by an obvious animus against modern (nineteenth-century) women who feel 'the impulse of genius like a command of Heaven within' and sacrifice the 'loveliness' of the sex to the urge to adopt a public role.[35] Amy Shrager Lang may well be right when she says that the Mrs Hutchinson of the sketch is guilty of resistance to lawful authority, yet to move from this judgement to a reading of *The Scarlet Letter* in which, in Lang's words, the town of Boston is 'authorized' to demand

[33] See Kearns (1965) for the theory that Hester Prynne was modelled on Margaret Fuller.   [34] See Baym (1971), p. 256.
[35] *Nathaniel Hawthorne: Tales and Sketches*, ed. Roy H. Pearce (Cambridge, 1974), p. 18.

conformity to its vision of the world and to argue—further—
that Hawthorne regards consensus as the prerequisite of
order,[36] is to beg the whole question of authority in a text that
problematizes it.

If we look beyond Hawthorne's published works (during his
lifetime) for evidence of his views and glance into the relative
privacy of his notebooks, we will find that his attitude to
Margaret Fuller's intellectual and spiritual aspirations could be
ungenerous and chauvinistic. In the notebook he kept while in
Rome in 1858, some eight years after Fuller's death,
Hawthorne looked back on her public career and on her
liaison with an Italian nobleman eleven years her junior and
vastly her inferior in intellect and culture. The relationship
with Ossoli, he decided, must have been 'purely sensual'; in
conceiving a child by him, Margaret had 'proved herself a very
woman, after all, and fell as the weakest of her sisters might'.[37]
To interpret *The Scarlet Letter* in the retroactive light of the
Roman notebook is to decide that the Antinomian allusions
are evidence, not of sympathy with those who live by the inner
light but, rather, of the author's allegiance to the consensus on
which public order depends. But to read the text in this way
would be to apply the concept of the author as a defence
against the proliferation of meaning and thus to close down a
text that, more than most, resists closure.[38]

Readers, Narratives, and Authority

The one feature of *The Scarlet Letter* that is beyond question is
that its readers have not been able to agree about its meaning.
From the beginning the published interpretations have been
diverse and—many of them—mutually incompatible. One of
the earliest critics of the book was the stern Orestes Brownson,
who stated, in October 1850, that 'Mr Hawthorne . . . seeks to

[36] Lang (1987), pp. 12; 181.
[37] *The French and Italian Notebooks*, ed. Woodson, CE, XIV (1980), p. 155.
[38] See Michel Foucault's 'What is an Author?', tr. J. V. Harari, in *Textual Strategies*, ed. Harari (1979).

excuse Hester Prynne, a married woman, for loving the Puritan minister, on the ground that she had no love for her husband.'[39] Equally shocked by the moral he thought he found in the text was Arthur Cleveland Coxe, who argued in January 1851 that Hester's 'frailty is philosophized into a natural and necessary result of the Scriptural law of marriage'. Coxe was distressed by what he called 'a provoking conceal-ment of the author's motive, from the beginning to the end of the story' as a consequence of which 'we wonder what he would be at'.[40] To this critic, therefore, goes the honour of being the earliest to respond to the curiously elusive nature of the moral judgement in the story, even if Coxe could only suspect that Hawthorne might be making fun of all religion. Both these moralistic critics believed, with differing degrees of certainty, that 'Hawthorne' endorsed Hester's immorality and challenged the biblical prohibition of adultery. A century later, many academic critics interpreted the story in a contrasting way, assuming that, in the words of more than one, 'Hawthorne disapproved of Hester'. Representative of these critics is Darel Abel (1952), who decided that Hester is to be held morally responsible for her wrongdoing. The reader, Abel believed, is expected to love Hester, but not to condone her fault.[41] When we confront the narrator's explicit moral judgements on Hester, Abel's version of the text seems plausible. Not only does the narrator tell us that, during her seven years of infamy, 'Shame, Despair, Solitude . . . taught her much amiss' (p. 200), he also states that society was more generous to her than she 'perchance . . . deserved' (p. 162). Such censorious remarks led Frederic Carpenter (1944) to believe that the romance was flawed by its author's moralistic and subjective criticism of Hester, though Carpenter also did

[39] Extracts from Brownson's review, which was originally published in his *Brownson's Quarterly Review* in 1850, are included in Crowley (1970), pp. 175–9.

[40] Coxe's review is reprinted from the *Church Review*, where it appeared in 1851, in Crowley's *The Critical Heritage* and in *The Recognition of Nathaniel Hawthorne*, ed. Cohen, p. 19.

[41] Abel (1952), pp. 303–9. The belief that Hawthorne disapproves of Hester is also maintained strongly by Cronin (1954).

justice to the complexity of the work by distinguishing three separate and mutually irreconcilable morals in it: an orthodox, traditional moral; a romantic moral, which endorses Hester's new morality of the human heart and of nature; and a transcendental moral, which finds in Hester's conscious purpose of permanent union with her lover an elevation above her romantic rejection of social morality.

The irreconcilable morals identified by Carpenter were later attributed by Austin Warren (1965) to diverse aspects of the author of *The Scarlet Letter*. Warren believed that Hawthorne's ambivalent feelings about Hester manifested themselves in a tangled relationship in the text between the Victorian commentator, who disapproved of the fallen woman, and the myth-maker who created in Hester a natural creature belonging to the pagan forest. Both are present in the forest scene where a celebration of Pearl's wild freedom is juxtaposed with the moralist's judgement on the 'unredeemed, unchristianized forest', which, being wild and heathen, was 'never subjugated by human law, nor illumined by higher truth (p. 203).

To explain the apparent contradictions in the text, Warren distinguished between what an author says through his characters and what he says as commentator. Neither voice, in this view, can be regarded as that of the 'total author', for the writer has the 'blessed gift' of being able to 'give voice to all the voices in him' without having finally to 'pull himself together too tightly into doctrinal consistency'. Following this insight, the next stage in the critical response to the problem of Hawthorne's narrator was to recognize that he could not simply be identified with 'Hawthorne' but had, instead, to be regarded in some sense as a character in the story.[42] Recent refinements of this approach have focused on the 'equivocations' of the narrator: on his reliance on hesitant and qualified statements: on his fondness for subjunctives. Responding to the narrator's style, Elaine Hansen has argued that, in making the narrative an exploration rather than a final statement, Hawthorne tests the artist's role as a moralist, forcing his

[42] Van Deusen (1966) was the first to expound this theory. There have been many reworkings and elaborations of it.

readers to examine the scope of the aesthetic capacity for moral vision.[43] In a yet more radical critique, David Leverenz comes to the conclusion that the narrator adopts a duplicitous stance to conceal the unresolved tensions in the story. Consequently, the reader must learn to see beyond the narrator's strategies to the *author*'s distrust of any authority, especially his own.[44]

We can best study the problematic nature of the narrative in the concluding chapters, and particularly in the chapter with the auspicious title 'The Revelation'. In a story that is, as one critic has it, a 'tissue of secrets'[45] this chapter promises resolutions and clarifications. After seven years of hypocrisy and moral cowardice, Arthur Dimmesdale publicly confesses, revealing the previously hidden stigmata on his breast and thus branding himself a sinner. When he does so, the narrator announces dramatically: 'It was revealed!' Presumably, the pronoun refers to the letter on Arthur's breast, but at this crucial point the narrator prefers not to be explicit. Instead he tells his readers that 'it were irreverent to describe that revelation' (p. 255). This note of 'reverence' is consistent with the delicacy the narrator has shown throughout the story. He drew back, we remember, from telling us exactly what Chillingworth saw when he peered at the breast of the sleeping Dimmesdale in the chapter with the somewhat sinister title 'The Leech and His Patient'. In the 'Conclusion', when the narrator attempts to sum up what happened at the 'Revelation', he tells us that the spectators (or most of them) 'testified to having seen, on the breast of the unhappy minister, a SCARLET LETTER—the very semblance of that worn by Hester Prynne— imprinted in the flesh' (p. 258). Various theories held by the spectators concerning the provenance of that letter are presented: the minister inflicted the wound on his own flesh in self torture; Chillingworth caused it to appear by using drugs; it was the physical manifestation of the minister's remorse. Here

---

[43] Hansen (1975), pp. 154–6. See also Van Leer (1985) for useful analysis of the problems of narrative voice in the text.

[44] Leverenz (1982–3), p. 553. On 'authority' in Hawthorne's short stories see Timms (1985).

[45] Moers (1984), p.53.

the narrator acts as a mere reporter, recording the opinions of those present at the scene. He then invites the reader to choose from the views noted, adding 'We have thrown all the light we could acquire upon the portent.' In other words, this narrator abdicates his authority; he renounces the power to pronounce conclusively (authoritatively) on the event—on its status and its meaning. Having done so, he reports that not all the spectators agreed on what they had seen. Some of them even 'denied that there was any mark whatever on his breast'. These witnesses also rejected the notion that Dimmesdale confessed to a personal sin. To them, his dying words did not acknowledge even a remote connection with Hester's guilt.

By adopting the role of a reporter who has limited access to the truth (to the events and to their significance) the narrator of course distinguishes his function from that of the author of a fiction whose authority over his creation is absolute and godlike. Sometimes, the narrator's hesitancy is so obviously a quirk of character—or even a mannerism of style—that it is disturbingly obtrusive. When he tells us that Dimmesdale's ability to climb the mountain peaks of faith and sanctity was thwarted by 'the burden, whatever it might be, of crime or anguish, beneath which it was his doom to totter' (p. 142), we might well ask how the narrator *cannot* know what that burden is, since, as he says in 'The Custom-House', he has imagined the motives and modes of passion of his characters. His tentativeness—his admissions of doubt—can also have serious consequences for the story that he tells. Mistress Hibbins (an historical figure, actually hanged as a witch in Boston in 1656) appears as a purely hypothetical presence in the narrative of *The Scarlet Letter* yet 'appears' in crucial scenes where her 'presence' is of great consequence for the meaning of Hester and—more importantly—of Pearl. Hibbins, the devotee of the Black Man, clearly enough represents one possible valuation of Hester and her daughter. In momentarily adopting the vulgar view of Pearl and talking of her 'eldritch scream' (p. 107) the narrator gives credence to the superstitions of the age that reinforced the male prejudice against women. The Revd Mr Wilson's good-humoured pleasantry—'The little baggage hath witchcraft in her' (p. 116)—is followed, in 'The Elf-Child and the Minister', by a characteristically non-committal reference to Mistress Hibbins on the part of the narrator: 'it is averred that . . . forth into the sunny day was thrust the face of Mistress Hibbins . . . who, a few years later, was executed as a witch.' The narrative method here is one that Hawthorne had used with similar effect on similar material in his story 'Young Goodman Brown',[46] for though the witch's presence is made hypothetical, her 'words' to Hester are quoted in the text and thus achieve a reality that has not been granted to her physical being. When Hibbins' presence is reported unequivocally by the narrator—she is drawn to her window by Dimmesdale's shriek on the midnight scaffold—he again lapses into the vulgar attitude and idiom, assuming 'beyond the shadow of a doubt' that she must have understood the minister's shout as 'the clamor of fiends and night-hags' (p. 149). Such a narrator is not just unreliable as a witness; he is distinctly dangerous, for the life of a Mistress Hibbins could depend on evidence such as his. She 'was well known', he tells us 'to make excursions into the forest' with such fiends as the one she may be supposed to have heard. Consequently, when the narrator talks of the 'witchcraft' in little Pearl's eyes as she glances at the minister with her elfish smile (p. 154), his apparently innocuous expressions could help to confirm the superstitions of those townspeople who decided that Pearl was 'a demon offspring' (p. 99). Sometimes the narator holds the superstitions and prejudices at arm's length, but not always. Pearl, he tells us, 'was a born outcast of the infantile world. An imp of evil, emblem and product of sin' (p. 93). In the narrative, Pearl is also the touchstone of truth and emotional honesty (she will not allow Hester or Dimmesdale to cast off the letter), but in making her a 'living hieroglyphic' (p. 207)—the scarlet letter personified—the narrator again presents the reader with the problem of interpreting signs.

[46] See 'Introduction', pp. xi–xii, to *Young Goodman Brown and Other Tales*, ed. Harding (Oxford, 1987).

Fathers, Authors, Clerics, Clerks

To consider the function of the narrator in *The Scarlet Letter* seriously, it is necessary to examine his role in 'The Custom-House'. To do that, it is essential to respond to the tone and style of the 'Nathaniel Hawthorne' who talks of himself in the introductory sketch. The voice that addresses the reader in the opening paragraphs of 'The Custom-House' speaks in urbane, sophisticated tones and exhibits a strong sense of literary propriety. The speaker is circumspect about the rights of the reader, whom he imagines to be a 'kind and apprehensive friend' listening sympathetically to his talk. In William Charvat's words, the sketch is 'on the surface . . . the kind of intimate journalism that the general audience like best' in Hawthorne's day. The Hawthorne pieces most admired and most often reprinted at the time, Charvat reminds us, were essayistic 'combinations of light humour, pathos, sentiment, and fancy'.[47] 'The Custom-House' is somewhat more astringent and ironic than 'Buds and Bird Voices' or 'A Rill from the Town Pump', but it belongs to the same genre. Another critic has drawn an analogy with the introductory essay to Lamb's *Essays of Elia*, itself an indulgent reminiscence about old times in a commercial centre that has long since lost its importance and vigour.[48] On the surface, too, this is a useful cross-reference, for contemporaries were often struck by what they thought to be similarities between the New England writer and the English essayist; but the likeness is deceptive, for Hawthorne's air of intimacy with his reader is illusory: it masks complexities of attitude that may include hostility.[49] The personal, even confessional, note sounded in 'The Custom-House' is qualified by the speaker's avowed resolution to 'keep the inmost Me behind its veil'. Since it is part of the introduction to a story about a man's hidden guilt, this metaphor must be significant.

The autobiographical impulse to which the speaker admits

[47] Charvat (1962), p. xx.   [48] Brumm (1975), p. 403.
[49] For the view that Hawthorne despised his readers, see Bayer (1980), p. 251.

in 'The Custom-House' is restrained, as he also makes clear, by his sense of literary propriety. Partly for this reason, the sketch serves to win the reader's trust. It also gains his confidence by explaining how the story came to be written and by making the reader acquainted with the author's—or rather editor's—official abode in his years as a surveyor. The authenticity of the account of life in the Custom House in a sense vouches for the authenticity of the story that will be told in *The Scarlet Letter*. In the course of his autobiographical revelations, the speaker in the sketch tells of his connection with Salem and so invites his readers to see parallels between himself and Hester Prynne when he later tells the story of her deep and mysterious ties to the town of Boston. Moreover, since the narrator of 'The Custom-House' will go on elaborately to embroider the tale he finds in Pue's manuscript, he will in a sense repeat Hester's embroidering of the letter she wears on her breast. He will also, of course, be found to share something with Arthur Dimmesdale, that rhetorician whose power to move his audience deeply depends on his own awareness of the significance of the letter 'A'. Like Chillingworth, too, the narrator will probe the depths of the human heart, though—unlike the sinister physician—he will feel guilty in so doing and will express his guilt in a somewhat demonstrative hesitancy and delicacy in his narrative. These main parallels between the narrator and the characters in the story he tells become obvious as one reads *The Scarlet Letter*, but there is a hidden link between the 'Nathaniel Hawthorne' of the sketch and the Arthur Dimmesdale of the story, for the former conceals a secret more effectively than the minister conceals his burning letter.

Early in the sketch the narrator explains that he was not a politician, and, though a faithful Democrat in principle, 'neither received nor held his office with any reference to political services' (p. 13). He was dismissed from office, as he later explains, because of the bloodthirstiness and cruelty of the Whigs (p. 41) who guillotined Democratic appointees when the Whig party was returned to power after the 1848 presidential election. In the sketch, the political innocence of

'Nathanial Hawthorne' is vigorously asserted yet, as Stephen Nissenbaum has conclusively demonstrated, the charge brought by the Salem Whigs—that he had used his office for partisan purposes—was substantiated by definite evidence.[50] Hawthorne had not been able to keep clear of party politics while in office at the Custom House because the very position he occupied was part of the Jacksonian patronage system. Democratic inspectors *were* paid more than their Whig colleagues while Hawthorne was surveyor and they *were* obliged to kick back half of their extra pay into local party funds. When they objected, two of the inspectors were suspended from office by Surveyor Hawthorne, whose signed notice to the men could be adduced as evidence. Though President Taylor had publicly eschewed partisan revenge on office holders of the Democratic party, he had made malfeasance a legitimate ground for dismissal. Nissenbaum's conclusion is that one function of the 'Custom House' sketch was to draw attention away from the facts of his appointment (Hawthorne had used the influence of his political allies to get the job in the first place) and to depoliticize the Custom House.

The disingenuousness of the narrator on the subject of 'Hawthorne's' political involvements and the legitimacy of his dismissal might cause the reader some unease, if he were aware of it, and might disturb his comfortable relationship with the genial—even bland—speaker in the sketch.[51] Yet that speaker's most agreeable characteristic remains his modesty, for he confides in the reader that he was 'happy to find a listener' or two when he published his earlier autobiographical essay by way of introduction to his *Mosses from an Old Manse*. What is more, he justifies his present intrusion on the reader's attention in part by adopting the role of editor rather than author. He explains that he *found* the story of Hester Prynne; that he did not invent it but discovered a manuscript in the hand of one Surveyor Pue, who preceded him in office by

[50] Nissenbaum (1978; 1984).
[51] Lee (1982) p. 53 insists that the self disclosed in 'The Custom-House' is from the outset a 'writerly' self.

some eighty years. In assuring the reader that the main facts of the story are 'authorized and authenticated by the document of Mr Surveyor Pue' the narrator seems already to be abdicating responsibility for the tale he is to tell. If he is not the author— the originator—of the story he cannot be held accountable for it; it is not his property.[52] Yet the story belongs to Pue only in the sense that he wrote the record of the events. Writing in the 1750s, Pue merely recorded the oral testimony of those aged citizens of Salem who could remember Hester Prynne as a very old woman in their youth. The degree of authority or authenticity is slight indeed, for the 'witnesses' encountered Hester long after the events that are to feature in her story. Since they were mere children when she was an old woman, their evidence can have been no more than hearsay and tradition.

Tenuous though the testimony is, the narrator imagines the dignified figure of Pue exhorting him to tell the story on the sacred consideration of his 'filial duty and reverence' towards his 'official ancestor'. Since one explicit topic of 'The Custom-House' is the narrator's relationship with his forefathers, his imagined relationship with Pue might be read as an exercise in literary filiopiety. Certainly, Pue is treated with something like reverence. He has the dignity (the narrator imagines) of one who has borne the commission of a king and so contrasts with the hangdog air of a republican official such as Nathaniel Hawthorne. But the extravagance of the deference that sees Pue 'illuminated by a ray of the splendor that shone . . . about the throne [of King George]' gives way to patent mockery in the allusion to the 'mouldy and moth-eaten lucubrations' (p. 33) contained in Pue's manuscript. All that survives of Pue's dignity is the majestic frizzle of his wig when it is disinterred; the 'venerable' skull of this literary ancestor is in a far less satisfactory state of preservation. The less-than-flattering term 'lucubrations' is used twice to refer to Pue's literary efforts in a sketch that smacks more of impiety than filial deference.

Though he modestly adopts the role of editor, the narrator

[52] On the etymological link between authorship and property, see Said (1975), p. 91.

negates the conventions he has been working with when he says that he has allowed himself almost as much liberty in imagining 'the motives and modes of passion that influenced the characters' in the story as if it had been his own invention entirely. Since the outline for whose authenticity the Pue manuscript is supposed to vouch can be no more than the 'facts' of Hester's public humiliation, Arthur's death, and the subsequent departure of mother and child for Europe, followed in turn by Hester's reappearance in Massachusetts, the attribution of authorship to Pue is a patently empty gesture.

The exercise in literary filiopiety proves, then, to be anything but solemn; it is, in fact, demonstrably comic, and this is portentous when we consider that one theme of *The Scarlet Letter* will be the authority of the fathers. What is more, the imagined encounter with the figure of Mr Surveyor Pue is preceded by the account of the narrator's relationship with the old gentlemen—former sea captains all—who, though his seniors in years, are his juniors (and dependants) in office. In his dealings with his elders, 'Hawthorne' finds himself playing judge and jury, sentencing more than one of these patriarchs to official (and, as it turns out, physical) death. The lightness of tone and the delicacy of the wit with which the incident is described cannot disguise the fact that—in parodic form—the narrator here is reversing the roles he has just imagined for himself and his own Hathorne ancestors.

When he imaginatively recreates his forefathers, 'Hawthorne' begins with that first ancestor, William Hathorne, who was 'a soldier, legislator, judge . . . a ruler in the Church' (p. 9). Obviously, this Hathorne could have stood with Bellingham on the balcony of the meeting house and looked down (literally and metaphorically) on Hester as she stood on the scaffold. The reference to William Hathorne's infamous cruelty to the Quaker Ann Coleman anticipates the punishment of Hester in *The Scarlet Letter*. Aligning himself with those his ancestors would have despised and condemned, the narrator of the sketch defines his art in terms of its unacceptability to his forefathers: he admits that he cannot break the links that bind him to them—those strong traits of their nature he finds in himself—but he also adopts the stance of the outlaw, for to the seventeenth-century Hathorne he would have been a mere idler, little better than a fiddler (p. 9).

In imagining his ancestors' contempt for his calling—that of a writer of story-books—the speaker in 'The Custom-House' could be understood to express his own lack of assurance about the value of his fictions. A tendency to self-derogation is, apparently, characteristic of this speaker, for in the first paragraph of the sketch he accuses himself of following the example of 'P. P., Clerk of This Parish' in burdening the reader with memoirs of his own life. The 'P. P.' of the 'Memoirs' (written by members of the Scriblerus Club) was a fool and a clown who absurdly imagined that his trivial and banal acts were important because in wearing the clerical band (as parish clerk), he had acquired 'ecclesiastical dignity' as a 'shred of the vestment of Aaron'.[53] This allusion can be read as witty self-deprecation on Hawthorne's part and as consistent with his usual authorial modesty; but it is possible that the repeated allusions to 'P. P.' in 'The Custom-House' signal something other than the writer's low valuation of his art. The 'Memoirs of P. P.' were, in fact, a satirical squib which ridiculed the self-importance of a man who had actually been an eminent cleric (a bishop) in his lifetime. The *Scriblerus Papers*, of which the 'Memoirs' formed an undistinguished part, demonstrated *not* the insignificance or triviality of 'clerks' (men of letters) but their subversive power when they practised the irreverent art of satire. Though *The Scarlet Letter* is closer to tragedy than to satire, its account of the men of God who ruled Massachusetts in Hester Prynne's day may be less reverent than many of its readers have supposed.

In 'The Procession', the chapter which provides a climax to the public theme, the early leaders of the Bay colony are described in their 'ponderous sobriety', their 'fortitude and self-reliance'. They display a cliff-like firmness in their defence of the state against all tempestuous onslaughts (p. 238). The Fathers have 'a demeanour of natural authority', though they

[53] See below, note to p. 3.

are the foremost men in a democracy. The roll-call of eminent men—'Bradstreet, Endicott, Dudley, Bellingham'—sounds so imposing that the passage has been read as an eloquent tribute to the nobility of the founders.[54] Yet, in the final paragraph of the chapter, the 'sainted minister in the church' and the 'woman of the scarlet letter in the market-place' are brought together by the *irreverent* imagination of the writer (p. 247). None of the pious citizens of Boston who 'drew back reverently' to let pass the 'Governor and magistrates, the old and wise men, the holy ministers, and all that were eminent and renowned' could possibly have been 'irreverent enough to surmise that the same scorching stigma was on them [Hester and Arthur] both'. To the people of Massachusetts, who 'possessed, by hereditary right, the quality of reverence' (p. 237), the preacher is 'admirable' and his strength is 'angelic', while the fallen woman is nothing more than an adulteress. Though the explicit comment of the narrator is that loss of the reverential spirit has been a mixed blessing for New England (and, by extension we must suppose, for the United States), he has told his story in such a way that his own interpretation is put into question. The issue becomes an urgent one in the case of the Revd Mr Dimmesdale's sermon. As Michael Bell has noted,[55] this Election Sermon sounds more like the orations with which nineteenth-century American politicians flattered their audiences than the Jeremiads with which seventeenth-century Puritan ministers strove to activate the consciences of their congregations. With characteristic elusiveness, the narrator merely states that Dimmesdale foretold a 'high and glorious destiny' for the people of New England (p. 249). Whether we label it 'evasion' or 'equivocation' the narrator's strategy here denies to the reader an unproblematic response to Dimmesdale's local patriotism and to the future for New England that he prophesied. The

[54] See M. D. Bell (1971), p. 140 for such a reading.
[55] Bell (1971), p. 142. Though Bell describes the sermon as political rant, he does not believe that it undermines the narrator's tribute to the founders. In a later essay (1985), however, Bell stresses the subversiveness of *The Scarlet Letter*.

narrator's consistent withdrawal from judgement places the burden of judgement, which is inextricable from the problem of interpretation, on the reader.

Only two years after the publication of *The Scarlet Letter* Hawthorne wrote a campaign biography for his friend Franklin Pierce, the Democratic Party's nominee for the presidency of the United States. The man offered for approval in the biography is a realist; a statesman who is superior to the 'mere theorist' and who values the 'great and sacred reality' of the Union above the 'mistiness of a philanthropic theory'—that is the theory of anti-slavery. Not only does the *Life of Franklin Pierce* substitute strength of character for political principle, as Jonathan Arac has noted;[56] it also pays conventional tribute to the eminent men of antebellum American politics. Pierce entered the Senate when Van Buren was President and when, we are told, Calhoun, Webster, Clay, and Benton were great figures in the political firmament. The roll-call suggests a respectful, even reverential, attitude. Since the work in which it appears is a campaign biography, there is no reason to suspect its author of any subversive intention; but should not *The Scarlet Letter* have taught us to attribute the respect for public eminence and for authority to one of Hawthorne's voices rather than to 'Hawthorne'?

[56] Arac (1986), p. 253.

NOTE ON THE TEXT

The text of this volume is that of *The Scarlet Letter,* Volume I of the *Centenary Edition of the Works of Nathaniel Hawthorne,* published in 1962 by the Ohio State University Press for the Ohio State University Center for Textual Studies. The Centenary text was established by the application of bibliographical and analytical criticism to the evidence of the various documentary forms in which the text had appeared. It is a critical, unmodernized reconstruction of Hawthorne's text, and is approved by the Center for Editions of the Modern Language Association of America.

A CHRONOLOGY OF
NATHANIEL HAWTHORNE

1804   4 July: born in Salem, Massachusetts, second of three children of Elizabeth (*née* Manning) and Nathaniel Hathorne.

1808   Father, a ship's captain, dies of yellow fever at Surinam (Dutch Guiana). The Hathornes move to the Manning family home in Salem.

1813   November: a foot injury causes lameness and keeps Nathaniel from school for fourteen months.

1818   October: the Hathorne family moves to Raymond, Maine, which is still a wilderness area. Nathaniel hunts, fishes, and runs wild.

1819   July: Nathaniel returns to Salem to live with his mother's family, under the guardianship of his uncle Robert Manning. His mother stays in Maine.

1820   Prepares for college under Benjamin L. Oliver in Salem.

1821   October: enters Bowdoin College, Brunswick, Maine. College friendships with Horatio Bridge, Franklin Pierce, Jonathan Cilley.

1822   H. W. Longfellow enters Bowdoin. He and Hawthorne meet.

1825   September: graduates from Bowdoin. Returns to live with family in Salem. According to his sister Elizabeth, Nathaniel has completed 'Seven Tales of My Native Land' by the time he graduates from Bowdoin.

1828   October: *Fanshawe* published anonymously and at the author's expense. By now Nathaniel has added the 'w' to his family name.

1829   Plans a second collection of stories, to be called 'Provincial Tales', and submits manuscript to S. G. Goodrich, editor of *The Token*, an annual.

1830   12 November and 21 December: 'The Hollow of the Three Hills' and 'An Old Woman's Tale'—Hawthorne's first known tales to appear in print—published in *Salem Gazette*.

1831   Releases some tales intended for 'Provincial Tales' for publication in *The Token*, dated 1832: 'The Gentle Boy', 'The Wives of the Dead', 'Roger Malvin's Burial', 'My Kinsman, Major Molineux'.

1832   Plans a third collection, to be called 'The Story Teller'. September–October: makes extensive journeys in Vermont and New York State, gathering literary materials.

1834   November and December: 'The Story Teller, Nos I and II' published in *New England Magazine*.

1835   'The Minister's Black Veil', 'The Maypole of Merry Mount', and 'The Wedding-Knell' published in *The Token* for 1836.

1836   January: moves to Boston to edit *American Magazine of Useful and Entertaining Knowledge*. March: first issue with Nathaniel Hawthorne as editor. His salary is not paid. Magazine goes bankrupt in May. May to September: writes—with the help of Elizabeth—*Peter Parley's Universal History, on the Basis of Geography*.

1837   March: *Twice-told Tales* published. Unknown to Hawthorne, Horatio Bridge has given financial guarantee to publisher. July: Longfellow's highly favourable review of *Twice-told Tales* appears in the *North American Review*. November: meets Sophia Amelia Peabody. October: begins his association with John L. O'Sullivan's *Democratic Review*. Eight Hawthorne pieces appear there in fifteen months.

1838   July–September: begins three months of seclusion in North Adams, Massachusetts, with trips to the Berkshires, upstate New York, Vermont, Connecticut.

1839   January: takes up appointment as measurer in the Boston Custom House. 6 March: writes first surviving love-letter to Sophia Peabody.

1840   November: resigns from Custom House with effect from 1 January 1841. December: *Grandfather's Chair* published, dated 1841, a children's history of New England.

1841   January: returns to Salem. *Famous Old People* published. March: *The Liberty Tree* published. April: joins the Brook

Farm Associationist experiment at West Roxbury, near Boston, as working member. Becomes a paying boarder at the Farm, with no work commitments, in the autumn. September: buys two shares in the Brook Farm project, planning to bring Sophia to live there when they are married. October: leaves the Farm for Boston.

1842   January: second edition of *Twice-told Tales* published, with additional volume containing sixteen recent tales and sketches together with five that antedate the 1837 collection. 9 July: Hawthorne and Sophia Peabody married. They move to Concord, Mass., where they rent the Old Manse. October: withdraws from the Brook Farm project and requests return of his stock.

1844   3 March: daughter (Una) born.

1845   January–April: edits Horatio Bridge's *Journal of an African Cruiser*. October: the Hawthornes move to Herbert Street, Salem, as the owner wants Old Manse.

1846   9 April: sworn in a surveyor at Salem Custom House, having been nominated by President Polk, the new Democratic President. June: *Mosses from an Old Manse* published in two volumes. A critical, but not a financial, success. 22 June: Julian Hawthorne born. August: Hawthornes move to Salem.

1848   November: becomes manager and corresponding secretary of Salem Lyceum. Invites Emerson, Thoreau, Theodore Parker, Horace Mann, Louis Agassiz to lecture.

1849   7 June: removed from office in Custom House, following election of Whig President, Zachary Taylor, in 1848. 31 July: Mother dies. September: begins writing *The Scarlet Letter* and 'The Custom-House'.

1850   16 March: *The Scarlet Letter* published in edition of 2,500 copies. April: second edition published. May: Hawthornes move to 'Red Cottage', Lenox, Massachusetts. 5 August: Hawthorne meets Melville at a literary picnic. August: begins *The House of the Seven Gables*. 17 and 24 August: Melville's 'Hawthorne and His Mosses' appears anonymously in *The Literary World*. November: *True Stories* (reissue of *Grandfather's Chair* and *Biographical Stories*) published, dated 1851.

1851   April: *The House of the Seven Gables* published. March: third edition of *Twice-told Tales* published, with preface. 20 May: Rose Hawthorne born. November: *A Wonder Book for Girls and Boys* published, dated 1852. December: *The Snow-Image* published, dated 1852.

1852   April: buys the Alcott House in Concord, naming it 'The Wayside'. July: *The Blithedale Romance* published. September: *Life of Franklin Pierce*—a campaign biography of the Presidential candidate—published.

1853   March: nominated to consulship at Liverpool and Manchester by President Pierce. Appointment confirmed by US Senate. July: sails for England with family. September: *Tanglewood Tales* published.

1853–7 While working as consul, Hawthorne keeps note-books in which he records his English experiences and impressions.

1854   Revised edition of *Mosses* published.

1856   November: Melville visits Hawthorne in Liverpool on way to the Holy Land. He also meets Hawthorne briefly on return journey in May 1857.

1857   October: gives up consulship.

1858   January: travels to Italy by way of France. Takes up residence in Rome. Keeps notebooks on his Italian experiences and begins work on an English romance, never to be completed, but published posthumously as *The Ancestral Footstep*. May to October: the Hawthornes live in Florence. He begins work on romance with an Italian theme.

1859   June: returns to England, where he rewrites the Italian romance.

1860   February: *The Transformation* published in England; in March the romance is published in America with the title *The Marble Faun*. June: returns to America and settles at 'The Wayside', Concord, where he begins work on a second version of his English romance.

1861   Abandons the romance, after making seven studies for the story. The fragment is published posthumously as *Dr Grimshaw's Secret*. Autumn: begins work on series of English essays. Begins a new romance on theme of the elixir of life but abandons this in 1862. Set at the time of the

Revolution, the fragment is published posthumously as *Septimius Felton*.

1863   September: *Our Old Home* published—the collected essays on England—most of which had appeared separately in the *Atlantic Monthly*.

1864   19 May: dies at Plymouth, New Hampshire, having written three chapters of another romance about the elixir of life, which is posthumously published as *The Dolliver Romance*.

THE SCARLET LETTER

PREFACE

MUCH to the author's surprise, and (if he may say so without additional offence) considerably to his amusement, he finds that his sketch of official life, introductory to THE SCARLET LETTER, has created an unprecedented excitement in the respectable community* immediately around him. It could hardly have been more violent, indeed, had he burned down the Custom-House, and quenched its last smoking ember in the blood of a certain venerable personage, against whom he is supposed to cherish a peculiar malevolence. As the public disapprobation would weigh very heavily on him, were he conscious of deserving it, the author begs leave to say, that he has carefully read over the introductory pages, with a purpose to alter or expunge whatever might be found amiss, and to make the best reparation in his power for the atrocities of which he has been adjudged guilty. But it appears to him, that the only remarkable features of the sketch are its frank and genuine good-humor, and the general accuracy with which he has conveyed his sincere impressions of the characters therein described. As to enmity, or ill-feeling of any kind, personal or political, he utterly disclaims such motives. The sketch might, perhaps, have been wholly omitted, without loss to the public, or detriment to the book; but, having undertaken to write it, he conceives that it could not have been done in a better or a kindlier spirit,* nor, so far as his abilities availed, with a livelier effect of truth.

The author is constrained, therefore, to republish his introductory sketch without the change of a word.

SALEM, *March* 30, 1850.

THE CUSTOM-HOUSE

INTRODUCTORY TO "THE SCARLET LETTER"

I T IS a little remarkable, that—though disinclined to talk
overmuch of myself and my affairs at the fireside, and to
my personal friends—an autobiographical impulse should
twice in my life have taken possession of me, in addressing the
public. The first time* was three or four years since, when I
favored the reader—inexcusably, and for no earthly reason,
that either the indulgent reader or the intrusive author could
imagine—with a description of my way of life in the deep quietude of an Old Manse. And now—because, beyond my de-
serts, I was happy enough to find a listener or two on the
former occasion—I again seize the public by the button, and
talk of my three years' experience in a Custom-House. The
example of the famous "P. P., Clerk of this Parish,"* was never
more faithfully followed. The truth seems to be, however,
that, when he casts his leaves forth upon the wind, the author
addresses, not the many who will fling aside his volume, or
never take it up, but the few who will understand him, better
than most of his schoolmates and lifemates. Some authors, indeed, do far more than this, and indulge themselves in such
confidential depths of revelation as could fittingly be addressed, only and exclusively, to the one heart and mind of
perfect sympathy; as if the printed book, thrown at large on
the wide world, were certain to find out the divided segment

of the writer's own nature, and complete his circle of existence by bringing him into communion with it. It is scarcely decorous, however, to speak all, even where we speak impersonally. But—as thoughts are frozen and utterance benumbed, unless the speaker stand in some true relation with his audience—it may be pardonable to imagine that a friend, a kind and apprehensive, though not the closest friend, is listening to our talk; and then, a native reserve being thawed by this genial consciousness, we may prate of the circumstances that lie around us, and even of ourself, but still keep the inmost Me behind its veil.* To this extent and within these limits, an author, methinks, may be autobiographical, without violating either the reader's rights or his own.

It will be seen, likewise, that this Custom-House sketch has a certain propriety, of a kind always recognized in literature, as explaining how a large portion of the following pages came into my possession, and as offering proofs of the authenticity of a narrative therein contained. This, in fact,—a desire to put myself in my true position as editor, or very little more, of the most prolix among the tales that make up my volume,*—this, and no other, is my true reason for assuming a personal relation with the public. In accomplishing the main purpose, it has appeared allowable, by a few extra touches, to give a faint representation of a mode of life not heretofore described, together with some of the characters that move in it, among whom the author happened to make one.

In my native town of Salem, at the head of what, half a century ago, in the days of old King Derby,* was a bustling wharf,—but which is now burdened with decayed wooden warehouses, and exhibits few or no symptoms of commercial life; except, perhaps, a bark or brig, half-way down its melancholy length, discharging hides; or, nearer at hand, a Nova Scotia schooner, pitching out her cargo of firewood,—at the head, I say, of this dilapidated wharf, which the tide often overflows, and along which, at the base and in the rear of the row of buildings, the track of many languid years is seen in a border of unthrifty grass,—here, with a view from its front windows adown this not very enlivening prospect, and thence across the harbour, stands a spacious edifice of brick. From the loftiest point of its roof, during precisely three and a half hours of each forenoon, floats or droops, in breeze or calm, the banner of the republic; but with the thirteen stripes turned vertically, instead of horizontally, and thus indicating that a civil, and not a military post of Uncle Sam's government, is here established. Its front is ornamented with a portico of half a dozen wooden pillars, supporting a balcony, beneath which a flight of wide granite steps descends towards the street. Over the entrance hovers an enormous specimen of the American eagle, with outspread wings, a shield before her breast, and, if I recollect aright, a bunch of intermingled thunderbolts and barbed arrows in each claw. With the customary infirmity of temper that characterizes this unhappy fowl, she appears, by the fierceness of her beak and eye and the general truculency of her attitude, to threaten mischief to the inoffensive community; and especially to warn all citizens, careful of their safety, against intruding on the premises which she overshadows with her wings. Nevertheless, vixenly as she looks, many people are seeking, at this very moment, to shelter themselves under the wing of the federal eagle; imagining, I presume, that her bosom has all the softness and snugness of an eider-down pillow. But she has no great tenderness, even in her best of moods, and, sooner or later,—oftener soon than late,—is apt to fling off her nestlings with a scratch of her claw, a dab of her beak, or a rankling wound from her barbed arrows.

The pavement round about the above-described edifice—which we may as well name at once as the Custom-House of the port—has grass enough growing in its chinks to show that it has not, of late days, been worn by any multitudinous resort of business. In some months of the year, however, there often chances a forenoon when affairs move onward with a livelier tread. Such occasions might remind the elderly citizen of that period, before the last war with England,* when Salem was a port by itself; not scorned, as she is now, by her own merchants and ship-owners, who permit her wharves to crumble to ruin, while their ventures go to swell, needlessly and imperceptibly, the mighty flood of commerce at New York or Boston. On some such morning, when three or four vessels happen to have arrived at once,—usually from Africa or South America,—or to be on the verge of their departure thitherward, there is a sound of frequent feet, passing briskly up and down the granite steps. Here, before his own wife has greeted him, you may greet the sea-flushed ship-master, just in port, with his vessel's papers under his arm in a tarnished tin box. Here, too, comes his owner, cheerful or sombre, gracious or in the sulks, accordingly as his scheme of the now accomplished voyage has been realized in merchandise that will readily be turned to gold, or has buried him under a bulk of incommodities, such as nobody will care to rid him of. Here, likewise,—the germ of the wrinkle-browed, grizzly-bearded, careworn merchant,—we have the smart young clerk, who gets the taste of traffic as a wolf-cub does of blood, and already sends adventures* in his master's ships, when he had better be sailing mimic boats upon a mill-pond. Another figure in the scene is the outward-bound sailor, in quest of a protection;* or the recently arrived one, pale and feeble, seeking a passport to the hospital. Nor must we forget the captains of the rusty little schooners that bring firewood from the British provinces; a rough-looking set of tarpaulins, without the alertness of the Yankee aspect, but contributing an item of no slight importance to our decaying trade.

Cluster all these individuals together, as they sometimes were, with other miscellaneous ones to diversify the group, and, for the time being, it made the Custom-House a stirring scene. More frequently, however, on ascending the steps, you would discern—in the entry, if it were summer time, or in their appropriate rooms, if wintry or inclement weather—a row of venerable figures, sitting in old-fashioned chairs, which were tipped on their hind legs back against the wall. Oftentimes they were asleep, but occasionally might be heard talking together, in voices between speech and a snore, and with that lack of energy that distinguishes the occupants of alms-houses, and all other human beings who depend for subsistence on charity, on monopolized labor, or any thing else but their own independent exertions. These old gentlemen—seated, like Matthew, at the receipt of custom,* but not very liable to be summoned thence, like him, for apostolic errands—were Custom-House officers.

Furthermore, on the left hand as you enter the front door, is a certain room or office, about fifteen feet square, and of a lofty height; with two of its arched windows commanding a view of the aforesaid dilapidated wharf, and the third looking across a narrow lane, and along a portion of Derby Street. All three give glimpses of the shops of grocers, block-makers, slop-sellers,* and ship-chandlers; around the doors of which are generally to be seen, laughing and gossiping, clusters of old salts, and such other wharf-rats as haunt the Wapping* of a seaport. The room itself is cobwebbed, and dingy with old paint; its floor is strewn with gray sand, in a fashion that has elsewhere fallen into long disuse; and it is easy to conclude, from the general slovenliness of the place, that this is a sanctuary into which womankind, with her tools of magic, the broom and mop, has very infrequent access. In the way of furniture, there is a stove with a voluminous funnel; an old pine desk, with a three-legged stool beside it; two or three wooden-bottom chairs, exceedingly decrepit and infirm; and, —not to forget the library,—on some shelves, a score or two of volumes of the Acts of Congress, and a bulky Digest of the Revenue Laws. A tin pipe ascends through the ceiling, and forms a medium of vocal communication with other parts of the edifice. And here, some six months ago,—pacing from corner to corner, or lounging on the long-legged stool, with his elbow on the desk, and his eyes wandering up and down the columns of the morning newspaper,—you might have recognized, honored reader, the same individual who welcomed you into his cheery little study, where the sunshine glimmered so pleasantly through the willow branches, on the western side of the Old Manse. But now, should you go thither to seek him, you would inquire in vain for the Loco-foco* Surveyor. The besom of reform has swept him out of office; and a worthier successor wears his dignity and pockets his emoluments.

This old town of Salem—my native place, though I have dwelt much away from it, both in boyhood and maturer years —possesses, or did possess, a hold on my affections, the force of which I have never realized during my seasons of actual residence here. Indeed, so far as its physical aspect is concerned, with its flat, unvaried surface, covered chiefly with wooden houses, few or none of which pretend to architectural beauty,—its irregularity, which is neither picturesque nor quaint, but only tame,—its long and lazy street, lounging wearisomely through the whole extent of the peninsula, with Gallows Hill*and New Guinea*at one end, and a view of the alms-house at the other,—such being the features of my native town, it would be quite as reasonable to form a sentimental attachment to a disarranged checkerboard. And yet, though invariably happiest elsewhere, there is within me a feeling for old Salem, which, in lack of a better phrase, I must be content to call affection. The sentiment is probably assignable to the deep and aged roots which my family has struck into the soil. It is now nearly two centuries and a quarter since the original Briton, the earliest emigrant of my name,* made his appearance in the wild and forest-bordered settlement, which has since become a city. And here his descendants have been born and died, and have mingled their earthy substance with the soil; until no small portion of it must necessarily be akin to the mortal frame wherewith, for a little while, I walk the streets. In part, therefore, the attachment which I speak of is the mere sensuous sympathy of dust for dust. Few of my countrymen can know what it is; nor, as frequent transplantation is perhaps better for the stock, need they consider it desirable to know.

But the sentiment has likewise its moral quality. The figure of that first ancestor,* invested by family tradition with a dim and dusky grandeur, was present to my boyish imagination, as far back as I can remember. It still haunts me, and induces a sort of home-feeling with the past, which I scarcely claim in reference to the present phase of the town. I seem to have a stronger claim to a residence here on account of this grave, bearded, sable-cloaked, and steeple-crowned progenitor,— who came so early, with his Bible and his sword, and trode the unworn street with such a stately port, and made so large a figure, as a man of war and peace,—a stronger claim than for myself, whose name is seldom heard and my face hardly known. He was a soldier, legislator, judge; he was a ruler in the Church; he had all the Puritanic traits, both good and evil. He was likewise a bitter persecutor; as witness the Quakers, who have remembered him in their histories,* and relate an incident of his hard severity towards a woman of their sect, which will last longer, it is to be feared, than any record of his better deeds, although these were many. His son,* too, inherited the persecuting spirit, and made himself so conspic-uous in the martyrdom of the witches, that their blood may fairly be said to have left a stain upon him. So deep a stain, indeed, that his old dry bones, in the Charter Street burial-ground, must still retain it, if they have not crumbled utterly to dust! I know not whether these ancestors of mine bethought themselves to repent, and ask pardon of Heaven for their cruelties; or whether they are now groaning under the heavy consequences of them, in another state of being. At all events, I, the present writer, as their representative, hereby take shame upon myself for their sakes, and pray that any curse incurred by them—as I have heard, and as the dreary and unprosperous condition of the race, for many a long year back, would argue to exist—may be now and henceforth removed.

Doubtless, however, either of these stern and black-browed Puritans would have thought it quite a sufficient retribution for his sins, that, after so long a lapse of years, the old trunk of the family tree, with so much venerable moss upon it, should have borne, as its topmost bough, an idler like myself. No aim, that I have ever cherished, would they recognize as laudable; no success of mine—if my life, beyond its domestic scope, had ever been brightened by success—would they deem otherwise than worthless, if not positively disgraceful. "What is he?" murmurs one gray shadow of my forefathers to the other. "A writer of story-books! What kind of a business in life,—what mode of glorifying God, or being serviceable to mankind in his day and generation,—may that be? Why, the degenerate fellow might as well have been a fiddler!" Such are the compliments bandied between my great-grandsires and myself, across the gulf of time! And yet, let them scorn me as they will, strong traits of their nature have intertwined themselves with mine.

Planted deep, in the town's earliest infancy and childhood, by these two earnest and energetic men, the race has ever since subsisted here; always, too, in respectability; never, so far as I have known, disgraced by a single unworthy member; but seldom or never, on the other hand, after the first two generations, performing any memorable deed, or so much as putting forward a claim to public notice. Gradually, they have sunk almost out of sight; as old houses, here and there about the streets, get covered half-way to the eaves by the accumulation of new soil. From father to son, for above a hundred years, they followed the sea; a gray-headed shipmaster, in each generation, retiring from the quarter-deck to the homestead, while a boy of fourteen took the hereditary place before the mast, confronting the salt spray and the gale, which had blustered against his sire and grandsire. The boy, also, in due time, passed from the forecastle to the cabin, spent a tempestuous manhood, and returned from his world-wanderings, to grow old, and die, and mingle his dust with the natal earth. This long connection of a family with one spot, as its place of birth and burial, creates a kindred between the human being and the locality, quite independent of any charm in the scenery or moral circumstances that surround him. It is not love, but instinct. The new inhabitant—who came himself from a foreign land, or whose father or grandfather came—has little claim to be called a Salemite; he has no conception of the oyster-like tenacity with which an old settler, over whom his third century is creeping, clings to the spot where his successive generations have been imbedded. It is no matter that the place is joyless for him; that he is weary of the old wooden houses, the mud and dust, the dead level of site and sentiment, the chill east wind, and the chillest of social atmospheres;—all these, and whatever faults besides he may see or imagine, are nothing to the purpose. The spell survives,* and just as powerfully as if the natal spot were an earthly paradise. So has it been in my case. I felt it almost as a destiny to make Salem my home; so that the mould of features and cast of character which had all along been familiar here—ever, as one representative of the race lay down in his grave, another assuming, as it were, his sentry-march along the Main Street—might still in my little day be seen and recognized in the old town. Nevertheless, this very sentiment is an evidence that the connection, which has become an unhealthy one, should at last be severed. Human nature will not flourish, any more than a potato, if it be planted and replanted, for too long a series of generations, in the same worn-out soil. My children have had other birth-places, and, so far as their fortunes may be within my control, shall strike their roots into unaccustomed earth.

On emerging from the Old Manse,* it was chiefly this strange, indolent, unjoyous attachment for my native town, that brought me to fill a place in Uncle Sam's brick edifice, when I might as well, or better, have gone somewhere else. My doom was on me. It was not the first time, nor the second, that I had gone away,—as it seemed, permanently,—but yet returned, like the bad half-penny; or as if Salem were for me the inevitable centre of the universe. So, one fine morning, I ascended the flight of granite steps, with the President's commission* in my pocket, and was introduced to the corps of gentlemen who were to aid me in my weighty responsibility, as chief executive officer of the Custom-House.

I doubt greatly—or rather, I do not doubt at all—whether any public functionary of the United States, either in the civil or military line, has ever had such a patriarchal body of veterans under his orders as myself. The whereabouts of the Oldest Inhabitant was at once settled, when I looked at them. For upwards of twenty years before this epoch, the independ-ent position of the Collector had kept the Salem Custom-House out of the whirlpool of political vicissitude, which makes the tenure of office generally so fragile. A soldier,—New England's most distinguished soldier,—he stood firmly on the pedestal of his gallant services; and, himself secure in the wise liberality of the successive administrations through which he had held office, he had been the safety of his subordinates in many an hour of danger and heart-quake. General Miller* was radically conservative; a man over whose kindly nature habit had no slight influence; attaching himself strongly to familiar faces, and with difficulty moved to change, even when change might have brought unquestionable im-provement. Thus, on taking charge of my department, I found few but aged men. They were ancient sea-captains, for the most part, who, after being tost on every sea, and standing up sturdily against life's tempestuous blast, had finally drifted into this quiet nook; where, with little to disturb them, except the periodical terrors of a Presidential election, they one and all acquired a new lease of existence. Though by no means less liable than their fellow-men to age and infirmity, they had evidently some talisman or other that kept death at bay. Two or three of their number, as I was assured, being gouty and rheumatic, or perhaps bed-ridden, never dreamed of making their appearance at the Custom-House, during a large part of the year; but, after a torpid winter, would creep out into the warm sunshine of May or June, go lazily about what they termed duty, and, at their own leisure and convenience, betake themselves to bed again. I must plead guilty to the charge of abbreviating the official breath of more than one of these venerable servants of the republic. They were allowed, on my representation, to rest from their arduous labors, and soon afterwards—as if their sole principle of life had been zeal for their country's service; as I verily believe it was—withdrew to a better world. It is a pious consolation to me, that, through my interference, a sufficient space was allowed them for repentance of the evil and corrupt practices, into which, as a matter of course, every Custom-House officer must be supposed to fall. Neither the front nor the back entrance of the Custom-House opens on the road to Paradise.

The greater part of my officers were Whigs.* It was well for their venerable brotherhood, that the new Surveyor was not a politician, and, though a faithful Democrat in principle, neither received nor held his office with any reference to political services.* Had it been otherwise,—had an active politician been put into this influential post, to assume the easy task of making head against a Whig Collector, whose infirmities withheld him from the personal administration of his office,—hardly a man of the old corps would have drawn

THE SCARLET LETTER

the breath of official life, within a month after the extermina-
ting angel had come up the Custom-House steps. According
to the received code in such matters, it would have been
nothing short of duty, in a politician, to bring every one of
those white heads under the axe of the guillotine. It was
plain enough to discern, that the old fellows dreaded some
such discourtesy at my hands. It pained, and at the same time
amused me, to behold the terrors that attended my advent; to
see a furrowed cheek, weather-beaten by half a century of
storm, turn ashy pale at the glance of so harmless an individual as myself; to detect, as one or another addressed me, the
tremor of a voice, which, in long-past days, had been wont
to bellow through a speaking-trumpet, hoarsely enough to
frighten Boreas*himself to silence. They knew, these excellent old persons, that, by all established rule,—and, as regarded some of them, weighed by their own lack of efficiency
for business,—they ought to have given place to younger
men, more orthodox in politics, and altogether fitter than
themselves to serve our common Uncle. I knew it too, but
could never quite find in my heart to act upon the knowledge.
Much and deservedly to my own discredit, therefore, and
considerably to the detriment of my official conscience, they
continued, during my incumbency, to creep about the
wharves, and loiter up and down the Custom-House steps.
They spent a good deal of time, also, asleep in their accustomed corners, with their chairs tilted back against the wall;
awaking, however, once or twice in a forenoon, to bore one
another with the several thousandth repetition of old sea-
stories, and mouldy jokes, that had grown to be pass-words and
countersigns among them.

The discovery was soon made, I imagine, that the new
Surveyor had no great harm in him. So, with lightsome hearts,
and the happy consciousness of being usefully employed,—
in their own behalf, at least, if not for our beloved country,—
these good old gentlemen went through the various formalities

of office. Sagaciously, under their spectacles, did they peep into the holds of vessels! Mighty was their fuss about little matters, and marvellous, sometimes, the obtuseness that allowed greater ones to slip between their fingers! Whenever such a mischance occurred,—when a wagon-load of valuable merchandise had been smuggled ashore, at noonday, perhaps, and directly beneath their unsuspicious noses,—nothing could exceed the vigilance and alacrity with which they proceeded to lock, and double-lock, and secure with tape and sealing-wax, all the avenues of the delinquent vessel. Instead of a reprimand for their previous negligence, the case seemed rather to require an eulogium on their praiseworthy caution, after the mischief had happened; a grateful recognition of the promptitude of their zeal, the moment that there was no longer any remedy!

Unless people are more than commonly disagreeable, it is my foolish habit to contract a kindness for them. The better part of my companion's character, if it have a better part, is that which usually comes uppermost in my regard, and forms the type whereby I recognize the man. As most of these old Custom-House officers had good traits, and as my position in reference to them, being paternal and protective, was favorable to the growth of friendly sentiments, I soon grew to like them all. It was pleasant, in the summer forenoons,—when the fervent heat, that almost liquefied the rest of the human family, merely communicated a genial warmth to their half-torpid systems,—it was pleasant to hear them chatting in the back entry, a row of them all tipped against the wall, as usual; while the frozen witticisms of past generations were thawed out, and came bubbling with laughter from their lips. Externally, the jollity of aged men has much in common with the mirth of children; the intellect, any more than a deep sense of humor, has little to do with the matter; it is, with both, a gleam that plays upon the surface, and imparts a sunny and cheery aspect alike to the green branch, and gray, mouldering trunk. In one case, however, it is real sunshine; in the other, it more resembles the phosphorescent glow of decaying wood.

It would be sad injustice, the reader must understand, to represent all my excellent old friends as in their dotage. In the first place, my coadjutors were not invariably old; there were men among them in their strength and prime, of marked ability and energy, and altogether superior to the sluggish and dependent mode of life on which their evil stars had cast them. Then, moreover, the white locks of age were sometimes found to be the thatch of an intellectual tenement in good repair. But, as respects the majority of my corps of veterans, there will be no wrong done, if I characterize them generally as a set of wearisome old souls, who had gathered nothing worth preservation from their varied experience of life. They seemed to have flung away all the golden grain of practical wisdom, which they had enjoyed so many opportunities of harvesting, and most carefully to have stored their memories with the husks. They spoke with far more interest and unction of their morning's breakfast, or yesterday's, to-day's, or to-morrow's dinner, than of the shipwreck of forty or fifty years ago, and all the world's wonders which they had witnessed with their youthful eyes.

The father of the Custom-House—the patriarch, not only of this little squad of officials, but, I am bold to say, of the respectable body of tide-waiters all over the United States—was a certain permanent Inspector.* He might truly be termed a legitimate son of the revenue system, dyed in the wool, or rather, born in the purple; since his sire, a Revolutionary colonel, and formerly collector of the port, had created an office for him, and appointed him to fill it, at a period of the early ages which few living men can now remember. This Inspector, when I first knew him, was a man of fourscore years, or thereabouts, and certainly one of the most wonderful specimens of winter-green that you would be likely to discover in a lifetime's search. With his florid cheek, his compact figure, smartly arrayed in a bright-buttoned blue coat, his brisk and vigorous step, and his hale and hearty aspect, altogether, he seemed—not young, indeed—but a kind of new contrivance of Mother Nature in the shape of man, whom age and infirmity had no business to touch. His voice and laugh, which perpetually reëchoed through the Custom-House, had nothing of the tremulous quaver and cackle of an old man's utterance; they came strutting out of his lungs, like the crow of a cock, or the blast of a clarion. Looking at him merely as an animal,—and there was very little else to look at,—he was a most satisfactory object, from the thorough healthfulness and wholesomeness of his system, and his capacity, at that extreme age, to enjoy all, or nearly all, the delights which he had ever aimed at, or conceived of. The careless security of his life in the Custom-House, on a regular income, and with but slight and infrequent apprehensions of removal, had no doubt contributed to make time pass lightly over him. The original and more potent causes, however, lay in the rare perfection of his animal nature, the moderate proportion of intellect, and the very trifling admixture of moral and spiritual ingredients; these latter qualities, indeed, being in barely enough measure to keep the old gentleman from walking on all-fours. He possessed no power of thought, no depth of feeling, no troublesome sensibilities; nothing, in short, but a few commonplace instincts, which, aided by the cheerful temper that grew inevitably out of his physical well-being, did duty very respectably, and to general acceptance, in lieu of a heart. He had been the husband of three wives, all long since dead; the father of twenty children, most of whom, at every age of childhood or maturity, had likewise returned to dust. Here, one would suppose, might have been sorrow enough to imbue the sunniest disposition, through and through, with a sable tinge. Not so with our old Inspector! One brief sigh sufficed to carry off the entire burden of these dismal reminiscences. The next moment, he was as ready for sport as any unbreeched infant; far readier than the Collector's junior clerk, who, at nineteen years, was much the elder and graver man of the two.

I used to watch and study this patriarchal personage with, I think, livelier curiosity than any other form of humanity there presented to my notice. He was, in truth, a rare phenomenon; so perfect in one point of view; so shallow, so delusive, so impalpable, such an absolute nonentity, in every other. My conclusion was that he had no soul, no heart, no mind; nothing, as I have already said, but instincts; and yet, withal, so cunningly had the few materials of his character been put together, that there was no painful perception of deficiency, but, on my part, an entire contentment with what I found in him. It might be difficult—and it was so—to conceive how he should exist hereafter, so earthy and sensuous did he seem; but surely his existence here, admitting that it was to terminate with his last breath, had been not unkindly given; with no higher moral responsibilities than the beasts of the field, but with a larger scope of enjoyment than theirs, and with all their blessed immunity from the dreariness and duskiness of age.

One point, in which he had vastly the advantage over his four-footed brethren, was his ability to recollect the good dinners which it had made no small portion of the happiness of his life to eat. His gourmandism was a highly agreeable trait; and to hear him talk of roast-meat was as appetizing as a pickle or an oyster. As he possessed no higher attribute, and neither sacrificed nor vitiated any spiritual endowment by devoting all his energies and ingenuities to subserve the delight and profit of his maw, it always pleased and satisfied me to hear him expatiate on fish, poultry, and butcher's meat, and the most eligible methods of preparing them for the table. His reminiscences of good cheer, however ancient the date of the actual banquet, seemed to bring the savor of pig or turkey under one's very nostrils. There were flavors on his palate, that had lingered there not less than sixty or seventy years, and were still apparently as fresh as that of the mutton-chop which he had just devoured for his breakfast. I have heard him smack his lips over dinners, every guest at which, except himself, had long been food for worms. It was marvel-lous to observe how the ghosts of bygone meals were continu-ally rising up before him; not in anger or retribution, but as if grateful for his former appreciation, and seeking to reduplicate an endless series of enjoyment, at once shadowy and sensual. A tenderloin of beef, a hind-quarter of veal, a spare-rib of pork, a particular chicken, or a remarkably praiseworthy turkey, which had perhaps adorned his board in the days of the elder Adams,* would be remembered; while all the subse-quent experience of our race, and all the events that bright-ened or darkened his individual career, had gone over him with as little permanent effect as the passing breeze. The chief tragic event of the old man's life, so far as I could judge, was his mishap with a certain goose, which lived and died some twenty or forty years ago; a goose of most promising figure, but which, at table, proved so inveterately tough that the carving-knife would make no impression on its carcass; and it could only be divided with an axe and handsaw.

But it is time to quit this sketch; on which, however, I should be glad to dwell at considerably more length, because, of all men whom I have ever known, this individual was fittest to be a Custom-House officer. Most persons, owing to causes which I may not have space to hint at, suffer moral detriment from this peculiar mode of life. The old Inspector was incapable of it, and, were he to continue in office to the end of time, would be just as good as he was then, and sit down to dinner with just as good an appetite.

There is one likeness, without which my gallery of Custom-House portraits would be strangely incomplete; but which my comparatively few opportunities for observation enable me to sketch only in the merest outline. It is that of the Collector, our gallant old General, who, after his brilliant military service, subsequently to which he had ruled over a wild Western territory,* had come hither, twenty years before, to spend the decline of his varied and honorable life. The brave soldier had already numbered, nearly or quite, his threescore years and ten, and was pursuing the remainder of his earthly march, burdened with infirmities which even the martial music of his own spirit-stirring recollections could do little towards lightening. The step was palsied now, that had been foremost in the charge. It was only with the assistance of a servant, and by leaning his hand heavily on the iron balustrade, that he could slowly and painfully ascend the Custom-House steps, and, with a toilsome progress across the floor, attain his customary chair beside the fireplace. There he used to sit, gazing with a somewhat dim serenity of aspect at the figures that came and went; amid the rustle of papers, the administering of oaths, the discussion of business, and the casual talk of the office; all which sounds and circumstances seemed but indistinctly to impress his senses, and hardly to make their way into his inner sphere of contemplation. His countenance, in this repose, was mild and kindly. If his notice was sought, an expression of courtesy and interest gleamed out upon his features; proving that there was light within him, and that it was only the outward medium of the intellectual lamp that obstructed the rays in their passage. The closer you penetrated to the substance of his mind, the sounder it appeared. When no longer called upon to speak, or listen, either of which operations cost him an evident effort, his face would briefly subside into its former not uncheerful quietude. It was not painful to behold this look; for, though dim, it had not the imbecility of decaying age. The framework of his nature, originally strong and massive, was not yet crumbled into ruin.

To observe and define his character, however, under such disadvantages, was as difficult a task as to trace out and build up anew, in imagination, an old fortress, like Ticonderoga,* from a view of its gray and broken ruins. Here and there, perchance, the walls may remain almost complete; but elsewhere may be only a shapeless mound, cumbrous with its very strength, and overgrown, through long years of peace and neglect, with grass and alien weeds.

Nevertheless, looking at the old warrior with affection,—for, slight as was the communication between us, my feeling towards him, like that of all bipeds and quadrupeds who knew him, might not improperly be termed so,—I could discern the main points of his portrait. It was marked with the noble and heroic qualities which showed it to be not by a mere accident, but of good right, that he had won a distinguished name. His spirit could never, I conceive, have been characterized by an uneasy activity; it must, at any period of his life, have required an impulse to set him in motion; but, once stirred up, with obstacles to overcome, and an adequate object to be attained, it was not in the man to give out or fail. The heat that had formerly pervaded his nature, and which was not yet extinct, was never of the kind that flashes and flickers in a blaze, but, rather, a deep, red glow, as of iron in a furnace. Weight, solidity, firmness; this was the expression of his repose, even in such decay as had crept untimely over him, at the period of which I speak. But I could imagine, even then, that, under some excitement which should go deeply into his consciousness,—roused by a trumpet-peal, loud enough to awaken all of his energies that were not dead, but only slumbering,—he was yet capable of flinging off his infirmities like a sick man's gown, dropping the staff of age to seize a battle sword, and starting up once more a warrior. And, in so intense a moment, his demeanour would have still been calm. Such an exhibition, however, was but to be pictured in fancy; not to be anticipated, nor desired. What I saw in him—as evidently as the indestructible ramparts of Old Ticonderoga, already cited as the most appropriate simile—were the features of stubborn and ponderous endurance, which might well have amounted to obstinacy in his earlier days; of integrity, that, like most of his other endowments, lay in a somewhat heavy mass, and was just as unmalleable and unmanageable as a ton of iron ore; and of benevolence, which, fiercely as he led the bayonets on at Chippewa or Fort Erie,* I take to be of quite as genuine a stamp as what actuates any or all the polemical philanthropists of the age. He had slain men with his own hand, for aught I know;—certainly, they had fallen, like blades of grass at the sweep of the scythe, before the charge to which his spirit imparted its triumphant energy;—but, be that as it might, there was never in his heart so much cruelty as would have brushed the down off a butterfly's wing. I have not known the man, to whose innate kindliness I would more confidently make an appeal.

Many characteristics—and those, too, which contribute not the least forcibly to impart resemblance in a sketch—must have vanished, or been obscured, before I met the General. All merely graceful attributes are usually the most evanescent; nor does Nature adorn the human ruin with blossoms of new beauty, that have their roots and proper nutriment only in the chinks and crevices of decay, as she sows wall-flowers over the ruined fortress of Ticonderoga. Still, even in respect of grace and beauty, there were points well worth noting. A ray of humor, now and then, would make its way through the veil of dim obstruction, and glimmer pleasantly upon our faces. A trait of native elegance, seldom seen in the masculine character after childhood or early youth, was shown in the General's fondness for the sight and fragrance of flowers. An old soldier might be supposed to prize only the bloody laurel on his brow; but here was one, who seemed to have a young girl's appreciation of the floral tribe.

There, beside the fireplace, the brave old General used to sit; while the Surveyor—though seldom, when it could be avoided, taking upon himself the difficult task of engaging him in conversation—was fond of standing at a distance, and watching his quiet and almost slumberous countenance. He seemed away from us, although we saw him but a few yards off; remote, though we passed close beside his chair; unattainable, though we might have stretched forth our hands and touched his own. It might be, that he lived a more real life within his thoughts, than amid the unappropriate environment of the Collector's office. The evolutions of the parade; the tumult of the battle; the flourish of old, heroic music, heard thirty years before;—such scenes and sounds, perhaps, were all alive before his intellectual sense. Meanwhile, the merchants and ship-masters, the spruce clerks, and uncouth sailors, entered and departed; the bustle of this commercial and Custom-House life kept up its little murmur roundabout him; and neither with the men nor their affairs did the General appear to sustain the most distant relation. He was as much out of place as an old sword—now rusty, but which had flashed once in the battle's front, and showed still a bright gleam along its blade—would have been, among the inkstands, paper-folders, and mahogany rulers, on the Deputy Collector's desk.

There was one thing that much aided me in renewing and re-creating the stalwart soldier of the Niagara frontier,—the man of true and simple energy. It was the recollection of those memorable words of his,—"I'll try, Sir!"*—spoken on the very verge of a desperate and heroic enterprise, and breathing the soul and spirit of New England hardihood, comprehending all perils, and encountering all. If, in our country, valor were rewarded by heraldic honor, this phrase—which it seems so easy to speak, but which only he, with such

a task of danger and glory before him, has ever spoken—
would be the best and fittest of all mottoes for the General's
shield of arms.

It contributes greatly towards a man's moral and intellectual
health, to be brought into habits of companionship with
individuals unlike himself, who care little for his pursuits,
and whose sphere and abilities he must go out of himself
to appreciate. The accidents of my life have often afforded
me this advantage, but never with more fulness and variety
than during my continuance in office. There was one man,
especially, the observation of whose character gave me a new
idea of talent. His gifts were emphatically those of a man of
business;* prompt, acute, clear-minded; with an eye that saw
through all perplexities, and a faculty of arrangement that
made them vanish, as by the waving of an enchanter's wand.
Bred up from boyhood in the Custom-House, it was his
proper field of activity; and the many intricacies of business,
so harassing to the interloper, presented themselves before
him with the regularity of a perfectly comprehended system.
In my contemplation, he stood as the ideal of his class. He
was, indeed, the Custom-House in himself; or, at all events,
the main-spring that kept its variously revolving wheels in
motion; for, in an institution like this, where its officers are
appointed to subserve their own profit and convenience, and
seldom with a leading reference to their fitness for the duty
to be performed, they must perforce seek elsewhere the
dexterity which is not in them. Thus, by an inevitable necessity, as a magnet attracts steel-filings, so did our man of
business draw to himself the difficulties which everybody met
with. With an easy condescension, and kind forbearance
towards our stupidity,—which, to his order of mind, must
have seemed little short of crime,—would he forthwith, by
the merest touch of his finger, make the incomprehensible
as clear as daylight. The merchants valued him not less than
we, his esoteric friends. His integrity was perfect; it was a

law of nature with him, rather than a choice or a principle; nor can it be otherwise than the main condition of an intellect so remarkably clear and accurate as his, to be honest and regular in the administration of affairs. A stain on his conscience, as to any thing that came within the range of his vocation, would trouble such a man very much in the same way, though to a far greater degree, than an error in the balance of an account, or an ink-blot on the fair page of a book of record. Here, in a word,—and it is a rare instance in my life,—I had met with a person thoroughly adapted to the situation which he held.

Such were some of the people with whom I now found myself connected. I took it in good part at the hands of Providence, that I was thrown into a position so little akin to my past habits; and set myself seriously to gather from it whatever profit was to be had. After my fellowship of toil and impracticable schemes, with the dreamy brethren of Brook Farm;* after living for three years within the subtile influence of an intellect like Emerson's;* after those wild, free days on the Assabeth,* indulging fantastic speculations beside our fire of fallen boughs, with Ellery Channing;* after talking with Thoreau* about pine-trees and Indian relics, in his hermitage at Walden; after growing fastidious by sympathy with the classic refinement of Hillard's* culture; after becoming imbued with poetic sentiment at Longfellow's hearth-stone;*—it was time, at length, that I should exercise other faculties of my nature, and nourish myself with food for which I had hitherto had little appetite. Even the old Inspector was desirable, as a change of diet, to a man who had known Alcott.* I looked upon it as an evidence, in some measure, of a system naturally well balanced, and lacking no essential part of a thorough organization, that, with such associates to remember, I could mingle at once with men of altogether different qualities, and never murmur at the change.

Literature, its exertions and objects, were now of little

moment* in my regard. I cared not, at this period, for books; they were apart from me. Nature,—except it were human nature,—the nature that is developed in earth and sky, was, in one sense, hidden from me; and all the imaginative delight, wherewith it had been spiritualized, passed away out of my mind. A gift, a faculty, if it had not departed, was suspended and inanimate within me. There would have been something sad, unutterably dreary, in all this, had I not been conscious that it lay at my own option to recall whatever was valuable in the past. It might be true, indeed, that this was a life which could not, with impunity, be lived too long; else, it might make me permanently other than I had been, without trans- forming me into any shape which it would be worth my while to take. But I never considered it as other than a tran- sitory life. There was always a prophetic instinct, a low whisper in my ear, that, within no long period, and whenever a new change of custom should be essential to my good, a change would come.

Meanwhile, there I was, a Surveyor of the Revenue, and, so far as I have been able to understand, as good a Surveyor as need be. A man of thought, fancy, and sensibility, (had he ten times the Surveyor's proportion of those qualities,) may, at any time, be a man of affairs, if he will only choose to give himself the trouble. My fellow-officers, and the merchants and sea-captains with whom my official duties brought me into any manner of connection, viewed me in no other light, and probably knew me in no other character. None of them, I presume, had ever read a page of my inditing, or would have cared a fig the more for me, if they had read them all; nor would it have mended the matter, in the least, had those same unprofitable pages been written with a pen like that of Burns or of Chaucer,* each of whom was a Custom-House officer in his day, as well as I. It is a good lesson—though it may often be a hard one—for a man who has dreamed of literary fame, and of making for himself a rank among the world's dignitaries by such means, to step aside out of the narrow circle in which his claims are recognized, and to find how utterly devoid of significance, beyond that circle, is all that he achieves, and all he aims at. I know not that I especially needed the lesson, either in the way of warning or rebuke; but, at any rate, I learned it thoroughly; nor, it gives me pleasure to reflect, did the truth, as it came home to my perception, ever cost me a pang, or require to be thrown off in a sigh. In the way of literary talk, it is true, the Naval Officer —an excellent fellow, who came into office with me, and went out only a little later—would often engage me in a discussion about one or the other of his favorite topics, Napoleon or Shakspeare. The Collector's junior clerk, too,—a young gentleman who, it was whispered, occasionally covered a sheet of Uncle Sam's letter-paper with what, (at the distance of a few yards,) looked very much like poetry,—used now and then to speak to me of books, as matters with which I might possibly be conversant. This was my all of lettered intercourse; and it was quite sufficient for my necessities.

No longer seeking nor caring that my name should be blazoned abroad on title-pages, I smiled to think that it had now another kind of vogue. The Custom-House marker imprinted it, with a stencil and black paint, on pepper-bags, and baskets of anatto,* and cigar-boxes, and bales of all kinds of dutiable merchandise, in testimony that these commodities had paid the impost, and gone regularly through the office. Borne on such queer vehicle of fame, a knowledge of my existence, so far as a name conveys it, was carried where it had never been before, and, I hope, will never go again.

But the past was not dead. Once in a great while, the thoughts, that had seemed so vital and so active, yet had been put to rest so quietly, revived again. One of the most remarkable occasions, when the habit of bygone days awoke in me, was that which brings it within the law of literary propriety to offer the public the sketch which I am now writing.

In the second story of the Custom-House, there is a large room, in which the brick-work and naked rafters have never been covered with panelling and plaster. The edifice—originally projected on a scale adapted to the old commercial enterprise of the port, and with an idea of subsequent prosperity destined never to be realized—contains far more space than its occupants know what to do with. This airy hall, therefore, over the Collector's apartments, remains unfinished to this day, and, in spite of the aged cobwebs that festoon its dusky beams, appears still to await the labor of the carpenter and mason. At one end of the room, in a recess, were a number of barrels, piled one upon another, containing bundles of official documents. Large quantities of similar rubbish lay lumbering the floor. It was sorrowful to think how many days, and weeks, and months, and years of toil, had been wasted on these musty papers,* which were now only an encumbrance on earth, and were hidden away in this forgotten corner, never more to be glanced at by human eyes. But, then, what reams of other manuscripts—filled, not with the dulness of official formalities, but with the thought of inventive brains and the rich effusion of deep hearts—had gone equally to oblivion; and that, moreover, without serving a purpose in their day, as these heaped-up papers had, and—saddest of all—without purchasing for their writers the comfortable livelihood which the clerks of the Custom-House had gained by these worthless scratchings of the pen! Yet not altogether worthless, perhaps, as materials of local history. Here, no doubt, statistics of the former commerce of Salem might be discovered, and memorials of her princely merchants,—old King Derby,—old Billy Gray,*—old Simon Forrester,*—and many another magnate in his day; whose powdered head, however, was scarcely in the tomb, before his mountain-pile of wealth began to dwindle. The founders of the greater part of the families which now compose the aristocracy of Salem might here be traced, from the petty and obscure beginnings of their traffic, at periods generally much posterior to the Revolution, upward to what their children look upon as long-established rank.

Prior to the Revolution, there is a dearth of records; the earlier documents and archives of the Custom-House having, probably, been carried off to Halifax, when all the King's officials accompanied the British army in its flight from Boston.* It has often been a matter of regret with me; for, going back, perhaps, to the days of the Protectorate,* those papers must have contained many references to forgotten or remembered men, and to antique customs, which would have affected me with the same pleasure as when I used to pick up Indian arrow-heads in the field near the Old Manse.

But, one idle and rainy day, it was my fortune to make a discovery of some little interest. Poking and burrowing into the heaped-up rubbish in the corner; unfolding one and another document, and reading the names of vessels that had long ago foundered at sea or rotted at the wharves, and those of merchants, never heard of now on 'Change,* nor very readily decipherable on their mossy tombstones; glancing at such matters with the saddened, weary, half-reluctant interest which we bestow on the corpse of dead activity,—and exerting my fancy, sluggish with little use, to raise up from these dry bones an image of the old town's brighter aspect, when India was a new region, and only Salem knew the way thither,—I chanced to lay my hand on a small package, carefully done up in a piece of ancient yellow parchment. This envelope had the air of an official record of some period long past, when clerks engrossed their stiff and formal chirography on more substantial materials than at present. There was something about it that quickened an instinctive curiosity, and made me undo the faded red tape, that tied up the package, with the sense that a treasure would here be brought to light. Unbending the rigid folds of the parchment cover, I found it to be a commission, under the hand and seal of Governor Shirley,* in favor of one Jonathan Pue,* as Surveyor of his Majesty's Customs for the port of Salem, in the Province of Massachusetts Bay. I remembered to have read (probably in Felt's Annals) a notice of the decease of Mr. Surveyor Pue, about fourscore years ago; and likewise, in a newspaper of recent times, an account of the digging up of his remains in the little grave-yard of St. Peter's Church, during the renewal of that edifice. Nothing, if I rightly call to mind, was left of my respected predecessor, save an imperfect skeleton, and some fragments of apparel, and a wig of majestic frizzle; which, unlike the head that it once adorned, was in very satisfactory preservation. But, on examining the papers which the parchment commission served to envelop, I found more traces of Mr. Pue's mental part, and the internal operations of his head, than the frizzled wig had contained of the venerable skull itself.

They were documents, in short, not official, but of a private nature, or, at least, written in his private capacity, and apparently with his own hand. I could account for their being included in the heap of Custom-House lumber only by the fact, that Mr. Pue's death had happened suddenly; and that these papers, which he probably kept in his official desk, had never come to the knowledge of his heirs, or were supposed to relate to the business of the revenue. On the transfer of the archives to Halifax, this package, proving to be of no public concern, was left behind, and had remained ever since unopened.

The ancient Surveyor—being little molested, I suppose, at that early day, with business pertaining to his office—seems to have devoted some of his many leisure hours to researches as a local antiquarian, and other inquisitions of a similar nature. These supplied material for petty activity to a mind that would otherwise have been eaten up with rust. A portion of his facts, by the by, did me good service in the preparation of the article entitled "MAIN STREET,"*included in the present volume. The remainder may perhaps be applied to purposes equally valuable, hereafter; or not impossibly may be worked up, so far as they go, into a regular history of Salem, should my veneration for the natal soil ever impel me to so pious a task. Meanwhile, they shall be at the command of any gentleman, inclined, and competent, to take the unprofitable labor off my hands. As a final disposition, I contemplate depositing them with the Essex Historical Society.*

But the object that most drew my attention, in the mysterious package, was a certain affair of fine red cloth, much worn and faded. There were traces about it of gold embroidery, which, however, was greatly frayed and defaced; so that none, or very little, of the glitter was left. It had been wrought, as was easy to perceive, with wonderful skill of needlework; and the stitch (as I am assured by ladies conversant with such mysteries) gives evidence of a now forgotten art, not to be recovered even by the process of picking out the threads. This rag of scarlet cloth,—for time, and wear, and a sacrilegious moth, had reduced it to little other than a rag,—on careful examination, assumed the shape of a letter. It was the capital letter A. By an accurate measurement, each limb proved to be precisely three inches and a quarter in length. It had been intended, there could be no doubt, as an ornamental article of dress; but how it was to be worn, or what rank, honor, and dignity, in by-past times, were signified by it, was a riddle which (so evanescent are the fashions of the world in these particulars) I saw little hope of solving. And yet it strangely interested me. My eyes fastened themselves upon the old scarlet letter, and would not be turned aside. Certainly, there was some deep meaning in it, most worthy of interpretation, and which, as it were, streamed forth from the mystic symbol, subtly communicating itself to my sensibilities, but evading the analysis of my mind.

While thus perplexed,—and cogitating, among other hypotheses, whether the letter might not have been one of those decorations which the white men used to contrive, in order to take the eyes of Indians,—I happened to place it on my breast. It seemed to me,—the reader may smile, but must not doubt my word,—it seemed to me, then, that I experienced a sensation not altogether physical, yet almost so, as of burning heat; and as if the letter were not of red cloth, but red-hot iron. I shuddered, and involuntarily let it fall upon the floor.

In the absorbing contemplation of the scarlet letter, I had hitherto neglected to examine a small roll of dingy paper, around which it had been twisted. This I now opened, and had the satisfaction to find, recorded by the old Surveyor's pen, a reasonably complete explanation of the whole affair. There were several foolscap sheets, containing many particulars respecting the life and conversation of one Hester Prynne, who appeared to have been rather a noteworthy personage in the view of our ancestors. She had flourished during a period between the early days of Massachusetts and the close of the seventeenth century. Aged persons, alive in the time of Mr. Surveyor Pue, and from whose oral testimony he had made up his narrative, remembered her, in their youth, as a very old, but not decrepit woman, of a stately and solemn aspect. It had been her habit, from an almost immemorial date, to go about the country as a kind of voluntary nurse, and doing whatever miscellaneous good she might; taking upon herself, likewise, to give advice in all matters, especially those of the heart; by which means, as a person of such propensities inevitably must, she gained from many people the reverence due to an angel, but, I should imagine, was looked upon by others as an intruder and a nuisance. Prying farther into the manuscript, I found the record of other doings and sufferings of this singular woman, for most of which the reader is referred to the story entitled "THE SCARLET LETTER"; and it should be borne carefully in mind, that the main facts of that story are authorized and authenticated by the document of Mr. Surveyor Pue. The original papers, together with the scarlet letter itself,—a most curious relic,—are still in my possession, and shall be freely exhibited to whomsoever, induced by the great interest of the narrative, may desire a sight of them. I must not be understood as affirming, that, in the dressing up of the tale, and imagining the motives and modes of passion that influenced the characters who figure in it, I have invariably confined myself within the limits of the old Surveyor's half a dozen sheets of foolscap. On the contrary, I have allowed myself, as to such points, nearly or altogether as much license as if the facts had been entirely of my own invention. What I contend for is the authenticity of the outline.

This incident recalled my mind, in some degree, to its old track. There seemed to be here the groundwork of a tale. It impressed me as if the ancient Surveyor, in his garb of a hundred years gone by, and wearing his immortal wig,—which was buried with him, but did not perish in the grave,—had met me in the deserted chamber of the Custom-House. In his port was the dignity of one who had borne his Majesty's commission, and who was therefore illuminated by a ray of the splendor that shone so dazzlingly about the throne. How unlike, alas! the hang-dog look of a republican official, who, as the servant of the people, feels himself less than the least, and below the lowest, of his masters. With his own ghostly hand, the obscurely seen, but majestic, figure had imparted to me the scarlet symbol, and the little roll of explanatory manuscript. With his own ghostly voice, he had exhorted me, on the sacred consideration of my filial duty and reverence towards him,—who might reasonably regard himself as my official ancestor,—to bring his mouldy and moth-eaten lucubrations before the public. "Do this," said the ghost of Mr. Surveyor Pue, emphatically nodding the head that looked so imposing within its memorable wig, "do this, and the profit shall be all your own! You will shortly need it; for it is not in your days as it was in mine, when a man's office was a life-lease, and oftentimes an heirloom. But, I charge you, in this matter of old

Mistress Prynne, give to your predecessor's memory the credit which will be rightfully its due!" And I said to the ghost of Mr. Surveyor Pue,—"I will!"

On Hester Prynne's story, therefore, I bestowed much thought. It was the subject of my meditations for many an hour, while pacing to and fro across my room, or traversing, with a hundredfold repetition, the long extent from the front-door of the Custom-House to the side-entrance, and back again. Great were the weariness and annoyance of the old Inspector and the Weighers and Gaugers, whose slumbers were disturbed by the unmercifully lengthened tramp of my passing and returning footsteps. Remembering their own former habits, they used to say that the Surveyor was walking the quarter-deck. They probably fancied that my sole object—and, indeed, the sole object for which a sane man could ever put himself into voluntary motion—was, to get an appetite for dinner. And to say the truth, an appetite, sharpened by the east-wind that generally blew along the passage, was the only valuable result of so much indefatigable exercise. So little adapted is the atmosphere of a Custom-House to the delicate harvest of fancy and sensibility, that, had I remained there through ten Presidencies yet to come, I doubt whether the tale of "The Scarlet Letter" would ever have been brought before the public eye. My imagination was a tarnished mirror. It would not reflect, or only with miserable dimness, the figures with which I did my best to people it. The characters of the narrative would not be warmed and rendered malleable, by any heat that I could kindle at my intellectual forge. They would take neither the glow of passion nor the tenderness of sentiment, but retained all the rigidity of dead corpses, and stared me in the face with a fixed and ghastly grin of contemptuous defiance. "What have you to do with us?" that expression seemed to say. "The little power you might once have possessed over the tribe of unrealities is gone! You have bartered it for a pittance of the public gold. Go, then, and earn your wages!" In short, the almost torpid creatures of my own fancy twitted me with imbecility, and not without fair occasion.

It was not merely during the three hours and a half which Uncle Sam claimed as his share of my daily life, that this wretched numbness held possession of me. It went with me on my sea-shore walks and rambles into the country, whenever—which was seldom and reluctantly—I bestirred myself to seek that invigorating charm of Nature, which used to give me such freshness and activity of thought, the moment that I stepped across the threshold of the Old Manse. The same torpor, as regarded the capacity for intellectual effort, accompanied me home, and weighed upon me in the chamber which I most absurdly termed my study. Nor did it quit me, when, late at night, I sat in the deserted parlour, lighted only by the glimmering coal-fire and the moon, striving to picture forth imaginary scenes, which, the next day, might flow out on the brightening page in many-hued description.

If the imaginative faculty refused to act at such an hour, it might well be deemed a hopeless case. Moonlight, in a familiar room, falling so white upon the carpet, and showing all its figures so distinctly,—making every object so minutely visible, yet so unlike a morning or noontide visibility,—is a medium the most suitable for a romance-writer to get acquainted with his illusive guests. There is the little domestic scenery of the well-known apartment; the chairs, with each its separate individuality; the centre-table, sustaining a work-basket, a volume or two, and an extinguished lamp; the sofa; the book-case; the picture on the wall;—all these details, so completely seen, are so spiritualized by the unusual light, that they seem to lose their actual substance, and become things of intellect. Nothing is too small or too trifling to undergo this change, and acquire dignity thereby. A child's shoe; the doll, seated in her little wicker carriage; the hobby-horse;—whatever, in a word, has been used or played with, during the day, is now invested with a quality of strangeness and remoteness, though still almost as vividly present as by daylight. Thus, therefore, the floor of our familiar room has become a neutral territory, somewhere between the real world and fairy-land, where the Actual and the Imaginary may meet, and each imbue itself with the nature of the other. Ghosts might enter here, without affrighting us. It would be too much in keeping with the scene to excite surprise, were we to look about us and discover a form, beloved, but gone hence, now sitting quietly in a streak of this magic moonshine, with an aspect that would make us doubt whether it had returned from afar, or had never once stirred from our fireside.

The somewhat dim coal-fire has an essential influence in producing the effect which I would describe. It throws its unobtrusive tinge throughout the room, with a faint ruddiness upon the walls and ceiling, and a reflected gleam from the polish of the furniture. This warmer light mingles itself with the cold spirituality of the moonbeams, and communicates, as it were, a heart and sensibilities of human tenderness to the forms which fancy summons up. It converts them from snow-images into men and women. Glancing at the looking-glass, we behold—deep within its haunted verge—the smouldering glow of the half-extinguished anthracite, the white moonbeams on the floor, and a repetition of all the gleam and shadow of the picture, with one remove farther from the actual, and nearer to the imaginative. Then, at such an hour, and with this scene before him, if a man, sitting all alone, cannot dream strange things, and make them look like truth, he need never try to write romances.

But, for myself, during the whole of my Custom-House experience, moonlight and sunshine, and the glow of fire-light, were just alike in my regard; and neither of them was of one whit more avail than the twinkle of a tallow-candle. An entire class of susceptibilities, and a gift connected with them, —of no great richness or value, but the best I had,—was gone from me.

It is my belief, however, that, had I attempted a different order of composition, my faculties would not have been found so pointless and inefficacious. I might, for instance, have contented myself with writing out the narratives of a veteran shipmaster,* one of the Inspectors, whom I should be most ungrateful not to mention; since scarcely a day passed that he did not stir me to laughter and admiration by his marvellous gifts as a story-teller. Could I have preserved the picturesque force of his style, and the humorous coloring which nature taught him how to throw over his descriptions, the result, I honestly believe, would have been something new in literature. Or I might readily have found a more serious task. It was a folly, with the materiality of this daily life pressing so intrusively upon me, to attempt to fling myself back into another age; or to insist on creating the semblance of a world out of airy matter, when, at every moment, the impalpable beauty of my soap-bubble was broken by the rude contact of some actual circumstance. The wiser effort would have been, to diffuse thought and imagination through the opaque substance of to-day, and thus to make it a bright transparency; to spiritualize the burden that began to weigh so heavily; to seek, resolutely, the true and indestructible value that lay hidden in the petty and wearisome incidents, and ordinary characters, with which I was now conversant. The fault was mine. The page of life that was spread out before me seemed dull and commonplace, only because I had not fathomed its deeper import. A better book than I shall ever write was there; leaf after leaf presenting itself to me, just as it was written out by the reality of the flitting hour, and vanishing as fast as written, only because my brain wanted the insight and my hand the cunning to transcribe it. At some future day, it may be, I shall remember a few scattered fragments and broken paragraphs, and write them down, and find the letters turn to gold upon the page.

These perceptions have come too late. At the instant, I was

only conscious that what would have been a pleasure once was now a hopeless toil. There was no occasion to make much moan about this state of affairs. I had ceased to be a writer of tolerably poor tales and essays, and had become a tolerably good Surveyor of the Customs. That was all. But, nevertheless, it is any thing but agreeable to be haunted by a suspicion that one's intellect is dwindling away; or exhaling, without your consciousness, like ether out of a phial; so that, at every glance, you find a smaller and less volatile residuum. Of the fact, there could be no doubt; and, examining myself and others, I was led to conclusions in reference to the effect of public office on the character, not very favorable to the mode of life in question. In some other form, perhaps, I may hereafter develop these effects. Suffice it here to say, that a Custom-House officer, of long continuance, can hardly be a very praiseworthy or respectable personage, for many reasons; one of them, the tenure by which he holds his situation, and another, the very nature of his business, which—though, I trust, an honest one—is of such a sort that he does not share in the united effort of mankind.

An effect—which I believe to be observable, more or less, in every individual who has occupied the position—is, that, while he leans on the mighty arm of the Republic, his own proper strength departs from him. He loses, in an extent proportioned to the weakness or force of his original nature, the capability of self-support. If he possess an unusual share of native energy, or the enervating magic of place do not operate too long upon him, his forfeited powers may be redeemable. The ejected officer—fortunate in the unkindly shove that sends him forth betimes, to struggle amid a struggling world —may return to himself, and become all that he has ever been. But this seldom happens. He usually keeps his ground just long enough for his own ruin, and is then thrust out, with sinews all unstrung, to totter along the difficult footpath of life as he best may. Conscious of his own infirmity,—that his tempered steel and elasticity are lost,—he for ever afterwards looks wistfully about him in quest of support external to himself. His pervading and continual hope—a hallucination, which, in the face of all discouragement, and making light of impossibilities, haunts him while he lives, and, I fancy, like the convulsive throes of the cholera, torments him for a brief space after death—is, that, finally, and in no long time, by some happy coincidence of circumstances, he shall be restored to office. This faith, more than any thing else, steals the pith and availability out of whatever enterprise he may dream of undertaking. Why should he toil and moil, and be at so much trouble to pick himself up out of the mud, when, in a little while hence, the strong arm of his Uncle will raise and support him? Why should he work for his living here, or go to dig gold in California,* when he is so soon to be made happy, at monthly intervals, with a little pile of glittering coin out of his Uncle's pocket? It is sadly curious to observe how slight a taste of office suffices to infect a poor fellow with this singular disease. Uncle Sam's gold—meaning no disrespect to the worthy old gentleman—has, in this respect, a quality of enchantment like that of the Devil's wages. Whoever touches it should look well to himself, or he may find the bargain to go hard against him, involving, if not his soul, yet many of its better attributes; its sturdy force, its courage and constancy, its truth,* its self-reliance, and all that gives the emphasis to manly character.

Here was a fine prospect in the distance! Not that the Surveyor brought the lesson home to himself, or admitted that he could be so utterly undone, either by continuance in office, or ejectment. Yet my reflections were not the most comfortable. I began to grow melancholy and restless; continually prying into my mind, to discover which of its poor properties were gone, and what degree of detriment had already accrued to the remainder. I endeavoured to calculate how much longer I could stay in the Custom-House, and yet go forth a

man. To confess the truth, it was my greatest apprehension,
—as it would never be a measure of policy to turn out so quiet
an individual as myself, and it being hardly in the nature of a
public officer to resign,—it was my chief trouble, therefore,
that I was likely to grow gray and decrepit in the Surveyorship, and become much such another animal as the old Inspector. Might it not, in the tedious lapse of official life that lay
before me, finally be with me as it was with this venerable
friend,—to make the dinner-hour the nucleus of the day, and
to spend the rest of it, as an old dog spends it, asleep in the
sunshine or the shade? A dreary look-forward this, for a man
who felt it to be the best definition of happiness to live
throughout the whole range of his faculties and sensibilities!
But, all this while, I was giving myself very unnecessary
alarm. Providence had meditated better things for me than I
could possibly imagine for myself.

A remarkable event of the third year of my Surveyorship—
to adopt the tone of "P.P."—was the election of General Taylor* to the Presidency. It is essential, in order to form a complete estimate of the advantages of official life, to view the in-
cumbent at the in-coming of a hostile administration. His position is then one of the most singularly irksome, and, in every
contingency, disagreeable, that a wretched mortal can possibly
occupy; with seldom an alternative of good, on either hand, although what presents itself to him as the worst event may
very probably be the best. But it is a strange experience, to a
man of pride and sensibility, to know that his interests are
within the control of individuals who neither love nor understand him, and by whom, since one or the other must needs
happen, he would rather be injured than obliged. Strange, too,
for one who has kept his calmness throughout the contest, to
observe the bloodthirstiness that is developed in the hour of
triumph, and to be conscious that he is himself among its objects! There are few uglier traits of human nature than this
tendency—which I now witnessed in men no worse than their

neighbours—to grow cruel, merely because they possessed the power of inflicting harm. If the guillotine,* as applied to office-holders, were a literal fact, instead of one of the most apt of metaphors, it is my sincere belief, that the active members of the victorious party were sufficiently excited to have chopped off all our heads, and have thanked Heaven for the opportunity! It appears to me—who have been a calm and curious observer, as well in victory as defeat—that this fierce and bitter spirit of malice and revenge has never distinguished the many triumphs of my own party as it now did that of the Whigs. The Democrats take the offices,* as a general rule, because they need them, and because the practice of many years has made it the law of political warfare, which, unless a different system be proclaimed, it were weakness and coward-ice to murmur at. But the long habit of victory has made them generous. They know how to spare, when they see occasion; and when they strike, the axe may be sharp, indeed, but its edge is seldom poisoned with ill-will; nor is it their custom ignominiously to kick the head which they have just struck off.

In short, unpleasant as was my predicament, at best, I saw much reason to congratulate myself that I was on the losing side, rather than the triumphant one. If, heretofore, I had been none of the warmest of partisans, I began now, at this season of peril and adversity, to be pretty acutely sensible with which party my predilections lay; nor was it without something like regret and shame, that, according to a rea-sonable calculation of chances, I saw my own prospect of re-taining office to be better than those of my Democratic brethren. But who can see an inch into futurity, beyond his nose? My own head was the first that fell!*

The moment when a man's head drops off is seldom or never, I am inclined to think, precisely the most agreeable of his life. Nevertheless, like the greater part of our misfortunes, even so serious a contingency brings its remedy and consola-tion with it, if the sufferer will but make the best, rather than the worst, of the accident which has befallen him. In my particular case, the consolatory topics were close at hand, and, indeed, had suggested themselves to my meditations a considerable time before it was requisite to use them. In view of my previous weariness of office, and vague thoughts of resignation, my fortune somewhat resembled that of a person who should entertain an idea of committing suicide, and, altogether beyond his hopes, meet with the good hap to be murdered. In the Custom-House, as before in the Old Manse, I had spent three years; a term long enough to rest a weary brain; long enough to break off old intellectual habits, and make room for new ones; long enough, and too long, to have lived in an unnatural state, doing what was really of no advantage nor delight to any human being, and withholding myself from toil that would, at least, have stilled an unquiet impulse in me. Then, moreover, as regarded his unceremonious ejectment, the late Surveyor was not altogether ill-pleased to be recognized by the Whigs as an enemy;*since his inactivity in political affairs,—his tendency to roam, at will, in that broad and quiet field where all mankind may meet, rather than confine himself to those narrow paths where brethren of the same household must diverge from one another,—had sometimes made it questionable with his brother Democrats whether he was a friend. Now, after he had won the crown of martyrdom, (though with no longer a head to wear it on,) the point might be looked upon as settled. Finally, little heroic as he was, it seemed more decorous to be overthrown in the downfall of the party with which he had been content to stand, than to remain a forlorn survivor, when so many worthier men were falling; and, at last, after subsisting for four years on the mercy of a hostile administration, to be compelled then to define his position anew, and claim the yet more humiliating mercy of a friendly one.

Meanwhile, the press had taken up my affair,*and kept me, for a week or two, careering through the public prints, in my decapitated state, like Irving's Headless Horseman;* ghastly and grim, and longing to be buried, as a politically dead man ought. So much for my figurative self. The real human being, all this time, with his head safely on his shoulders, had brought himself to the comfortable conclusion, that every thing was for the best; and, making an investment in ink, paper, and steel-pens, had opened his long-disused writing-desk, and was again a literary man.

Now it was, that the lucubrations of my ancient predecessor, Mr. Surveyor Pue, came into play. Rusty through long idleness, some little space was requisite before my intellectual machinery could be brought to work upon the tale, with an effect in any degree satisfactory. Even yet, though my thoughts were ultimately much absorbed in the task, it wears, to my eye, a stern and sombre aspect; too much ungladdened by genial sunshine; too little relieved by the tender and familiar influences which soften almost every scene of nature and real life, and, undoubtedly, should soften every picture of them. This uncaptivating effect is perhaps due to the period of hardly accomplished revolution, and still seething turmoil, in which the story shaped itself. It is no indication, however, of a lack of cheerfulness in the writer's mind; for he was happier, while straying through the gloom of these sunless fantasies, than at any time since he had quitted the Old Manse.* Some of the briefer articles, which contribute to make up the volume, have likewise been written since my involuntary withdrawal from the toils and honors of public life, and the remainder are gleaned from annuals and magazines, of such antique date that they have gone round the circle, and come back to novelty again.* Keeping up the metaphor of the political guillotine, the whole may be considered as the POSTHUMOUS PAPERS OF A DECAPITATED SURVEYOR; and the sketch

---

* At the time of writing this article, the author intended to publish, along with "The Scarlet Letter," several shorter tales and sketches. These it has been thought advisable to defer.

which I am now bringing to a close, if too autobiographical for a modest person to publish in his lifetime, will readily be excused in a gentleman who writes from beyond the grave. Peace be with all the world! My blessing on my friends! My forgiveness to my enemies! For I am in the realm of quiet!

The life of the Custom-House lies like a dream behind me. The old Inspector,—who, by the by, I regret to say, was overthrown and killed by a horse, some time ago; else he would certainly have lived for ever,—he, and all those other venerable personages who sat with him at the receipt of custom, are but shadows in my view; white-headed and wrinkled images, which my fancy used to sport with, and has now flung aside for ever. The merchants,—Pingree, Phillips, Shepard, Upton, Kimball, Bertram, Hunt,—these, and many other names, which had such a classic familiarity for my ear six months ago,—these men of traffic, who seemed to occupy so important a position in the world,—how little time has it required to disconnect me from them all, not merely in act, but recollection! It is with an effort that I recall the figures and appellations of these few. Soon, likewise, my old native town will loom upon me through the haze of memory, a mist brooding over and around it; as if it were no portion of the real earth, but an overgrown village in cloud-land, with only imaginary inhabitants to people its wooden houses, and walk its homely lanes, and the unpicturesque prolixity of its main street. Henceforth, it ceases to be a reality of my life. I am a citizen of somewhere else. My good townspeople will not much regret me; for—though it has been as dear an object as any, in my literary efforts, to be of some importance in their eyes, and to win myself a pleasant memory in this abode and burial-place of so many of my forefathers—there has never been, for me, the genial atmosphere which a literary man requires, in order to ripen the best harvest of his mind. I shall do better amongst other faces; and these familiar ones, it need hardly be said, will do just as well without me.

It may be, however,—O, transporting and triumphant thought!—that the great-grandchildren of the present race may sometimes think kindly of the scribbler of bygone days, when the antiquary of days to come, among the sites memorable in the town's history, shall point out the locality of THE TOWN-PUMP!*

THE SCARLET LETTER

I

THE PRISON-DOOR

A THRONG of bearded men, in sad-colored garments and gray, steeple-crowned hats, intermixed with women, some wearing hoods, and others bareheaded, was assembled in front of a wooden edifice, the door of which was heavily timbered with oak, and studded with iron spikes.

The founders of a new colony, whatever Utopia of human virtue and happiness they might originally project, have invariably recognized it among their earliest practical necessities to allot a portion of the virgin soil as a cemetery, and another portion as the site of a prison. In accordance with this rule, it may safely be assumed that the forefathers of Boston had built the first prison-house, somewhere in the vicinity of Cornhill,* almost as seasonably as they marked out the first burial-ground, on Isaac Johnson's lot,* and round about his grave, which subsequently became the nucleus of all the congregated sepulchres in the old church-yard of King's Chapel.* Certain it is, that, some fifteen or twenty years*after the settlement of the town, the wooden jail was already marked with weather-stains and other indications of age,* which gave a yet darker aspect to its beetle-browed and gloomy front. The rust on the ponderous iron-work of its oaken door looked more antique than any thing else in the new world. Like all that pertains to crime, it seemed never to have known a youthful era. Before this ugly edifice, and between it and the wheel-track of the street, was a grass-plot, much overgrown with burdock, pig-weed, apple-peru, and such unsightly vegetation, which evidently found something congenial in the soil that had so early borne the black flower of civilized society, a prison. But, on one side of the portal, and rooted almost at the threshold, was a wild rose-bush,* covered, in this month of June, with its delicate gems, which might be imagined to offer their fragrance and fragile beauty to the prisoner as he went in, and to the condemned criminal as he came forth to his doom, in token that the deep heart of Nature could pity and be kind to him.

This rose-bush, by a strange chance, has been kept alive in history; but whether it had merely survived out of the stern old wilderness, so long after the fall of the gigantic pines and oaks that originally overshadowed it,—or whether, as there is fair authority for believing, it had sprung up under the foot-steps of the sainted Ann Hutchinson,* as she entered the prison-door,—we shall not take upon us to determine. Finding it so directly on the threshold of our narrative, which is now about to issue from that inauspicious portal, we could hardly do otherwise than pluck one of its flowers and present it to the reader. It may serve, let us hope, to symbolize some sweet moral blossom, that may be found along the track, or relieve the darkening close of a tale of human frailty and sorrow.

II

THE MARKET-PLACE

T HE grass-plot before the jail, in Prison Lane, on a certain summer morning, not less than two centuries ago, was occupied by a pretty large number of the inhabitants of Boston; all with their eyes intently fastened on the iron-clamped oaken door. Amongst any other population, or at a later period in the history of New England, the grim rigidity that petrified the bearded physiognomies of these good people would have augured some awful business in hand. It could have betokened nothing short of the anticipated execution of some noted culprit, on whom the sentence of a legal tribunal had but confirmed the verdict of public sentiment. But, in that early severity of the Puritan character, an inference of this kind could not so indubitably be drawn. It might be that a sluggish bond-servant, or an undutiful child, whom his parents had given over to the civil authority, was to be corrected at the whipping-post. It might be, that an Antinomian,* a Quaker,* or other heterodox religionist, was to be scourged out of the town, or an idle and vagrant Indian, whom the white man's fire-water had made riotous about the streets, was to be driven with stripes into the shadow of the forest. It might be, too, that a witch, like old Mistress Hibbins,* the bitter-tempered widow of the magistrate, was to die upon the gallows. In either case, there was very much the same solemnity of demeanour on the part of the spectators; as befitted a people amongst whom religion and law were almost identical, and in whose character both were so thoroughly interfused, that the mildest and the severest acts of public discipline were alike made venerable and awful. Meagre, indeed, and cold, was the sympathy that a transgressor might look for, from such bystanders at the scaffold. On the other hand, a penalty which, in our days, would infer a degree of mocking infamy and ridicule, might then be invested with almost as stern a dignity as the punishment of death itself.

It was a circumstance to be noted, on the summer morning when our story begins its course, that the women, of whom there were several in the crowd, appeared to take a peculiar interest in whatever penal infliction might be expected to ensue. The age had not so much refinement, that any sense of impropriety restrained the wearers of petticoat and farthingale from stepping forth into the public ways, and wedging their not unsubstantial persons, if occasion were, into the throng nearest to the scaffold at an execution. Morally, as well as materially, there was a coarser fibre in those wives and maidens of old English birth and breeding, than in their fair descendants, separated from them by a series of six or seven generations; for, throughout that chain of ancestry, every successive mother has transmitted to her child a fainter bloom, a more delicate and briefer beauty, and a slighter physical frame, if not a character of less force and solidity, than her own. The women, who were now standing about the prison-door, stood within less than half a century of the period when the man-like Elizabeth* had been the not altogether unsuitable representative of the sex. They were her countrywomen; and the beef and ale of their native land, with a moral diet not a whit more refined, entered largely into their composition. The bright morning sun, therefore, shone on broad shoulders and well-developed busts, and on round and ruddy cheeks, that had ripened in the far-off island, and had hardly yet grown paler or thinner in the atmosphere of New England. There was, moreover, a boldness and rotundity of speech among these matrons, as most of them seemed to be, that would startle us at the present day, whether in respect to its purport or its volume of tone.

"Goodwives," said a hard-featured dame of fifty, "I'll tell ye a piece of my mind. It would be greatly for the public behoof, if we women, being of mature age and church-members in good repute, should have the handling of such malefactresses as this Hester Prynne. What think ye, gossips? If the hussy stood up for judgment before us five, that are now here in a knot together, would she come off with such a sentence as the worshipful magistrates have awarded? Marry, I trow not!"

"People say," said another, "that the Reverend Master Dimmesdale, her godly pastor, takes it very grievously to heart that such a scandal should have come upon his congregation."

"The magistrates are God-fearing gentlemen, but merciful overmuch,—that is a truth," added a third autumnal matron. "At the very least, they should have put the brand of a hot iron on Hester Prynne's forehead. Madam Hester would have winced at that, I warrant me. But she,—the naughty baggage,—little will she care what they put upon the bodice of her gown! Why, look you, she may cover it with a brooch, or such like heathenish adornment, and so walk the streets as brave as ever!"

"Ah, but," interposed, more softly, a young wife, holding a child by the hand, "let her cover the mark as she will, the pang of it will be always in her heart."

"What do we talk of marks and brands, whether on the bodice of her gown, or the flesh of her forehead?" cried another female, the ugliest as well as the most pitiless of these self-constituted judges. "This woman has brought shame upon us all, and ought to die. Is there not law for it? Truly there is, both in the Scripture and the statute-book.* Then let the magistrates, who have made it of no effect, thank themselves if their own wives and daughters go astray!"

"Mercy on us, goodwife," exclaimed a man in the crowd, "is there no virtue in woman, save what springs from a wholesome fear of the gallows? That is the hardest word yet! Hush, now, gossips; for the lock is turning in the prison-door, and here comes Mistress Prynne herself."

The door of the jail being flung open from within, there appeared, in the first place, like a black shadow emerging into the sunshine, the grim and grisly presence of the town-beadle, with a sword by his side and his staff of office in his hand. This personage prefigured and represented in his aspect the whole dismal severity of the Puritanic code of law, which it was his business to administer in its final and closest application to the offender. Stretching forth the official staff in his left hand, he laid his right upon the shoulder of a young woman, whom he thus drew forward; until, on the threshold of the prison-door, she repelled him, by an action marked with natural dignity and force of character, and stepped into the open air, as if by her own free-will. She bore in her arms a child, a baby of some three months old, who winked and turned aside its little face from the too vivid light of day; because its existence, heretofore, had brought it acquainted only with the gray twilight of a dungeon, or other darksome apartment of the prison.

When the young woman—the mother of this child—stood fully revealed before the crowd, it seemed to be her first impulse to clasp the infant closely to her bosom; not so much by an impulse of motherly affection, as that she might thereby conceal a certain token, which was wrought or fastened into her dress. In a moment, however, wisely judging that one token of her shame would but poorly serve to hide another, she took the baby on her arm, and, with a burning blush, and yet a haughty smile, and a glance that would not be abashed, looked around at her townspeople and neighbours. On the breast of her gown, in fine red cloth, surrounded with an elaborate embroidery and fantastic flourishes of gold thread, appeared the letter A. It was so artistically done, and with so much fertility and gorgeous luxuriance of fancy, that it had all the effect of a last and fitting decoration to the apparel which she wore; and which was of a splendor in accordance with the taste of the age, but greatly beyond what was allowed by the sumptuary regulations of the colony.

The young woman was tall, with a figure of perfect elegance, on a large scale. She had dark and abundant hair, so glossy that it threw off the sunshine with a gleam, and a face which, besides being beautiful from regularity of feature and richness of complexion, had the impressiveness belonging to a marked brow and deep black eyes. She was lady-like, too, after the manner of the feminine gentility of those days; characterized by a certain state and dignity, rather than by the delicate, evanescent, and indescribable grace, which is now recognized as its indication. And never had Hester Prynne appeared more lady-like, in the antique interpretation of the term, than as she issued from the prison. Those who had before known her, and had expected to behold her dimmed and obscured by a disastrous cloud, were astonished, and even startled, to perceive how her beauty shone out, and made a halo of the misfortune and ignominy in which she was enveloped. It may be true, that, to a sensitive observer, there was something exquisitely painful in it. Her attire, which, indeed, she had wrought for the occasion, in prison, and had modelled much after her own fancy, seemed to express the attitude of her spirit, the desperate recklessness of her mood, by its wild and picturesque peculiarity. But the point which drew all eyes, and, as it were, transfigured the wearer,—so that both men and women, who had been familiarly acquainted with Hester Prynne, were now impressed as if they beheld her for the first time,—was that SCARLET LETTER,* so fantastically embroidered and illuminated upon her bosom. It had the effect of a spell, taking her out of the ordinary relations with humanity, and inclosing her in a sphere by herself.

"She hath good skill at her needle, that's certain," remarked one of the female spectators; "but did ever a woman, before this brazen hussy, contrive such a way of showing it! Why, gossips, what is it but to laugh in the faces of our godly magistrates, and make a pride out of what they, worthy gentlemen, meant for a punishment?"

"It were well," muttered the most iron-visaged of the old dames, "if we stripped Madam Hester's rich gown off her dainty shoulders; and as for the red letter, which she hath stitched so curiously, I'll bestow a rag of mine own rheumatic flannel, to make a fitter one!"

"O, peace, neighbours, peace!" whispered their youngest companion. "Do not let her hear you! Not a stitch in that embroidered letter, but she has felt it in her heart."

The grim beadle now made a gesture with his staff.

"Make way, good people, make way, in the King's name," cried he. "Open a passage; and, I promise ye, Mistress Prynne shall be set where man, woman, and child may have a fair sight of her brave apparel, from this time till an hour past meridian. A blessing on the righteous Colony of the Massachusetts, where iniquity is dragged out into the sunshine! Come along, Madam Hester, and show your scarlet letter in the market-place!"

A lane was forthwith opened through the crowd of spectators. Preceded by the beadle, and attended by an irregular procession of stern-browed men and unkindly-visaged women, Hester Prynne set forth towards the place appointed for her punishment. A crowd of eager and curious schoolboys, understanding little of the matter in hand, except that it gave them a half-holiday, ran before her progress, turning their heads continually to stare into her face, and at the winking baby in her arms, and at the ignominious letter on her breast. It was no great distance, in those days, from the prison-door to the market-place. Measured by the prisoner's experience, however, it might be reckoned a journey of some length; for, haughty as her demeanour was, she perchance underwent an agony from every footstep of those that thronged to see her, as if her heart had been flung into the street for them all to spurn and trample upon. In our nature, however, there is a provision, alike marvellous and merciful, that the sufferer should never know the intensity of what he endures by its present torture, but chiefly by the pang that rankles after it. With almost a serene deportment, therefore, Hester Prynne passed through this portion of her ordeal, and came to a sort of scaffold,* at the western extremity of the market-place. It stood nearly beneath the eaves of Boston's earliest church, and appeared to be a fixture there.

In fact, this scaffold constituted a portion of a penal machine, which now, for two or three generations past, has been merely historical and traditionary among us, but was held, in the old time, to be as effectual an agent in the promotion of good citizenship, as ever was the guillotine among the terrorists of France. It was, in short, the platform of the pillory; and above it rose the framework of that instrument of discipline, so fashioned as to confine the human head in its tight grasp, and thus hold it up to the public gaze. The very ideal of ignominy was embodied and made manifest in this contrivance of wood and iron. There can be no outrage, methinks, against our common nature,—whatever be the delinquencies of the individual,—no outrage more flagrant than to forbid the culprit to hide his face for shame; as it was the essence of this punishment to do. In Hester Prynne's instance, however, as not unfrequently in other cases, her sentence bore, that she should stand a certain time upon the platform, but without undergoing that gripe about the neck and confinement of the head, the proneness to which was the most devilish characteristic of this ugly engine. Knowing well her part, she ascended a flight of wooden steps, and was thus displayed to the surrounding multitude, at about the height of a man's shoulders above the street.

Had there been a Papist among the crowd of Puritans, he might have seen in this beautiful woman, so picturesque in her attire and mien, and with the infant at her bosom, an object to remind him of the image of Divine Maternity,* which so many illustrious painters have vied with one another to represent; something which should remind him, indeed, but only by contrast, of that sacred image of sinless motherhood, whose infant was to redeem the world. Here, there was the taint of deepest sin in the most sacred quality of human life, working such effect, that the world was only the darker for this woman's beauty, and the more lost for the infant that she had borne.

The scene was not without a mixture of awe, such as must always invest the spectacle of guilt and shame in a fellow-creature, before society shall have grown corrupt enough to smile, instead of shuddering, at it. The witnesses of Hester Prynne's disgrace had not yet passed beyond their simplicity. They were stern enough to look upon her death, had that been the sentence, without a murmur at its severity, but had none of the heartlessness of another social state, which would find only a theme for jest in an exhibition like the present. Even had there been a disposition to turn the matter into ridicule, it must have been repressed and overpowered by the solemn presence of men no less dignified than the Governor, and several of his counsellors, a judge, a general, and the ministers of the town; all of whom sat or stood in a balcony of the meeting-house, looking down upon the platform. When such personages could constitute a part of the spectacle, without risking the majesty or reverence of rank and office, it was safely to be inferred that the infliction of a legal sentence would have an earnest and effectual meaning. Accordingly, the crowd was sombre and grave. The unhappy culprit sustained herself as best a woman might, under the heavy weight of a thousand unrelenting eyes, all fastened upon her, and concentred at her bosom. It was almost intolerable to be borne. Of an impulsive and passionate nature, she had fortified herself to encounter the stings and venomous stabs of public contumely, wreaking itself in every variety of insult; but there was a quality so much more terrible in the solemn mood of the popular mind, that she longed rather to behold all those rigid countenances contorted with scornful merriment, and herself the object. Had a roar of laughter burst from the multitude,—each man, each woman, each little shrill-voiced child, contributing their individual parts,—Hester Prynne might have repaid them all with a bitter and disdainful smile. But, under the leaden infliction which it was her doom to endure, she felt, at moments, as if she must needs shriek out with the full power of her lungs, and cast herself from the scaffold down upon the ground, or else go mad at once.

Yet there were intervals when the whole scene, in which she was the most conspicuous object, seemed to vanish from her eyes, or, at least, glimmered indistinctly before them, like a mass of imperfectly shaped and spectral images. Her mind, and especially her memory, was preternaturally active, and kept bringing up other scenes than this roughly hewn street of a little town, on the edge of the Western wilderness;*other faces than were lowering upon her from beneath the brims of those steeple-crowned hats. Reminiscences, the most trifling and immaterial, passages of infancy and school-days, sports, childish quarrels, and the little domestic traits of her maiden years, came swarming back upon her, intermingled with recollections of whatever was gravest in her subsequent life; one picture precisely as vivid as another; as if all were of similar importance, or all alike a play. Possibly, it was an instinctive device of her spirit, to relieve itself, by the exhibition of these phantasmagoric forms, from the cruel weight and hardness of the reality.

Be that as it might, the scaffold of the pillory was a point of view that revealed to Hester Prynne the entire track along which she had been treading, since her happy infancy. Standing on that miserable eminence, she saw again her native village, in Old England, and her paternal home; a decayed house of gray stone, with a poverty-stricken aspect, but retaining a half-obliterated shield of arms over the portal, in token of antique gentility. She saw her father's face, with its bald brow, and reverend white beard, that flowed over the old-fashioned Elizabethan ruff; her mother's, too, with the look of heedful and anxious love which it always wore in her remembrance, and which, even since her death, had so often laid the impediment of a gentle remonstrance in her daughter's pathway. She saw her own face, glowing with girlish beauty, and illuminating all the interior of the dusky mirror in which she had been wont to gaze at it. There she beheld another countenance, of a man well stricken in years, a pale, thin, scholar-like visage, with eyes dim and bleared by the lamp-light that had served them to pore over many ponderous books. Yet those same bleared optics had a strange, penetrating power, when it was their owner's purpose to read the human soul. This figure of the study and the cloister, as Hester Prynne's womanly fancy failed not to recall, was slightly deformed, with the left shoulder a trifle higher than the right. Next rose before her, in memory's picture-gallery, the intricate and narrow thoroughfares, the tall, gray houses, the huge cathedrals, and the public edifices, ancient in date and quaint in architecture, of a Continental city;*where a new life had awaited her, still in connection with the misshapen scholar; a new life, but feeding itself on time-worn materials, like a tuft of green moss on a crumbling wall. Lastly, in lieu of these shifting scenes, came back the rude market-place of the Puritan settlement, with all the townspeople assembled and levelling their stern regards at Hester Prynne,—yes, at herself,—who stood on the scaffold of the pillory, an infant on her arm, and the letter A, in scarlet, fantastically embroidered with gold thread, upon her bosom!

Could it be true? She clutched the child so fiercely to her breast, that it sent forth a cry; she turned her eyes downward at the scarlet letter, and even touched it with her finger, to assure herself that the infant and the shame were real. Yes!—these were her realities,—all else had vanished!

III

THE RECOGNITION

FROM this intense consciousness of being the object of severe and universal observation, the wearer of the scarlet letter was at length relieved by discerning, on the outskirts of the crowd, a figure which irresistibly took possession of her thoughts. An Indian, in his native garb, was standing there; but the red men were not so infrequent visitors of the English settlements, that one of them would have attracted any notice from Hester Prynne, at such a time; much less would he have excluded all other objects and ideas from her mind. By the Indian's side, and evidently sustaining a companionship with him, stood a white man, clad in a strange disarray of civilized and savage costume.

He was small in stature, with a furrowed visage, which, as yet, could hardly be termed aged. There was a remarkable intelligence in his features, as of a person who had so cultivated his mental part that it could not fail to mould the physical to itself, and become manifest by unmistakable tokens. Although, by a seemingly careless arrangement of his heterogeneous garb, he had endeavoured to conceal or abate the peculiarity, it was sufficiently evident to Hester Prynne, that one of this man's shoulders rose higher than the other. Again, at the first instant of perceiving that thin visage, and the slight deformity of the figure, she pressed her infant to her bosom, with so convulsive a force that the poor babe uttered another cry of pain. But the mother did not seem to hear it.

At his arrival in the market-place, and some time before she saw him, the stranger had bent his eyes on Hester Prynne. It was carelessly, at first, like a man chiefly accustomed to look inward, and to whom external matters are of little value and import, unless they bear relation to something within his mind. Very soon, however, his look became keen and penetrative. A writhing horror twisted itself across his features, like a snake gliding swiftly over them, and making one little pause, with all its wreathed intervolutions in open sight. His face darkened with some powerful emotion, which, nevertheless, he so instantaneously controlled by an effort of his will, that, save at a single moment, its expression might have passed for calmness. After a brief space, the convulsion grew almost imperceptible, and finally subsided into the depths of his nature. When he found the eyes of Hester Prynne fastened on his own, and saw that she appeared to recognize him, he slowly and calmly raised his finger, made a gesture with it in the air, and laid it on his lips.

Then, touching the shoulder of a townsman who stood next to him, he addressed him in a formal and courteous manner.

"I pray you, good Sir," said he, "who is this woman?—and wherefore is she here set up to public shame?"

"You must needs be a stranger in this region, friend," answered the townsman, looking curiously at the questioner and his savage companion; "else you would surely have heard of Mistress Hester Prynne, and her evil doings. She hath raised a great scandal, I promise you, in godly Master Dimmesdale's church."

"You say truly," replied the other. "I am a stranger, and have been a wanderer, sorely against my will. I have met with grievous mishaps by sea and land, and have been long held in bonds among the heathen-folk, to the southward; and am now brought hither by this Indian, to be redeemed out of my captivity. Will it please you, therefore, to tell me of Hester Prynne's,—have I her name rightly?—of this woman's offences, and what has brought her to yonder scaffold?"

"Truly, friend, and methinks it must gladden your heart, after your troubles and sojourn in the wilderness," said the townsman, "to find yourself, at length, in a land where iniquity is searched out, and punished in the sight of rulers and people; as here in our godly New England. Yonder woman, Sir, you must know, was the wife of a certain learned man, English by birth, but who had long dwelt in Amsterdam, whence, some good time agone, he was minded to cross over and cast in his lot with us of the Massachusetts. To this purpose, he sent his wife before him, remaining himself to look after some necessary affairs. Marry, good Sir, in some two years, or less, that the woman has been a dweller here in Boston, no tidings have come of this learned gentleman, Master Prynne; and his young wife, look you, being left to her own misguidance——"

"Ah!—aha!—I conceive you," said the stranger, with a bitter smile. "So learned a man as you speak of should have learned this too in his books. And who, by your favor, Sir, may be the father of yonder babe—it is some three or four months old, I should judge—which Mistress Prynne is holding in her arms?"

"Of a truth, friend, that matter remaineth a riddle; and the Daniel*who shall expound it is yet a-wanting," answered the townsman. "Madam Hester absolutely refuseth to speak, and the magistrates have laid their heads together in vain. Peradventure the guilty one stands looking on at this sad spectacle, unknown of man, and forgetting that God sees him."

"The learned man," observed the stranger, with another smile, "should come himself to look into the mystery."

"It behooves him well, if he be still in life," responded the townsman. "Now, good Sir, our Massachusetts magistracy, bethinking themselves that this woman is youthful and fair, and doubtless was strongly tempted to her fall;—and that, moreover, as is most likely, her husband may be at the bottom of the sea;—they have not been bold to put in force the extremity of our righteous law against her. The penalty thereof is death.* But, in their great mercy and tenderness of heart, they have doomed Mistress Prynne to stand only a space of three hours on the platform of the pillory, and then and thereafter, for the remainder of her natural life, to wear a mark of shame upon her bosom."

"A wise sentence!" remarked the stranger, gravely bowing his head. "Thus she will be a living sermon against sin, until the ignominious letter be engraved upon her tombstone. It irks me, nevertheless, that the partner of her iniquity should not, at least, stand on the scaffold by her side. But he will be known!—he will be known!—he will be known!"

He bowed courteously to the communicative townsman, and, whispering a few words to his Indian attendant, they both made their way through the crowd.

While this passed, Hester Prynne had been standing on her pedestal, still with a fixed gaze towards the stranger; so fixed a gaze, that, at moments of intense absorption, all other objects in the visible world seemed to vanish, leaving only him and her. Such an interview, perhaps, would have been more terrible than even to meet him as she now did, with the hot, mid-day sun burning down upon her face, and lighting up its shame; with the scarlet token of infamy on her breast; with the sin-born infant in her arms; with a whole people, drawn forth as to a festival, staring at the features that should have been seen only in the quiet gleam of the fireside, in the happy shadow of a home, or beneath a matronly veil, at church. Dreadful as it was, she was conscious of a shelter in the presence of these thousand witnesses. It was better to stand thus, with so many betwixt him and her, than to greet him, face to face, they two alone. She fled for refuge, as it were, to the public exposure, and dreaded the moment when its protection should be withdrawn from her. Involved in these thoughts, she scarcely heard a voice behind her, until it had repeated her name more than once, in a loud and solemn tone, audible to the whole multitude.

"Hearken unto me, Hester Prynne!" said the voice.

It has already been noticed, that directly over the platform on which Hester Prynne stood was a kind of balcony, or open gallery, appended to the meeting-house. It was the place whence proclamations were wont to be made, amidst an assemblage of the magistracy, with all the ceremonial that attended such public observances in those days. Here, to witness the scene which we are describing, sat Governor Bellingham* himself, with four sergeants about his chair, bearing halberds, as a guard of honor. He wore a dark feather in his hat, a border of embroidery on his cloak, and a black velvet tunic beneath; a gentleman advanced in years, and with a hard experience written in his wrinkles. He was not ill fitted to be the head and representative of a community, which owed its origin and progress, and its present state of development, not to the impulses of youth, but to the stern and tempered energies of manhood, and the sombre sagacity of age; accomplishing so much, precisely because it imagined and hoped so little. The other eminent characters, by whom the chief ruler was surrounded, were distinguished by a dignity of mien, belonging to a period when the forms of authority were felt to possess the sacredness of divine institutions. They were, doubtless, good men, just, and sage. But, out of the whole human family, it would not have been easy to select the same number of wise and virtuous persons, who should be less capable of sitting in judgment on an erring woman's heart, and disentangling its mesh of good and evil, than the sages of rigid aspect towards whom Hester Prynne now turned her face. She seemed conscious, indeed, that whatever sympathy she might expect lay in the larger and warmer heart of the multitude; for, as she lifted her eyes towards the balcony, the unhappy woman grew pale and trembled.

The voice which had called her attention was that of the reverend and famous John Wilson,* the eldest clergyman of Boston, a great scholar, like most of his contemporaries in the profession, and withal a man of kind and genial spirit. This last attribute, however, had been less carefully developed than his intellectual gifts, and was, in truth, rather a matter of shame than self-congratulation with him. There he stood, with a border of grizzled locks beneath his skull-cap; while his gray eyes, accustomed to the shaded light of his study, were winking, like those of Hester's infant, in the unadulterated sunshine. He looked like the darkly engraved portraits which we see prefixed to old volumes of sermons; and had no more right than one of those portraits would have, to step forth, as he now did, and meddle with a question of human guilt, passion, and anguish.

"Hester Prynne," said the clergyman, "I have striven with my young brother here, under whose preaching of the word you have been privileged to sit,"—here Mr. Wilson laid his hand on the shoulder of a pale young man beside him,—"I have sought, I say, to persuade this godly youth, that he should deal with you, here in the face of Heaven, and before these wise and upright rulers, and in hearing of all the people, as touching the vileness and blackness of your sin. Knowing your natural temper better than I, he could the better judge what arguments to use, whether of tenderness or terror, such as might prevail over your hardness and obstinacy; insomuch that you should no longer hide the name of him who tempted you to this grievous fall. But he opposes to me, (with a young man's oversoftness, albeit wise beyond his years,) that it were wronging the very nature of woman to force her to lay open her heart's secrets in such broad daylight, and in presence of so great a multitude. Truly, as I sought to convince him, the shame lay in the commission of the sin, and not in the showing of it forth. What say you to it, once again, brother Dimmesdale? Must it be thou or I that shall deal with this poor sinner's soul?"

There was a murmur among the dignified and reverend occupants of the balcony; and Governor Bellingham gave expression to its purport, speaking in an authoritative voice, although tempered with respect towards the youthful clergyman whom he addressed.

"Good Master Dimmesdale," said he, "the responsibility of this woman's soul lies greatly with you. It behooves you, therefore, to exhort her to repentance, and to confession, as a proof and consequence thereof."

The directness of this appeal drew the eyes of the whole crowd upon the Reverend Mr. Dimmesdale; a young clergyman, who had come from one of the great English universities, bringing all the learning of the age into our wild forest-land. His eloquence and religious fervor had already given the earnest of high eminence in his profession. He was a person of very striking aspect, with a white, lofty, and impending brow, large, brown, melancholy eyes, and a mouth which, unless when he forcibly compressed it, was apt to be tremulous, expressing both nervous sensibility and a vast power of self-restraint. Notwithstanding his high native gifts and scholar-like attainments, there was an air about this young minister,—an apprehensive, a startled, a half-frightened look,—as of a being who felt himself quite astray and at a loss in the pathway of human existence, and could only be at ease in some seclusion of his own. Therefore, so far as his duties would permit, he trode in the shadowy by-paths, and thus kept himself simple and childlike; coming forth, when occasion was, with a freshness, and fragrance, and dewy purity of thought, which, as many people said, affected them like the speech of an angel.*

Such was the young man whom the Reverend Mr. Wilson and the Governor had introduced so openly to the public notice, bidding him speak, in the hearing of all men, to that mystery of a woman's soul, so sacred even in its pollution. The trying nature of his position drove the blood from his cheek, and made his lips tremulous.

"Speak to the woman, my brother," said Mr. Wilson. "It is of moment to her soul, and therefore, as the worshipful Governor says, momentous to thine own, in whose charge hers is. Exhort her to confess the truth!"

The Reverend Mr. Dimmesdale bent his head, in silent prayer, as it seemed, and then came forward.

"Hester Prynne," said he, leaning over the balcony, and looking down stedfastly into her eyes, "thou hearest what this good man says, and seest the accountability under which I labor. If thou feelest it to be for thy soul's peace, and that thy earthly punishment will thereby be made more effectual to salvation, I charge thee to speak out the name of thy fellow-sinner and fellow-sufferer! Be not silent from any mistaken pity and tenderness for him; for, believe me, Hester, though he were to step down from a high place, and stand there beside thee, on thy pedestal of shame, yet better were it so, than to hide a guilty heart through life. What can thy silence do for him, except it tempt him—yea, compel him, as it were—to add hypocrisy to sin? Heaven hath granted thee an open ignominy, that thereby thou mayest work out an open triumph over the evil within thee, and the sorrow without. Take heed how thou deniest to him*—who, perchance, hath not the courage to grasp it for himself—the bitter, but wholesome, cup that is now presented to thy lips!"

The young pastor's voice was tremulously sweet, rich, deep, and broken. The feeling that it so evidently manifested, rather than the direct purport of the words, caused it to vibrate within all hearts, and brought the listeners into one accord of sympathy. Even the poor baby, at Hester's bosom, was affected by the same influence; for it directed its hitherto vacant gaze towards Mr. Dimmesdale, and held up its little arms, with a half pleased, half plaintive murmur. So powerful seemed the minister's appeal, that the people could not believe but that Hester Prynne would speak out the guilty name; or else that the guilty one himself, in whatever high or lowly place he stood, would be drawn forth by an inward and inevitable necessity, and compelled to ascend the scaffold.

Hester shook her head.

"Woman, transgress not beyond the limits of Heaven's mercy!" cried the Reverend Mr. Wilson, more harshly than before. "That little babe hath been gifted with a voice, to second and confirm the counsel which thou hast heard. Speak out the name! That, and thy repentance, may avail to take the scarlet letter off thy breast."

"Never!" replied Hester Prynne, looking, not at Mr. Wilson, but into the deep and troubled eyes of the younger clergyman. "It is too deeply branded. Ye cannot take it off. And would that I might endure his agony, as well as mine!"

"Speak, woman!" said another voice, coldly and sternly, proceeding from the crowd about the scaffold. "Speak; and give your child a father!"

"I will not speak!" answered Hester, turning pale as death, but responding to this voice, which she too surely recognized. "And my child must seek a heavenly Father; she shall never know an earthly one!"

"She will not speak!" murmured Mr. Dimmesdale, who, leaning over the balcony, with his hand upon his heart, had awaited the result of his appeal. He now drew back, with a long respiration. "Wondrous strength and generosity of a woman's heart! She will not speak!"

Discerning the impracticable state of the poor culprit's mind, the elder clergyman, who had carefully prepared himself for the occasion, addressed to the multitude a discourse on sin, in all its branches, but with continual reference to the ignominious letter. So forcibly did he dwell upon this symbol, for the hour or more during which his periods were rolling over the people's heads, that it assumed new terrors in their imagination, and seemed to derive its scarlet hue from the flames of the infernal pit. Hester Prynne, meanwhile, kept her place upon the pedestal of shame, with glazed eyes, and an air of weary indifference. She had borne, that morning, all that nature could endure; and as her temperament was not of the order that escapes from too intense suffering by a swoon, her spirit could only shelter itself beneath a stony crust of insensibility, while the faculties of animal life remained entire. In this state, the voice of the preacher thundered remorselessly, but unavailingly, upon her ears. The infant, during the latter portion of her ordeal, pierced the air with its wailings and screams; she strove to hush it, mechanically, but seemed scarcely to sympathize with its trouble. With the same hard demeanour, she was led back to prison, and vanished from the public gaze within its iron-clamped portal. It was whispered, by those who peered after her, that the scarlet letter threw a lurid gleam along the dark passage-way of the interior.

IV

THE INTERVIEW

AFTER her return to the prison, Hester Prynne was found to be in a state of nervous excitement that demanded constant watchfulness, lest she should perpetrate violence on herself, or do some half-frenzied mischief to the poor babe. As night approached, it proving impossible to quell her insubordination by rebuke or threats of punishment, Master Brackett,* the jailer, thought fit to introduce a physician. He described him as a man of skill in all Christian modes of physical science, and likewise familiar with whatever the savage people could teach, in respect to medicinal herbs and roots that grew in the forest. To say the truth, there was much need of professional assistance, not merely for Hester herself, but still more urgently for the child; who, drawing its sustenance from the maternal bosom, seemed to have drank in with it all the turmoil, the anguish, and despair, which pervaded the mother's system. It now writhed in convulsions of pain, and was a forcible type, in its little frame, of the moral agony which Hester Prynne had borne throughout the day.

Closely following the jailer into the dismal apartment, appeared that individual, of singular aspect, whose presence in the crowd had been of such deep interest to the wearer of the scarlet letter. He was lodged in the prison, not as suspected of any offence, but as the most convenient and suitable mode of disposing of him, until the magistrates should have conferred with the Indian sagamores* respecting his ransom. His name was announced as Roger Chillingworth. The jailer, after ushering him into the room, remained a moment, marvelling at the comparative quiet that followed his entrance; for Hester Prynne had immediately become as still as death, although the child continued to moan.

"Prithee, friend, leave me alone with my patient," said the practitioner. "Trust me, good jailer, you shall briefly have peace in your house; and, I promise you, Mistress Prynne shall hereafter be more amenable to just authority than you may have found her heretofore."

"Nay, if your worship can accomplish that," answered Master Brackett, "I shall own you for a man of skill indeed! Verily, the woman hath been like a possessed one; and there lacks little, that I should take in hand to drive Satan out of her with stripes."

The stranger had entered the room with the characteristic quietude of the profession to which he announced himself as belonging. Nor did his demeanour change, when the withdrawal of the prison-keeper left him face to face with the woman, whose absorbed notice of him, in the crowd, had intimated so close a relation between himself and her. His first care was given to the child; whose cries, indeed, as she lay writhing on the trundle-bed, made it of peremptory necessity to postpone all other business to the task of soothing her. He examined the infant carefully, and then proceeded to unclasp a leathern case, which he took from beneath his dress. It appeared to contain certain medical preparations, one of which he mingled with a cup of water.

"My old studies in alchemy,"*observed he, "and my sojourn, for above a year past, among a people well versed in the kindly properties of simples,* have made a better physician of me than many that claim the medical degree. Here, woman!

The child is yours,—she is none of mine,—neither will she recognize my voice or aspect as a father's. Administer this draught, therefore, with thine own hand."

Hester repelled the offered medicine, at the same time gazing with strongly marked apprehension into his face.

"Wouldst thou avenge thyself on the innocent babe?" whispered she.

"Foolish woman!" responded the physician, half coldly, half soothingly. "What should ail me to harm this misbegotten and miserable babe? The medicine is potent for good; and were it my child,—yea, mine own, as well as thine!—I could do no better for it."

As she still hesitated, being, in fact, in no reasonable state of mind, he took the infant in his arms, and himself administered the draught. It soon proved its efficacy, and redeemed the leech's pledge. The moans of the little patient subsided; its convulsive tossings gradually ceased; and in a few moments, as is the custom of young children after relief from pain, it sank into a profound and dewy slumber. The physician, as he had a fair right to be termed, next bestowed his attention on the mother. With calm and intent scrutiny, he felt her pulse, looked into her eyes,—a gaze that made her heart shrink and shudder, because so familiar, and yet so strange and cold, —and, finally, satisfied with his investigation, proceeded to mingle another draught.

"I know not Lethe nor Nepenthe,"*remarked he; "but I have learned many new secrets in the wilderness, and here is one of them,—a recipe that an Indian taught me, in requital of some lessons of my own, that were as old as Paracelsus.* Drink it! It may be less soothing than a sinless conscience. That I cannot give thee. But it will calm the swell and heaving of thy passion, like oil thrown on the waves of a tempestuous sea."

He presented the cup to Hester, who received it with a

slow, earnest look into his face; not precisely a look of fear, yet full of doubt and questioning, as to what his purposes might be. She looked also at her slumbering child.

"I have thought of death," said she,—"have wished for it,—would even have prayed for it, were it fit that such as I should pray for any thing. Yet, if death be in this cup, I bid thee think again, ere thou beholdest me quaff it. See! It is even now at my lips."

"Drink, then," replied he, still with the same cold composure. "Dost thou know me so little, Hester Prynne? Are my purposes wont to be so shallow? Even if I imagine a scheme of vengeance, what could I do better for my object than to let thee live,—than to give thee medicines against all harm and peril of life,—so that this burning shame may still blaze upon thy bosom?"—As he spoke, he laid his long forefinger on the scarlet letter, which forthwith seemed to scorch into Hester's breast, as if it had been red-hot. He noticed her involuntary gesture, and smiled.—"Live, therefore, and bear about thy doom with thee, in the eyes of men and women,—in the eyes of him whom thou didst call thy husband,—in the eyes of yonder child! And, that thou mayest live, take off this draught."

Without further expostulation or delay, Hester Prynne drained the cup, and, at the motion of the man of skill, seated herself on the bed where the child was sleeping; while he drew the only chair which the room afforded, and took his own seat beside her. She could not but tremble at these preparations; for she felt that—having now done all that humanity, or principle, or, if so it were, a refined cruelty, impelled him to do, for the relief of physical suffering—he was next to treat with her as the man whom she had most deeply and irreparably injured.

"Hester," said he, "I ask not wherefore, nor how, thou hast fallen into the pit, or say rather, thou hast ascended to the pedestal of infamy, on which I found thee. The reason is not far to seek. It was my folly, and thy weakness. I,—a man of thought,—the book-worm of great libraries,—a man already in decay, having given my best years to feed the hungry dream of knowledge,—what had I to do with youth and beauty like thine own! Misshapen from my birth-hour, how could I delude myself with the idea that intellectual gifts might veil physical deformity in a young girl's fantasy! Men call me wise. If sages were ever wise in their own behoof, I might have foreseen all this. I might have known that, as I came out of the vast and dismal forest, and entered this settlement of Christian men, the very first object to meet my eyes would be thyself, Hester Prynne, standing up, a statue of ignominy, before the people. Nay, from the moment when we came down the old church-steps together, a married pair, I might have beheld the bale-fire* of that scarlet letter blazing at the end of our path!"

"Thou knowest," said Hester,—for, depressed as she was, she could not endure this last quiet stab at the token of her shame,—"thou knowest that I was frank with thee. I felt no love, nor feigned any."

"True!" replied he. "It was my folly! I have said it. But, up to that epoch of my life, I had lived in vain. The world had been so cheerless! My heart was a habitation large enough for many guests, but lonely and chill, and without a household fire. I longed to kindle one! It seemed not so wild a dream,— old as I was, and sombre as I was, and misshapen as I was, —that the simple bliss, which is scattered far and wide, for all mankind to gather up, might yet be mine. And so, Hester, I drew thee into my heart, into its innermost chamber, and sought to warm thee by the warmth which thy presence made there!"

"I have greatly wronged thee," murmured Hester.

"We have wronged each other," answered he. "Mine was

the first wrong, when I betrayed thy budding youth into a false and unnatural relation with my decay. Therefore, as a man who has not thought and philosophized in vain, I seek no vengeance, plot no evil against thee. Between thee and me, the scale hangs fairly balanced. But, Hester, the man lives who has wronged us both! Who is he?"

"Ask me not!" replied Hester Prynne, looking firmly into his face. "That thou shalt never know!"

"Never, sayest thou?" rejoined he, with a smile of dark and self-relying intelligence. "Never know him! Believe me, Hester, there are few things,—whether in the outward world, or, to a certain depth, in the invisible sphere of thought,— few things hidden from the man, who devotes himself earnestly and unreservedly to the solution of a mystery. Thou mayest cover up thy secret from the prying multitude. Thou mayest conceal it, too, from the ministers and magistrates, even as thou didst this day, when they sought to wrench the name out of thy heart, and give thee a partner on thy pedestal. But, as for me, I come to the inquest with other senses than they possess. I shall seek this man, as I have sought truth in books; as I have sought gold in alchemy. There is a sympathy that will make me conscious of him. I shall see him tremble. I shall feel myself shudder, suddenly and unawares. Sooner or later, he must needs be mine!"

The eyes of the wrinkled scholar glowed so intensely upon her, that Hester Prynne clasped her hands over her heart, dreading lest he should read the secret there at once.

"Thou wilt not reveal his name? Not the less he is mine," resumed he, with a look of confidence, as if destiny were at one with him. "He bears no letter of infamy wrought into his garment, as thou dost; but I shall read it on his heart. Yet fear not for him! Think not that I shall interfere with Heaven's own method of retribution, or, to my own loss, betray him to the gripe of human law. Neither do thou imagine that I shall contrive aught against his life; no, nor against his fame, if, as I judge, he be a man of fair repute. Let him live! Let him hide himself in outward honor, if he may! Not the less he shall be mine!"

"Thy acts are like mercy," said Hester, bewildered and appalled. "But thy words interpret thee as a terror!"

"One thing, thou that wast my wife, I would enjoin upon thee," continued the scholar. "Thou hast kept the secret of thy paramour. Keep, likewise, mine! There are none in this land that know me. Breathe not, to any human soul, that thou didst ever call me husband! Here, on this wild outskirt of the earth, I shall pitch my tent; for, elsewhere a wanderer, and isolated from human interests, I find here a woman, a man, a child, amongst whom and myself there exist the closest ligaments. No matter whether of love or hate; no matter whether of right or wrong! Thou and thine, Hester Prynne, belong to me. My home is where thou art, and where he is. But betray me not!"

"Wherefore dost thou desire it?" inquired Hester, shrinking, she hardly knew why, from this secret bond. "Why not announce thyself openly, and cast me off at once?"

"It may be," he replied, "because I will not encounter the dishonor that besmirches the husband of a faithless woman. It may be for other reasons. Enough, it is my purpose to live and die unknown. Let, therefore, thy husband be to the world as one already dead, and of whom no tidings shall ever come. Recognize me not, by word, by sign, by look! Breathe not the secret, above all, to the man thou wottest of. Shouldst thou fail me in this, beware! His fame, his position, his life, will be in my hands. Beware!"

"I will keep thy secret, as I have his," said Hester.

"Swear it!" rejoined he.

And she took the oath.

"And now, Mistress Prynne," said old Roger Chillingworth, as he was hereafter to be named, "I leave thee alone;

alone with thy infant, and the scarlet letter! How is it, Hester? Doth thy sentence bind thee to wear the token in thy sleep? Art thou not afraid of nightmares and hideous dreams?"

"Why dost thou smile so at me?" inquired Hester, troubled at the expression of his eyes. "Art thou like the Black Man that haunts the forest*round about us? Hast thou enticed me into a bond that will prove the ruin of my soul?"

"Not thy soul," he answered, with another smile. "No, not thine!"

HESTER AT HER NEEDLE

H ESTER PRYNNE'S term of confinement was now at an end. Her prison-door was thrown open, and she came forth into the sunshine, which, falling on all alike, seemed, to her sick and morbid heart, as if meant for no other purpose than to reveal the scarlet letter on her breast. Perhaps there was a more real torture in her first unattended footsteps from the threshold of the prison, than even in the procession and spectacle that have been described, where she was made the common infamy, at which all mankind was summoned to point its finger. Then, she was supported by an unnatural tension of the nerves, and by all the combative energy of her character, which enabled her to convert the scene into a kind of lurid triumph. It was, moreover, a separate and insulated event, to occur but once in her lifetime, and to meet which, therefore, reckless of economy, she might call up the vital strength that would have sufficed for many quiet years. The very law that condemned her—a giant of stern features, but with vigor to support, as well as to annihilate, in his iron arm—had held her up, through the terrible ordeal of her ignominy. But now, with this unattended walk from her prison-door, began the daily custom, and she must either sustain and carry it forward by the ordinary resources of her nature, or sink beneath it. She could no longer borrow from the future, to help her through the present grief. To-morrow would bring its own trial with it; so would the next day, and so would the next; each its own trial, and yet the very same that was now so unutterably grievous to be borne. The days of the far-off future would toil onward, still with the same burden for her to take up, and bear along with her, but never to fling down; for the accumulating days, and added years, would pile up their misery upon the heap of shame. Throughout them all, giving up her individuality, she would become the general symbol at which the preacher and moralist might point, and in which they might vivify and embody their images of woman's frailty and sinful passion. Thus the young and pure would be taught to look at her, with the scarlet letter flaming on her breast,—at her, the child of honorable parents,—at her, the mother of a babe, that would hereafter be a woman,—at her, who had once been innocent, —as the figure, the body, the reality of sin. And over her grave, the infamy that she must carry thither would be her only monument.

It may seem marvellous, that, with the world before her,— kept by no restrictive clause of her condemnation within the limits of the Puritan settlement, so remote and so obscure,— free to return to her birthplace, or to any other European land, and there hide her character and identity under a new exterior, as completely as if emerging into another state of being,—and having also the passes of the dark, inscrutable forest open to her, where the wildness of her nature might assimilate itself with a people whose customs and life were alien from the law* that had condemned her,—it may seem marvellous, that this woman should still call that place her home, where, and where only, she must needs be the type of shame. But there is a fatality, a feeling so irresistible and inevitable that it has the force of doom, which almost invariably compels human beings to linger around and haunt, ghost-like, the spot where some great and marked event has given the color to their lifetime; and still the more irresistibly, the darker the tinge that saddens it. Her sin, her ignominy, were the roots which she had struck into the soil. It was as if a new birth, with stronger assimilations than the first, had converted the forest-land, still so uncongenial to every other pilgrim and wanderer, into Hester Prynne's wild and dreary, but life-long home. All other scenes of earth—even that village of rural England, where happy infancy and stainless maidenhood seemed yet to be in her mother's keeping, like garments put off long ago—were foreign to her, in comparison. The chain that bound her here was of iron links, and galling to her inmost soul, but never could be broken.

It might be, too,—doubtless it was so, although she hid the secret from herself, and grew pale whenever it struggled out of her heart, like a serpent from its hole,—it might be that another feeling kept her within the scene and pathway that had been so fatal. There dwelt, there trode the feet of one with whom she deemed herself connected in a union, that, unrecognized on earth, would bring them together before the bar of final judgment, and make that their marriage-altar, for a joint futurity of endless retribution. Over and over again, the tempter of souls had thrust this idea upon Hester's contemplation, and laughed at the passionate and desperate joy with which she seized, and then strove to cast it from her. She barely looked the idea in the face, and hastened to bar it in its dungeon. What she compelled herself to believe,— what, finally, she reasoned upon, as her motive for continuing a resident of New England,—was half a truth, and half a self-delusion. Here, she said to herself, had been the scene of her guilt, and here should be the scene of her earthly punishment; and so, perchance, the torture of her daily shame would at length purge her soul, and work out another purity than that which she had lost; more saint-like, because the result of martyrdom.

Hester Prynne, therefore, did not flee. On the outskirts of the town, within the verge of the peninsula, but not in close vicinity to any other habitation, there was a small thatched cottage. It had been built by an earlier settler, and abandoned, because the soil about it was too sterile for cultivation, while its comparative remoteness put it out of the sphere of that social activity which already marked the habits of the emigrants. It stood on the shore, looking across a basin of the sea at the forest-covered hills, towards the west. A clump of scrubby trees, such as alone grew on the peninsula, did not so much conceal the cottage from view, as seem to denote that here was some object which would fain have been, or at least ought to be, concealed. In this little, lonesome dwelling, with some slender means that she possessed, and by the license of the magistrates, who still kept an inquisitorial watch over her, Hester established herself, with her infant child. A mystic shadow of suspicion immediately attached itself to the spot. Children, too young to comprehend wherefore this woman should be shut out from the sphere of human charities, would creep nigh enough to behold her plying her needle at the cottage-window, or standing in the door-way, or laboring in her little garden, or coming forth along the pathway that led townward; and, discerning the scarlet letter on her breast, would scamper off, with a strange, contagious fear.

Lonely as was Hester's situation, and without a friend on earth who dared to show himself, she, however, incurred no risk of want. She possessed an art that sufficed, even in a land that afforded comparatively little scope for its exercise, to supply food for her thriving infant and herself. It was the art—then, as now, almost the only one within a woman's grasp—of needle-work. She bore on her breast, in the curiously embroidered letter, a specimen of her delicate and imaginative skill, of which the dames of a court might gladly have availed themselves, to add the richer and more spiritual adornment of human ingenuity to their fabrics of silk and gold. Here, indeed, in the sable simplicity that generally characterized the Puritanic modes of dress, there might be an infrequent call for the finer productions of her handiwork. Yet the taste of the age, demanding whatever was elaborate in compositions of this kind, did not fail to extend its influence over our stern progenitors, who had cast behind them so many fashions which it might seem harder to dispense with. Public ceremonies, such as ordinations, the installation of magistrates, and all that could give majesty to the forms in which a new government manifested itself to the people, were, as a matter of policy, marked by a stately and well-conducted ceremonial, and a sombre, but yet a studied magnificence. Deep ruffs, painfully wrought bands, and gorgeously embroidered gloves, were all deemed necessary to the official state of men assuming the reins of power; and were readily allowed to individuals dignified by rank or wealth, even while sumptuary laws forbade these and similar extravagances to the plebeian order. In the array of funerals, too,—whether for the apparel of the dead body, or to typify, by manifold emblematic devices of sable cloth and snowy lawn, the sorrow of the survivors,— there was a frequent and characteristic demand for such labor as Hester Prynne could supply. Baby-linen—for babies then wore robes of state—afforded still another possibility of toil and emolument.

By degrees, nor very slowly, her handiwork became what would now be termed the fashion. Whether from commisera-tion for a woman of so miserable a destiny; or from the morbid curiosity that gives a fictitious value even to common or worthless things; or by whatever other intangible circumstance was then, as now, sufficient to bestow, on some persons, what others might seek in vain; or because Hester really filled a gap which must otherwise have remained vacant; it is certain that she had ready and fairly requited employment for as many hours as she saw fit to occupy with her needle. Vanity, it may be, chose to mortify itself, by putting on, for ceremonials of pomp and state, the garments that had been wrought by her sinful hands. Her needle-work was seen on the ruff of the Governor; military men wore it on their scarfs, and the minister on his band; it decked the baby's little cap; it was shut up, to be mildewed and moulder away, in the coffins of the dead. But it is not recorded that, in a single instance, her skill was called in aid to embroider the white veil which was to cover the pure blushes of a bride. The exception indicated the ever relentless vigor with which society frowned upon her sin.

Hester sought not to acquire any thing beyond a subsistence, of the plainest and most ascetic description, for herself, and a simple abundance for her child. Her own dress was of the coarsest materials and the most sombre hue; with only that one ornament,—the scarlet letter,—which it was her doom to wear. The child's attire, on the other hand, was distinguished by a fanciful, or, we might rather say, a fantastic ingenuity, which served, indeed, to heighten the airy charm that early began to develop itself in the little girl, but which appeared to have also a deeper meaning. We may speak further of it hereafter. Except for that small expenditure in the decoration of her infant, Hester bestowed all her superfluous means in charity, on wretches less miserable than herself, and who not unfrequently insulted the hand that fed them. Much of the time, which she might readily have applied to the better efforts of her art, she employed in making coarse garments for the poor. It is probable that there was an idea of penance in this mode of occupation, and that she offered up a real sacrifice of enjoyment, in devoting so many hours to such rude handiwork. She had in her nature a rich, voluptuous, Oriental* characteristic,—a taste for the gorgeously beautiful, which, save in the exquisite productions of her needle, found nothing else, in all the possibilities of her life, to exercise itself upon. Women derive a pleasure, incomprehensible to the other sex, from the delicate toil of the needle. To Hester Prynne it might have been a mode of expressing, and therefore soothing, the passion of her life. Like all other joys, she rejected it as sin. This morbid meddling of conscience with an immaterial matter betokened, it is to be feared, no genuine and stedfast penitence, but something doubtful, something that might be deeply wrong, beneath.

In this manner, Hester Prynne came to have a part to perform in the world. With her native energy of character, and rare capacity, it could not entirely cast her off, although it had set a mark upon her, more intolerable to a woman's heart than that which branded the brow of Cain.* In all her intercourse with society, however, there was nothing that made her feel as if she belonged to it. Every gesture, every word, and even the silence of those with whom she came in contact, implied, and often expressed, that she was banished, and as much alone as if she inhabited another sphere, or communicated with the common nature by other organs and senses than the rest of human kind. She stood apart from mortal interests, yet close beside them, like a ghost that revisits the familiar fireside, and can no longer make itself seen or felt; no more smile with the household joy, nor mourn with the kindred sorrow; or, should it succeed in manifesting its forbidden sympathy, awakening only terror and horrible repugnance. These emotions, in fact, and its bitterest scorn besides, seemed to be the sole portion that she retained in the universal heart. It was not an age of delicacy; and her position, although she understood it well, and was in little danger of forgetting it, was often brought before her vivid self-perception, like a new anguish, by the rudest touch upon the tenderest spot. The poor, as we have already said, whom she sought out to be the objects of her bounty, often reviled the hand that was stretched forth to succor them. Dames of elevated rank, likewise, whose doors she entered in the way of her occupation, were accustomed to distil drops of bitterness into her heart; sometimes through that alchemy of quiet malice, by which women can concoct a subtile poison from ordinary trifles; and sometimes, also, by a coarser expression, that fell upon the sufferer's defenceless breast like a rough blow upon an ulcerated wound. Hester had schooled herself long and well; she never responded to these attacks, save by a flush of crimson that rose irrepressibly over her pale cheek, and again subsided into the depths of her bosom. She was patient,—a martyr, indeed,—but she forbore to pray for her enemies; lest, in spite of her forgiving aspirations, the words of the blessing should stubbornly twist themselves into a curse.

Continually, and in a thousand other ways, did she feel the innumerable throbs of anguish that had been so cunningly contrived for her by the undying, the ever-active sentence of the Puritan tribunal. Clergymen paused in the street to address words of exhortation, that brought a crowd, with its mingled grin and frown, around the poor, sinful woman. If she entered a church, trusting to share the Sabbath smile of the Universal Father, it was often her mishap to find herself the text of the discourse. She grew to have a dread of children; for they had imbibed from their parents a vague idea of something horrible in this dreary woman, gliding silently through the town, with never any companion but one only child. Therefore, first allowing her to pass, they pursued her at a distance with shrill cries, and the utterance of a word that had no distinct purport to their own minds, but was none the less terrible to her, as proceeding from lips that babbled it unconsciously. It seemed to argue so wide a diffusion of her shame, that all nature knew of it; it could have caused her no deeper pang, had the leaves of the trees whispered the dark story among themselves,—had the summer breeze murmured about it,—had the wintry blast shrieked it aloud! Another peculiar torture was felt in the gaze of a new eye. When strangers looked curiously at the scarlet letter,—and none ever failed to do so,—they branded it afresh into Hester's soul; so that, oftentimes, she could scarcely refrain, yet always did refrain, from covering the symbol with her hand. But then, again, an accustomed eye had likewise its own anguish to inflict. Its cool stare of familiarity was intolerable. From first to last, in short, Hester Prynne had always this dreadful agony in feeling a human eye upon the token; the spot never grew callous; it seemed, on the contrary, to grow more sensitive with daily torture.

But sometimes, once in many days, or perchance in many months, she felt an eye—a human eye—upon the ignominious brand, that seemed to give a momentary relief, as if half of her agony were shared. The next instant, back it all rushed again, with still a deeper throb of pain; for, in that brief interval, she had sinned anew. Had Hester sinned alone?

Her imagination was somewhat affected, and, had she been of a softer moral and intellectual fibre, would have been still more so, by the strange and solitary anguish of her life. Walking to and fro, with those lonely footsteps, in the little world with which she was outwardly connected, it now and then appeared to Hester,—if altogether fancy, it was nevertheless too potent to be resisted,—she felt or fancied, then, that the scarlet letter had endowed her with a new sense. She shuddered to believe, yet could not help believing, that it gave her a sympathetic knowledge of the hidden sin in other hearts.* She was terror-stricken by the revelations that were thus made. What were they? Could they be other than the insidious whispers of the bad angel, who would fain have persuaded the struggling woman, as yet only half his victim, that the outward guise of purity was but a lie, and that, if truth were everywhere to be shown, a scarlet letter would blaze forth on many a bosom besides Hester Prynne's? Or, must she receive those intimations—so obscure, yet so distinct—as truth? In all her miserable experience, there was nothing else so awful and so loathsome as this sense. It perplexed, as well as shocked her, by the irreverent inopportuneness of the occasions that brought it into vivid action. Sometimes, the red infamy upon her breast would give a sympathetic throb, as she passed near a venerable minister or magistrate, the model of piety and justice, to whom that age of antique reverence looked up, as to a mortal man in fellowship with angels. "What evil thing is at hand?" would Hester say to herself. Lifting her reluctant eyes, there would be nothing human within the scope of view, save the form of this earthly saint! Again, a mystic sister-hood would contumaciously assert itself, as she met the sancti-fied frown of some matron, who, according to the rumor of all tongues, had kept cold snow within her bosom throughout life. That unsunned snow in the matron's bosom, and the burning shame on Hester Prynne's,—what had the two in common? Or, once more, the electric thrill would give her warning,—"Behold, Hester, here is a companion!"—and, looking up, she would detect the eyes of a young maiden glancing at the scarlet letter, shyly and aside, and quickly averted, with a faint, chill crimson in her cheeks; as if her purity were somewhat sullied by that momentary glance. O Fiend, whose talisman was that fatal symbol, wouldst thou leave nothing, whether in youth or age, for this poor sinner to revere?—Such loss of faith is ever one of the saddest results of sin. Be it accepted as a proof that all was not corrupt in this poor victim of her own frailty, and man's hard law, that Hester Prynne yet struggled to believe that no fellow-mortal was guilty like herself.

The vulgar, who, in those dreary old times, were always contributing a grotesque horror to what interested their imaginations, had a story about the scarlet letter which we might readily work up into a terrific legend. They averred, that the symbol was not mere scarlet cloth, tinged in an earthly dye-pot, but was red-hot with infernal fire, and could be seen glowing all alight, whenever Hester Prynne walked abroad in the night-time. And we must needs say, it seared Hester's bosom so deeply, that perhaps there was more truth in the rumor than our modern incredulity may be inclined to admit.

VI

PEARL

WE HAVE as yet hardly spoken of the infant; that little creature, whose innocent life had sprung, by the inscrutable decree of Providence, a lovely and immortal flower, out of the rank luxuriance of a guilty passion. How strange it seemed to the sad woman, as she watched the growth, and the beauty that became every day more brilliant, and the intelligence that threw its quivering sunshine over the tiny features of this child! Her Pearl!— For so had Hester called her; not as a name expressive of her aspect, which had nothing of the calm, white, unimpassioned lustre that would be indicated by the comparison. But she named the infant "Pearl," as being of great price,*—purchased with all she had,—her mother's only treasure! How strange, indeed! Man had marked this woman's sin by a scarlet letter, which had such potent and disastrous efficacy that no human sympathy could reach her, save it were sinful like herself. God, as a direct consequence of the sin which man thus punished, had given her a lovely child, whose place was on that same dishonored bosom, to connect her parent for ever with the race and descent of mortals, and to be finally a blessed soul in heaven! Yet these thoughts affected Hester Prynne less with hope than apprehension. She knew that her deed had been evil; she could have no faith, therefore, that its result would be for good. Day after day, she looked fearfully into the child's expanding nature; ever dreading to detect some dark and wild peculiarity, that should correspond with the guiltiness to which she owed her being.

Certainly, there was no physical defect. By its perfect shape, its vigor, and its natural dexterity in the use of all its untried limbs, the infant was worthy to have been brought forth in Eden; worthy to have been left there, to be the plaything of the angels, after the world's first parents were driven out. The child had a native grace which does not invariably coexist with faultless beauty; its attire, however simple, always impressed the beholder as if it were the very garb that precisely became it best. But little Pearl was not clad in rustic weeds. Her mother, with a morbid purpose that may be better understood hereafter, had bought the richest tissues that could be procured, and allowed her imaginative faculty its full play in the arrangement and decoration of the dresses which the child wore, before the public eye. So magnificent was the small figure, when thus arrayed, and such was the splendor of Pearl's own proper beauty, shining through the gorgeous robes which might have extinguished a paler loveliness, that there was an absolute circle of radiance around her, on the darksome cottage-floor. And yet a russet gown, torn and soiled with the child's rude play, made a picture of her just as perfect. Pearl's aspect was imbued with a spell of infinite variety; in this one child there were many children, comprehending the full scope between the wild-flower prettiness of a peasant-baby, and the pomp, in little, of an infant princess. Throughout all, however, there was a trait of passion, a certain depth of hue, which she never lost; and if, in any of her changes, she had grown fainter or paler, she would have ceased to be herself;—it would have been no longer Pearl!

This outward mutability indicated, and did not more than fairly express, the various properties of her inner life. Her nature appeared to possess depth, too, as well as variety; but—

or else Hester's fears deceived her—it lacked reference and adaptation to the world into which she was born. The child could not be made amenable to rules.* In giving her existence, a great law had been broken; and the result was a being, whose elements were perhaps beautiful and brilliant, but all in disorder; or with an order peculiar to themselves, amidst which the point of variety and arrangement was difficult or impossible to be discovered. Hester could only account for the child's character—and even then, most vaguely and imperfectly—by recalling what she herself had been, during that momentous period while Pearl was imbibing her soul from the spiritual world, and her bodily frame from its material of earth. The mother's impassioned state had been the medium through which were transmitted to the unborn infant the rays of its moral life; and, however white and clear originally, they had taken the deep stains of crimson and gold, the fiery lustre, the black shadow, and the untempered light, of the intervening substance. Above all, the warfare of Hester's spirit, at that epoch, was perpetuated in Pearl. She could recognize her wild, desperate, defiant mood, the flightiness of her temper, and even some of the very cloud-shapes of gloom and despondency that had brooded in her heart. They were now illuminated by the morning radiance of a young child's disposition, but, later in the day of earthly existence, might be prolific of the storm and whirlwind.

The discipline of the family, in those days, was of a far more rigid kind than now. The frown, the harsh rebuke, the frequent application of the rod, enjoined by Scriptural authority, were used, not merely in the way of punishment for actual offences, but as a wholesome regimen for the growth and promotion of all childish virtues. Hester Prynne, nevertheless, the lonely mother of this one child, ran little risk of erring on the side of undue severity. Mindful, however, of her own errors and misfortunes, she early sought to impose a tender, but strict, control over the infant immortality that was committed to her charge. But the task was beyond her skill. After testing both smiles and frowns, and proving that neither mode of treatment possessed any calculable influence, Hester was ultimately compelled to stand aside, and permit the child to be swayed by her own impulses. Physical compulsion or restraint was effectual, of course, while it lasted. As to any other kind of discipline, whether addressed to her mind or heart, little Pearl might or might not be within its reach, in accordance with the caprice that ruled the moment. Her mother, while Pearl was yet an infant, grew acquainted with a certain peculiar look, that warned her when it would be labor thrown away to insist, persuade, or plead. It was a look so intelligent, yet inexplicable, so perverse, sometimes so malicious, but generally accompanied by a wild flow of spirits, that Hester could not help questioning, at such moments, whether Pearl was a human child. She seemed rather an airy sprite, which, after playing its fantastic sports for a little while upon the cottage-floor, would flit away with a mocking smile. Whenever that look appeared in her wild, bright, deeply black eyes, it invested her with a strange remoteness and intangibility; it was as if she were hovering in the air and might vanish, like a glimmering light that comes we know not whence, and goes we know not whither. Beholding it, Hester was constrained to rush towards the child,—to pursue the little elf in the flight which she invariably began,—to snatch her to her bosom, with a close pressure and earnest kisses,—not so much from overflowing love, as to assure herself that Pearl was flesh and blood, and not utterly delusive. But Pearl's laugh, when she was caught, though full of merriment and music, made her mother more doubtful than before.

Heart-smitten at this bewildering and baffling spell, that so often came between herself and her sole treasure, whom she had bought so dear, and who was all her world, Hester sometimes burst into passionate tears. Then, perhaps,—for there was no foreseeing how it might affect her,—Pearl would frown, and clench her little fist, and harden her small features into a stern, unsympathizing look of discontent. Not seldom, she would laugh anew, and louder than before, like a thing incapable and unintelligent of human sorrow.* Or—but this more rarely happened—she would be convulsed with a rage of grief, and sob out her love for her mother, in broken words, and seem intent on proving that she had a heart, by breaking it. Yet Hester was hardly safe in confiding herself to that gusty tenderness; it passed, as suddenly as it came. Brooding over all these matters, the mother felt like one who has evoked a spirit, but, by some irregularity in the process of conjuration, has failed to win the master-word that should control this new and incomprehensible intelligence. Her only real comfort was when the child lay in the placidity of sleep. Then she was sure of her, and tasted hours of quiet, sad, delicious happiness; until—perhaps with that perverse expression glimmering from beneath her opening lids—little Pearl awoke!

How soon—with what strange rapidity, indeed!—did Pearl arrive at an age that was capable of social intercourse, beyond the mother's ever-ready smile and nonsense-words! And then what a happiness would it have been, could Hester Prynne have heard her clear, bird-like voice mingling with the uproar of other childish voices, and have distinguished and un-ravelled her own darling's tones, amid all the entangled outcry of a group of sportive children! But this could never be. Pearl was a born outcast of the infantile world. An imp of evil, emblem and product of sin,* she had no right among christened infants. Nothing was more remarkable than the instinct, as it seemed, with which the child comprehended her loneliness; the destiny that had drawn an inviolable circle round about her; the whole peculiarity, in short, of her posi-tion in respect to other children. Never, since her release from prison, had Hester met the public gaze without her. In all her walks about the town, Pearl, too, was there; first as the babe in arms, and afterwards as the little girl, small companion of her mother, holding a forefinger with her whole grasp, and tripping along at the rate of three or four footsteps to one of Hester's. She saw the children of the settlement, on the grassy margin of the street, or at the domestic thresholds, disporting themselves in such grim fashion as the Puritanic nurture would permit; playing at going to church, perchance; or at scourging Quakers;* or taking scalps in a sham-fight with the Indians; or scaring one another with freaks of imitative witchcraft. Pearl saw, and gazed intently, but never sought to make acquaintance. If spoken to, she would not speak again. If the children gathered about her, as they sometimes did, Pearl would grow positively terrible in her puny wrath, snatching up stones to fling at them, with shrill, incoherent exclamations that made her mother tremble, because they had so much the sound of a witch's anathemas in some unknown tongue.

The truth was, that the little Puritans, being of the most intolerant brood that ever lived, had got a vague idea of something outlandish, unearthly, or at variance with ordinary fashions, in the mother and child; and therefore scorned them in their hearts, and not unfrequently reviled them with their tongues. Pearl felt the sentiment, and requited it with the bitterest hatred that can be supposed to rankle in a childish bosom. These outbreaks of a fierce temper had a kind of value, and even comfort, for her mother; because there was at least an intelligible earnestness in the mood, instead of the fitful caprice that so often thwarted her in the child's manifestations. It appalled her, nevertheless, to discern here, again, a shadowy reflection of the evil that had existed in herself. All this enmity and passion had Pearl inherited, by inalienable right, out of Hester's heart. Mother and daughter stood together in the same circle of seclusion from human society; and in the nature of the child seemed to be perpetuated those unquiet elements that had distracted Hester Prynne before Pearl's birth, but had since begun to be soothed away by the softening influences of maternity.

At home, within and around her mother's cottage, Pearl wanted not a wide and various circle of acquaintance. The spell of life went forth from her ever creative spirit, and communicated itself to a thousand objects, as a torch kindles a flame wherever it may be applied. The unlikeliest materials, a stick, a bunch of rags, a flower, were the puppets of Pearl's witchcraft, and, without undergoing any outward change, became spiritually adapted to whatever drama occupied the stage of her inner world. Her one baby-voice served a multitude of imaginary personages, old and young, to talk withal. The pine-trees, aged, black, and solemn, and flinging groans and other melancholy utterances on the breeze, needed little transformation to figure as Puritan elders; the ugliest weeds of the garden were their children, whom Pearl smote down and uprooted, most unmercifully. It was wonderful, the vast variety of forms into which she threw her intellect, with no continuity, indeed, but darting up and dancing, always in a state of preternatural activity,—soon sinking down, as if exhausted by so rapid and feverish a tide of life,—and succeeded by other shapes of a similar wild energy. It was like nothing so much as the phantasmagoric play of the northern lights. In the mere exercise of the fancy, however, and the sportiveness of a growing mind, there might be little more than was observable in other children of bright faculties; except as Pearl, in the dearth of human playmates, was thrown more upon the visionary throng which she created. The singularity lay in the hostile feelings with which the child regarded all these offspring of her own heart and mind. She never created a friend, but seemed always to be sowing broadcast the dragon's teeth, whence sprung a harvest of armed enemies, against whom she rushed to battle. It was inexpressibly sad—then what depth of sorrow to a mother, who felt in her own heart the cause!—to observe, in one so young, this constant recognition of an adverse world, and so fierce a training of the energies that were to make good her cause, in the contest that must ensue.

Gazing at Pearl, Hester Prynne often dropped her work upon her knees, and cried out, with an agony which she would fain have hidden, but which made utterance for itself, betwixt speech and a groan,—"O Father in Heaven,—if Thou art still my Father,—what is this being which I have brought into the world!" And Pearl, overhearing the ejaculation, or aware, through some more subtile channel, of those throbs of anguish, would turn her vivid and beautiful little face upon her mother, smile with sprite-like intelligence, and resume her play.

One peculiarity of the child's deportment remains yet to be told. The very first thing which she had noticed, in her life, was—what?—not the mother's smile, responding to it, as other babies do, by that faint, embryo smile of the little mouth, remembered so doubtfully afterwards, and with such fond discussion whether it were indeed a smile. By no means! But that first object of which Pearl seemed to become aware was—shall we say it?—the scarlet letter on Hester's bosom! One day, as her mother stooped over the cradle, the infant's eyes had been caught by the glimmering of the gold embroidery about the letter; and, putting up her little hand, she grasped at it, smiling, not doubtfully, but with a decided gleam that gave her face the look of a much older child. Then, gasping for breath, did Hester Prynne clutch the fatal token, instinctively endeavouring to tear it away; so infinite was the torture inflicted by the intelligent touch of Pearl's baby-hand. Again, as if her mother's agonized gesture were meant only to make sport for her, did little Pearl look into her eyes, and smile! From that epoch, except when the child was asleep, Hester had never felt a moment's safety; not a moment's calm enjoyment of her. Weeks, it is true, would sometimes elapse, during which Pearl's gaze might never once be fixed upon the scarlet letter; but then, again, it would come at unawares, like the stroke of sudden death, and always with that peculiar smile, and odd expression of the eyes.

Once, this freakish, elfish cast came into the child's eyes, while Hester was looking at her own image in them, as mothers are fond of doing; and, suddenly,—for women in solitude, and with troubled hearts, are pestered with unaccountable delusions,—she fancied that she beheld, not her own miniature portrait, but another face in the small black mirror of Pearl's eye. It was a face, fiend-like, full of smiling malice, yet bearing the semblance of features that she had known full well, though seldom with a smile, and never with malice, in them. It was as if an evil spirit possessed the child, and had just then peeped forth in mockery. Many a time afterwards had Hester been tortured, though less vividly, by the same illusion.

In the afternoon of a certain summer's day, after Pearl grew big enough to run about, she amused herself with gathering handfuls of wild-flowers, and flinging them, one by one, at her mother's bosom; dancing up and down, like a little elf, whenever she hit the scarlet letter. Hester's first motion had been to cover her bosom with her clasped hands. But, whether from pride or resignation, or a feeling that her penance might best be wrought out by this unutterable pain, she resisted the impulse, and sat erect, pale as death, looking sadly into little Pearl's wild eyes. Still came the battery of flowers, almost invariably hitting the mark, and covering the mother's breast with hurts for which she could find no balm in this world, nor knew how to seek it in another. At last, her shot being all expended, the child stood still and gazed at Hester, with that little, laughing image of a fiend peeping out —or, whether it peeped or no, her mother so imagined it— from the unsearchable abyss of her black eyes.

"Child, what art thou?" cried the mother.

"O, I am your little Pearl!" answered the child.

But, while she said it, Pearl laughed and began to dance up and down, with the humorsome gesticulation of a little imp, whose next freak might be to fly up the chimney.

"Art thou my child, in very truth?" asked Hester.

Nor did she put the question altogether idly, but, for the moment, with a portion of genuine earnestness; for, such was Pearl's wonderful intelligence, that her mother half doubted whether she were not acquainted with the secret spell of her existence, and might not now reveal herself.

"Yes; I am little Pearl!" repeated the child, continuing her antics.

"Thou art not my child! Thou art no Pearl of mine!" said the mother, half playfully; for it was often the case that a sportive impulse came over her, in the midst of her deepest suffering. "Tell me, then, what thou art, and who sent thee hither?"

"Tell me, mother!" said the child, seriously, coming up to Hester, and pressing herself close to her knees. "Do thou tell me!"

"Thy Heavenly Father sent thee!" answered Hester Prynne.

But she said it with a hesitation that did not escape the acuteness of the child. Whether moved only by her ordinary freakishness, or because an evil spirit prompted her, she put up her small forefinger, and touched the scarlet letter.

"He did not send me!" cried she, positively. "I have no Heavenly Father!"

"Hush, Pearl, hush! Thou must not talk so!" answered the mother, suppressing a groan. "He sent us all into this world. He sent even me, thy mother. Then, much more, thee! Or, if not, thou strange and elfish child, whence didst thou come?"

"Tell me! Tell me!" repeated Pearl, no longer seriously, but laughing, and capering about the floor. "It is thou that must tell me!"

But Hester could not resolve the query, being herself in a

dismal labyrinth of doubt. She remembered—betwixt a smile and a shudder—the talk of the neighbouring townspeople; who, seeking vainly elsewhere for the child's paternity, and observing some of her odd attributes, had given out that poor little Pearl was a demon offspring;* such as, ever since old Catholic times, had occasionally been seen on earth, through the agency of their mothers' sin, and to promote some foul and wicked purpose. Luther, according to the scandal of his monkish enemies, was a brat of that hellish breed; nor was Pearl the only child to whom this inauspicious origin was assigned, among the New England Puritans.

VII

THE GOVERNOR'S HALL

H ESTER PRYNNE went, one day, to the mansion of
Governor Bellingham, with a pair of gloves, which
she had fringed and embroidered to his order, and
which were to be worn on some great occasion of state; for,
though the chances of a popular election had caused this former ruler to descend a step or two from the highest rank, he
still held an honorable and influential place among the colonial magistracy.

Another and far more important reason than the delivery of
a pair of embroidered gloves impelled Hester, at this time, to
seek an interview with a personage of so much power and activity in the affairs of the settlement. It had reached her ears,
that there was a design on the part of some of the leading inhabitants, cherishing the more rigid order of principles in religion and government, to deprive her of her child. On the sup-
position that Pearl, as already hinted, was of demon origin,
these good people not unreasonably argued that a Chr:stian
interest in the mother's soul required them to remove such a
stumbling-block from her path. If the child, on the other hand,
were really capable of moral and religious growth, and possessed the elements of ultimate salvation, then, surely, it
would enjoy all the fairer prospect of these advantages by being transferred to wiser and better guardianship than Hester

Prynne's. Among those who promoted the design, Governor Bellingham was said to be one of the most busy. It may appear singular, and, indeed, not a little ludicrous, that an affair of this kind, which, in later days, would have been referred to no higher jurisdiction than that of the selectmen*of the town, should then have been a question publicly discussed, and on which statesmen of eminence took sides. At that epoch of pristine simplicity, however, matters of even slighter public interest, and of far less intrinsic weight than the welfare of Hester and her child, were strangely mixed up with the deliberations of legislators and acts of state. The period was hardly, if at all, earlier than that of our story, when a dispute concerning the right of property in a pig,* not only caused a fierce and bitter contest in the legislative body of the colony, but resulted in an important modification of the framework itself of the legislature.

Full of concern, therefore,—but so conscious of her own right, that it seemed scarcely an unequal match between the public, on the one side, and a lonely woman, backed by the sympathies of nature, on the other,—Hester Prynne set forth from her solitary cottage. Little Pearl, of course, was her companion. She was now of an age to run lightly along by her mother's side, and, constantly in motion from morn till sunset, could have accomplished a much longer journey than that before her. Often, nevertheless, more from caprice than necessity, she demanded to be taken up in arms, but was soon as imperious to be set down again, and frisked onward before Hester on the grassy pathway, with many a harmless trip and tumble. We have spoken of Pearl's rich and luxuriant beauty; a beauty that shone with deep and vivid tints; a bright complexion, eyes possessing intensity both of depth and glow, and hair already of a deep, glossy brown, and which, in after years, would be nearly akin to black. There was fire in her and throughout her; she seemed the unpremeditated offshoot of a passionate moment. Her mother, in contriving the child's

garb, had allowed the gorgeous tendencies of her imagination
their full play; arraying her in a crimson velvet tunic, of a peculiar cut, abundantly embroidered with fantasies and flourishes of gold thread. So much strength of coloring, which must
have given a wan and pallid aspect to cheeks of a fainter
bloom, was admirably adapted to Pearl's beauty, and made her
the very brightest little jet of flame that ever danced upon the
earth.

But it was a remarkable attribute of this garb, and, indeed,
of the child's whole appearance, that it irresistibly and inevitably reminded the beholder of the token which Hester
Prynne was doomed to wear upon her bosom. It was the scarlet letter in another form; the scarlet letter endowed with life!
The mother herself—as if the red ignominy were so deeply
scorched into her brain, that all her conceptions assumed its
form—had carefully wrought out the similitude; lavishing
many hours of morbid ingenuity, to create an analogy between the object of her affection, and the emblem of her guilt
and torture. But, in truth, Pearl was the one, as well as the
other; and only in consequence of that identity had Hester
contrived so perfectly to represent the scarlet letter in her appearance.

As the two wayfarers came within the precincts of the town,
the children of the Puritans looked up from their play,—or
what passed for play with those sombre little urchins,—and
spake gravely one to another:—

"Behold, verily, there is the woman of the scarlet letter; and,
of a truth, moreover, there is the likeness of the scarlet letter
running along by her side! Come, therefore, and let us fling
mud at them!"

But Pearl, who was a dauntless child, after frowning, stamping her foot, and shaking her little hand with a variety of
threatening gestures, suddenly made a rush at the knot of her
enemies, and put them all to flight. She resembled, in her
fierce pursuit of them, an infant pestilence,—the scarlet fever,

or some such half-fledged angel of judgment,—whose mission was to punish the sins of the rising generation. She screamed and shouted, too, with a terrific volume of sound, which doubtless caused the hearts of the fugitives to quake within them. The victory accomplished, Pearl returned quietly to her mother, and looked up smiling into her face.

Without further adventure, they reached the dwelling of Governor Bellingham. This was a large wooden house, built in a fashion of which there are specimens still extant in the streets of our elder towns; now moss-grown, crumbling to decay, and melancholy at heart with the many sorrowful or joyful occurrences, remembered or forgotten, that have happened, and passed away, within their dusky chambers. Then, however, there was the freshness of the passing year on its exterior, and the cheerfulness, gleaming forth from the sunny windows, of a human habitation into which death had never entered. It had indeed a very cheery aspect; the walls being overspread with a kind of stucco, in which fragments of broken glass were plentifully intermixed; so that, when the sunshine fell aslant-wise over the front of the edifice, it glittered and sparkled as if diamonds had been flung against it by the double handful. The brilliancy might have befitted Aladdin's palace, rather than the mansion of a grave old Puritan ruler. It was further decorated with strange and seemingly cabalistic figures and diagrams, suitable to the quaint taste of the age, which had been drawn in the stucco when newly laid on, and had now grown hard and durable, for the admiration of after times.

Pearl, looking at this bright wonder of a house, began to caper and dance, and imperatively required that the whole breadth of sunshine should be stripped off its front, and given her to play with.

"No, my little Pearl!" said her mother. "Thou must gather thine own sunshine. I have none to give thee!"

They approached the door; which was of an arched form,

and flanked on each side by a narrow tower or projection of
the edifice, in both of which were lattice-windows, with
wooden shutters to close over them at need. Lifting the iron
hammer that hung at the portal, Hester Prynne gave a summons, which was answered by one of the Governor's bond-
servants; a free-born Englishman, but now a seven years' slave.*
During that term he was to be the property of his master,
and as much a commodity of bargain and sale as an ox, or a
joint-stool. The serf wore the blue coat, which was the customary garb of serving-men at that period, and long before, in
the old hereditary halls of England.

"Is the worshipful Governor Bellingham within?" inquired
Hester.

"Yea, forsooth," replied the bond-servant, staring with wide-
open eyes at the scarlet letter, which, being a new-comer in the
country, he had never before seen. "Yea, his honorable worship is within. But he hath a godly minister or two with him,
and likewise a leech. Ye may not see his worship now."

"Nevertheless, I will enter," answered Hester Prynne; and
the bond-servant, perhaps judging from the decision of her air
and the glittering symbol in her bosom, that she was a great
lady in the land, offered no opposition.

So the mother and little Pearl were admitted into the hall
of entrance. With many variations, suggested by the nature of
his building-materials, diversity of climate, and a different
mode of social life, Governor Bellingham had planned his new
habitation after the residences of gentlemen of fair estate in
his native land. Here, then, was a wide and reasonably lofty
hall, extending through the whole depth of the house, and
forming a medium of general communication, more or less directly, with all the other apartments. At one extremity, this
spacious room was lighted by the windows of the two towers,
which formed a small recess on either side of the portal. At the
other end, though partly muffled by a curtain, it was more
powerfully illuminated by one of those embowed hall-win-

dows which we read of in old books, and which was provided
with a deep and cushioned seat. Here, on the cushion, lay a
folio tome, probably of the Chronicles of England,* or other
such substantial literature; even as, in our own days, we scatter
gilded volumes on the centre-table, to be turned over by the
casual guest. The furniture of the hall consisted of some ponderous chairs, the backs of which were elaborately carved with
wreaths of oaken flowers; and likewise a table in the same
taste; the whole being of the Elizabethan age, or perhaps earlier, and heirlooms, transferred hither from the Governor's
paternal home. On the table—in token that the sentiment of
old English hospitality had not been left behind—stood a
large pewter tankard, at the bottom of which, had Hester or
Pearl peeped into it, they might have seen the frothy remnant
of a recent draught of ale.

On the wall hung a row of portraits, representing the forefathers of the Bellingham lineage, some with armour on their
breasts, and others with stately ruffs and robes of peace. All
were characterized by the sternness and severity which old
portraits so invariably put on; as if they were the ghosts,
rather than the pictures, of departed worthies, and were gazing with harsh and intolerant criticism at the pursuits and en-
joyments of living men.

At about the centre of the oaken panels, that lined the hall,
was suspended a suit of mail, not, like the pictures, an ancestral relic, but of the most modern date; for it had been manu-
factured by a skilful armorer in London, the same year in
which Governor Bellingham came over to New England.
There was a steel head-piece, a cuirass, a gorget, and greaves,
with a pair of gauntlets and a sword hanging beneath; all, and
especially the helmet and breastplate, so highly burnished as
to glow with white radiance, and scatter an illumination
everywhere about upon the floor. This bright panoply was not
meant for mere idle show, but had been worn by the Governor
on many a solemn muster and training field, and had glittered,

moreover, at the head of a regiment in the Pequod war.* For, though bred a lawyer, and accustomed to speak of Bacon, Coke, Noye, and Finch,* as his professional associates, the exigencies of this new country had transformed Governor Bellingham into a soldier, as well as a statesman and ruler.

Little Pearl—who was as greatly pleased with the gleaming armour as she had been with the glittering frontispiece of the house—spent some time looking into the polished mirror of the breastplate.

"Mother," cried she, "I see you here. Look! Look!"

Hester looked, by way of humoring the child; and she saw that, owing to the peculiar effect of this convex mirror, the scarlet letter was represented in exaggerated and gigantic proportions, so as to be greatly the most prominent feature of her appearance. In truth, she seemed absolutely hidden behind it. Pearl pointed upward, also, at a similar picture in the head-piece; smiling at her mother, with the elfish intelligence that was so familiar an expression on her small physiognomy. That look of naughty merriment was likewise reflected in the mirror, with so much breadth and intensity of effect, that it made Hester Prynne feel as if it could not be the image of her own child, but of an imp who was seeking to mould itself into Pearl's shape.

"Come along, Pearl!" said she, drawing her away. "Come and look into this fair garden. It may be, we shall see flowers there; more beautiful ones than we find in the woods."

Pearl, accordingly, ran to the bow-window, at the farther end of the hall, and looked along the vista of a garden-walk, carpeted with closely shaven grass, and bordered with some rude and immature attempt at shrubbery. But the proprietor appeared already to have relinquished, as hopeless, the effort to perpetuate on this side of the Atlantic, in a hard soil and amid the close struggle for subsistence, the native English taste for ornamental gardening. Cabbages grew in plain sight; and a pumpkin vine, rooted at some distance, had run across the intervening space, and deposited one of its gigantic products directly beneath the hall-window; as if to warn the Governor that this great lump of vegetable gold was as rich an ornament as New England earth would offer him. There were a few rose-bushes, however, and a number of apple-trees, probably the descendants of those planted by the Reverend Mr. Blackstone,* the first settler of the peninsula; that half mythological personage who rides through our early annals, seated on the back of a bull.

Pearl, seeing the rose-bushes, began to cry for a red rose, and would not be pacified.

"Hush, child, hush!" said her mother earnestly. "Do not cry, dear little Pearl! I hear voices in the garden. The Governor is coming, and gentlemen along with him!"

In fact, adown the vista of the garden-avenue, a number of persons were seen approaching towards the house. Pearl, in utter scorn of her mother's attempt to quiet her, gave an eldritch* scream, and then became silent; not from any notion of obedience, but because the quick and mobile curiosity of her disposition was excited by the appearance of these new personages.

VIII

THE ELF-CHILD AND THE MINISTER

GOVERNOR BELLINGHAM, in a loose gown and easy cap,—such as elderly gentlemen loved to indue themselves with, in their domestic privacy,—walked foremost, and appeared to be showing off his estate, and expatiating on his projected improvements. The wide circumference of an elaborate ruff, beneath his gray beard, in the antiquated fashion of King James's reign, caused his head to look not a little like that of John the Baptist in a charger. The impression made by his aspect, so rigid and severe, and frost-bitten with more than autumnal age, was hardly in keeping with the appliances of worldly enjoyment wherewith he had evidently done his utmost to surround himself. But it is an error to suppose that our grave forefathers—though accustomed to speak and think of human existence as a state merely of trial and warfare, and though unfeignedly prepared to sacrifice goods and life at the behest of duty—made it a matter of conscience to reject such means of comfort, or even luxury, as lay fairly within their grasp. This creed was never taught, for instance, by the venerable pastor, John Wilson,* whose beard, white as a snow-drift, was seen over Governor Bellingham's shoulder; while its wearer suggested that pears and peaches might yet be naturalized in the New England climate, and that purple grapes might possibly be compelled to flourish, against the sunny garden-wall. The old clergyman, nurtured at the rich bosom of the English Church, had a long established and legitimate taste for all good and comfortable things; and however stern he might show himself in the pulpit, or in his public reproof of such transgressions as that of Hester Prynne, still, the genial benevolence of his private life had won him warmer affection than was accorded to any of his professional contemporaries.

Behind the Governor and Mr. Wilson came two other guests; one, the Reverend Arthur Dimmesdale, whom the reader may remember, as having taken a brief and reluctant part in the scene of Hester Prynne's disgrace; and, in close companionship with him, old Roger Chillingworth, a person of great skill in physic, who, for two or three years past, had been settled in the town. It was understood that this learned man was the physician as well as friend of the young minister, whose health had severely suffered, of late, by his too unreserved self-sacrifice to the labors and duties of the pastoral relation.

The Governor, in advance of his visitors, ascended one or two steps, and, throwing open the leaves of the great hall-window, found himself close to little Pearl. The shadow of the curtain fell on Hester Prynne, and partially concealed her.

"What have we here?" said Governor Bellingham, looking with surprise at the scarlet little figure before him. "I profess, I have never seen the like, since my days of vanity, in old King James's time,* when I was wont to esteem it a high favor to be admitted to a court mask! There used to be a swarm of these small apparitions, in holiday-time; and we called them children of the Lord of Misrule.* But how gat such a guest into my hall?"

"Ay, indeed!" cried good old Mr. Wilson. "What little bird of scarlet plumage may this be? Methinks I have seen just such figures, when the sun has been shining through a richly painted window, and tracing out the golden and crimson images across the floor. But that was in the old land. Prithee, young one, who art thou, and what has ailed thy mother to bedizen thee in this strange fashion? Art thou a Christian child,—ha? Dost know thy catechism? Or art thou one of those naughty elfs or fairies, whom we thought to have left behind us, with other relics of Papistry, in merry old England?"

"I am mother's child," answered the scarlet vision, "and my name is Pearl!"

"Pearl?—Ruby, rather!—or Coral!—or Red Rose, at the very least, judging from thy hue!" responded the old minister, putting forth his hand in a vain attempt to pat little Pearl on the cheek. "But where is this mother of thine? Ah! I see," he added; and, turning to Governor Bellingham, whispered,— "This is the selfsame child of whom we have held speech together; and behold here the unhappy woman, Hester Prynne, her mother!"

"Sayest thou so?" cried the Governor. "Nay, we might have judged that such a child's mother must needs be a scarlet woman, and a worthy type of her of Babylon!*But she comes at a good time; and we will look into this matter forthwith."

Governor Bellingham stepped through the window into the hall, followed by his three guests.

"Hester Prynne," said he, fixing his naturally stern regard on the wearer of the scarlet letter, "there hath been much question concerning thee, of late. The point hath been weightily discussed, whether we, that are of authority and influence, do well discharge our consciences by trusting an immortal soul, such as there is in yonder child, to the guidance of one who hath stumbled and fallen, amid the pitfalls of this world. Speak thou, the child's own mother! Were it not, thinkest thou, for thy little one's temporal and eternal welfare, that she be taken out of thy charge, and clad soberly, and disciplined strictly, and instructed in the truths of heaven and earth? What canst thou do for the child, in this kind?"

"I can teach my little Pearl what I have learned from this!" answered Hester Prynne, laying her finger on the red token.

"Woman, it is thy badge of shame!" replied the stern magistrate. "It is because of the stain which that letter indicates, that we would transfer thy child to other hands."

"Nevertheless," said the mother calmly, though growing more pale, "this badge hath taught me,—it daily teaches me, —it is teaching me at this moment,—lessons whereof my child may be the wiser and better, albeit they can profit nothing to myself."

"We will judge warily," said Bellingham, "and look well what we are about to do. Good Master Wilson, I pray you, examine this Pearl,—since that is her name,—and see whether she hath had such Christian nurture as befits a child of her age."

The old minister seated himself in an arm-chair, and made an effort to draw Pearl betwixt his knees. But the child, unaccustomed to the touch or familiarity of any but her mother, escaped through the open window and stood on the upper step, looking like a wild, tropical bird, of rich plumage, ready to take flight into the upper air. Mr. Wilson, not a little astonished at this outbreak,—for he was a grandfatherly sort of personage, and usually a vast favorite with children,—essayed, however, to proceed with the examination.

"Pearl," said he, with great solemnity, "thou must take heed to instruction, that so, in due season, thou mayest wear in thy bosom the pearl of great price. Canst thou tell me, my child, who made thee?"

Now Pearl knew well enough who made her; for Hester Prynne, the daughter of a pious home, very soon after her talk with the child about her Heavenly Father, had begun to inform her of those truths which the human spirit, at whatever stage of immaturity, imbibes with such eager interest. Pearl, therefore, so large were the attainments of her three years' lifetime, could have borne a fair examination in the New Eng-

land Primer,* or the first column of the Westminster Catechism,* although unacquainted with the outward form of
either of those celebrated works. But that perversity, which
all children have more or less of, and of which little Pearl had
a tenfold portion, now, at the most inopportune moment,
took thorough possession of her, and closed her lips, or impelled her to speak words amiss. After putting her finger in
her mouth, with many ungracious refusals to answer good Mr.
Wilson's question, the child finally announced that she had
not been made at all, but had been plucked by her mother off
the bush of wild roses,* that grew by the prison-door.

This fantasy was probably suggested by the near proximity
of the Governor's red roses, as Pearl stood outside of the window; together with her recollection of the prison rose-bush,
which she had passed in coming hither.

Old Roger Chillingworth, with a smile on his face, whispered something in the young clergyman's ear. Hester Prynne
looked at the man of skill, and even then, with her fate hanging in the balance, was startled to perceive what a change had
come over his features,—how much uglier they were,—how
his dark complexion seemed to have grown duskier, and his
figure more misshapen,—since the days when she had familiarly known him. She met his eyes for an instant, but was immediately constrained to give all her attention to the scene
now going forward.

"This is awful!" cried the Governor, slowly recovering from
the astonishment into which Pearl's response had thrown him.
"Here is a child of three years old, and she cannot tell who
made her! Without question, she is equally in the dark as to
her soul, its present depravity,* and future destiny!*Methinks,
gentlemen, we need inquire no further."

Hester caught hold of Pearl, and drew her forcibly into her
arms, confronting the old Puritan magistrate with almost a
fierce expression. Alone in the world, cast off by it, and with
this sole treasure to keep her heart alive, she felt that she pos-

sessed indefeasible rights against the world, and was ready to defend them to the death.

"God gave me the child!" cried she. "He gave her, in requital of all things else, which ye had taken from me. She is my happiness!—she is my torture, none the less! Pearl keeps me here in life! Pearl punishes me too! See ye not, she is the scarlet letter, only capable of being loved, and so endowed with a million-fold the power of retribution for my sin? Ye shall not take her! I will die first!"

"My poor woman," said the not unkind old minister, "the child shall be well cared for!—far better than thou canst do it."

"God gave her into my keeping," repeated Hester Prynne, raising her voice almost to a shriek. "I will not give her up!"— And here, by a sudden impulse, she turned to the young clergyman, Mr. Dimmesdale, at whom, up to this moment, she had seemed hardly so much as once to direct her eyes.— "Speak thou for me!" cried she. "Thou wast my pastor, and hadst charge of my soul, and knowest me better than these men can. I will not lose the child! Speak for me! Thou knowest,—for thou hast sympathies which these men lack!—thou knowest what is in my heart, and what are a mother's rights, and how much the stronger they are, when that mother has but her child and the scarlet letter! Look thou to it! I will not lose the child! Look to it!"

At this wild and singular appeal, which indicated that Hester Prynne's situation had provoked her to little less than madness, the young minister at once came forward, pale, and holding his hand over his heart, as was his custom whenever his peculiarly nervous temperament was thrown into agitation. He looked now more careworn and emaciated than as we described him at the scene of Hester's public ignominy; and whether it were his failing health, or whatever the cause might be, his large dark eyes had a world of pain in their troubled and melancholy depth.

"There is truth in what she says," began the minister, with

a voice sweet, tremulous, but powerful, insomuch that the hall reëchoed, and the hollow armour rang with it,—"truth in what Hester says, and in the feeling which inspires her! God gave her the child, and gave her, too, an instinctive knowledge of its nature and requirements,—both seemingly so peculiar,— which no other mortal being can possess. And, moreover, is there not a quality of awful sacredness in the relation between this mother and this child?"

"Ay!—how is that, good Master Dimmesdale?" interrupted the Governor. "Make that plain, I pray you!"

"It must be even so," resumed the minister. "For, if we deem it otherwise, do we not thereby say that the Heavenly Father, the Creator of all flesh, hath lightly recognized a deed of sin, and made of no account the distinction between unhallowed lust and holy love? This child of its father's guilt and its mother's shame hath come from the hand of God, to work in many ways upon her heart, who pleads so earnestly, and with such bitterness of spirit, the right to keep her. It was meant for a blessing; for the one blessing of her life! It was meant, doubtless, as the mother herself hath told us, for a retribution too; a torture, to be felt at many an unthought of moment; a pang, a sting, an ever-recurring agony, in the midst of a troubled joy! Hath she not expressed this thought in the garb of the poor child, so forcibly reminding us of that red symbol which sears her bosom?"

"Well said, again!" cried good Mr. Wilson. "I feared the woman had no better thought than to make a mountebank of her child!"

"O, not so!—not so!" continued Mr. Dimmesdale. "She recognizes, believe me, the solemn miracle which God hath wrought, in the existence of that child. And may she feel, too, —what, methinks, is the very truth,—that this boon was meant, above all things else, to keep the mother's soul alive, and to preserve her from blacker depths of sin into which Satan might else have sought to plunge her! Therefore it is good for this poor, sinful woman that she hath an infant immortality, a being capable of eternal joy or sorrow, confided to her care,—to be trained up by her to righteousness,—to remind her, at every moment, of her fall,—but yet to teach her, as it were by the Creator's sacred pledge, that, if she bring the child to heaven, the child also will bring its parent thither! Herein is the sinful mother happier than the sinful father. For Hester Prynne's sake, then, and no less for the poor child's sake, let us leave them as Providence hath seen fit to place them!"

"You speak, my friend, with a strange earnestness," said old Roger Chillingworth, smiling at him.

"And there is weighty import in what my young brother hath spoken," added the Reverend Mr. Wilson. "What say you, worshipful Master Bellingham? Hath he not pleaded well for the poor woman?"

"Indeed hath he," answered the magistrate, "and hath adduced such arguments, that we will even leave the matter as it now stands; so long, at least, as there shall be no further scandal in the woman. Care must be had, nevertheless, to put the child to due and stated examination in the catechism at thy hands or Master Dimmesdale's. Moreover, at a proper season, the tithing-men* must take heed that she go both to school and to meeting."

The young minister, on ceasing to speak, had withdrawn a few steps from the group, and stood with his face partially concealed in the heavy folds of the window-curtain; while the shadow of his figure, which the sunlight cast upon the floor, was tremulous with the vehemence of his appeal. Pearl, that wild and flighty little elf, stole softly towards him, and, taking his hand in the grasp of both her own, laid her cheek against it; a caress so tender, and withal so unobtrusive, that her mother, who was looking on, asked herself,— "Is that my Pearl?" Yet she knew that there was love in the child's heart, although it mostly revealed itself in passion, and hardly twice in her lifetime had been softened by such gentleness as now.

The minister,—for, save the long-sought regards of woman, nothing is sweeter than these marks of childish preference, accorded spontaneously by a spiritual instinct, and therefore seeming to imply in us something truly worthy to be loved,—the minister looked round, laid his hand on the child's head, hesitated an instant, and then kissed her brow. Little Pearl's unwonted mood of sentiment lasted no longer; she laughed, and went capering down the hall, so airily, that old Mr. Wilson raised a question whether even her tiptoes touched the floor.

"The little baggage hath witchcraft in her, I profess," said he to Mr. Dimmesdale. "She needs no old woman's broomstick to fly withal!"

"A strange child!" remarked old Roger Chillingworth. "It is easy to see the mother's part in her. Would it be beyond a philosopher's research, think ye, gentlemen, to analyze that child's nature, and, from its make and mould, to give a shrewd guess at the father?"

"Nay; it would be sinful, in such a question, to follow the clew of profane philosophy," said Mr. Wilson. "Better to fast and pray upon it; and still better, it may be, to leave the mystery as we find it, unless Providence reveal it of its own accord. Thereby, every good Christian man hath a title to show a father's kindness towards the poor, deserted babe."

The affair being so satisfactorily concluded, Hester Prynne, with Pearl, departed from the house. As they descended the steps, it is averred that the lattice of a chamber-window was thrown open, and forth into the sunny day was thrust the face of Mistress Hibbins, Governor Bellingham's bitter-tempered sister, and the same who, a few years later, was executed as a witch.

"Hist, hist!" said she, while her ill-omened physiognomy seemed to cast a shadow over the cheerful newness of the house. "Wilt thou go with us to-night? There will be a merry company in the forest; and I wellnigh promised the Black Man that comely Hester Prynne should make one."

"Make my excuse to him, so please you!" answered Hester, with a triumphant smile. "I must tarry at home, and keep watch over my little Pearl. Had they taken her from me, I would willingly have gone with thee into the forest, and signed my name in the Black Man's book too, and that with mine own blood!"

"We shall have thee there anon!" said the witch-lady, frowning, as she drew back her head.

But here—if we suppose this interview betwixt Mistress Hibbins and Hester Prynne to be authentic, and not a parable —was already an illustration of the young minister's argument against sundering the relation of a fallen mother to the off-spring of her frailty. Even thus early had the child saved her from Satan's snare.

IX

THE LEECH

UNDER the appellation of Roger Chillingworth, the reader will remember, was hidden another name, which its former wearer had resolved should never more be spoken. It has been related, how, in the crowd that witnessed Hester Prynne's ignominious exposure, stood a man, elderly, travel-worn, who, just emerging from the perilous wilderness, beheld the woman, in whom he hoped to find embodied the warmth and cheerfulness of home, set up as a type of sin before the people. Her matronly fame was trodden under all men's feet. Infamy was babbling around her in the public market-place. For her kindred, should the tidings ever reach them, and for the companions of her unspotted life, there remained nothing but the contagion of her dishonor; which would not fail to be distributed in strict accordance and proportion with the intimacy and sacredness of their previous relationship. Then why—since the choice was with himself— should the individual, whose connection with the fallen woman had been the most intimate and sacred of them all, come forward to vindicate his claim to an inheritance so little desirable? He resolved not to be pilloried beside her on her pedestal of shame. Unknown to all but Hester Prynne, and possessing the lock and key of her silence, he chose to withdraw his name from the roll of mankind, and, as regarded his former ties and interests, to vanish out of life as completely as if he indeed lay at the bottom of the ocean, whither rumor had long ago consigned him. This purpose once effected, new interests would immediately spring up, and likewise a new purpose; dark, it is true, if not guilty, but of force enough to engage the full strength of his faculties.

In pursuance of this resolve, he took up his residence in the Puritan town, as Roger Chillingworth, without other introduction than the learning and intelligence of which he possessed more than a common measure. As his studies, at a previous period of his life, had made him extensively acquainted with the medical science of the day, it was as a physician that he presented himself, and as such was cordially received. Skilful men, of the medical and chirurgical profession, were of rare occurrence in the colony. They seldom, it would appear, partook of the religious zeal that brought other emigrants across the Atlantic. In their researches into the human frame, it may be that the higher and more subtile faculties of such men were materialized,[*] and that they lost the spiritual view of existence amid the intricacies of that wondrous mechanism, which seemed to involve art enough to comprise all of life within itself. At all events, the health of the good town of Boston, so far as medicine had aught to do with it, had hitherto lain in the guardianship of an aged deacon and apothecary, whose piety and godly deportment were stronger testimonials in his favor, than any that he could have produced in the shape of a diploma. The only surgeon was one who combined the occasional exercise of that noble art with the daily and habitual flourish of a razor. To such a professional body Roger Chillingworth was a brilliant acquisition. He soon manifested his familiarity with the ponderous and imposing machinery of antique physic; in which every remedy contained a multitude of far-fetched and heterogeneous ingredients, as elaborately compounded as if the proposed result had been the Elixir of Life.[*] In his Indian captivity, moreover, he had gained much knowledge of the properties of native herbs and roots; nor did he conceal from his patients, that these simple medicines, Nature's boon to the untutored savage, had quite as large a share of his own confidence as the European pharmacopœia, which so many learned doctors had spent centuries in elaborating.

This learned stranger was exemplary, as regarded at least the outward forms of a religious life, and, early after his arrival, had chosen for his spiritual guide the Reverend Mr. Dimmesdale. The young divine, whose scholar-like renown still lived in Oxford, was considered by his more fervent admirers as little less than a heaven-ordained apostle, destined, should he live and labor for the ordinary term of life, to do as great deeds for the now feeble New England Church, as the early Fathers had achieved for the infancy of the Christian faith. About this period, however, the health of Mr. Dimmesdale had evidently begun to fail. By those best acquainted with his habits, the paleness of the young minister's cheek was accounted for by his too earnest devotion to study, his scrupulous fulfilment of parochial duty, and, more than all, by the fasts and vigils of which he made a frequent practice, in order to keep the grossness of this earthly state from clogging and obscuring his spiritual lamp. Some declared, that, if Mr. Dimmesdale were really going to die, it was cause enough, that the world was not worthy to be any longer trodden by his feet. He himself, on the other hand, with characteristic humility, avowed his belief, that, if Providence should see fit to remove him, it would be because of his own unworthiness to perform its humblest mission here on earth. With all this difference of opinion as to the cause of his decline, there could be no question of the fact. His form grew emaciated; his voice, though still rich and sweet, had a certain melancholy prophecy of decay in it; he was often observed, on any slight alarm or other sudden accident, to put his hand over his heart, with first a flush and then a paleness, indicative of pain.

Such was the young clergyman's condition, and so imminent the prospect that his dawning light would be extinguished, all untimely, when Roger Chillingworth made his advent to the town. His first entry on the scene, few people could tell whence, dropping down, as it were, out of the sky, or starting from the nether earth, had an aspect of mystery, which was easily heightened to the miraculous. He was now known to be a man of skill; it was observed that he gathered herbs, and the blossoms of wild-flowers, and dug up roots and plucked off twigs from the forest-trees, like one acquainted with hidden virtues in what was valueless to common eyes. He was heard to speak of Sir Kenelm Digby,* and other famous men,—whose scientific attainments were esteemed hardly less than supernatural,—as having been his correspondents or associates. Why, with such rank in the learned world, had he come hither? What could he, whose sphere was in great cities, be seeking in the wilderness? In answer to this query, a rumor gained ground,—and, however absurd, was entertained by some very sensible people,—that Heaven had wrought an absolute miracle, by transporting an eminent Doctor of Physic, from a German university, bodily through the air, and setting him down at the door of Mr. Dimmesdale's study! Individuals of wiser faith, indeed, who knew that Heaven promotes its purposes without aiming at the stage-effect of what is called miraculous interposition, were inclined to see a providential hand in Roger Chillingworth's so opportune arrival.

This idea was countenanced by the strong interest which the physician ever manifested in the young clergyman; he attached himself to him as a parishioner, and sought to win a friendly regard and confidence from his naturally reserved sensibility. He expressed great alarm at his pastor's state of health, but was anxious to attempt the cure, and, if early undertaken, seemed not despondent of a favorable result. The elders, the deacons, the motherly dames, and the young and fair maidens, of Mr. Dimmesdale's flock, were alike importunate that he should make trial of the physician's frankly offered skill. Mr. Dimmesdale gently repelled their entreaties.

"I need no medicine," said he.

But how could the young minister say so, when, with every successive Sabbath, his cheek was paler and thinner, and his voice more tremulous than before,—when it had now become a constant habit, rather than a casual gesture, to press his hand over his heart? Was he weary of his labors? Did he wish to die? These questions were solemnly propounded to Mr. Dimmesdale by the elder ministers of Boston and the deacons of his church, who, to use their own phrase, "dealt with him" on the sin of rejecting the aid which Providence so manifestly held out. He listened in silence, and finally promised to confer with the physician.

"Were it God's will," said the Reverend Mr. Dimmesdale, when, in fulfilment of this pledge, he requested old Roger Chillingworth's professional advice, "I could be well content, that my labors, and my sorrows, and my sins, and my pains, should shortly end with me, and what is earthly of them be buried in my grave, and the spiritual go with me to my eternal state, rather than that you should put your skill to the proof in my behalf."

"Ah," replied Roger Chillingworth, with that quietness which, whether imposed or natural, marked all his deportment, "it is thus that a young clergyman is apt to speak. Youthful men, not having taken a deep root, give up their hold of life so easily! And saintly men, who walk with God on earth, would fain be away, to walk with him on the golden pavements of the New Jerusalem."*

"Nay," rejoined the young minister, putting his hand to his heart, with a flush of pain flitting over his brow, "were I worthier to walk there, I could be better content to toil here."

"Good men ever interpret themselves too meanly," said the physician.

In this manner, the mysterious old Roger Chillingworth became the medical adviser of the Reverend Mr. Dimmesdale.
As not only the disease interested the physician, but he was
strongly moved to look into the character and qualities of the
patient, these two men, so different in age, came gradually to
spend much time together. For the sake of the minister's
health, and to enable the leech to gather plants with healing
balm in them, they took long walks on the sea-shore, or in the
forest; mingling various talk with the plash and murmur of the
waves, and the solemn wind-anthem among the tree-tops.
Often, likewise, one was the guest of the other, in his place of
study and retirement. There was a fascination for the minister
in the company of the man of science, in whom he recognized
an intellectual cultivation of no moderate depth or scope; together with a range and freedom of ideas,* that he would have
vainly looked for among the members of his own profession.
In truth, he was startled, if not shocked, to find this attribute
in the physician. Mr. Dimmesdale was a true priest, a true religionist, with the reverential sentiment largely developed, and
an order of mind that impelled itself powerfully along the
track of a creed, and wore its passage continually deeper with
the lapse of time. In no state of society would he have been
what is called a man of liberal views; it would always be essential to his peace to feel the pressure of a faith about him, supporting, while it confined him within its iron framework. Not
the less, however, though with a tremulous enjoyment, did he
feel the occasional relief of looking at the universe through
the medium of another kind of intellect than those with
which he habitually held converse. It was as if a window were
thrown open, admitting a freer atmosphere into the close and
stifled study, where his life was wasting itself away, amid
lamp-light, or obstructed day-beams, and the musty fragrance,
be it sensual or moral, that exhales from books. But the air was
too fresh and chill to be long breathed, with comfort. So the
minister, and the physician with him, withdrew again within

the limits of what their church defined as orthodox.

Thus Roger Chillingworth scrutinized his patient carefully, both as he saw him in his ordinary life, keeping an accustomed pathway in the range of thoughts familiar to him, and as he appeared when thrown amidst other moral scenery, the novelty of which might call out something new to the surface of his character. He deemed it essential, it would seem, to know the man, before attempting to do him good. Wherever there is a heart and an intellect, the diseases of the physical frame are tinged with the peculiarities of these. In Arthur Dimmesdale, thought and imagination were so active, and sensibility so intense, that the bodily infirmity would be likely to have its groundwork there. So Roger Chillingworth—the man of skill, the kind and friendly physician—strove to go deep into his patient's bosom, delving among his principles, prying into his recollections, and probing every thing with a cautious touch, like a treasure-seeker in a dark cavern. Few secrets can escape an investigator, who has opportunity and license to undertake such a quest, and skill to follow it up. A man burdened with a secret should especially avoid the intimacy of his physician. If the latter possess native sagacity, and a nameless something more,—let us call it intuition; if he show no intrusive egotism, nor disagreeably prominent characteristics of his own; if he have the power, which must be born with him, to bring his mind into such affinity with his patient's, that this last shall unawares have spoken what he imagines himself only to have thought; if such revelations be received without tumult, and acknowledged not so often by an uttered sympathy, as by silence, an inarticulate breath, and here and there a word, to indicate that all is understood; if, to these qualifications of a confidant be joined the advantages afforded by his recognized character as a physician;—then, at some inevitable moment, will the soul of the sufferer be dissolved, and flow forth in a dark, but transparent stream, bringing all its mysteries into the daylight.

Roger Chillingworth possessed all, or most, of the attributes above enumerated. Nevertheless, time went on; a kind of intimacy, as we have said, grew up between these two cultivated minds, which had as wide a field as the whole sphere of human thought and study, to meet upon; they discussed every topic of ethics and religion, of public affairs, and private character; they talked much, on both sides, of matters that seemed personal to themselves; and yet no secret, such as the physician fancied must exist there, ever stole out of the minister's consciousness into his companion's ear. The latter had his suspicions, indeed, that even the nature of Mr. Dimmesdale's bodily disease had never fairly been revealed to him. It was a strange reserve!

After a time, at a hint from Roger Chillingworth, the friends of Mr. Dimmesdale effected an arrangement by which the two were lodged in the same house; so that every ebb and flow of the minister's life-tide might pass under the eye of his anxious and attached physician. There was much joy throughout the town, when this greatly desirable object was attained. It was held to be the best possible measure for the young clergyman's welfare; unless, indeed, as often urged by such as felt authorized to do so, he had selected some one of the many blooming damsels, spiritually devoted to him, to become his devoted wife. This latter step, however, there was no present prospect that Arthur Dimmesdale would be prevailed upon to take; he rejected all suggestions of the kind, as if priestly celibacy were one of his articles of church-discipline. Doomed by his own choice, therefore, as Mr. Dimmesdale so evidently was, to eat his unsavory morsel always at another's board, and endure the life-long chill which must be his lot who seeks to warm himself only at another's fireside, it truly seemed that this sagacious, experienced, benevolent, old physician, with his concord of paternal and reverential love for the young pastor, was the very man, of all mankind, to be constantly within reach of his voice.

The new abode of the two friends was with a pious widow, of good social rank, who dwelt in a house covering pretty nearly the site on which the venerable structure of King's Chapel*has since been built. It had the grave-yard, originally Isaac Johnson's home-field, on one side, and so was well adapted to call up serious reflections, suited to their respective employments, in both minister and man of physic. The motherly care of the good widow assigned to Mr. Dimmesdale a front apartment, with a sunny exposure, and heavy window-curtains to create a noontide shadow, when desirable. The walls were hung round with tapestry, said to be from the Gobelin looms,* and, at all events, representing the Scriptural story of David and Bathsheba,* and Nathan the Prophet,* in colors still unfaded, but which made the fair woman of the scene almost as grimly picturesque as the woe-denouncing seer. Here, the pale clergyman piled up his library, rich with parchment-bound folios of the Fathers, and the lore of Rabbis,* and monkish erudition, of which the Protestant divines, even while they vilified and decried that class of writers, were yet constrained often to avail themselves. On the other side of the house, old Roger Chillingworth arranged his study and laboratory; not such as a modern man of science would reckon even tolerably complete, but provided with a distilling apparatus, and the means of compounding drugs and chemicals, which the practised alchemist knew well how to turn to purpose. With such commodiousness of situation, these two learned persons sat themselves down, each in his own domain, yet familiarly passing from one apartment to the other, and bestowing a mutual and not incurious inspection into one another's business.

And the Reverend Arthur Dimmesdale's best discerning friends, as we have intimated, very reasonably imagined that the hand of Providence had done all this, for the purpose—besought in so many public, and domestic, and secret prayers—of restoring the young minister to health. But—it must now be said—another portion of the community had latterly begun to take its own view of the relation betwixt Mr. Dimmesdale and the mysterious old physician. When an uninstructed multitude attempts to see with its eyes, it is exceedingly apt to be deceived. When, however, it forms its judgment, as it usually does, on the intuitions of its great and warm heart, the conclusions thus attained are often so profound and so unerring, as to possess the character of truths supernaturally revealed. The people, in the case of which we speak, could justify its prejudice against Roger Chillingworth by no fact or argument worthy of serious refutation. There was an aged handicraftsman, it is true, who had been a citizen of London at the period of Sir Thomas Overbury's murder,* now some thirty years agone; he testified to having seen the physician, under some other name, which the narrator of the story had now forgotten, in company with Doctor Forman,* the famous old conjurer, who was implicated in the affair of Overbury. Two or three individuals hinted, that the man of skill, during his Indian captivity, had enlarged his medical attainments by joining in the incantations of the savage priests; who were universally acknowledged to be powerful enchanters, often performing seemingly miraculous cures by their skill in the black art. A large number—and many of these were persons of such sober sense and practical observation, that their opinions would have been valuable, in other matters—affirmed that Roger Chillingworth's aspect had undergone a remarkable change while he had dwelt in town, and especially since his abode with Mr. Dimmesdale. At first, his expression had been calm, meditative, scholar-like. Now, there was something ugly and evil in his face, which they had not previously noticed, and which grew still the more obvious to sight, the oftener they looked upon him. According to the vulgar idea, the fire in his laboratory had been brought from the lower regions, and was fed with infernal fuel; and so, as might be expected, his visage was getting sooty with the smoke.

To sum up the matter, it grew to be a widely diffused opinion, that the Reverend Arthur Dimmesdale, like many other personages of especial sanctity, in all ages of the Christian world, was haunted either by Satan himself, or Satan's emissary, in the guise of old Roger Chillingworth. This diabolical agent had the Divine permission, for a season, to burrow into the clergyman's intimacy, and plot against his soul. No sensible man, it was confessed, could doubt on which side the victory would turn. The people looked, with an unshaken hope, to see the minister come forth out of the conflict, transfigured with the glory which he would unquestionably win. Meanwhile, nevertheless, it was sad to think of the perchance mortal agony through which he must struggle towards his triumph.

Alas, to judge from the gloom and terror in the depths of the poor minister's eyes, the battle was a sore one, and the victory any thing but secure!

X

THE LEECH AND HIS PATIENT

OLD Roger Chillingworth, throughout life, had been calm in temperament, kindly, though not of warm affections, but ever, and in all his relations with the world, a pure and upright man. He had begun an investigation, as he imagined, with the severe and equal integrity of a judge, desirous only of truth, even as if the question involved no more than the air-drawn lines and figures of a geometrical problem, instead of human passions, and wrongs inflicted on himself. But, as he proceeded, a terrible fascination, a kind of fierce, though still calm, necessity seized the old man within its gripe, and never set him free again, until he had done all its bidding. He now dug into the poor clergyman's heart, like a miner searching for gold; or, rather, like a sexton delving into a grave, possibly in quest of a jewel that had been buried on the dead man's bosom, but likely to find nothing save mortality and corruption. Alas for his own soul, if these were what he sought!

Sometimes, a light glimmered out of the physician's eyes, burning blue and ominous, like the reflection of a furnace, or, let us say, like one of those gleams of ghastly fire that darted from Bunyan's awful door-way*in the hill-side, and quivered on the pilgrim's face. The soil where this dark miner was working had perchance shown indications that encouraged him.

"This man," said he, at one such moment, to himself, "pure as they deem him,—all spiritual as he seems,—hath inherited a strong animal nature from his father or his mother. Let us dig a little farther in the direction of this vein!"

Then, after long search into the minister's dim interior, and turning over many precious materials, in the shape of high aspirations for the welfare of his race, warm love of souls, pure sentiments, natural piety, strengthened by thought and study, and illuminated by revelation,—all of which invaluable gold was perhaps no better than rubbish to the seeker,—he would turn back, discouraged, and begin his quest towards another point. He groped along as stealthily, with as cautious a tread, and as wary an outlook, as a thief entering a chamber where a man lies only half asleep,—or, it may be, broad awake,—with purpose to steal the very treasure which this man guards as the apple of his eye. In spite of his premeditated carefulness, the floor would now and then creak; his garments would rustle; the shadow of his presence, in a forbidden proximity, would be thrown across his victim. In other words, Mr. Dimmesdale, whose sensibility of nerve often produced the effect of spiritual intuition, would become vaguely aware that something inimical to his peace had thrust itself into relation with him. But old Roger Chillingworth, too, had perceptions that were almost intuitive; and when the minister threw his startled eyes towards him, there the physician sat; his kind, watchful, sympathizing, but never intrusive friend.

Yet Mr. Dimmesdale would perhaps have seen this individual's character more perfectly, if a certain morbidness, to which sick hearts are liable, had not rendered him suspicious of all mankind. Trusting no man as his friend, he could not recognize his enemy when the latter actually appeared. He therefore still kept up a familiar intercourse with him, daily receiving the old physician in his study; or visiting the laboratory, and, for recreation's sake, watching the processes by which weeds were converted into drugs of potency.

One day, leaning his forehead on his hand, and his elbow on the sill of the open window, that looked towards the grave-yard, he talked with Roger Chillingworth, while the old man was examining a bundle of unsightly plants.

"Where," asked he, with a look askance at them,—for it was the clergyman's peculiarity that he seldom, now-a-days, looked straightforth at any object, whether human or inanimate,—"where, my kind doctor, did you gather those herbs, with such a dark, flabby leaf?"

"Even in the grave-yard, here at hand," answered the physician, continuing his employment. "They are new to me. I found them growing on a grave, which bore no tombstone, nor other memorial of the dead man, save these ugly weeds that have taken upon themselves to keep him in remembrance. They grew out of his heart, and typify, it may be, some hideous secret that was buried with him, and which he had done better to confess during his lifetime."

"Perchance," said Mr. Dimmesdale, "he earnestly desired it, but could not."

"And wherefore?" rejoined the physician. "Wherefore not; since all the powers of nature call so earnestly for the confession of sin, that these black weeds have sprung up out of a buried heart, to make manifest an unspoken crime?"

"That, good Sir, is but a fantasy of yours," replied the minister. "There can be, if I forebode aright, no power, short of the Divine mercy, to disclose, whether by uttered words, or by type or emblem, the secrets that may be buried with a human heart. The heart, making itself guilty of such secrets, must perforce hold them, until the day when all hidden things shall be revealed. Nor have I so read or interpreted Holy Writ,*as to understand that the disclosure of human thoughts and deeds, then to be made, is intended as a part of the retribution. That, surely, were a shallow view of it. No; these revelations, unless I greatly err, are meant merely to promote the intellectual satisfaction of all intelligent beings, who will stand waiting, on that day, to see the dark problem of this life made plain. A knowledge of men's hearts will be needful to the completest solution of that problem. And I conceive, moreover, that the hearts holding such miserable secrets as you speak of will yield them up, at that last day, not with reluctance, but with a joy unutterable."

"Then why not reveal them here?" asked Roger Chillingworth, glancing quietly aside at the minister. "Why should not the guilty ones sooner avail themselves of this unutterable solace?"

"They mostly do," said the clergyman, griping hard at his breast, as if afflicted with an importunate throb of pain. "Many, many a poor soul hath given its confidence to me, not only on the death-bed, but while strong in life, and fair in reputation. And ever, after such an outpouring, O, what a relief have I witnessed in those sinful brethren! even as in one who at last draws free air, after long stifling with his own polluted breath. How can it be otherwise? Why should a wretched man, guilty, we will say, of murder, prefer to keep the dead corpse buried in his own heart, rather than fling it forth at once, and let the universe take care of it!"

"Yet some men bury their secrets thus," observed the calm physician.

"True; there are such men," answered Mr. Dimmesdale. "But, not to suggest more obvious reasons, it may be that they are kept silent by the very constitution of their nature. Or,—can we not suppose it?—guilty as they may be, retaining, nevertheless, a zeal for God's glory and man's welfare, they shrink from displaying themselves black and filthy in the view of men; because, thenceforward, no good can be achieved by them; no evil of the past be redeemed by better service. So, to their own unutterable torment, they go about among their fellow-creatures, looking pure as new-fallen snow; while their hearts are all speckled and spotted with iniquity of which they cannot rid themselves."

"These men deceive themselves," said Roger Chillingworth, with somewhat more emphasis than usual, and making a slight gesture with his forefinger. "They fear to take up the shame that rightfully belongs to them. Their love for man, their zeal for God's service,—these holy impulses may or may not coexist in their hearts with the evil inmates to which their guilt has unbarred the door, and which must needs propagate a hellish breed within them. But, if they seek to glorify God, let them not lift heavenward their unclean hands! If they would serve their fellow-men, let them do it by making manifest the power and reality of conscience, in constraining them to penitential self-abasement! Wouldst thou have me to believe, O wise and pious friend, that a false show can be better—can be more for God's glory, or man's welfare—than God's own truth? Trust me, such men deceive themselves!"

"It may be so," said the young clergyman indifferently, as waiving a discussion that he considered irrelevant or unseasonable. He had a ready faculty, indeed, of escaping from any topic that agitated his too sensitive and nervous temperament. —"But, now, I would ask of my well-skilled physician, whether, in good sooth, he deems me to have profited by his kindly care of this weak frame of mine?"

Before Roger Chillingworth could answer, they heard the clear, wild laughter of a young child's voice, proceeding from the adjacent burial-ground. Looking instinctively from the open window,—for it was summer-time,—the minister beheld Hester Prynne and little Pearl passing along the footpath that traversed the inclosure. Pearl looked as beautiful as the day, but was in one of those moods of perverse merriment which, whenever they occurred, seemed to remove her entirely out of the sphere of sympathy or human contact. She now skipped irreverently from one grave to another; until, coming to the broad, flat, armorial tombstone of a departed worthy,—perhaps of Isaac Johnson himself,—she began to dance upon it. In reply to her mother's command and en-

treaty that she would behave more decorously, little Pearl
paused to gather the prickly burrs from a tall burdock, which
grew beside the tomb. Taking a handful of these, she arranged
them along the lines of the scarlet letter that decorated the
maternal bosom, to which the burrs, as their nature was, tena-
ciously adhered. Hester did not pluck them off.

Roger Chillingworth had by this time approached the window, and smiled grimly down.

"There is no law, nor reverence for authority, no regard for
human ordinances or opinions, right or wrong, mixed up with
that child's composition," remarked he, as much to himself as
to his companion. "I saw her, the other day, bespatter the
Governor himself with water, at the cattle-trough in Spring
Lane. What, in Heaven's name, is she? Is the imp altogether
evil? Hath she affections? Hath she any discoverable principle
of being?"

"None,—save the freedom of a broken law," answered Mr.
Dimmesdale, in a quiet way, as if he had been discussing the
point within himself. "Whether capable of good, I know not."

The child probably overheard their voices; for, looking up
to the window, with a bright, but naughty smile of mirth and
intelligence, she threw one of the prickly burrs at the Reverend Mr. Dimmesdale. The sensitive clergyman shrunk, with
nervous dread, from the light missile. Detecting his emotion,
Pearl clapped her little hands in the most extravagant ecstasy.
Hester Prynne, likewise, had involuntarily looked up; and all
these four persons, old and young, regarded one another in
silence, till the child laughed aloud, and shouted,—"Come
away, mother! Come away, or yonder old Black Man* will
catch you! He hath got hold of the minister already. Come
away, mother, or he will catch you! But he cannot catch little
Pearl!"

So she drew her mother away, skipping, dancing, and frisk-
ing fantastically among the hillocks of the dead people, like a
creature that had nothing in common with a bygone and

buried generation, nor owned herself akin to it. It was as if she had been made afresh, out of new elements, and must perforce be permitted to live her own life, and be a law unto herself, without her eccentricities being reckoned to her for a crime.

"There goes a woman," resumed Roger Chillingworth, after a pause, "who, be her demerits what they may, hath none of that mystery of hidden sinfulness which you deem so grievous to be borne. Is Hester Prynne the less miserable, think you, for that scarlet letter on her breast?"

"I do verily believe it," answered the clergyman. "Nevertheless, I cannot answer for her. There was a look of pain in her face, which I would gladly have been spared the sight of. But still, methinks, it must needs be better for the sufferer to be free to show his pain, as this poor woman Hester is, than to cover it all up in his heart."

There was another pause; and the physician began anew to examine and arrange the plants which he had gathered.

"You inquired of me, a little time agone," said he, at length, "my judgment as touching your health."

"I did," answered the clergyman, "and would gladly learn it. Speak frankly, I pray you, be it for life or death."

"Freely, then, and plainly," said the physician, still busy with his plants, but keeping a wary eye on Mr. Dimmesdale, "the disorder is a strange one; not so much in itself, nor as outwardly manifested,—in so far, at least, as the symptoms have been laid open to my observation. Looking daily at you, my good Sir, and watching the tokens of your aspect, now for months gone by, I should deem you a man sore sick, it may be, yet not so sick but that an instructed and watchful physician might well hope to cure you. But—I know not what to say—the disease is what I seem to know, yet know it not."

"You speak in riddles, learned Sir," said the pale minister, glancing aside out of the window.

"Then, to speak more plainly," continued the physician,

"and I crave pardon, Sir,—should it seem to require pardon, —for this needful plainness of my speech. Let me ask,—as your friend,—as one having charge, under Providence, of your life and physical well-being,—hath all the operation of this disorder been fairly laid open and recounted to me?"

"How can you question it?" asked the minister. "Surely, it were child's play to call in a physician, and then hide the sore!"

"You would tell me, then, that I know all?" said Roger Chillingworth, deliberately, and fixing an eye, bright with intense and concentrated intelligence, on the minister's face. "Be it so! But, again! He to whom only the outward and physical evil is laid open knoweth, oftentimes, but half the evil which he is called upon to cure. A bodily disease, which we look upon as whole and entire within itself, may, after all, be but a symptom of some ailment in the spiritual part. Your pardon, once again, good Sir, if my speech give the shadow of offence. You, Sir, of all men whom I have known, are he whose body is the closest conjoined, and imbued, and identified, so to speak, with the spirit whereof it is the instrument."

"Then I need ask no further," said the clergyman, somewhat hastily rising from his chair. "You deal not, I take it, in medicine for the soul!"

"Thus, a sickness," continued Roger Chillingworth, going on, in an unaltered tone, without heeding the interruption,— but standing up, and confronting the emaciated and white-cheeked minister with his low, dark, and misshapen figure, —"a sickness, a sore place, if we may so call it, in your spirit, hath immediately its appropriate manifestation in your bodily frame. Would you, therefore, that your physician heal the bodily evil? How may this be, unless you first lay open to him the wound or trouble in your soul?"

"No!—not to thee!—not to an earthly physician!" cried Mr. Dimmesdale, passionately, and turning his eyes, full and bright, and with a kind of fierceness, on old Roger Chillingworth. "Not to thee! But, if it be the soul's disease, then do I commit myself to the one Physician of the soul! He, if it stand with his good pleasure, can cure; or he can kill! Let him do with me as, in his justice and wisdom, he shall see good. But who art thou, that meddlest in this matter?—that dares thrust himself between the sufferer and his God?"

With a frantic gesture, he rushed out of the room.

"It is as well to have made this step," said Roger Chillingworth to himself, looking after the minister with a grave smile. "There is nothing lost. We shall be friends again anon. But see, now, how passion takes hold upon this man, and hurrieth him out of himself! As with one passion, so with another! He hath done a wild thing ere now, this pious Master Dimmesdale, in the hot passion of his heart!"

It proved not difficult to reëstablish the intimacy of the two companions, on the same footing and in the same degree as heretofore. The young clergyman, after a few hours of privacy, was sensible that the disorder of his nerves had hurried him into an unseemly outbreak of temper, which there had been nothing in the physician's words to excuse or palliate. He marvelled, indeed, at the violence with which he had thrust back the kind old man, when merely proffering the advice which it was his duty to bestow, and which the minister himself had expressly sought. With these remorseful feelings, he lost no time in making the amplest apologies, and besought his friend still to continue the care, which, if not successful in restoring him to health, had, in all probability, been the means of prolonging his feeble existence to that hour. Roger Chillingworth readily assented, and went on with his medical supervision of the minister; doing his best for him, in all good faith, but always quitting the patient's apartment, at the close of a professional interview, with a mysterious and puzzled smile upon his lips. This expression was invisible in Mr. Dimmesdale's presence, but grew strongly evident as the physician crossed the threshold.

"A rare case!" he muttered. "I must needs look deeper into it. A strange sympathy betwixt soul and body! Were it only for the art's sake, I must search this matter to the bottom!"

It came to pass, not long after the scene above recorded, that the Reverend Mr. Dimmesdale, at noonday, and entirely unawares, fell into a deep, deep slumber, sitting in his chair, with a large black-letter*volume open before him on the table. It must have been a work of vast ability in the somniferous school of literature. The profound depth of the minister's repose was the more remarkable; inasmuch as he was one of those persons whose sleep, ordinarily, is as light, as fitful, and as easily scared away, as a small bird hopping on a twig. To such an unwonted remoteness, however, had his spirit now withdrawn into itself, that he stirred not in his chair, when old Roger Chillingworth, without any extraordinary precaution, came into the room. The physician advanced directly in front of his patient, laid his hand upon his bosom, and thrust aside the vestment, that, hitherto, had always covered it even from the professional eye.

Then, indeed, Mr. Dimmesdale shuddered, and slightly stirred.

After a brief pause, the physician turned away.

But with what a wild look of wonder, joy, and horror! With what a ghastly rapture, as it were, too mighty to be expressed only by the eye and features, and therefore bursting forth through the whole ugliness of his figure, and making itself even riotously manifest by the extravagant gestures with which he threw up his arms towards the ceiling, and stamped his foot upon the floor! Had a man seen old Roger Chillingworth, at that moment of his ecstasy, he would have had no need to ask how Satan comports himself, when a precious human soul is lost to heaven, and won into his kingdom.

But what distinguished the physician's ecstasy from Satan's was the trait of wonder in it!

XI

THE INTERIOR OF A HEART

AFTER the incident last described, the intercourse between the clergyman and the physician, though externally the same, was really of another character than it had previously been. The intellect of Roger Chillingworth had now a sufficiently plain path before it. It was not, indeed, precisely that which he had laid out for himself to tread. Calm, gentle, passionless, as he appeared, there was yet, we fear, a quiet depth of malice, hitherto latent, but active now, in this unfortunate old man, which led him to imagine a more intimate revenge than any mortal had ever wreaked upon an enemy. To make himself the one trusted friend, to whom should be confided all the fear, the remorse, the agony, the ineffectual repentance, the backward rush of sinful thoughts, expelled in vain! All that guilty sorrow, hidden from the world, whose great heart would have pitied and forgiven, to be revealed to him, the Pitiless, to him, the Unforgiving! All that dark treasure to be lavished on the very man, to whom nothing else could so adequately pay the debt of vengeance!

The clergyman's shy and sensitive reserve had balked this scheme. Roger Chillingworth, however, was inclined to be hardly, if at all, less satisfied with the aspect of affairs, which Providence—using the avenger and his victim for its own pur-

THE SCARLET LETTER

poses, and, perchance, pardoning, where it seemed most to punish—had substituted for his black devices. A revelation, he could almost say, had been granted to him. It mattered little, for his object, whether celestial, or from what other region. By its aid, in all the subsequent relations betwixt him and Mr. Dimmesdale, not merely the external presence, but the very inmost soul of the latter seemed to be brought out before his eyes, so that he could see and comprehend its every movement. He became, thenceforth, not a spectator only, but a chief actor, in the poor minister's interior world. He could play upon him as he chose. Would he arouse him with a throb of agony? The victim was for ever on the rack; it needed only to know the spring that controlled the engine;—and the physician knew it well! Would he startle him with sudden fear? As at the waving of a magician's wand,* uprose a grisly phantom,—uprose a thousand phantoms,—in many shapes, of death, or more awful shame, all flocking round-about the clergyman, and pointing with their fingers at his breast!

All this was accomplished with a subtlety so perfect, that the minister, though he had constantly a dim perception of some evil influence watching over him, could never gain a knowledge of its actual nature. True, he looked doubtfully, fearfully,—even, at times, with horror and the bitterness of hatred,—at the deformed figure of the old physician. His gestures, his gait, his grizzled beard, his slightest and most indifferent acts, the very fashion of his garments, were odious in the clergyman's sight; a token, implicitly to be relied on, of a deeper antipathy in the breast of the latter than he was willing to acknowledge to himself. For, as it was impossible to assign a reason for such distrust and abhorrence, so Mr. Dimmesdale, conscious that the poison of one morbid spot was infecting his heart's entire substance, attributed all his presentiments to no other cause. He took himself to task for his bad sympathies in reference to Roger Chillingworth, disregarded the lesson that he should have drawn from them, and did his best to root them out. Unable to accomplish this, he nevertheless, as a matter of principle, continued his habits of social familiarity with the old man, and thus gave him constant opportunities for perfecting the purpose to which— poor, forlorn creature that he was, and more wretched than his victim—the avenger had devoted himself.

While thus suffering under bodily disease, and gnawed and tortured by some black trouble of the soul, and given over to the machinations of his deadliest enemy, the Reverend Mr. Dimmesdale had achieved a brilliant popularity in his sacred office. He won it, indeed, in great part, by his sorrows. His intellectual gifts, his moral perceptions, his power of experiencing and communicating emotion, were kept in a state of preternatural activity by the prick and anguish of his daily life. His fame, though still on its upward slope, already overshadowed the soberer reputations of his fellow-clergymen, eminent as several of them were. There were scholars among them, who had spent more years in acquiring abstruse lore, connected with the divine profession, than Mr. Dimmesdale had lived; and who might well, therefore, be more profoundly versed in such solid and valuable attainments than their youthful brother. There were men, too, of a sturdier texture of mind than his, and endowed with a far greater share of shrewd, hard, iron or granite understanding; which, duly mingled with a fair proportion of doctrinal ingredient, constitutes a highly respectable, efficacious, and unamiable variety of the clerical species. There were others, again, true saintly fathers, whose faculties had been elaborated by weary toil among their books, and by patient thought, and etherealized, moreover, by spiritual communications with the better world, into which their purity of life had almost introduced these holy personages, with their garments of mortality still clinging to them. All that they lacked was the gift that descended upon the chosen disciples, at Pentecost,* in tongues of flame;

symbolizing, it would seem, not the power of speech in foreign and unknown languages, but that of addressing the whole human brotherhood in the heart's native language.* These fathers, otherwise so apostolic, lacked Heaven's last and rarest attestation of their office, the Tongue of Flame.* They would have vainly sought—had they ever dreamed of seeking—to express the highest truths through the humblest medium of familiar words and images. Their voices came down, afar and indistinctly, from the upper heights where they habitually dwelt.

Not improbably, it was to this latter class of men that Mr. Dimmesdale, by many of his traits of character, naturally belonged. To their high mountain-peaks of faith and sanctity he would have climbed, had not the tendency been thwarted by the burden, whatever it might be, of crime or anguish, beneath which it was his doom to totter. It kept him down, on a level with the lowest; him, the man of ethereal attributes, whose voice the angels might else have listened to and answered! But this very burden it was, that gave him sympathies so intimate with the sinful brotherhood of mankind; so that his heart vibrated in unison with theirs, and received their pain into itself, and sent its own throb of pain through a thousand other hearts, in gushes of sad, persuasive eloquence. Oftenest persuasive, but sometimes terrible! The people knew not the power that moved them thus. They deemed the young clergyman a miracle of holiness. They fancied him the mouthpiece of Heaven's messages of wisdom, and rebuke, and love. In their eyes, the very ground on which he trod was sanctified. The virgins of his church grew pale around him, victims of a passion so imbued with religious sentiment that they imagined it to be all religion, and brought it openly, in their white bosoms, as their most acceptable sacrifice before the altar. The aged members of his flock, beholding Mr. Dimmesdale's frame so feeble, while they were themselves so rugged in their infirmity, believed that he would go heavenward before them, and enjoined it upon their children, that their old bones should be buried close to their young pastor's holy grave. And, all this time, perchance, when poor Mr. Dimmesdale was thinking of his grave, he questioned with himself whether the grass would ever grow on it, because an accursed thing must there be buried!

It is inconceivable, the agony with which this public veneration tortured him! It was his genuine impulse to adore the truth, and to reckon all things shadow-like, and utterly devoid of weight or value, that had not its divine essence as the life within their life. Then, what was he?—a substance?—or the dimmest of all shadows? He longed to speak out, from his own pulpit, at the full height of his voice, and tell the people what he was. "I, whom you behold in these black garments of the priesthood,—I, who ascend the sacred desk, and turn my pale face heavenward, taking upon myself to hold communion, in your behalf, with the Most High Omniscience,— I, in whose daily life you discern the sanctity of Enoch,*—I, whose footsteps, as you suppose, leave a gleam along my earthly track, whereby the pilgrims that shall come after me may be guided to the regions of the blest,—I, who have laid the hand of baptism upon your children,—I, who have breathed the parting prayer over your dying friends, to whom the Amen sounded faintly from a world which they had quitted,—I, your pastor, whom you so reverence and trust, am utterly a pollution and a lie!"

More than once, Mr. Dimmesdale had gone into the pulpit, with a purpose never to come down its steps, until he should have spoken words like the above. More than once, he had cleared his throat, and drawn in the long, deep, and tremulous breath, which, when sent forth again, would come burdened with the black secret of his soul. More than once —nay, more than a hundred times—he had actually spoken! Spoken! But how? He had told his hearers that he was altogether vile, a viler companion of the vilest, the worst of sinners, an abomination, a thing of unimaginable iniquity; and that the only wonder was, that they did not see his wretched body shrivelled up before their eyes, by the burning wrath of the Almighty! Could there be plainer speech than this? Would not the people start up in their seats, by a simultaneous impulse, and tear him down out of the pulpit which he defiled? Not so, indeed! They heard it all, and did but reverence him the more. They little guessed what deadly purport lurked in those self-condemning words. "The godly youth!" said they among themselves. "The saint on earth! Alas, if he discern such sinfulness in his own white soul, what horrid spectacle would he behold in thine or mine!" The minister well knew—subtle, but remorseful hypocrite that he was!—the light in which his vague confession would be viewed. He had striven to put a cheat upon himself by making the avowal of a guilty conscience, but had gained only one other sin, and a self-acknowledged shame, without the momentary relief of being self-deceived. He had spoken the very truth, and transformed it into the veriest falsehood. And yet, by the constitution of his nature, he loved the truth, and loathed the lie, as few men ever did. Therefore, above all things else, he loathed his miserable self!

His inward trouble drove him to practices, more in accordance with the old, corrupted faith of Rome, than with the better light of the church in which he had been born and bred. In Mr. Dimmesdale's secret closet, under lock and key, there was a bloody scourge. Oftentimes, this Protestant and Puritan divine had plied it on his own shoulders; laughing bitterly at himself the while, and smiting so much the more pitilessly, because of that bitter laugh. It was his custom, too, as it has been that of many other pious Puritans, to fast,— not, however, like them, in order to purify the body and render it the fitter medium of celestial illumination,—but rigorously, and until his knees trembled beneath him, as an act of penance. He kept vigils, likewise, night after night, sometimes in utter darkness; sometimes with a glimmering lamp; and sometimes, viewing his own face in a looking-glass, by the most powerful light which he could throw upon it. He thus typified the constant introspection wherewith he tortured, but could not purify, himself. In these lengthened vigils, his brain often reeled, and visions seemed to flit before him; perhaps seen doubtfully, and by a faint light of their own, in the remote dimness of the chamber, or more vividly, and close beside him, within the looking-glass. Now it was a herd of diabolic shapes, that grinned and mocked at the pale minister, and beckoned him away with them; now a group of shining angels, who flew upward heavily, as sorrow-laden, but grew more ethereal as they rose. Now came the dead friends of his youth, and his white-bearded father, with a saint-like frown, and his mother, turning her face away as she passed by. Ghost of a mother,—thinnest fantasy of a mother,—methinks she might yet have thrown a pitying glance towards her son! And now, through the chamber which these spectral thoughts had made so ghastly, glided Hester Prynne, leading along little Pearl, in her scarlet garb, and pointing her forefinger, first, at the scarlet letter on her bosom, and then at the clergyman's own breast.

None of these visions ever quite deluded him. At any moment, by an effort of his will, he could discern substances through their misty lack of substance, and convince himself that they were not solid in their nature, like yonder table of carved oak, or that big, square, leathern-bound and brazen-clasped volume of divinity. But, for all that, they were, in one sense, the truest and most substantial things which the poor minister now dealt with. It is the unspeakable misery of a life so false as his, that it steals the pith and substance out of whatever realities there are around us, and which were meant by Heaven to be the spirit's joy and nutriment. To the untrue man, the whole universe is false,—it is impalpable,—it shrinks to nothing within his grasp. And he himself, in so far as he shows himself in a false light, becomes a shadow, or, indeed, ceases to exist. The only truth, that continued to give Mr. Dimmesdale a real existence on this earth, was the anguish in his inmost soul, and the undissembled expression of it in his aspect. Had he once found power to smile, and wear a face of gayety, there would have been no such man!

On one of those ugly nights, which we have faintly hinted at, but forborne to picture forth, the minister started from his chair. A new thought had struck him. There might be a moment's peace in it. Attiring himself with as much care as if it had been for public worship, and precisely in the same manner, he stole softly down the staircase, undid the door, and issued forth.

XII

THE MINISTER'S VIGIL

WALKING in the shadow of a dream, as it were, and perhaps actually under the influence of a species of somnambulism, Mr. Dimmesdale reached the spot, where, now so long since, Hester Prynne had lived through her first hour of public ignominy. The same platform or scaffold, black and weather-stained with the storm or sunshine of seven long years, and foot-worn, too, with the tread of many culprits who had since ascended it, remained standing beneath the balcony of the meeting-house. The minister went up the steps.

It was an obscure night of early May. An unvaried pall of cloud muffled the whole expanse of sky from zenith to horizon. If the same multitude which had stood as eyewitnesses while Hester Prynne sustained her punishment could now have been summoned forth, they would have discerned no face above the platform, nor hardly the outline of a human shape, in the dark gray of the midnight. But the town was all asleep. There was no peril of discovery. The minister might stand there, if it so pleased him, until morning should redden in the east, without other risk than that the dank and chill night-air would creep into his frame, and stiffen his joints with rheumatism, and clog his throat with catarrh and cough; thereby defrauding the expectant audience of to-morrow's prayer and sermon. No eye could see him, save that ever-wakeful one which had seen him in his closet, wielding the bloody scourge. Why, then, had he come hither? Was it but the mockery of penitence? A mockery, indeed, but in which his soul trifled with itself! A mockery at which angels blushed and wept, while fiends rejoiced, with jeering laughter! He had been driven hither by the impulse of that Remorse which dogged him everywhere, and whose own sister and closely linked companion was that Cowardice which invariably drew him back, with her tremulous gripe, just when the other impulse had hurried him to the verge of a disclosure. Poor, miserable man! what right had infirmity like his to burden itself with crime? Crime is for the iron-nerved, who have their choice either to endure it, or, if it press too hard, to exert their fierce and savage strength for a good purpose, and fling it off at once! This feeble and most sensitive of spirits could do neither, yet continually did one thing or another, which intertwined, in the same inextricable knot, the agony of heaven-defying guilt and vain repentance.

And thus, while standing on the scaffold, in this vain show of expiation, Mr. Dimmesdale was overcome with a great horror of mind, as if the universe were gazing at a scarlet token on his naked breast, right over his heart. On that spot, in very truth, there was, and there had long been, the gnawing and poisonous tooth of bodily pain. Without any effort of his will, or power to restrain himself, he shrieked aloud; an outcry that went pealing through the night, and was beaten back from one house to another, and reverberated from the hills in the background; as if a company of devils, detecting so much misery and terror in it, had made a plaything of the sound, and were bandying it to and fro.

"It is done!" muttered the minister, covering his face with his hands. "The whole town will awake, and hurry forth, and find me here!"

But it was not so. The shriek had perhaps sounded with

a far greater power, to his own startled ears, than it actually possessed. The town did not awake; or, if it did, the drowsy slumberers mistook the cry either for something frightful in a dream, or for the noise of witches,* whose voices, at that period, were often heard to pass over the settlements or lonely cottages, as they rode with Satan through the air. The clergyman, therefore, hearing no symptoms of disturbance, uncovered his eyes and looked about him. At one of the chamber-windows of Governor Bellingham's mansion, which stood at some distance, on the line of another street, he beheld the appearance of the old magistrate himself, with a lamp in his hand, a white night-cap on his head, and a long white gown enveloping his figure. He looked like a ghost, evoked unseasonably from the grave. The cry had evidently startled him. At another window of the same house, moreover, appeared old Mistress Hibbins, the Governor's sister, also with a lamp, which, even thus far off, revealed the expression of her sour and discontented face. She thrust forth her head from the lattice, and looked anxiously upward. Beyond the shadow of a doubt, this venerable witch-lady had heard Mr. Dimmesdale's outcry, and interpreted it, with its multitudinous echoes and reverberations, as the clamor of the fiends and night-hags, with whom she was well known to make excursions into the forest.

Detecting the gleam of Governor Bellingham's lamp, the old lady quickly extinguished her own, and vanished. Possibly, she went up among the clouds. The minister saw nothing further of her motions. The magistrate, after a wary observation of the darkness—into which, nevertheless, he could see but little farther than he might into a mill-stone—retired from the window.

The minister grew comparatively calm. His eyes, however, were soon greeted by a little, glimmering light, which, at first a long way off, was approaching up the street. It threw a gleam of recognition on here a post, and there a garden-fence, and here a latticed window-pane, and there a pump, with its full trough of water, and here, again, an arched door of oak, with an iron knocker, and a rough log for the door-step. The Reverend Mr. Dimmesdale noted all these minute particulars, even while firmly convinced that the doom of his existence was stealing onward, in the footsteps which he now heard; and that the gleam of the lantern would fall upon him, in a few moments more, and reveal his long-hidden secret. As the light drew nearer, he beheld, within its illuminated circle, his brother clergyman,—or, to speak more accurately, his professional father, as well as highly valued friend,—the Reverend Mr. Wilson; who, as Mr. Dimmesdale now conjectured, had been praying at the bedside of some dying man. And so he had. The good old minister came freshly from the death-chamber of Governor Winthrop,* who had passed from earth to heaven within that very hour. And now, surrounded, like the saint-like personages of olden times, with a radiant halo, that glorified him amid this gloomy night of sin,—as if the departed Governor had left him an inheritance of his glory, or as if he had caught upon himself the distant shine of the celestial city, while looking thitherward to see the triumphant pilgrim pass within its gates,—now, in short, good Father Wilson was moving homeward, aiding his footsteps with a lighted lantern! The glimmer of this luminary suggested the above conceits to Mr. Dimmesdale, who smiled,—nay, almost laughed at them,—and then wondered if he were going mad.

As the Reverend Mr. Wilson passed beside the scaffold, closely muffling his Geneva cloak* about him with one arm, and holding the lantern before his breast with the other, the minister could hardly restrain himself from speaking.

"A good evening to you, venerable Father Wilson! Come up hither, I pray you, and pass a pleasant hour with me!"

Good heavens! Had Mr. Dimmesdale actually spoken? For one instant, he believed that these words had passed his lips.

But they were uttered only within his imagination. The venerable Father Wilson continued to step slowly onward, looking carefully at the muddy pathway before his feet, and never once turning his head towards the guilty platform. When the light of the glimmering lantern had faded quite away, the minister discovered, by the faintness which came over him, that the last few moments had been a crisis of terrible anxiety; although his mind had made an involuntary effort to relieve itself by a kind of lurid playfulness.

Shortly afterwards, the like grisly sense of the humorous again stole in among the solemn phantoms of his thought. He felt his limbs growing stiff with the unaccustomed chilliness of the night, and doubted whether he should be able to descend the steps of the scaffold. Morning would break, and find him there. The neighbourhood would begin to rouse itself. The earliest riser, coming forth in the dim twilight, would perceive a vaguely defined figure aloft on the place of shame; and, half crazed betwixt alarm and curiosity, would go, knocking from door to door, summoning all the people to behold the ghost—as he needs must think it—of some defunct transgressor. A dusky tumult would flap its wings from one house to another. Then—the morning light still waxing stronger—old patriarchs would rise up in great haste, each in his flannel gown, and matronly dames, without pausing to put off their night-gear. The whole tribe of decorous personages, who had never heretofore been seen with a single hair of their heads awry, would start into public view, with the disorder of a nightmare in their aspects. Old Governor Bellingham would come grimly forth, with his King James's ruff fastened askew; and Mistress Hibbins, with some twigs of the forest clinging to her skirts, and looking sourer than ever, as having hardly got a wink of sleep after her night ride; and good Father Wilson, too, after spending half the night at a death-bed, and liking ill to be disturbed, thus early, out of his dreams about the glorified saints. Hither, likewise, would come the elders and deacons of Mr. Dimmesdale's church, and the young virgins who so idolized their minister, and had made a shrine for him in their white bosoms; which, now, by the by, in their hurry and confusion, they would scantly have given themselves time to cover with their kerchiefs. All people, in a word, would come stumbling over their thresholds, and turning up their amazed and horror-stricken visages around the scaffold. Whom would they discern there, with the red eastern light upon his brow? Whom, but the Reverend Arthur Dimmesdale, half frozen to death, overwhelmed with shame, and standing where Hester Prynne had stood!

Carried away by the grotesque horror of this picture, the minister, unawares, and to his own infinite alarm, burst into a great peal of laughter. It was immediately responded to by a light, airy, childish laugh, in which, with a thrill of the heart,—but he knew not whether of exquisite pain, or pleasure as acute,—he recognized the tones of little Pearl.

"Pearl! Little Pearl!" cried he, after a moment's pause; then, suppressing his voice,—"Hester! Hester Prynne! Are you there?"

"Yes; it is Hester Prynne!" she replied, in a tone of surprise; and the minister heard her footsteps approaching from the sidewalk, along which she had been passing.—"It is I, and my little Pearl."

"Whence come you, Hester?" asked the minister. "What sent you hither?"

"I have been watching at a death-bed," answered Hester Prynne;—"at Governor Winthrop's death-bed, and have taken his measure for a robe, and am now going homeward to my dwelling."

"Come up hither, Hester, thou and little Pearl," said the Reverend Mr. Dimmesdale. "Ye have both been here before, but I was not with you. Come up hither once again, and we will stand all three together!"

She silently ascended the steps, and stood on the platform, holding little Pearl by the hand. The minister felt for the child's other hand, and took it. The moment that he did so, there came what seemed a tumultuous rush of new life, other life than his own, pouring like a torrent into his heart, and hurrying through all his veins, as if the mother and the child were communicating their vital warmth to his half-torpid system. The three formed an electric chain.

"Minister!" whispered little Pearl.

"What wouldst thou say, child?" asked Mr. Dimmesdale.

"Wilt thou stand here with mother and me, to-morrow noontide?" inquired Pearl.

"Nay; not so, my little Pearl!" answered the minister; for, with the new energy of the moment, all the dread of public exposure, that had so long been the anguish of his life, had returned upon him; and he was already trembling at the conjunction in which—with a strange joy, nevertheless—he now found himself. "Not so, my child. I shall, indeed, stand with thy mother and thee one other day, but not to-morrow!"

Pearl laughed, and attempted to pull away her hand. But the minister held it fast.

"A moment longer, my child!" said he.

"But wilt thou promise," asked Pearl, "to take my hand, and mother's hand, to-morrow noontide?"

"Not then, Pearl," said the minister, "but another time!"

"And what other time?" persisted the child.

"At the great judgment day!" whispered the minister,—and, strangely enough, the sense that he was a professional teacher of the truth impelled him to answer the child so. "Then, and there, before the judgment-seat, thy mother, and thou, and I, must stand together! But the daylight of this world shall not see our meeting!"

Pearl laughed again.

But, before Mr. Dimmesdale had done speaking, a light gleamed far and wide over all the muffled sky. It was doubtless caused by one of those meteors, which the night-watcher may so often observe burning out to waste, in the vacant regions of the atmosphere. So powerful was its radiance, that it thoroughly illuminated the dense medium of cloud betwixt the sky and earth. The great vault brightened, like the dome of an immense lamp. It showed the familiar scene of the street, with the distinctness of mid-day, but also with the awfulness that is always imparted to familiar objects by an unaccustomed light. The wooden houses, with their jutting stories and quaint gable-peaks; the doorsteps and thresholds, with the early grass springing up about them; the garden-plots, black with freshly turned earth; the wheel-track, little worn, and, even in the market-place, margined with green on either side;—all were visible, but with a singularity of aspect that seemed to give another moral interpretation to the things of this world than they had ever borne before. And there stood the minister, with his hand over his heart; and Hester Prynne, with the embroidered letter glimmering on her bosom; and little Pearl, herself a symbol, and the connecting link between those two. They stood in the noon of that strange and solemn splendor, as if it were the light that is to reveal all secrets, and the day-break that shall unite all who belong to one another.

There was witchcraft in little Pearl's eyes; and her face, as she glanced upward at the minister, wore that naughty smile which made its expression frequently so elfish. She withdrew her hand from Mr. Dimmesdale's, and pointed across the street. But he clasped both his hands over his breast, and cast his eyes towards the zenith.

Nothing was more common, in those days, than to interpret all meteoric appearances, and other natural phenomena, that occurred with less regularity than the rise and set of sun and moon, as so many revelations from a supernatural source. Thus, a blazing spear, a sword of flame, a bow, or a sheaf of arrows, seen in the midnight sky, prefigured Indian warfare. Pestilence was known to have been foreboded by a shower of crimson light. We doubt whether any marked event, for good or evil, ever befell New England, from its settlement down to Revolutionary times, of which the inhabitants had not been previously warned by some spectacle of this nature. Not seldom, it had been seen by multitudes. Oftener, however, its credibility rested on the faith of some lonely eyewitness, who beheld the wonder through the colored, magnifying, and distorting medium of his imagination, and shaped it more distinctly in his after-thought. It was, indeed, a majestic idea, that the destiny of nations should be revealed, in these awful hieroglyphics, on the cope of heaven. A scroll so wide might not be deemed too expansive for Providence to write a people's doom upon. The belief was a favorite one with our forefathers, as betokening that their infant commonwealth was under a celestial guardianship of peculiar intimacy and strictness. But what shall we say, when an individual discovers a revelation, addressed to himself alone, on the same vast sheet of record! In such a case, it could only be the symptom of a highly disordered mental state, when a man, rendered morbidly self-contemplative by long, intense, and secret pain, had extended his egotism over the whole expanse of nature, until the firmament itself should appear no more than a fitting page for his soul's history and fate.

We impute it, therefore, solely to the disease in his own eye and heart, that the minister, looking upward to the zenith, beheld there the appearance of an immense letter,—the letter A,—marked out in lines of dull red light. Not but the meteor may have shown itself at that point, burning duskily through a veil of cloud; but with no such shape as his guilty imagination gave it; or, at least, with so little definiteness, that another's guilt might have seen another symbol in it.

There was a singular circumstance that characterized Mr. Dimmesdale's psychological state, at this moment. All the time that he gazed upward to the zenith, he was, nevertheless, perfectly aware that little Pearl was pointing her finger towards old Roger Chillingworth, who stood at no great distance from the scaffold. The minister appeared to see him, with the same glance that discerned the miraculous letter. To his features, as to all other objects, the meteoric light imparted a new expression; or it might well be that the physician was not careful then, as at all other times, to hide the malevolence with which he looked upon his victim. Certainly, if the meteor kindled up the sky, and disclosed the earth, with an awfulness that admonished Hester Prynne and the clergyman of the day of judgment, then might Roger Chillingworth have passed with them for the arch-fiend, standing there, with a smile and scowl, to claim his own. So vivid was the expression, or so intense the minister's perception of it, that it seemed still to remain painted on the darkness, after the meteor had vanished, with an effect as if the street and all things else were at once annihilated.

"Who is that man, Hester?" gasped Mr. Dimmesdale, overcome with terror. "I shiver at him! Dost thou know the man? I hate him, Hester!"

She remembered her oath, and was silent.

"I tell thee, my soul shivers at him," muttered the minister again. "Who is he? Who is he? Canst thou do nothing for me? I have a nameless horror of the man."

"Minister," said little Pearl, "I can tell thee who he is!"

"Quickly, then, child!" said the minister, bending his ear close to her lips. "Quickly!—and as low as thou canst whisper."

Pearl mumbled something into his ear, that sounded, indeed, like human language, but was only such gibberish as children may be heard amusing themselves with, by the hour together. At all events, if it involved any secret information in regard to old Roger Chillingworth, it was in a tongue unknown to the erudite clergyman, and did but increase the bewilderment of his mind. The elfish child then laughed aloud.

"Dost thou mock me now?" said the minister.

"Thou wast not bold!—thou wast not true!" answered the child. "Thou wouldst not promise to take my hand, and mother's hand, to-morrow noontide!"

"Worthy Sir," said the physician, who had now advanced to the foot of the platform. "Pious Master Dimmesdale! can this be you? Well, well, indeed! We men of study, whose heads are in our books, have need to be straitly looked after! We dream in our waking moments, and walk in our sleep. Come, good Sir, and my dear friend, I pray you, let me lead you home!"

"How knewest thou that I was here?" asked the minister, fearfully.

"Verily, and in good faith," answered Roger Chillingworth, "I knew nothing of the matter. I had spent the better part of the night at the bedside of the worshipful Governor Winthrop, doing what my poor skill might to give him ease. He going home to a better world, I, likewise, was on my way homeward, when this strange light shone out. Come with me, I beseech you, Reverend Sir; else you will be poorly able to do Sabbath duty to-morrow. Aha! see now, how they trouble the brain,—these books!—these books! You should study less, good Sir, and take a little pastime; or these night-whimseys will grow upon you!"

"I will go home with you," said Mr. Dimmesdale.

With a chill despondency, like one awaking, all nerveless, from an ugly dream, he yielded himself to the physician, and was led away.

The next day, however, being the Sabbath, he preached a discourse which was held to be the richest and most powerful, and the most replete with heavenly influences, that had ever proceeded from his lips. Souls, it is said, more souls than one, were brought to the truth by the efficacy of that sermon, and vowed within themselves to cherish a holy gratitude towards Mr. Dimmesdale throughout the long hereafter. But, as he came down the pulpit-steps, the gray-bearded sexton met him, holding up a black glove, which the minister recognized as his own.

"It was found," said the sexton, "this morning, on the scaffold, where evil-doers are set up to public shame. Satan dropped it there, I take it, intending a scurrilous jest against your reverence. But, indeed, he was blind and foolish, as he ever and always is. A pure hand needs no glove to cover it!"

"Thank you, my good friend," said the minister gravely, but startled at heart; for, so confused was his remembrance, that he had almost brought himself to look at the events of the past night as visionary. "Yes, it seems to be my glove indeed!"

"And, since Satan saw fit to steal it, your reverence must needs handle him without gloves, henceforward," remarked the old sexton, grimly smiling. "But did your reverence hear of the portent that was seen last night? A great red letter in the sky,—the letter A,—which we interpret to stand for Angel. For, as our good Governor Winthrop was made an angel this past night, it was doubtless held fit that there should be some notice thereof!"

"No," answered the minister. "I had not heard of it."

XIII

ANOTHER VIEW OF HESTER

IN HER late singular interview with Mr. Dimmesdale, Hester Prynne was shocked at the condition to which she found the clergyman reduced. His nerve seemed absolutely destroyed. His moral force was abased into more than childish weakness. It grovelled helpless on the ground, even while his intellectual faculties retained their pristine strength, or had perhaps acquired a morbid energy, which disease only could have given them. With her knowledge of a train of circumstances hidden from all others, she could readily infer, that, besides the legitimate action of his own conscience, a terrible machinery had been brought to bear, and was still operating, on Mr. Dimmesdale's well-being and repose. Knowing what this poor, fallen man had once been, her whole soul was moved by the shuddering terror with which he had appealed to her,—the outcast woman,—for support against his instinctively discovered enemy. She decided, moreover, that he had a right to her utmost aid. Little accustomed, in her long seclusion from society, to measure her ideas of right and wrong by any standard external to herself, Hester saw —or seemed to see—that there lay a responsibility upon her, in reference to the clergyman, which she owed to no other, nor to the whole world besides. The links that united her to the rest of human kind—links of flowers, or silk, or gold, or whatever the material—had all been broken. Here was the iron link of mutual crime, which neither he nor she could break. Like all other ties, it brought along with it its obligations.

Hester Prynne did not now occupy precisely the same position in which we beheld her during the earlier periods of her ignominy. Years had come, and gone. Pearl was now seven years old. Her mother, with the scarlet letter on her breast, glittering in its fantastic embroidery, had long been a familiar object to the townspeople. As is apt to be the case when a person stands out in any prominence before the community, and, at the same time, interferes neither with public nor individual interests and convenience, a species of general regard had ultimately grown up in reference to Hester Prynne. It is to the credit of human nature, that, except where its selfishness is brought into play, it loves more readily than it hates. Hatred, by a gradual and quiet process, will even be transformed to love, unless the change be impeded by a continually new irritation of the original feeling of hostility. In this matter of Hester Prynne, there was neither irritation nor irksomeness. She never battled with the public, but submitted uncomplainingly to its worst usage; she made no claim upon it, in requital for what she suffered; she did not weigh upon its sympathies. Then, also, the blameless purity of her life, during all these years in which she had been set apart to infamy, was reckoned largely in her favor. With nothing now to lose, in the sight of mankind, and with no hope, and seemingly no wish, of gaining any thing, it could only be a genuine regard for virtue that had brought back the poor wanderer to its paths.

It was perceived, too, that, while Hester never put forward even the humblest title to share in the world's privileges,— farther than to breathe the common air, and earn daily bread for little Pearl and herself by the faithful labor of her hands, —she was quick to acknowledge her sisterhood with the race of man, whenever benefits were to be conferred. None so ready as she to give of her little substance to every demand of poverty; even though the bitter-hearted pauper threw back a gibe in requital of the food brought regularly to his door, or the garments wrought for him by the fingers that could have embroidered a monarch's robe. None so self-devoted as Hester, when pestilence stalked through the town. In all seasons of calamity, indeed, whether general or of individuals, the outcast of society at once found her place. She came, not as a guest, but as a rightful inmate, into the household that was darkened by trouble; as if its gloomy twilight were a medium in which she was entitled to hold intercourse with her fellow-creatures. There glimmered the embroidered letter, with comfort in its unearthly ray. Elsewhere the token of sin, it was the taper of the sick-chamber. It had even thrown its gleam, in the sufferer's hard extremity, across the verge of time. It had shown him where to set his foot, while the light of earth was fast becoming dim, and ere the light of futurity could reach him. In such emergencies, Hester's nature showed itself warm and rich; a well-spring of human tenderness, unfailing to every real demand, and inexhaustible by the largest. Her breast, with its badge of shame, was but the softer pillow for the head that needed one. She was self-ordained a Sister of Mercy; or, we may rather say, the world's heavy hand had so ordained her, when neither the world nor she looked forward to this result. The letter was the symbol of her calling. Such helpfulness was found in her,—so much power to do, and power to sympathize,—that many people refused to interpret the scarlet A by its original signification. They said that it meant Able;* so strong was Hester Prynne, with a woman's strength.

It was only the darkened house that could contain her. When sunshine came again, she was not there. Her shadow had faded across the threshold. The helpful inmate had departed, without one backward glance to gather up the meed of gratitude, if any were in the hearts of those whom she had served so zealously. Meeting them in the street, she never raised her head to receive their greeting. If they were resolute to accost her, she laid her finger on the scarlet letter, and passed on. This might be pride, but was so like humility, that it produced all the softening influence of the latter quality on the public mind. The public is despotic in its temper; it is capable of denying common justice, when too strenuously demanded as a right; but quite as frequently it awards more than justice, when the appeal is made, as despots love to have it made, entirely to its generosity. Interpreting Hester Prynne's deportment as an appeal of this nature, society was inclined to show its former victim a more benign countenance than she cared to be favored with, or, perchance, than she deserved.

The rulers, and the wise and learned men of the community, were longer in acknowledging the influence of Hester's good qualities than the people. The prejudices which they shared in common with the latter were fortified in themselves by an iron framework of reasoning, that made it a far tougher labor to expel them. Day by day, nevertheless, their sour and rigid wrinkles were relaxing into something which, in the due course of years, might grow to be an expression of almost benevolence. Thus it was with the men of rank, on whom their eminent position imposed the guardianship of the public morals. Individuals in private life, meanwhile, had quite forgiven Hester Prynne for her frailty; nay, more, they had begun to look upon the scarlet letter as the token, not of that one sin, for which she had borne so long and dreary a penance, but of her many good deeds since. "Do you see that woman with the embroidered badge?" they would say to strangers. "It is our Hester,—the town's own Hester,—who is so kind to the poor, so helpful to the sick, so comfortable to the afflicted!" Then, it is true, the propensity of human nature to tell the very worst of itself, when embodied in the person of

another, would constrain them to whisper the black scandal of
bygone years. It was none the less a fact, however, that, in
the eyes of the very men who spoke thus, the scarlet letter
had the effect of the cross on a nun's bosom.* It imparted to
the wearer a kind of sacredness, which enabled her to walk
securely amid all peril. Had she fallen among thieves, it would
have kept her safe. It was reported, and believed by many,
that an Indian had drawn his arrow against the badge, and
that the missile struck it, but fell harmless to the ground.

The effect of the symbol—or rather, of the position in respect to society that was indicated by it—on the mind of Hester Prynne herself, was powerful and peculiar. All the light
and graceful foliage of her character had been withered up by
this red-hot brand, and had long ago fallen away, leaving a
bare and harsh outline, which might have been repulsive,
had she possessed friends or companions to be repelled by it.
Even the attractiveness of her person had undergone a similar change. It might be partly owing to the studied austerity
of her dress, and partly to the lack of demonstration in her
manners. It was a sad transformation, too, that her rich and
luxuriant hair had either been cut off, or was so completely
hidden by a cap, that not a shining lock of it ever once gushed
into the sunshine. It was due in part to all these causes, but
still more to something else, that there seemed to be no longer
any thing in Hester's face for Love to dwell upon; nothing
in Hester's form, though majestic and statue-like, that Passion would ever dream of clasping in its embrace; nothing in
Hester's bosom, to make it ever again the pillow of Affection.
Some attribute had departed from her, the permanence of
which had been essential to keep her a woman. Such is frequently the fate, and such the stern development, of the feminine character and person, when the woman has encountered,
and lived through, an experience of peculiar severity. If she
be all tenderness, she will die. If she survive, the tenderness
will either be crushed out of her, or—and the outward sem-

blance is the same—crushed so deeply into her heart that it can never show itself more. The latter is perhaps the truest theory. She who has once been woman, and ceased to be so, might at any moment become a woman again, if there were only the magic touch to effect the transfiguration. We shall see whether Hester Prynne were ever afterwards so touched, and so transfigured.

Much of the marble coldness of Hester's impression was to be attributed to the circumstance that her life had turned, in a great measure, from passion and feeling, to thought. Standing alone in the world,—alone, as to any dependence on society, and with little Pearl to be guided and protected,—alone, and hopeless of retrieving her position, even had she not scorned to consider it desirable,—she cast away the fragments of a broken chain. The world's law was no law for her mind. It was an age in which the human intellect, newly emancipated, had taken a more active and a wider range than for many centuries before. Men of the sword had overthrown nobles and kings. Men bolder than these had overthrown and rearranged—not actually, but within the sphere of theory, which was their most real abode—the whole system of ancient prejudice, wherewith was linked much of ancient principle. Hester Prynne imbibed this spirit. She assumed a freedom of speculation, then common enough on the other side of the Atlantic, but which our forefathers, had they known of it, would have held to be a deadlier crime than that stigmatized by the scarlet letter. In her lonesome cottage, by the sea-shore, thoughts visited her, such as dared to enter no other dwelling in New England; shadowy guests, that would have been as perilous as demons to their entertainer, could they have been seen so much as knocking at her door.

It is remarkable, that persons who speculate the most boldly often conform with the most perfect quietude to the external regulations of society. The thought suffices them, without investing itself in the flesh and blood of action. So it seemed to be with Hester. Yet, had little Pearl never come to her from the spiritual world, it might have been far otherwise. Then, she might have come down to us in history, hand in hand with Ann Hutchinson, as the foundress of a religious sect. She might, in one of her phases, have been a prophetess.* She might, and not improbably would, have suffered death from the stern tribunals of the period, for attempting to undermine the foundations of the Puritan establishment. But, in the education of her child, the mother's enthusiasm of thought had something to wreak itself upon. Providence, in the person of this little girl, had assigned to Hester's charge the germ and blossom of womanhood, to be cherished and developed amid a host of difficulties. Every thing was against her. The world was hostile. The child's own nature had something wrong in it, which continually betokened that she had been born amiss,—the effluence of her mother's lawless passion,—and often impelled Hester to ask, in bitterness of heart, whether it were for ill or good that the poor little creature had been born at all.

Indeed, the same dark question often rose into her mind, with reference to the whole race of womanhood. Was existence worth accepting, even to the happiest among them? As concerned her own individual existence, she had long ago decided in the negative, and dismissed the point as settled. A tendency to speculation, though it may keep woman quiet, as it does man, yet makes her sad. She discerns, it may be, such a hopeless task before her. As a first step, the whole system of society is to be torn down, and built up anew. Then, the very nature of the opposite sex, or its long hereditary habit, which has become like nature, is to be essentially modified, before woman can be allowed to assume what seems a fair and suitable position. Finally, all other difficulties being obviated, woman cannot take advantage of these preliminary reforms, until she herself shall have undergone a still mightier change; in which, perhaps, the ethereal essence, wherein she has her truest life, will be found to have evaporated. A woman never overcomes these problems by any exercise of thought. They are not to be solved, or only in one way. If her heart chance to come uppermost, they vanish. Thus, Hester Prynne, whose heart had lost its regular and healthy throb, wandered without a clew in the dark labyrinth of mind; now turned aside by an insurmountable precipice; now starting back from a deep chasm. There was wild and ghastly scenery all around her, and a home and comfort nowhere. At times, a fearful doubt strove to possess her soul, whether it were not better to send Pearl at once to heaven, and go herself to such futurity as Eternal Justice should provide.

The scarlet letter had not done its office.

Now, however, her interview with the Reverend Mr. Dimmesdale, on the night of his vigil, had given her a new theme of reflection, and held up to her an object that appeared worthy of any exertion and sacrifice for its attainment. She had witnessed the intense misery beneath which the minister struggled, or, to speak more accurately, had ceased to struggle. She saw that he stood on the verge of lunacy, if he had not already stepped across it. It was impossible to doubt, that, whatever painful efficacy there might be in the secret sting of remorse, a deadlier venom had been infused into it by the hand that proffered relief. A secret enemy had been continually by his side, under the semblance of a friend and helper, and had availed himself of the opportunities thus afforded for tampering with the delicate springs of Mr. Dimmesdale's nature. Hester could not but ask herself, whether there had not originally been a defect of truth, courage, and loyalty, on her own part, in allowing the minister to be thrown into a position where so much evil was to be foreboded, and nothing auspicious to be hoped. Her only justification lay in the fact, that she had been able to discern no method of rescuing him from a blacker ruin than had overwhelmed herself, except by acquiescing in

Roger Chillingworth's scheme of disguise. Under that impulse, she had made her choice, and had chosen, as it now appeared, the more wretched alternative of the two. She determined to redeem her error, so far as it might yet be possible. Strengthened by years of hard and solemn trial, she felt herself no longer so inadequate to cope with Roger Chillingworth as on that night, abased by sin, and half maddened by the ignominy that was still new, when they had talked together in the prison-chamber. She had climbed her way, since then, to a higher point. The old man, on the other hand, had brought himself nearer to her level, or perhaps below it, by the revenge which he had stooped for.

In fine, Hester Prynne resolved to meet her former husband, and do what might be in her power for the rescue of the victim on whom he had so evidently set his gripe. The occasion was not long to seek. One afternoon, walking with Pearl in a retired part of the peninsula, she beheld the old physician, with a basket on one arm, and a staff in the other hand, stooping along the ground, in quest of roots and herbs to concoct his medicines withal.

XIV

HESTER AND THE PHYSICIAN

HESTER bade little Pearl run down to the margin of the water, and play with the shells and tangled seaweed, until she should have talked awhile with yonder gatherer of herbs. So the child flew away like a bird, and, making bare her small white feet, went pattering along the moist margin of the sea. Here and there, she came to a full stop, and peeped curiously into a pool, left by the retiring tide as a mirror for Pearl to see her face in. Forth peeped at her, out of the pool, with dark, glistening curls around her head, and an elf-smile in her eyes, the image of a little maid, whom Pearl, having no other playmate, invited to take her hand and run a race with her. But the visionary little maid, on her part, beckoned likewise, as if to say,—"This is a better place! Come thou into the pool!" And Pearl, stepping in, midleg deep, beheld her own white feet at the bottom; while, out of a still lower depth, came the gleam of a kind of fragmentary smile, floating to and fro in the agitated water.

Meanwhile, her mother had accosted the physician.

"I would speak a word with you," said she,—"a word that concerns us much."

"Aha! And is it Mistress Hester that has a word for old Roger Chillingworth?" answered he, raising himself from his stooping posture. "With all my heart! Why, Mistress, I hear good tidings of you on all hands! No longer ago than yester-eve, a magistrate, a wise and godly man, was discoursing of your affairs, Mistress Hester, and whispered me that there had been question concerning you in the council. It was debated whether or no, with safety to the common weal, yonder scarlet letter might be taken off your bosom. On my life, Hester, I made my entreaty to the worshipful magistrate that it might be done forthwith!"

"It lies not in the pleasure of the magistrates to take off this badge," calmly replied Hester. "Were I worthy to be quit of it, it would fall away of its own nature, or be transformed into something that should speak a different purport."

"Nay, then, wear it, if it suit you better," rejoined he. "A woman must needs follow her own fancy, touching the adorn-ment of her person. The letter is gayly embroidered, and shows right bravely on your bosom!"

All this while, Hester had been looking steadily at the old man, and was shocked, as well as wonder-smitten, to discern what a change had been wrought upon him within the past seven years. It was not so much that he had grown older; for though the traces of advancing life were visible, he bore his age well, and seemed to retain a wiry vigor and alertness. But the former aspect of an intellectual and studious man, calm and quiet, which was what she best remembered in him, had altogether vanished, and been succeeded by an eager, searching, almost fierce, yet carefully guarded look. It seemed to be his wish and purpose to mask this expression with a smile; but the latter played him false, and flickered over his visage so derisively, that the spectator could see his blackness all the better for it. Ever and anon, too, there came a glare of red light out of his eyes; as if the old man's soul were on fire, and kept on smouldering duskily within his breast, un-til, by some casual puff of passion, it was blown into a mo-mentary flame. This he repressed as speedily as possible, and strove to look as if nothing of the kind had happened.

In a word, old Roger Chillingworth was a striking evidence of man's faculty of transforming himself into a devil, if he will only, for a reasonable space of time, undertake a devil's office. This unhappy person had effected such a transformation by devoting himself, for seven years, to the constant analysis of a heart full of torture, and deriving his enjoyment thence, and adding fuel to those fiery tortures which he analyzed and gloated over.

The scarlet letter burned on Hester Prynne's bosom. Here was another ruin, the responsibility of which came partly home to her.

"What see you in my face," asked the physician, "that you look at it so earnestly?"

"Something that would make me weep, if there were any tears bitter enough for it," answered she. "But let it pass! It is of yonder miserable man that I would speak."

"And what of him?" cried Roger Chillingworth eagerly, as if he loved the topic, and were glad of an opportunity to discuss it with the only person of whom he could make a confidant. "Not to hide the truth, Mistress Hester, my thoughts happen just now to be busy with the gentleman. So speak freely; and I will make answer."

"When we last spake together," said Hester, "now seven years ago, it was your pleasure to extort a promise of secrecy, as touching the former relation betwixt yourself and me. As the life and good fame of yonder man were in your hands, there seemed no choice to me, save to be silent, in accordance with your behest. Yet it was not without heavy misgivings that I thus bound myself; for, having cast off all duty towards other human beings, there remained a duty towards him; and something whispered me that I was betraying it, in pledging myself to keep your counsel. Since that day, no man is so near to him as you. You tread behind his every footstep. You are beside him, sleeping and waking. You search his thoughts. You burrow and rankle in his heart! Your clutch is on his life, and you cause him to die daily a living death; and still he knows you not. In permitting this, I have surely acted a false part by the only man to whom the power was left me to be true!"

"What choice had you?" asked Roger Chillingworth. "My finger, pointed at this man, would have hurled him from his pulpit into a dungeon,—thence, peradventure, to the gallows!"

"It had been better so!" said Hester Prynne.

"What evil have I done the man?" asked Roger Chillingworth again. "I tell thee, Hester Prynne, the richest fee that ever physician earned from monarch could not have bought such care as I have wasted on this miserable priest! But for my aid, his life would have burned away in torments, within the first two years after the perpetration of his crime and thine. For, Hester, his spirit lacked the strength that could have borne up, as thine has, beneath a burden like thy scarlet letter. O, I could reveal a goodly secret! But enough! What art can do, I have exhausted on him. That he now breathes, and creeps about on earth, is owing all to me!"

"Better he had died at once!" said Hester Prynne.

"Yea, woman, thou sayest truly!" cried old Roger Chillingworth, letting the lurid fire of his heart blaze out before her eyes. "Better had he died at once! Never did mortal suffer what this man has suffered. And all, all, in the sight of his worst enemy! He has been conscious of me. He has felt an influence dwelling always upon him like a curse. He knew, by some spiritual sense,—for the Creator never made another being so sensitive as this,—he knew that no friendly hand was pulling at his heart-strings, and that an eye was looking curiously into him, which sought only evil, and found it. But he knew not that the eye and hand were mine! With the superstition common to his brotherhood, he fancied himself given over to a fiend, to be tortured with frightful dreams, and desperate thoughts, the sting of remorse, and despair of pardon; as a foretaste of what awaits him beyond the grave. But it was the constant shadow of my presence!—the closest propinquity of the man whom he had most vilely wronged! —and who had grown to exist only by this perpetual poison of the direst revenge! Yea, indeed!—he did not err!—there was a fiend at his elbow! A mortal man, with once a human heart, has become a fiend for his especial torment!"

The unfortunate physician, while uttering these words, lifted his hands with a look of horror, as if he had beheld some frightful shape, which he could not recognize, usurping the place of his own image in a glass. It was one of those moments—which sometimes occur only at the interval of years—when a man's moral aspect is faithfully revealed to his mind's eye. Not improbably, he had never before viewed himself as he did now.

"Hast thou not tortured him enough?" said Hester, noticing the old man's look. "Has he not paid thee all?"

"No!—no!—He has but increased the debt!" answered the physician; and, as he proceeded, his manner lost its fiercer characteristics, and subsided into gloom. "Dost thou remember me, Hester, as I was nine years agone? Even then, I was in the autumn of my days, nor was it the early autumn. But all my life had been made up of earnest, studious, thoughtful, quiet years, bestowed faithfully for the increase of mine own knowledge, and faithfully, too, though this latter object was but casual to the other,—faithfully for the advancement of human welfare. No life had been more peaceful and innocent than mine; few lives so rich with benefits conferred. Dost thou remember me? Was I not, though you might deem me cold, nevertheless a man thoughtful for others, craving little for himself,—kind, true, just, and of constant, if not warm affections? Was I not all this?"

"All this, and more," said Hester.

"And what am I now?" demanded he, looking into her face, and permitting the whole evil within him to be written on his features. "I have already told thee what I am! A fiend! Who made me so?"

"It was myself!" cried Hester, shuddering. "It was I, not less than he. Why hast thou not avenged thyself on me?"

"I have left thee to the scarlet letter," replied Roger Chillingworth. "If that have not avenged me, I can do no more!"

He laid his finger on it, with a smile.

"It has avenged thee!" answered Hester Prynne.

"I judged no less," said the physician. "And now, what wouldst thou with me touching this man?"

"I must reveal the secret," answered Hester, firmly. "He must discern thee in thy true character. What may be the result, I know not. But this long debt of confidence, due from me to him, whose bane and ruin I have been, shall at length be paid. So far as concerns the overthrow or preservation of his fair fame and his earthly state, and perchance his life, he is in thy hands. Nor do I,—whom the scarlet letter has disciplined to truth, though it be the truth of red-hot iron, entering into the soul,—nor do I perceive such advantage in his living any longer a life of ghastly emptiness, that I shall stoop to implore thy mercy. Do with him as thou wilt! There is no good for him,—no good for me,—no good for thee! There is no good for little Pearl! There is no path to guide us out of this dismal maze!"

"Woman, I could wellnigh pity thee!" said Roger Chillingworth, unable to restrain a thrill of admiration too; for there was a quality almost majestic in the despair which she expressed. "Thou hadst great elements. Peradventure, hadst thou met earlier with a better love than mine, this evil had not been. I pity thee, for the good that has been wasted in thy nature!"

"And I thee," answered Hester Prynne, "for the hatred that has transformed a wise and just man to a fiend! Wilt thou yet purge it out of thee, and be once more human? If not for his sake, then doubly for thine own! Forgive, and leave his further retribution to the Power that claims it! I said, but now, that there could be no good event for him, or thee, or me, who are here wandering together in this gloomy maze of evil, and stumbling, at every step, over the guilt wherewith we have strewn our path. It is not so! There might be good for thee, and thee alone, since thou hast been deeply wronged, and hast it at thy will to pardon. Wilt thou give up that only privilege? Wilt thou reject that priceless benefit?"

"Peace, Hester, peace!" replied the old man, with gloomy sternness. "It is not granted me to pardon. I have no such power as thou tellest me of. My old faith, long forgotten, comes back to me, and explains all that we do, and all we suffer. By thy first step awry, thou didst plant the germ of evil; but, since that moment, it has all been a dark necessity.* Ye that have wronged me are not sinful, save in a kind of typical illusion; neither am I fiend-like, who have snatched a fiend's office from his hands. It is our fate. Let the black flower blossom as it may! Now go thy ways, and deal as thou wilt with yonder man."

He waved his hand, and betook himself again to his employment of gathering herbs.

XV

HESTER AND PEARL

S O ROGER CHILLINGWORTH—a deformed old figure, with a face that haunted men's memories longer
than they liked—took leave of Hester Prynne, and
went stooping away along the earth. He gathered here and
there an herb, or grubbed up a root, and put it into the basket
on his arm. His gray beard almost touched the ground, as he
crept onward. Hester gazed after him a little while, looking
with a half-fantastic curiosity to see whether the tender grass
of early spring would not be blighted beneath him, and
show the wavering track of his footsteps, sere and brown,
across its cheerful verdure. She wondered what sort of herbs
they were, which the old man was so sedulous to gather.
Would not the earth, quickened to an evil purpose by the
sympathy of his eye, greet him with poisonous shrubs, of
species hitherto unknown, that would start up under his fingers? Or might it suffice him, that every wholesome growth
should be converted into something deleterious and malignant at his touch? Did the sun, which shone so brightly everywhere else, really fall upon him? Or was there, as it
rather seemed, a circle of ominous shadow moving along with
his deformity, whichever way he turned himself? And whither
was he now going? Would he not suddenly sink into the
earth, leaving a barren and blasted spot, where, in due course

of time, would be seen deadly nightshade, dogwood, hen-bane,* and whatever else of vegetable wickedness the climate could produce, all flourishing with hideous luxuriance? Or would he spread bat's wings and flee away, looking so much the uglier, the higher he rose towards heaven?

"Be it sin or no," said Hester Prynne bitterly, as she still gazed after him, "I hate the man!"

She upbraided herself for the sentiment, but could not over-come or lessen it. Attempting to do so, she thought of those long-past days, in a distant land, when he used to emerge at eventide from the seclusion of his study, and sit down in the fire-light of their home, and in the light of her nuptial smile. He needed to bask himself in that smile, he said, in order that the chill of so many lonely hours among his books might be taken off the scholar's heart. Such scenes had once ap-peared not otherwise than happy, but now, as viewed through the dismal medium of her subsequent life, they classed them-selves among her ugliest remembrances. She marvelled how such scenes could have been! She marvelled how she could ever have been wrought upon to marry him! She deemed it her crime most to be repented of, that she had ever endured, and reciprocated, the lukewarm grasp of his hand, and had suffered the smile of her lips and eyes to mingle and melt into his own. And it seemed a fouler offence committed by Roger Chillingworth, than any which had since been done him, that, in the time when her heart knew no better, he had persuaded her to fancy herself happy by his side.

"Yes, I hate him!" repeated Hester, more bitterly than be-fore. "He betrayed me! He has done me worse wrong than I did him!"

Let men tremble to win the hand of woman, unless they win along with it the utmost passion of her heart! Else it may be their miserable fortune, as it was Roger Chilling-worth's, when some mightier touch than their own may have awakened all her sensibilities, to be reproached even for the calm content, the marble image of happiness, which they will have imposed upon her as the warm reality. But Hester ought long ago to have done with this injustice. What did it betoken? Had seven long years, under the torture of the scarlet letter, inflicted so much of misery, and wrought out no repentance?

The emotions of that brief space, while she stood gazing after the crooked figure of old Roger Chillingworth, threw a dark light on Hester's state of mind, revealing much that she might not otherwise have acknowledged to herself.

He being gone, she summoned back her child.

"Pearl! Little Pearl! Where are you?"

Pearl, whose activity of spirit never flagged, had been at no loss for amusement while her mother talked with the old gatherer of herbs. At first, as already told, she had flirted fancifully with her own image in a pool of water, beckoning the phantom forth, and—as it declined to venture—seeking a passage for herself into its sphere of impalpable earth and unattainable sky. Soon finding, however, that either she or the image was unreal, she turned elsewhere for better pastime. She made little boats out of birch-bark, and freighted them with snail-shells, and sent out more ventures on the mighty deep than any merchant in New England; but the larger part of them foundered near the shore. She seized a live horseshoe by the tail, and made prize of several five-fingers, and laid out a jelly-fish to melt in the warm sun. Then she took up the white foam, that streaked the line of the advancing tide, and threw it upon the breeze, scampering after it with winged footsteps, to catch the great snow-flakes ere they fell. Perceiving a flock of beach-birds, that fed and fluttered along the shore, the naughty child picked up her apron full of pebbles, and, creeping from rock to rock after these small sea-fowl, displayed remarkable dexterity in pelting them. One little gray bird, with a white breast, Pearl was almost sure, had been hit by a pebble, and fluttered away with a broken wing. But then the elf-child sighed, and gave up her sport; because it grieved her to have done harm to a little being that was as wild as the sea-breeze, or as wild as Pearl herself.

Her final employment was to gather sea-weed, of various kinds, and make herself a scarf, or mantle, and a head-dress, and thus assume the aspect of a little mermaid. She inherited her mother's gift for devising drapery and costume. As the last touch to her mermaid's garb, Pearl took some eel-grass, and imitated, as best she could, on her own bosom, the decoration with which she was so familiar on her mother's. A letter, —the letter A,—but freshly green, instead of scarlet! The child bent her chin upon her breast, and contemplated this device with strange interest; even as if the one only thing for which she had been sent into the world was to make out its hidden import.

"I wonder if mother will ask me what it means!" thought Pearl.

Just then, she heard her mother's voice, and, flitting along as lightly as one of the little sea-birds, appeared before Hester Prynne, dancing, laughing, and pointing her finger to the ornament upon her bosom.

"My little Pearl," said Hester, after a moment's silence, "the green letter, and on thy childish bosom, has no purport. But dost thou know, my child, what this letter means which thy mother is doomed to wear?"

"Yes, mother," said the child. "It is the great letter A. Thou hast taught it me in the horn-book."*

Hester looked steadily into her little face; but, though there was that singular expression which she had so often remarked in her black eyes, she could not satisfy herself whether Pearl really attached any meaning to the symbol. She felt a morbid desire to ascertain the point.

"Dost thou know, child, wherefore thy mother wears this letter?"

"Truly do I!" answered Pearl, looking brightly into her

mother's face. "It is for the same reason that the minister keeps his hand over his heart!"

"And what reason is that?" asked Hester, half smiling at the absurd incongruity of the child's observation; but, on second thoughts, turning pale. "What has the letter to do with any heart, save mine?"

"Nay, mother, I have told all I know," said Pearl, more seriously than she was wont to speak. "Ask yonder old man whom thou hast been talking with! It may be he can tell. But in good earnest now, mother dear, what does this scarlet letter mean?—and why dost thou wear it on thy bosom?—and why does the minister keep his hand over his heart?"

She took her mother's hand in both her own, and gazed into her eyes with an earnestness that was seldom seen in her wild and capricious character. The thought occurred to Hester, that the child might really be seeking to approach her with childlike confidence, and doing what she could, and as intelligently as she knew how, to establish a meeting-point of sympathy. It showed Pearl in an unwonted aspect. Heretofore, the mother, while loving her child with the intensity of a sole affection, had schooled herself to hope for little other return than the waywardness of an April breeze; which spends its time in airy sport, and has its gusts of inexplicable passion, and is petulant in its best of moods, and chills oftener than caresses you, when you take it to your bosom; in requital of which misdemeanours, it will sometimes, of its own vague purpose, kiss your cheek with a kind of doubtful tenderness, and play gently with your hair, and then begone about its other idle business, leaving a dreamy pleasure at your heart. And this, moreover, was a mother's estimate of the child's disposition. Any other observer might have seen few but unamiable traits, and have given them a far darker coloring. But now the idea came strongly into Hester's mind, that Pearl, with her remarkable precocity and acuteness, might already have approached the age when she could be made a friend, and intrusted with as much of her mother's sorrows as could be imparted, without irreverence either to the parent or the child. In the little chaos of Pearl's character, there might be seen emerging—and could have been, from the very first—the stedfast principles of an unflinching courage,—an uncontrollable will,—a sturdy pride, which might be disciplined into self-respect,—and a bitter scorn of many things, which, when examined, might be found to have the taint of falsehood in them. She possessed affections, too, though hitherto acrid and disagreeable, as are the richest flavors of unripe fruit. With all these sterling attributes, thought Hester, the evil which she inherited from her mother must be great indeed, if a noble woman do not grow out of this elfish child.

Pearl's inevitable tendency to hover about the enigma of the scarlet letter seemed an innate quality of her being. From the earliest epoch of her conscious life, she had entered upon this as her appointed mission.* Hester had often fancied that Providence had a design of justice and retribution, in endowing the child with this marked propensity; but never, until now, had she bethought herself to ask, whether, linked with that design, there might not likewise be a purpose of mercy and beneficence. If little Pearl were entertained with faith and trust, as a spirit-messenger no less than an earthly child, might it not be her errand to soothe away the sorrow that lay cold in her mother's heart, and converted it into a tomb?—and to help her to overcome the passion, once so wild, and even yet neither dead nor asleep, but only imprisoned within the same tomb-like heart?

Such were some of the thoughts that now stirred in Hester's mind, with as much vivacity of impression as if they had actually been whispered into her ear. And there was little Pearl, all this while, holding her mother's hand in both her own, and turning her face upward, while she put these searching questions, once, and again, and still a third time.

"What does the letter mean, mother?—and why dost thou

wear it?—and why does the minister keep his hand over his heart?"

"What shall I say?" thought Hester to herself.—"No! If this be the price of the child's sympathy, I cannot pay it!"

Then she spoke aloud.

"Silly Pearl," said she, "what questions are these? There are many things in this world that a child must not ask about. What know I of the minister's heart? And as for the scarlet letter, I wear it for the sake of its gold thread!"

In all the seven bygone years, Hester Prynne had never before been false to the symbol on her bosom. It may be that it was the talisman of a stern and severe, but yet a guardian spirit, who now forsook her; as recognizing that, in spite of his strict watch over her heart, some new evil had crept into it, or some old one had never been expelled. As for little Pearl, the earnestness soon passed out of her face.

But the child did not see fit to let the matter drop. Two or three times, as her mother and she went homeward, and as often at supper-time, and while Hester was putting her to bed, and once after she seemed to be fairly asleep, Pearl looked up, with mischief gleaming in her black eyes.

"Mother," said she, "what does the scarlet letter mean?"

And the next morning, the first indication the child gave of being awake was by popping up her head from the pillow, and making that other inquiry, which she had so unaccountably connected with her investigations about the scarlet letter:—

"Mother!—Mother!—Why does the minister keep his hand over his heart?"

"Hold thy tongue, naughty child!" answered her mother, with an asperity that she had never permitted to herself before. "Do not tease me; else I shall shut thee into the dark closet!"

XVI

A FOREST WALK

HESTER PRYNNE remained constant in her resolve to make known to Mr. Dimmesdale, at whatever risk of present pain or ulterior consequences, the true character of the man who had crept into his intimacy. For several days, however, she vainly sought an opportunity of addressing him in some of the meditative walks which she knew him to be in the habit of taking, along the shores of the peninsula, or on the wooded hills of the neighbouring country. There would have been no scandal, indeed, nor peril to the holy whiteness of the clergyman's good fame, had she visited him in his own study; where many a penitent, ere now, had confessed sins of perhaps as deep a dye as the one betokened by the scarlet letter. But, partly that she dreaded the secret or undisguised interference of old Roger Chillingworth, and partly that her conscious heart imputed suspicion where none could have been felt, and partly that both the minister and she would need the whole wide world to breathe in, while they talked together,—for all these reasons, Hester never thought of meeting him in any narrower privacy than beneath the open sky.

At last, while attending in a sick-chamber, whither the Reverend Mr. Dimmesdale had been summoned to make a prayer, she learnt that he had gone, the day before, to visit

the Apostle Eliot,* among his Indian converts. He would probably return, by a certain hour, in the afternoon of the mor-
row. Betimes, therefore, the next day, Hester took little Pearl,
—who was necessarily the companion of all her mother's ex-
peditions, however inconvenient her presence,—and set forth.

The road, after the two wayfarers had crossed from the
peninsula to the mainland, was no other than a footpath. It
straggled onward into the mystery of the primeval forest.* This
hemmed it in so narrowly, and stood so black and dense on
either side, and disclosed such imperfect glimpses of the sky
above, that, to Hester's mind, it imaged not amiss the moral
wilderness in which she had so long been wandering. The
day was chill and sombre. Overhead was a gray expanse of
cloud, slightly stirred, however, by a breeze; so that a gleam
of flickering sunshine might now and then be seen at its solitary play along the path. This flitting cheerfulness was always
at the farther extremity of some long vista through the forest.
The sportive sunlight—feebly sportive, at best, in the pre-
dominant pensiveness of the day and scene—withdrew itself
as they came nigh, and left the spots where it had danced
the drearier, because they had hoped to find them bright.

"Mother," said little Pearl, "the sunshine does not love you.
It runs away and hides itself, because it is afraid of something
on your bosom. Now, see! There it is, playing, a good way
off. Stand you here, and let me run and catch it. I am but
a child. It will not flee from me; for I wear nothing on my
bosom yet!"

"Nor ever will, my child, I hope," said Hester.

"And why not, mother?" asked Pearl, stopping short, just
at the beginning of her race. "Will not it come of its own
accord, when I am a woman grown?"

"Run away, child," answered her mother, "and catch the
sunshine! It will soon be gone."

Pearl set forth, at a great pace, and, as Hester smiled to
perceive, did actually catch the sunshine, and stood laughing

in the midst of it, all brightened by its splendor, and scintillating with the vivacity excited by rapid motion. The light lingered about the lonely child, as if glad of such a playmate, until her mother had drawn almost nigh enough to step into the magic circle too.

"It will go now!" said Pearl, shaking her head.

"See!" answered Hester, smiling. "Now I can stretch out my hand, and grasp some of it."

As she attempted to do so, the sunshine vanished; or, to judge from the bright expression that was dancing on Pearl's features, her mother could have fancied that the child had absorbed it into herself, and would give it forth again, with a gleam about her path, as they should plunge into some gloomier shade. There was no other attribute that so much impressed her with a sense of new and untransmitted vigor in Pearl's nature, as this never-failing vivacity of spirits; she had not the disease of sadness, which almost all children, in these latter days, inherit, with the scrofula,* from the troubles of their ancestors. Perhaps this too was a disease, and but the reflex of the wild energy with which Hester had fought against her sorrows, before Pearl's birth. It was certainly a doubtful charm, imparting a hard, metallic lustre to the child's character. She wanted—what some people want throughout life—a grief that should deeply touch her, and thus humanize and make her capable of sympathy. But there was time enough yet for little Pearl!

"Come, my child!" said Hester, looking about her, from the spot where Pearl had stood still in the sunshine. "We will sit down a little way within the wood, and rest ourselves."

"I am not aweary, mother," replied the little girl. "But you may sit down, if you will tell me a story meanwhile."

"A story, child!" said Hester. "And about what?"

"O, a story about the Black Man!" answered Pearl, taking hold of her mother's gown, and looking up, half earnestly, half mischievously, into her face. "How he haunts this forest, and carries a book* with him,—a big, heavy book, with iron clasps; and how this ugly Black Man offers his book and an iron pen to every body that meets him here among the trees; and they are to write their names with their own blood. And then he sets his mark on their bosoms! Didst thou ever meet the Black Man, mother?"

"And who told you this story, Pearl?" asked her mother, recognizing a common superstition of the period.

"It was the old dame in the chimney-corner, at the house where you watched last night," said the child. "But she fancied me asleep while she was talking of it. She said that a thousand and a thousand people had met him here, and had written in his book, and have his mark on them. And that ugly-tempered lady, old Mistress Hibbins, was one. And, mother, the old dame said that this scarlet letter was the Black Man's mark on thee, and that it glows like a red flame when thou meetest him at midnight, here in the dark wood. Is it true, mother? And dost thou go to meet him in the night-time?"

"Didst thou ever awake, and find thy mother gone?" asked Hester.

"Not that I remember," said the child. "If thou fearest to leave me in our cottage, thou mightest take me along with thee. I would very gladly go! But, mother, tell me now! Is there such a Black Man? And didst thou ever meet him? And is this his mark?"

"Wilt thou let me be at peace, if I once tell thee?" asked her mother.

"Yes, if thou tellest me all," answered Pearl.

"Once in my life I met the Black Man!" said her mother. "This scarlet letter is his mark!"*

Thus conversing, they entered sufficiently deep into the wood to secure themselves from the observation of any casual passenger along the forest-track. Here they sat down on a luxuriant heap of moss; which, at some epoch of the preceding

THE SCARLET LETTER

century, had been a gigantic pine, with its roots and trunk in
the darksome shade, and its head aloft in the upper atmosphere. It was a little dell where they had seated themselves,
with a leaf-strewn bank rising gently on either side, and a
brook flowing through the midst, over a bed of fallen and
drowned leaves. The trees impending over it had flung down
great branches, from time to time, which choked up the
current, and compelled it to form eddies and black depths at
some points; while, in its swifter and livelier passages, there
appeared a channel-way of pebbles, and brown, sparkling
sand. Letting the eyes follow along the course of the stream,
they could catch the reflected light from its water, at some
short distance within the forest, but soon lost all traces of it
amid the bewilderment of tree-trunks and underbrush, and
here and there a huge rock, covered over with gray lichens.
All these giant trees and boulders of granite seemed intent on
making a mystery of the course of this small brook; fearing,
perhaps, that, with its never-ceasing loquacity, it should
whisper tales out of the heart of the old forest whence it
flowed, or mirror its revelations on the smooth surface of a
pool. Continually, indeed, as it stole onward, the streamlet
kept up a babble, kind, quiet, soothing, but melancholy, like
the voice of a young child that was spending its infancy without playfulness, and knew not how to be merry among sad
acquaintance and events of sombre hue.

"O brook! O foolish and tiresome little brook!" cried Pearl,
after listening awhile to its talk. "Why art thou so sad? Pluck
up a spirit, and do not be all the time sighing and murmuring!"

But the brook, in the course of its little lifetime among the
forest-trees, had gone through so solemn an experience that
it could not help talking about it, and seemed to have nothing
else to say. Pearl resembled the brook, inasmuch as the current of her life gushed from a well-spring as mysterious, and
had flowed through scenes shadowed as heavily with gloom.

But, unlike the little stream, she danced and sparkled, and prattled airily along her course.

"What does this sad little brook say, mother?" inquired she.

"If thou hadst a sorrow of thine own, the brook might tell thee of it," answered her mother, "even as it is telling me of mine! But now, Pearl, I hear a footstep along the path, and the noise of one putting aside the branches. I would have thee betake thyself to play, and leave me to speak with him that comes yonder."

"Is it the Black Man?" asked Pearl.

"Wilt thou go and play, child?" repeated her mother. "But do not stray far into the wood. And take heed that thou come at my first call."

"Yes, mother," answered Pearl. "But, if it be the Black Man, wilt thou not let me stay a moment, and look at him, with his big book under his arm?"

"Go, silly child!" said her mother, impatiently. "It is no Black Man! Thou canst see him now through the trees. It is the minister!"

"And so it is!" said the child. "And, mother, he has his hand over his heart! Is it because, when the minister wrote his name in the book, the Black Man set his mark in that place? But why does he not wear it outside his bosom, as thou dost, mother?"

"Go now, child, and thou shalt tease me as thou wilt another time!" cried Hester Prynne. "But do not stray far. Keep where thou canst hear the babble of the brook."

The child went singing away, following up the current of the brook, and striving to mingle a more lightsome cadence with its melancholy voice. But the little stream would not be comforted, and still kept telling its unintelligible secret of some very mournful mystery that had happened—or making a prophetic lamentation about something that was yet to happen—within the verge of the dismal forest. So Pearl, who had enough of shadow in her own little life, chose to break off all acquaintance with this repining brook. She set herself, therefore, to gathering violets and wood-anemones, and some scarlet columbines that she found growing in the crevices of a high rock.

When her elf-child had departed, Hester Prynne made a step or two towards the track that led through the forest, but still remained under the deep shadow of the trees. She beheld the minister advancing along the path, entirely alone, and leaning on a staff which he had cut by the way-side. He looked haggard and feeble, and betrayed a nerveless despondency in his air, which had never so remarkably characterized him in his walks about the settlement, nor in any other situation where he deemed himself liable to notice. Here it was wofully visible, in this intense seclusion of the forest, which of itself would have been a heavy trial to the spirits. There was a list-lessness in his gait; as if he saw no reason for taking one step farther, nor felt any desire to do so, but would have been glad, could he be glad of any thing, to fling himself down at the root of the nearest tree, and lie there passive for evermore. The leaves might bestrew him, and the soil gradually accumulate and form a little hillock over his frame, no matter whether there were life in it or no. Death was too definite an object to be wished for, or avoided.

To Hester's eye, the Reverend Mr. Dimmesdale exhibited no symptom of positive and vivacious suffering, except that, as little Pearl had remarked, he kept his hand over his heart.

XVII

THE PASTOR AND HIS PARISHIONER

SLOWLY as the minister walked, he had almost gone by, before Hester Prynne could gather voice enough to attract his observation. At length, she succeeded.

"Arthur Dimmesdale!" she said, faintly at first; then louder, but hoarsely. "Arthur Dimmesdale!"

"Who speaks?" answered the minister.

Gathering himself quickly up, he stood more erect, like a man taken by surprise in a mood to which he was reluctant to have witnesses. Throwing his eyes anxiously in the direction of the voice, he indistinctly beheld a form under the trees, clad in garments so sombre, and so little relieved from the gray twilight into which the clouded sky and the heavy foliage had darkened the noontide, that he knew not whether it were a woman or a shadow. It may be, that his pathway through life was haunted thus, by a spectre that had stolen out from among his thoughts.

He made a step nigher, and discovered the scarlet letter.

"Hester! Hester Prynne!" said he. "Is it thou? Art thou in life?"

"Even so!" she answered. "In such life as has been mine these seven years past! And thou, Arthur Dimmesdale, dost thou yet live?"

It was no wonder that they thus questioned one another's

actual and bodily existence, and even doubted of their own. So strangely did they meet, in the dim wood, that it was like the first encounter, in the world beyond the grave, of two spirits who had been intimately connected in their former life, but now stood coldly shuddering, in mutual dread; as not yet familiar with their state, nor wonted to the companionship of disembodied beings. Each a ghost, and awe-stricken at the other ghost! They were awe-stricken likewise at themselves; because the crisis flung back to them their consciousness, and revealed to each heart its history and experience, as life never does, except at such breathless epochs. The soul beheld its features in the mirror of the passing moment. It was with fear, and tremulously, and, as it were, by a slow, reluctant necessity, that Arthur Dimmesdale put forth his hand, chill as death, and touched the chill hand of Hester Prynne. The grasp, cold as it was, took away what was dreariest in the interview. They now felt themselves, at least, inhabitants of the same sphere.

Without a word more spoken,—neither he nor she assuming the guidance, but with an unexpressed consent,—they glided back into the shadow of the woods, whence Hester had emerged, and sat down on the heap of moss where she and Pearl had before been sitting. When they found voice to speak, it was, at first, only to utter remarks and inquiries such as any two acquaintance might have made, about the gloomy sky, the threatening storm, and, next, the health of each. Thus they went onward, not boldly, but step by step, into the themes that were brooding deepest in their hearts. So long estranged by fate and circumstances, they needed something slight and casual to run before, and throw open the doors of intercourse, so that their real thoughts might be led across the threshold.

After a while, the minister fixed his eyes on Hester Prynne's.

"Hester," said he, "hast thou found peace?"

She smiled drearily, looking down upon her bosom.

"Hast thou?" she asked.

"None!—nothing but despair!" he answered. "What else could I look for, being what I am, and leading such a life as mine? Were I an atheist,—a man devoid of conscience,—a wretch with coarse and brutal instincts,—I might have found peace, long ere now. Nay, I never should have lost it! But, as matters stand with my soul, whatever of good capacity there originally was in me, all of God's gifts that were the choicest have become the ministers of spiritual torment. Hester, I am most miserable!"

"The people reverence thee," said Hester. "And surely thou workest good among them! Doth this bring thee no comfort?"

"More misery, Hester!—only the more misery!" answered the clergyman, with a bitter smile. "As concerns the good which I may appear to do, I have no faith in it. It must needs be a delusion. What can a ruined soul, like mine, effect towards the redemption of other souls?—or a polluted soul, towards their purification? And as for the people's reverence, would that it were turned to scorn and hatred! Canst thou deem it, Hester, a consolation, that I must stand up in my pulpit, and meet so many eyes turned upward to my face, as if the light of heaven were beaming from it!—must see my flock hungry for the truth, and listening to my words as if a tongue of Pentecost were speaking!—and then look inward, and discern the black reality of what they idolize? I have laughed, in bitterness and agony of heart, at the contrast between what I seem and what I am! And Satan laughs at it!"

"You wrong yourself in this," said Hester, gently. "You have deeply and sorely repented. Your sin is left behind you, in the days long past. Your present life is not less holy, in very truth, than it seems in people's eyes. Is there no reality in the penitence thus sealed and witnessed by good works? And wherefore should it not bring you peace?"

"No, Hester, no!" replied the clergyman. "There is no sub-stance in it! It is cold and dead, and can do nothing for me! Of penance I have had enough! Of penitence there has been none! Else, I should long ago have thrown off these garments of mock holiness, and have shown myself to man-kind as they will see me at the judgment-seat. Happy are you, Hester, that wear the scarlet letter openly upon your bosom! Mine burns in secret! Thou little knowest what a relief it is, after the torment of a seven years' cheat, to look into an eye that recognizes me for what I am! Had I one friend,—or were it my worst enemy!—to whom, when sickened with the praises of all other men, I could daily betake myself, and be known as the vilest of all sinners, methinks my soul might keep itself alive thereby. Even thus much of truth would save me! But, now, it is all falsehood!—all emptiness!—all death!"

Hester Prynne looked into his face, but hesitated to speak. Yet, uttering his long-restrained emotions so vehemently as he did, his words here offered her the very point of circum-stances in which to interpose what she came to say. She con-quered her fears, and spoke.

"Such a friend as thou hast even now wished for," said she, "with whom to weep over thy sin, thou hast in me, the part-ner of it!"—Again she hesitated, but brought out the words with an effort.—"Thou hast long had such an enemy, and dwellest with him under the same roof!"

The minister started to his feet, gasping for breath, and clutching at his heart as if he would have torn it out of his bosom.

"Ha! What sayest thou?" cried he. "An enemy! And under mine own roof! What mean you?"

Hester Prynne was now fully sensible of the deep injury for which she was responsible to this unhappy man, in per-mitting him to lie for so many years, or, indeed, for a single moment, at the mercy of one, whose purposes could not be other than malevolent. The very contiguity of his enemy, beneath whatever mask the latter might conceal himself, was enough to disturb the magnetic sphere of a being so sensitive as Arthur Dimmesdale. There had been a period when Hester was less alive to this consideration; or, perhaps, in the misanthropy of her own trouble, she left the minister to bear what she might picture to herself as a more tolerable doom. But of late, since the night of his vigil, all her sympathies towards him had been both softened and invigorated. She now read his heart more accurately. She doubted not, that the continual presence of Roger Chillingworth,—the secret poison of his malignity, infecting all the air about him,—and his authorized interference, as a physician, with the minister's physical and spiritual infirmities,—that these bad opportunities had been turned to a cruel purpose. By means of them, the sufferer's conscience had been kept in an irritated state, the tendency of which was, not to cure by wholesome pain, but to disorganize and corrupt his spiritual being. Its result, on earth, could hardly fail to be insanity, and hereafter, that eternal alienation from the Good and True, of which madness is perhaps the earthly type.

Such was the ruin to which she had brought the man, once,—nay, why should we not speak it?*—still so passionately loved! Hester felt that the sacrifice of the clergyman's good name, and death itself, as she had already told Roger Chillingworth, would have been infinitely preferable to the alternative which she had taken upon herself to choose. And now, rather than have had this grievous wrong to confess, she would gladly have lain down on the forest-leaves, and died there, at Arthur Dimmesdale's feet.

"O Arthur," cried she, "forgive me! In all things else, I have striven to be true! Truth was the one virtue which I might have held fast, and did hold fast through all extremity; save when thy good,—thy life,—thy fame,—were put in question! Then I consented to a deception. But a lie is never good, even though death threaten on the other side! Dost thou not see what I would say? That old man!—the physician!—he whom they call Roger Chillingworth!—he was my husband!"

The minister looked at her, for an instant, with all that violence of passion, which—intermixed, in more shapes than one, with his higher, purer, softer qualities—was, in fact, the portion of him which the Devil claimed, and through which he sought to win the rest. Never was there a blacker or a fiercer frown, than Hester now encountered. For the brief space that it lasted, it was a dark transfiguration. But his character had been so much enfeebled by suffering, that even its lower energies were incapable of more than a temporary struggle. He sank down on the ground, and buried his face in his hands.

"I might have known it!" murmured he. "I did know it! Was not the secret told me in the natural recoil of my heart, at the first sight of him, and as often as I have seen him since? Why did I not understand? O Hester Prynne, thou little, little knowest all the horror of this thing! And the shame!—the indelicacy!—the horrible ugliness of this exposure of a sick and guilty heart to the very eye that would gloat over it! Woman, woman, thou art accountable for this! I cannot forgive thee!"

"Thou shalt forgive me!" cried Hester, flinging herself on the fallen leaves beside him. "Let God punish! Thou shalt forgive!"

With sudden and desperate tenderness, she threw her arms around him, and pressed his head against her bosom; little caring though his cheek rested on the scarlet letter. He would have released himself, but strove in vain to do so. Hester would not set him free, lest he should look her sternly in the face. All the world had frowned on her,—for seven long years had it frowned upon this lonely woman,—and still she bore it all, nor ever once turned away her firm, sad eyes. Heaven, likewise, had frowned upon her, and she had not died. But the frown of this pale, weak, sinful, and sorrow-stricken man was what Hester could not bear, and live!

"Wilt thou yet forgive me?" she repeated, over and over again. "Wilt thou not frown? Wilt thou forgive?"

"I do forgive you, Hester," replied the minister, at length, with a deep utterance out of an abyss of sadness, but no anger. "I freely forgive you now. May God forgive us both! We are not, Hester, the worst sinners in the world. There is one worse than even the polluted priest! That old man's revenge has been blacker than my sin. He has violated, in cold blood, the sanctity of a human heart. Thou and I, Hester, never did so!"

"Never, never!" whispered she. "What we did had a consecration of its own. We felt it so! We said so to each other! Hast thou forgotten it?"

"Hush, Hester!" said Arthur Dimmesdale, rising from the ground. "No; I have not forgotten!"

They sat down again, side by side, and hand clasped in hand, on the mossy trunk of the fallen tree. Life had never brought them a gloomier hour; it was the point whither their pathway had so long been tending, and darkening ever, as it stole along;—and yet it inclosed a charm that made them linger upon it, and claim another, and another, and, after all, another moment. The forest was obscure around them, and creaked with a blast that was passing through it. The boughs were tossing heavily above their heads; while one solemn old tree groaned dolefully to another, as if telling the sad story of the pair that sat beneath, or constrained to forebode evil to come.

And yet they lingered. How dreary looked the forest-track that led backward to the settlement, where Hester Prynne must take up again the burden of her ignominy, and the minister the hollow mockery of his good name! So they lingered an instant longer. No golden light had ever been so precious as the gloom of this dark forest. Here, seen only by his eyes, the scarlet letter need not burn into the bosom of the fallen woman! Here, seen only by her eyes, Arthur Dimmesdale, false to God and man, might be, for one moment, true!

He started at a thought that suddenly occurred to him.

"Hester," cried he, "here is a new horror! Roger Chillingworth knows your purpose to reveal his true character. Will he continue, then, to keep our secret? What will now be the course of his revenge?"

"There is a strange secrecy in his nature," replied Hester, thoughtfully; "and it has grown upon him by the hidden practices of his revenge. I deem it not likely that he will betray the secret. He will doubtless seek other means of satiating his dark passion."

"And I!—how am I to live longer, breathing the same air with this deadly enemy?" exclaimed Arthur Dimmesdale, shrinking within himself, and pressing his hand nervously against his heart,—a gesture that had grown involuntary with him. "Think for me, Hester! Thou art strong. Resolve for me!"

"Thou must dwell no longer with this man," said Hester, slowly and firmly. "Thy heart must be no longer under his evil eye!"

"It were far worse than death!" replied the minister. "But how to avoid it? What choice remains to me? Shall I lie down again on these withered leaves, where I cast myself when thou didst tell me what he was? Must I sink down there, and die at once?"

"Alas, what a ruin has befallen thee!" said Hester, with the tears gushing into her eyes. "Wilt thou die for very weakness? There is no other cause!"

"The judgment of God is on me," answered the conscience-stricken priest. "It is too mighty for me to struggle with!"

"Heaven would show mercy," rejoined Hester, "hadst thou but the strength to take advantage of it."

"Be thou strong for me!" answered he. "Advise me what to do."

"Is the world then so narrow?" exclaimed Hester Prynne, fixing her deep eyes on the minister's, and instinctively exercising a magnetic power* over a spirit so shattered and subdued, that it could hardly hold itself erect. "Doth the universe lie within the compass of yonder town, which only a little time ago was but a leaf-strewn desert, as lonely as this around us? Whither leads yonder forest-track? Backward to the settlement, thou sayest! Yes; but onward, too! Deeper it goes, and deeper, into the wilderness, less plainly to be seen at every step; until, some few miles hence, the yellow leaves will show no vestige of the white man's tread. There thou art free! So brief a journey would bring thee from a world where thou hast been most wretched, to one where thou mayest still be happy! Is there not shade enough in all this boundless forest to hide thy heart from the gaze of Roger Chillingworth?"

"Yes, Hester; but only under the fallen leaves!" replied the minister, with a sad smile.

"Then there is the broad pathway of the sea!" continued Hester. "It brought thee hither. If thou so choose, it will bear thee back again. In our native land, whether in some remote rural village or in vast London,—or, surely, in Germany, in France, in pleasant Italy,—thou wouldst be beyond his power and knowledge! And what hast thou to do with all these iron men,* and their opinions? They have kept thy better part in bondage too long already!"

"It cannot be!" answered the minister, listening as if he were called upon to realize a dream. "I am powerless to go. Wretched and sinful as I am, I have had no other thought than to drag on my earthly existence in the sphere where Providence hath placed me. Lost as my own soul is, I would still do what I may for other human souls! I dare not quit my post, though an unfaithful sentinel, whose sure reward is death and dishonor, when his dreary watch shall come to an end!"

"Thou art crushed under this seven years' weight of misery," replied Hester, fervently resolved to buoy him up with her own energy. "But thou shalt leave it all behind thee! It shall not cumber thy steps, as thou treadest along the forest-path; neither shalt thou freight the ship with it, if thou prefer to cross the sea. Leave this wreck and ruin here where it hath happened! Meddle no more with it! Begin all anew! Hast thou exhausted possibility in the failure of this one trial? Not so! The future is yet full of trial and success. There is happiness to be enjoyed! There is good to be done! Exchange this false life of thine for a true one. Be, if thy spirit summon thee to such a mission, the teacher and apostle of the red men.* Or,—as is more thy nature,—be a scholar and a sage among the wisest and the most renowned of the cultivated world. Preach! Write! Act! Do any thing, save to lie down and die! Give up this name of Arthur Dimmesdale, and make thyself another, and a high one, such as thou canst wear without fear or shame. Why shouldst thou tarry so much as one other day in the torments that have so gnawed into thy life!—that have made thee feeble to will and to do!—that will leave thee powerless even to repent! Up, and away!"

"O Hester!" cried Arthur Dimmesdale, in whose eyes a fitful light, kindled by her enthusiasm, flashed up and died away, "thou tellest of running a race to a man whose knees are tottering beneath him! I must die here. There is not the strength or courage left me to venture into the wide, strange, difficult world, alone!"

It was the last expression of the despondency of a broken spirit. He lacked energy to grasp the better fortune that seemed within his reach.

He repeated the word.

"Alone, Hester!"

"Thou shalt not go alone!" answered she, in a deep whisper.

Then, all was spoken!

XVIII

A FLOOD OF SUNSHINE

ARTHUR DIMMESDALE gazed into Hester's face with a look in which hope and joy shone out, indeed, but with fear betwixt them, and a kind of horror at her boldness, who had spoken what he vaguely hinted at, but dared not speak.

But Hester Prynne, with a mind of native courage and activity, and for so long a period not merely estranged, but outlawed, from society, had habituated herself to such latitude of speculation as was altogether foreign to the clergyman. She had wandered, without rule or guidance, in a moral wilderness; as vast, as intricate and shadowy, as the untamed forest, amid the gloom of which they were now holding a colloquy that was to decide their fate. Her intellect and heart had their home, as it were, in desert places, where she roamed as freely as the wild Indian in his woods. For years past she had looked from this estranged point of view at human institutions, and whatever priests or legislators had established; criticizing all with hardly more reverence than the Indian would feel for the clerical band, the judicial robe, the pillory, the gallows, the fireside, or the church. The tendency of her fate and fortunes had been to set her free. The scarlet letter was her passport into regions where other women dared not tread. Shame, Despair, Solitude! These had been her teachers,—stern and wild ones,—and they had made her strong, but taught her much amiss.

The minister, on the other hand, had never gone through an experience calculated to lead him beyond the scope of generally received laws; although, in a single instance, he had so fearfully transgressed one of the most sacred of them. But this had been a sin of passion, not of principle, nor even purpose. Since that wretched epoch, he had watched, with morbid zeal and minuteness, not his acts,—for those it was easy to arrange,—but each breath of emotion, and his every thought. At the head of the social system, as the clergymen of that day stood, he was only the more trammelled by its regulations, its principles, and even its prejudices. As a priest, the framework of his order inevitably hemmed him in. As a man who had once sinned, but who kept his conscience all alive and painfully sensitive by the fretting of an unhealed wound, he might have been supposed safer within the line of virtue, than if he had never sinned at all.

Thus, we seem to see that, as regarded Hester Prynne, the whole seven years of outlaw and ignominy had been little other than a preparation for this very hour. But Arthur Dimmesdale! Were such a man once more to fall, what plea could be urged in extenuation of his crime? None; unless it avail him somewhat, that he was broken down by long and ex- quisite suffering; that his mind was darkened and confused by the very remorse which harrowed it; that, between fleeing as an avowed criminal, and remaining as a hypocrite, conscience might find it hard to strike the balance; that it was human to avoid the peril of death and infamy, and the inscrutable machinations of an enemy; that, finally, to this poor pilgrim, on his dreary and desert path, faint, sick, miserable, there appeared a glimpse of human affection and sympathy, a new life, and a true one, in exchange for the heavy doom which he was now expiating. And be the stern and sad truth spoken, that the breach which guilt has once made into the human soul is never, in this mortal state, repaired. It may be watched and guarded; so that the enemy shall not force his way again into the citadel, and might even, in his subsequent assaults, select some other avenue, in preference to that where he had formerly succeeded. But there is still the ruined wall, and, near it, the stealthy tread of the foe that would win over again his unforgotten triumph.

The struggle, if there were one, need not be described. Let it suffice, that the clergyman resolved to flee, and not alone.

"If, in all these past seven years," thought he, "I could recall one instant of peace or hope, I would yet endure, for the sake of that earnest of Heaven's mercy. But now,—since I am irrevocably doomed,—wherefore should I not snatch the solace allowed to the condemned culprit before his execution? Or, if this be the path to a better life, as Hester would persuade me, I surely give up no fairer prospect by pursuing it! Neither can I any longer live without her companionship; so powerful is she to sustain,—so tender to soothe! O Thou to whom I dare not lift mine eyes, wilt Thou yet pardon me!"

"Thou wilt go!" said Hester calmly, as he met her glance.

The decision once made, a glow of strange enjoyment threw its flickering brightness over the trouble of his breast. It was the exhilarating effect—upon a prisoner just escaped from the dungeon of his own heart—of breathing the wild, free atmosphere of an unredeemed, unchristianized, lawless region.* His spirit rose, as it were, with a bound, and attained a nearer prospect of the sky, than throughout all the misery which had kept him grovelling on the earth. Of a deeply religious temperament, there was inevitably a tinge of the devotional in his mood.

"Do I feel joy again?" cried he, wondering at himself. "Methought the germ of it was dead in me! O Hester, thou art my better angel! I seem to have flung myself—sick, sinstained, and sorrow-blackened—down upon these forest-leaves, and to have risen up all made anew, and with new powers to glorify Him that hath been merciful! This is already the better life! Why did we not find it sooner?"

"Let us not look back," answered Hester Prynne. "The past is gone! Wherefore should we linger upon it now? See! With this symbol, I undo it all, and make it as it had never been!"

So speaking, she undid the clasp that fastened the scarlet letter, and, taking it from her bosom, threw it to a distance among the withered leaves. The mystic token alighted on the hither verge of the stream. With a hand's breadth farther flight it would have fallen into the water, and have given the little brook another woe to carry onward, besides the unintelligible tale which it still kept murmuring about. But there lay the embroidered letter, glittering like a lost jewel, which some ill-fated wanderer might pick up, and thenceforth be haunted by strange phantoms of guilt, sinkings of the heart, and unaccountable misfortune.

The stigma gone, Hester heaved a long, deep sigh, in which the burden of shame and anguish departed from her spirit. O exquisite relief! She had not known the weight, until she felt the freedom! By another impulse, she took off the formal cap that confined her hair; and down it fell upon her shoulders, dark and rich, with at once a shadow and a light in its abundance, and imparting the charm of softness to her features. There played around her mouth, and beamed out of her eyes, a radiant and tender smile, that seemed gushing from the very heart of womanhood. A crimson flush was glowing on her cheek, that had been long so pale. Her sex, her youth, and the whole richness of her beauty, came back from what men call the irrevocable past, and clustered themselves, with her maiden hope, and a happiness before unknown, within the magic circle of this hour. And, as if the gloom of the earth and sky had been but the effluence of these two mortal hearts, it vanished with their sorrow. All at once, as with a sudden smile of heaven, forth burst the sunshine, pouring a very flood into the obscure forest, gladdening each green leaf, transmuting the yellow fallen ones to gold, and gleaming adown the gray trunks of the solemn trees. The objects that had made a shadow hitherto, embodied the brightness now. The course of the little brook might be traced by its merry gleam afar into the wood's heart of mystery, which had become a mystery of joy.

Such was the sympathy of Nature—that wild, heathen Nature of the forest, never subjugated by human law, nor illumined by higher truth—with the bliss of these two spirits! Love, whether newly born, or aroused from a deathlike slumber, must always create a sunshine, filling the heart so full of radiance, that it overflows upon the outward world. Had the forest still kept its gloom, it would have been bright in Hester's eyes, and bright in Arthur Dimmesdale's!

Hester looked at him with the thrill of another joy.

"Thou must know Pearl!" said she. "Our little Pearl! Thou hast seen her,—yes, I know it!—but thou wilt see her now with other eyes. She is a strange child! I hardly comprehend her! But thou wilt love her dearly, as I do, and wilt advise me how to deal with her."

"Dost thou think the child will be glad to know me?" asked the minister, somewhat uneasily. "I have long shrunk from children, because they often show a distrust,—a backwardness to be familiar with me. I have even been afraid of little Pearl!"

"Ah, that was sad!" answered the mother. "But she will love thee dearly, and thou her. She is not far off. I will call her! Pearl! Pearl!"

"I see the child," observed the minister. "Yonder she is, standing in a streak of sunshine, a good way off, on the other side of the brook. So thou thinkest the child will love me?"

Hester smiled, and again called to Pearl, who was visible, at some distance, as the minister had described her, like a bright-apparelled vision, in a sunbeam, which fell down upon her through an arch of boughs. The ray quivered to and fro, making her figure dim or distinct,—now like a real child, now like a child's spirit,—as the splendor went and came again. She heard her mother's voice, and approached slowly through the forest.

Pearl had not found the hour pass wearisomely, while her mother sat talking with the clergyman. The great black forest —stern as it showed itself to those who brought the guilt and troubles of the world into its bosom—became the playmate of the lonely infant, as well as it knew how. Sombre as it was, it put on the kindest of its moods to welcome her. It offered her the partridge-berries, the growth of the preceding autumn, but ripening only in the spring, and now red as drops of blood upon the withered leaves. These Pearl gathered, and was pleased with their wild flavor. The small denizens of the wilderness hardly took pains to move out of her path. A partridge, indeed, with a brood of ten behind her, ran forward threateningly, but soon repented of her fierceness, and clucked to her young ones not to be afraid. A pigeon, alone on a low branch, allowed Pearl to come beneath, and uttered a sound as much of greeting as alarm. A squirrel, from the lofty depths of his domestic tree, chattered either in anger or merriment,—for a squirrel is such a choleric and humorous little personage that it is hard to distinguish between his moods,—so he chattered at the child, and flung down a nut upon her head. It was a last year's nut, and already gnawed by his sharp tooth. A fox, startled from his sleep by her light footstep on the leaves, looked inquisitively at Pearl, as doubting whether it were better to steal off, or renew his nap on the same spot. A wolf, it is said,—but here the tale has surely lapsed into the improbable,—came up, and smelt of Pearl's robe, and offered his savage head to be patted by her hand. The truth seems to be, however, that the mother-forest, and these wild things which it nourished, all recognized a kindred wildness in the human child.

And she was gentler here than in the grassy-margined streets of the settlement, or in her mother's cottage. The flowers appeared to know it; and one and another whispered, as she passed, "Adorn thyself with me, thou beautiful child, adorn thyself with me!"—and, to please them, Pearl gathered the violets, and anemones, and columbines, and some twigs of the freshest green, which the old trees held down before her eyes. With these she decorated her hair, and her young waist, and became a nymph-child, or an infant dryad,* or whatever else was in closest sympathy with the antique wood. In such guise had Pearl adorned herself, when she heard her mother's voice, and came slowly back.

Slowly; for she saw the clergyman!

XIX

THE CHILD AT THE BROOK-SIDE

"THOU wilt love her dearly," repeated Hester Prynne, as she and the minister sat watching little Pearl. "Dost thou not think her beautiful? And see with what natural skill she has made those simple flowers adorn her! Had she gathered pearls, and diamonds, and rubies, in the wood, they could not have become her better. She is a splendid child! But I know whose brow she has!"

"Dost thou know, Hester," said Arthur Dimmesdale, with an unquiet smile, "that this dear child, tripping about always at thy side, hath caused me many an alarm? Methought— O Hester, what a thought is that, and how terrible to dread it!—that my own features were partly repeated in her face, and so strikingly that the world might see them! But she is mostly thine!"

"No, no! Not mostly!" answered the mother with a tender smile. "A little longer, and thou needest not to be afraid to trace whose child she is. But how strangely beautiful she looks, with those wild flowers in her hair! It is as if one of the fairies, whom we left in our dear old England,* had decked her out to meet us."

It was with a feeling which neither of them had ever before experienced, that they sat and watched Pearl's slow advance. In her was visible the tie that united them. She had been offered to the world, these seven years past, as the living hieroglyphic,* in which was revealed the secret they so darkly sought to hide,—all written in this symbol,—all plainly manifest,—had there been a prophet or magician skilled to read the character of flame! And Pearl was the oneness of their being. Be the foregone evil what it might, how could they doubt that their earthly lives and future destinies were conjoined, when they beheld at once the material union, and the spiritual idea, in whom they met, and were to dwell immortally together? Thoughts like these—and perhaps other thoughts, which they did not acknowledge or define—threw an awe about the child, as she came onward.

"Let her see nothing strange—no passion nor eagerness—in thy way of accosting her," whispered Hester. "Our Pearl is a fitful and fantastic little elf, sometimes. Especially, she is seldom tolerant of emotion, when she does not fully comprehend the why and wherefore. But the child hath strong affections! She loves me, and will love thee!"

"Thou canst not think," said the minister, glancing aside at Hester Prynne, "how my heart dreads this interview, and yearns for it! But, in truth, as I already told thee, children are not readily won to be familiar with me. They will not climb my knee, nor prattle in my ear, nor answer to my smile; but stand apart, and eye me strangely. Even little babes, when I take them in my arms, weep bitterly. Yet Pearl, twice in her little lifetime, hath been kind to me! The first time,—thou knowest it well! The last was when thou ledst her with thee to the house of yonder stern old Governor."

"And thou didst plead so bravely in her behalf and mine!" answered the mother. "I remember it; and so shall little Pearl. Fear nothing! She may be strange and shy at first, but will soon learn to love thee!"

By this time Pearl had reached the margin of the brook, and stood on the farther side, gazing silently at Hester and the clergyman, who still sat together on the mossy tree-trunk, waiting to receive her. Just where she had paused the brook chanced to form a pool, so smooth and quiet that it reflected a perfect image of her little figure, with all the brilliant picturesqueness of her beauty, in its adornment of flowers and wreathed foliage, but more refined and spiritualized than the reality. This image, so nearly identical with the living Pearl, seemed to communicate somewhat of its own shadowy and intangible quality to the child herself. It was strange, the way in which Pearl stood, looking so stedfastly at them through the dim medium of the forest-gloom; herself, meanwhile, all glorified with a ray of sunshine, that was attracted thitherward as by a certain sympathy. In the brook beneath stood another child,—another and the same,—with likewise its ray of golden light. Hester felt herself, in some indistinct and tantalizing manner, estranged from Pearl; as if the child, in her lonely ramble through the forest, had strayed out of the sphere in which she and her mother dwelt together, and was now vainly seeking to return to it.

There was both truth and error in the impression; the child and mother were estranged, but through Hester's fault, not Pearl's. Since the latter rambled from her side, another inmate had been admitted within the circle of the mother's feelings, and so modified the aspect of them all, that Pearl, the returning wanderer, could not find her wonted place, and hardly knew where she was.

"I have a strange fancy," observed the sensitive minister, "that this brook is the boundary between two worlds, and that thou canst never meet thy Pearl again. Or is she an elfish spirit, who, as the legends of our childhood taught us, is forbidden to cross a running stream? Pray hasten her; for this delay has already imparted a tremor to my nerves."

"Come, dearest child!" said Hester encouragingly, and stretching out both her arms. "How slow thou art! When hast thou been so sluggish before now? Here is a friend of mine, who must be thy friend also. Thou wilt have twice as much love, henceforward, as thy mother alone could give thee! Leap across the brook and come to us. Thou canst leap like a young deer!"

Pearl, without responding in any manner to these honey-sweet expressions, remained on the other side of the brook. Now she fixed her bright, wild eyes* on her mother, now on the minister, and now included them both in the same glance; as if to detect and explain to herself the relation which they bore to one another. For some unaccountable reason, as Arthur Dimmesdale felt the child's eyes upon himself, his hand—with that gesture so habitual as to have become involuntary—stole over his heart. At length, assuming a singular air of authority, Pearl stretched out her hand, with the small forefinger extended, and pointing evidently towards her mother's breast. And beneath, in the mirror of the brook, there was the flower-girdled and sunny image of little Pearl, pointing her small forefinger too.

"Thou strange child, why dost thou not come to me?" exclaimed Hester.

Pearl still pointed with her forefinger; and a frown gathered on her brow; the more impressive from the childish, the almost baby-like aspect of the features that conveyed it. As her mother still kept beckoning to her, and arraying her face in a holiday suit of unaccustomed smiles, the child stamped her foot with a yet more imperious look and gesture. In the brook, again, was the fantastic beauty of the image, with its reflected frown, its pointed finger, and imperious gesture, giving emphasis to the aspect of little Pearl.

"Hasten, Pearl; or I shall be angry with thee!" cried Hester Prynne, who, however inured to such behaviour on the elf-child's part at other seasons, was naturally anxious for a more seemly deportment now. "Leap across the brook, naughty child, and run hither! Else I must come to thee!"

But Pearl, not a whit startled at her mother's threats, any more than mollified by her entreaties, now suddenly burst into a fit of passion, gesticulating violently, and throwing her small figure into the most extravagant contortions. She accompanied this wild outbreak with piercing shrieks, which the woods reverberated on all sides; so that, alone as she was in her childish and unreasonable wrath, it seemed as if a hidden multitude were lending her their sympathy and encouragement. Seen in the brook, once more, was the shadowy wrath of Pearl's image, crowned and girdled with flowers, but stamping its foot, wildly gesticulating, and, in the midst of all, still pointing its small forefinger at Hester's bosom!

"I see what ails the child," whispered Hester to the clergyman, and turning pale in spite of a strong effort to conceal her trouble and annoyance. "Children will not abide any, the slightest, change in the accustomed aspect of things that are daily before their eyes. Pearl misses something which she has always seen me wear!"

"I pray you," answered the minister, "if thou hast any means of pacifying the child, do it forthwith! Save it were the cankered wrath of an old witch, like Mistress Hibbins," added he, attempting to smile, "I know nothing that I would not sooner encounter than this passion in a child. In Pearl's young beauty, as in the wrinkled witch, it has a preternatural effect. Pacify her, if thou lovest me!"

Hester turned again towards Pearl, with a crimson blush upon her cheek, a conscious glance aside at the clergyman, and then a heavy sigh; while, even before she had time to speak, the blush yielded to a deadly pallor.

"Pearl," said she, sadly, "look down at thy feet! There!—before thee!—on the hither side of the brook!"

The child turned her eyes to the point indicated; and there lay the scarlet letter, so close upon the margin of the stream, that the gold embroidery was reflected in it

"Bring it hither!" said Hester.

"Come thou and take it up!" answered Pearl.

"Was ever such a child!" observed Hester aside to the minister. "O, I have much to tell thee about her. But, in very truth, she is right as regards this hateful token. I must bear its torture yet a little longer,—only a few days longer,—until we shall have left this region, and look back hither as to a land which we have dreamed of. The forest cannot hide it! The mid-ocean shall take it from my hand, and swallow it up for ever!"

With these words, she advanced to the margin of the brook, took up the scarlet letter, and fastened it again into her bosom. Hopefully, but a moment ago, as Hester had spoken of drowning it in the deep sea, there was a sense of inevitable doom upon her, as she thus received back this deadly symbol from the hand of fate. She had flung it into infinite space!—she had drawn an hour's free breath!—and here again was the scarlet misery, glittering on the old spot! So it ever is, whether thus typified or no, that an evil deed invests itself with the character of doom. Hester next gathered up the heavy tresses of her hair, and confined them beneath her cap. As if there were a withering spell in the sad letter, her beauty, the warmth and richness of her womanhood, departed, like fading sunshine; and a gray shadow seemed to fall across her.

When the dreary change was wrought, she extended her hand to Pearl.

"Dost thou know thy mother now, child?" asked she, reproachfully, but with a subdued tone. "Wilt thou come across the brook, and own thy mother, now that she has her shame upon her,—now that she is sad?"

"Yes; now I will!" answered the child, bounding across the brook, and clasping Hester in her arms. "Now thou art my mother indeed! And I am thy little Pearl!"

In a mood of tenderness that was not usual with her, she drew down her mother's head, and kissed her brow and both her cheeks. But then—by a kind of necessity that always impelled this child to alloy whatever comfort she might chance to give with a throb of anguish—Pearl put up her mouth, and kissed the scarlet letter too!

"That was not kind!" said Hester. "When thou hast shown me a little love, thou mockest me!"

"Why doth the minister sit yonder?" asked Pearl.

"He waits to welcome thee," replied her mother. "Come thou, and entreat his blessing! He loves thee, my little Pearl, and loves thy mother too. Wilt thou not love him? Come! he longs to greet thee!"

"Doth he love us?" said Pearl, looking up with acute intelligence into her mother's face. "Will he go back with us, hand in hand, we three together, into the town?"

"Not now, dear child," answered Hester. "But in days to come he will walk hand in hand with us. We will have a home and fireside of our own; and thou shalt sit upon his knee; and he will teach thee many things, and love thee dearly. Thou wilt love him; wilt thou not?"

"And will he always keep his hand over his heart?" inquired Pearl.

"Foolish child, what a question is that!" exclaimed her mother. "Come and ask his blessing!"

But, whether influenced by the jealousy that seems instinctive with every petted child towards a dangerous rival, or from whatever caprice of her freakish nature, Pearl would show no favor to the clergyman. It was only by an exertion of force that her mother brought her up to him, hanging back, and manifesting her reluctance by odd grimaces; of which, ever since her babyhood, she had possessed a singular variety and could transform her mobile physiognomy into a series of different aspects, with a new mischief in them, each and all. The minister—painfully embarrassed, but hoping that a kiss might prove a talisman to admit him into the child's kindlier regards—bent forward, and impressed one on her brow. Hereupon, Pearl broke away from her mother, and

running to the brook, stooped over it, and bathed her forehead, until the unwelcome kiss was quite washed off, and
diffused through a long lapse of the gliding water. She then
remained apart, silently watching Hester and the clergyman;
while they talked together, and made such arrangements as
were suggested by their new position, and the purposes soon
to be fulfilled.

And now this fateful interview had come to a close. The
dell was to be left a solitude among its dark, old trees, which,
with their multitudinous tongues, would whisper long of
what had passed there, and no mortal be the wiser. And the
melancholy brook would add this other tale to the mystery
with which its little heart was already overburdened, and
whereof it still kept up a murmuring babble, with not a whit
more cheerfulness of tone than for ages heretofore.

XX

THE MINISTER IN A MAZE

A S THE minister departed, in advance of Hester Prynne and little Pearl, he threw a backward glance; half expecting that he should discover only some faintly traced features or outline of the mother and the child, slowly fading into the twilight of the woods. So great a vicissitude in his life could not at once be received as real. But there was Hester, clad in her gray robe, still standing beside the tree-trunk, which some blast had overthrown a long antiquity ago, and which time had ever since been covering with moss, so that these two fated ones, with earth's heaviest burden on them, might there sit down together, and find a single hour's rest and solace. And there was Pearl, too, lightly dancing from the margin of the brook,—now that the intrusive third person was gone,—and taking her old place by her mother's side. So the minister had not fallen asleep, and dreamed!

In order to free his mind from this indistinctness and duplicity of impression, which vexed it with a strange disquietude, he recalled and more thoroughly defined the plans which Hester and himself had sketched for their departure. It had been determined between them, that the Old World, with its crowds and cities, offered them a more eligible shelter and concealment than the wilds of New England, or all America, with its alternatives of an Indian wigwam, or the few settlements of Europeans, scattered thinly along the seaboard. Not to speak of the clergyman's health, so inadequate to sustain the hardships of a forest life, his native gifts, his culture, and his entire development would secure him a home only in the midst of civilization and refinement; the higher the state, the more delicately adapted to it the man. In furtherance of this choice, it so happened that a ship lay in the harbour; one of those questionable cruisers, frequent at that day, which, without being absolutely outlaws of the deep, yet roamed over its surface with a remarkable irresponsibility of character. This vessel had recently arrived from the Spanish Main, and, within three days' time, would sail for Bristol. Hester Prynne—whose vocation, as a self-enlisted Sister of Charity, had brought her acquainted with the captain and crew—could take upon herself to secure the passage of two individuals and a child, with all the secrecy which circumstances rendered more than desirable.

The minister had inquired of Hester, with no little interest, the precise time at which the vessel might be expected to depart. It would probably be on the fourth day from the present. "That is most fortunate!" he had then said to himself. Now, why the Reverend Mr. Dimmesdale considered it so very fortunate, we hesitate to reveal.* Nevertheless,—to hold nothing back from the reader,—it was because, on the third day from the present, he was to preach the Election Sermon;* and, as such an occasion formed an honorable epoch in the life of a New England clergyman, he could not have chanced upon a more suitable mode and time of terminating his professional career. "At least, they shall say of me," thought this exemplary man, "that I leave no public duty unperformed, nor ill performed!" Sad, indeed, that an introspection so profound and acute as this poor minister's should be so miserably deceived! We have had, and may still have, worse things to tell of him; but none, we apprehend, so pitiably weak; no evidence, at once so slight and irrefragable, of a subtle disease, that had long since begun to eat into the real substance of his character. No man, for any considerable period, can wear one face to himself, and another to the multitude, without finally getting bewildered as to which may be the true.

The excitement of Mr. Dimmesdale's feelings, as he returned from his interview with Hester, lent him unaccustomed physical energy, and hurried him townward at a rapid pace. The pathway among the woods seemed wilder, more uncouth with its rude natural obstacles, and less trodden by the foot of man, than he remembered it on his outward journey. But he leaped across the plashy places, thrust himself through* the clinging underbrush, climbed the ascent, plunged into the hollow, and overcame, in short, all the difficulties of the track, with an unweariable activity that astonished him. He could not but recall how feebly, and with what frequent pauses for breath, he had toiled over the same ground only two days before. As he drew near the town, he took an impression of change from the series of familiar objects that presented themselves. It seemed not yesterday, not one, nor two, but many days, or even years ago, since he had quitted them. There, indeed, was each former trace of the street, as he remembered it, and all the peculiarities of the houses, with the due multitude of gable-peaks, and a weathercock at every point where his memory suggested one. Not the less, however, came this importunately obtrusive sense of change. The same was true as regarded the acquaintances whom he met, and all the well-known shapes of human life, about the little town. They looked neither older nor younger, now; the beards of the aged were no whiter, nor could the creeping babe of yesterday walk on his feet to-day; it was impossible to describe in what respect they differed from the individuals on whom he had so recently bestowed a parting glance; and yet the minister's deepest sense seemed to inform him of their mutability. A similar impression struck him most remarkably, as he passed under the walls of his own church. The edifice had so very strange, and yet so familiar, an aspect, that Mr. Dimmesdale's mind vibrated between two ideas; either that he had seen it only in a dream hitherto, or that he was merely dreaming about it now.

This phenomenon, in the various shapes which it assumed, indicated no external change, but so sudden and important a change in the spectator of the familiar scene, that the intervening space of a single day had operated on his consciousness like the lapse of years. The minister's own will, and Hester's will, and the fate that grew between them, had wrought this transformation. It was the same town as heretofore; but the same minister returned not from the forest. He might have said to the friends who greeted him,—"I am not the man for whom you take me! I left him yonder in the forest, withdrawn into a secret dell, by a mossy tree-trunk, and near a melancholy brook! Go, seek your minister, and see if his emaciated figure, his thin cheek, his white, heavy, pain-wrinkled brow, be not flung down there like a cast-off garment!" His friends, no doubt, would still have insisted with him,—"Thou art thyself the man!"—but the error would have been their own, not his.

Before Mr. Dimmesdale reached home, his inner man gave him other evidences of a revolution in the sphere of thought and feeling. In truth, nothing short of a total change of dynasty and moral code, in that interior kingdom, was adequate to account for the impulses now communicated to the unfortunate and startled minister. At every step he was incited to do some strange, wild, wicked thing or other, with a sense that it would be at once involuntary and intentional; in spite of himself, yet growing out of a profounder self than that which opposed the impulse. For instance, he met one of his own deacons. The good old man addressed him with the paternal affection and patriarchal privilege, which his venerable age, his upright and holy character, and his station in the Church, entitled him to use; and, conjoined with this, the deep, almost worshipping respect, which the minister's professional and private claims alike demanded. Never was there a more beautiful example of how the majesty of age and wisdom may comport with the obeisance and respect enjoined upon it, as from a lower social rank and inferior order of endowment, towards a higher. Now, during a conversation of some two or three moments between the Reverend Mr. Dimmesdale and this excellent and hoary-bearded deacon, it was only by the most careful self-control that the former could refrain from uttering certain blasphemous suggestions that rose into his mind, respecting the communion-supper. He absolutely trembled and turned pale as ashes, lest his tongue should wag itself, in utterance of these horrible matters, and plead his own consent for so doing, without his having fairly given it. And, even with this terror in his heart, he could hardly avoid laughing to imagine how the sanctified old patriarchal deacon would have been petrified by his minister's impiety!

Again, another incident of the same nature. Hurrying along the street, the Reverend Mr. Dimmesdale encountered the eldest female member of his church; a most pious and exemplary old dame; poor, widowed, lonely, and with a heart as full of reminiscences about her dead husband and children, and her dead friends of long ago, as a burial-ground is full of storied grave-stones. Yet all this, which would else have been such heavy sorrow, was made almost a solemn joy to her devout old soul by religious consolations and the truths of Scripture, wherewith she had fed herself continually for more than thirty years. And, since Mr. Dimmesdale had taken her in charge, the good grandam's chief earthly comfort— which, unless it had been likewise a heavenly comfort, could have been none at all—was to meet her pastor, whether casually, or of set purpose, and be refreshed with a word of warm, fragrant, heaven-breathing Gospel truth from his beloved lips into her dulled, but rapturously attentive ear. But, on this occasion, up to the moment of putting his lips to the old woman's ear, Mr. Dimmesdale, as the great enemy of souls would have it, could recall no text of Scripture, nor aught else, except a brief, pithy, and, as it then appeared to him, unanswerable argument against the immortality of the human soul. The instilment thereof into her mind would probably have caused this aged sister to drop down dead, at once, as by the effect of an intensely poisonous infusion. What he really did whisper, the minister could never afterwards recollect. There was, perhaps, a fortunate disorder in his utterance, which failed to impart any distinct idea to the good widow's comprehension, or which Providence interpreted after a method of its own. Assuredly, as the minister looked back, he beheld an expression of divine gratitude and ecstasy that seemed like the shine of the celestial city on her face, so wrinkled and ashy pale.

Again, a third instance. After parting from the old church-member, he met the youngest sister of them all. It was a maiden newly won—and won by the Reverend Mr. Dimmesdale's own sermon, on the Sabbath after his vigil—to barter the transitory pleasures of the world for the heavenly hope, that was to assume brighter substance as life grew dark around her, and which would gild the utter gloom with final glory. She was fair and pure as a lily that had bloomed in Paradise. The minister knew well that he was himself enshrined within the stainless sanctity of her heart, which hung its snowy curtains about his image, imparting to religion the warmth of love, and to love a religious purity. Satan, that afternoon, had surely led the poor young girl away from her mother's side, and thrown her into the pathway of this sorely tempted, or—shall we not rather say?—this lost and desperate man. As she drew nigh, the arch-fiend whispered him to condense into small compass and drop into her tender bosom a germ of evil that would be sure to blossom darkly soon, and bear black fruit betimes. Such was his sense of power over this virgin soul, trusting him as she did, that the minister felt potent to blight all the field of innocence with but one wicked look, and develop all its opposite with but a word. So—with a mightier struggle than he had yet sustained—he held his Geneva cloak before his face, and hurried onward, making no sign of recognition, and leaving the young sister to digest his rudeness as she might. She ransacked her conscience,— which was full of harmless little matters, like her pocket or her work-bag,—and took herself to task, poor thing, for a thousand imaginary faults; and went about her household duties with swollen eyelids the next morning.

Before the minister had time to celebrate his victory over this last temptation, he was conscious of another impulse, more ludicrous, and almost as horrible. It was,—we blush to tell it,—it was to stop short in the road, and teach some very wicked words to a knot of little Puritan children who were playing there, and had but just begun to talk. Denying himself this freak, as unworthy of his cloth, he met a drunken seaman, one of the ship's crew from the Spanish Main. And, here, since he had so valiantly forborne all other wickedness, poor Mr. Dimmesdale longed, at least, to shake hands with the tarry blackguard, and recreate himself with a few improper jests, such as dissolute sailors so abound with, and a volley of good, round, solid, satisfactory, and heaven-defying oaths! It was not so much a better principle, as partly his natural good taste, and still more his buckramed habit of clerical decorum, that carried him safely through the latter crisis.

"What is it that haunts and tempts me thus?" cried the minister to himself, at length, pausing in the street, and striking his hand against his forehead. "Am I mad? or am I given over utterly to the fiend? Did I make a contract with him in the forest, and sign it with my blood? And does he now

summon me to its fulfilment, by suggesting the performance
of every wickedness which his most foul imagination can conceive?"

At the moment when the Reverend Mr. Dimmesdale thus
communed with himself, and struck his forehead with his
hand, old Mistress Hibbins, the reputed witch-lady, is said
to have been passing by. She made a very grand appearance;
having on a high head-dress, a rich gown of velvet, and a ruff
done up with the famous yellow starch, of which Ann Turner,*
her especial friend, had taught her the secret, before this last
good lady had been hanged for Sir Thomas Overbury's murder. Whether the witch had read the minister's thoughts,
or no, she came to a full stop, looked shrewdly into his face,
smiled craftily, and—though little given to converse with
clergymen—began a conversation.

"So, reverend Sir, you have made a visit into the forest,"
observed the witch-lady, nodding her high head-dress at him.
"The next time, I pray you to allow me only a fair warning,
and I shall be proud to bear you company. Without taking
overmuch upon myself, my good word will go far towards
gaining any strange gentleman a fair reception from yonder
potentate you wot of!"

"I profess, madam," answered the clergyman, with a grave
obeisance, such as the lady's rank demanded, and his own
good-breeding made imperative,—"I profess, on my conscience and character, that I am utterly bewildered as touching
the purport of your words! I went not into the forest to seek
a potentate; neither do I, at any future time, design a visit
thither, with a view to gaining the favor of such personage.
My one sufficient object was to greet that pious friend of
mine, the Apostle Eliot, and rejoice with him over the many
precious souls he hath won from heathendom!"

"Ha, ha, ha!" cackled the old witch-lady, still nodding her
high head-dress at the minister. "Well, well, we must needs

talk thus in the daytime! You carry it off like an old hand! But at midnight, and in the forest, we shall have other talk together!"

She passed on with her aged stateliness, but often turning back her head and smiling at him, like one willing to recognize a secret intimacy of connection.

"Have I then sold myself," thought the minister, "to the fiend whom, if men say true, this yellow-starched and velveted old hag has chosen for her prince and master!"

The wretched minister! He had made a bargain very like it! Tempted by a dream of happiness, he had yielded himself with deliberate choice, as he had never done before, to what he knew was deadly sin. And the infectious poison of that sin had been thus rapidly diffused throughout his moral system. It had stupefied all blessed impulses, and awakened into vivid life the whole brotherhood of bad ones. Scorn, bitterness, unprovoked malignity, gratuitous desire of ill, ridicule of whatever was good and holy, all awoke, to tempt, even while they frightened him. And his encounter with old Mistress Hibbins, if it were a real incident, did but show his sympathy and fellowship with wicked mortals and the world of perverted spirits.

He had by this time reached his dwelling, on the edge of the burial-ground, and, hastening up the stairs, took refuge in his study. The minister was glad to have reached this shelter, without first betraying himself to the world by any of those strange and wicked eccentricities to which he had been continually impelled while passing through the streets. He entered the accustomed room, and looked around him on its books, its windows, its fireplace, and the tapestried comfort of the walls, with the same perception of strangeness that had haunted him throughout his walk from the forest-dell into the town, and thitherward. Here he had studied and written; here, gone through fast and vigil, and come forth half alive; here, striven to pray; here, borne a hundred thousand agonies!

There was the Bible, in its rich old Hebrew, with Moses and the Prophets speaking to him, and God's voice through all! There, on the table, with the inky pen beside it, was an unfinished sermon, with a sentence broken in the midst, where his thoughts had ceased to gush out upon the page two days before. He knew that it was himself, the thin and white-cheeked minister, who had done and suffered these things, and written thus far into the Election Sermon! But he seemed to stand apart, and eye this former self with scornful, pitying, but half-envious curiosity. That self was gone! Another man had returned out of the forest; a wiser one; with a knowledge of hidden mysteries which the simplicity of the former never could have reached. A bitter kind of knowledge that!

While occupied with these reflections, a knock came at the door of the study, and the minister said, "Come in!"—not wholly devoid of an idea that he might behold an evil spirit. And so he did! It was old Roger Chillingworth that entered. The minister stood, white and speechless, with one hand on the Hebrew Scriptures, and the other spread upon his breast.

"Welcome home, reverend Sir!" said the physician. "And how found you that godly man, the Apostle Eliot? But methinks, dear Sir, you look pale; as if the travel through the wilderness had been too sore for you. Will not my aid be requisite to put you in heart and strength to preach your Election Sermon?"

"Nay, I think not so," rejoined the Reverend Mr. Dimmesdale. "My journey, and the sight of the holy Apostle yonder, and the free air which I have breathed, have done me good, after so long confinement in my study. I think to need no more of your drugs, my kind physician, good though they be, and administered by a friendly hand."

All this time, Roger Chillingworth was looking at the minister with the grave and intent regard of a physician towards his patient. But, in spite of this outward show, the latter

was almost convinced of the old man's knowledge, or, at least,
his confident suspicion, with respect to his own interview with
Hester Prynne. The physician knew, then, that, in the minister's regard, he was no longer a trusted friend, but his bitterest enemy. So much being known, it would appear natural
that a part of it should be expressed. It is singular, however,
how long a time often passes before words embody things;
and with what security two persons, who choose to avoid
a certain subject, may approach its very verge, and retire
without disturbing it. Thus, the minister felt no apprehension
that Roger Chillingworth would touch, in express words,
upon the real position which they sustained towards one another. Yet did the physician, in his dark way, creep frightfully
near the secret.

"Were it not better," said he, "that you use my poor skill
to-night? Verily, dear Sir, we must take pains to make you
strong and vigorous for this occasion of the Election discourse.
The people look for great things from you; apprehending that
another year may come about, and find their pastor gone."

"Yea, to another world," replied the minister, with pious
resignation. "Heaven grant it be a better one; for, in good
sooth, I hardly think to tarry with my flock through the flitting
seasons of another year! But, touching your medicine, kind
Sir, in my present frame of body I need it not."

"I joy to hear it," answered the physician. "It may be that
my remedies, so long administered in vain, begin now to take
due effect. Happy man were I, and well deserving of New
England's gratitude, could I achieve this cure!"

"I thank you from my heart, most watchful friend," said
the Reverend Mr. Dimmesdale, with a solemn smile. "I thank
you, and can but requite your good deeds with my prayers."

"A good man's prayers are golden recompense!" rejoined
old Roger Chillingworth, as he took his leave. "Yea, they are
the current gold coin of the New Jerusalem,* with the King's
own mint-mark* on them!"

Left alone, the minister summoned a servant of the house, and requested food, which, being set before him, he ate with ravenous appetite. Then, flinging the already written pages of the Election Sermon into the fire, he forthwith began another, which he wrote with such an impulsive flow of thought and emotion, that he fancied himself inspired; and only wondered that Heaven should see fit to transmit the grand and solemn music of its oracles through so foul an organ-pipe as he. However, leaving that mystery to solve itself, or go unsolved for ever, he drove his task onward, with earnest haste and ecstasy. Thus the night fled away, as if it were a winged steed, and he careering on it; morning came, and peeped blushing through the curtains; and at last sunrise threw a golden beam into the study, and laid it right across the minister's bedazzled eyes. There he was, with the pen still between his fingers, and a vast, immeasurable tract of written space behind him!

XXI

THE NEW ENGLAND HOLIDAY

ETIMES in the morning of the day on which the new
Governor was to receive his office at the hands of the
people, Hester Prynne and little Pearl came into the
market-place. It was already thronged with the craftsmen and
other plebeian inhabitants of the town, in considerable numbers; among whom, likewise, were many rough figures, whose
attire of deer-skins marked them as belonging to some of the
forest settlements, which surrounded the little metropolis of
the colony.

On this public holiday, as on all other occasions, for seven
years past, Hester was clad in a garment of coarse gray cloth.
Not more by its hue than by some indescribable peculiarity
in its fashion, it had the effect of making her fade personally
out of sight and outline; while, again, the scarlet letter
brought her back from this twilight indistinctness, and revealed her under the moral aspect of its own illumination.
Her face, so long familiar to the townspeople, showed the
marble quietude which they were accustomed to behold there.
It was like a mask; or rather, like the frozen calmness of a
dead woman's features; owing this dreary resemblance to the
fact that Hester was actually dead, in respect to any claim
of sympathy, and had departed out of the world with which
she still seemed to mingle.

It might be, on this one day, that there was an expression unseen before, nor, indeed, vivid enough to be detected now; unless some preternaturally gifted observer should have first read the heart, and have afterwards sought a corresponding development in the countenance and mien. Such a spiritual seer might have conceived, that, after sustaining the gaze of the multitude through seven miserable years as a necessity, a penance, and something which it was a stern religion to endure, she now, for one last time more, encountered it freely and voluntarily, in order to convert what had so long been agony into a kind of triumph. "Look your last on the scarlet letter and its wearer!"—the people's victim and life-long bond-slave, as they fancied her, might say to them. "Yet a little while, and she will be beyond your reach! A few hours longer, and the deep, mysterious ocean will quench and hide for ever the symbol which ye have caused to burn upon her bosom!" Nor were it an inconsistency too improbable to be assigned to human nature, should we suppose a feeling of regret in Hester's mind, at the moment when she was about to win her freedom from the pain which had been thus deeply incorporated with her being. Might there not be an irresistible desire to quaff a last, long, breathless draught of the cup of wormwood and aloes, with which nearly all her years of womanhood had been perpetually flavored? The wine of life, henceforth to be presented to her lips, must be indeed rich, delicious, and exhilarating, in its chased and golden beaker; or else leave an inevitable and weary languor, after the lees of bitterness wherewith she had been drugged, as with a cordial of intensest potency.

Pearl was decked out with airy gayety. It would have been impossible to guess that this bright and sunny apparition owed its existence to the shape of gloomy gray; or that a fancy, at once so gorgeous and so delicate as must have been requisite to contrive the child's apparel, was the same that had achieved a task perhaps more difficult, in imparting so distinct a peculiarity to Hester's simple robe. The dress, so proper was it to little Pearl, seemed an effluence, or inevitable development and outward manifestation of her character, no more to be separated from her than the many-hued brilliancy from a butterfly's wing, or the painted glory from the leaf of a bright flower. As with these, so with the child; her garb was all of one idea with her nature. On this eventful day, moreover, there was a certain singular inquietude and excitement in her mood, resembling nothing so much as the shimmer of a diamond, that sparkles and flashes with the varied throbbings of the breast on which it is displayed. Children have always a sympathy in the agitations of those connected with them; always, especially, a sense of any trouble or impending revolution, of whatever kind, in domestic circumstances; and therefore Pearl, who was the gem on her mother's unquiet bosom, betrayed, by the very dance of her spirits, the emotions which none could detect in the marble passiveness of Hester's brow.

This effervescence made her flit with a bird-like movement, rather than walk by her mother's side. She broke continually into shouts of a wild, inarticulate, and sometimes piercing music. When they reached the market-place, she became still more restless, on perceiving the stir and bustle that enlivened the spot; for it was usually more like the broad and lonesome green before a village meeting-house, than the centre of a town's business.

"Why, what is this, mother?" cried she. "Wherefore have all the people left their work to-day? Is it a play-day for the whole world? See, there is the blacksmith! He has washed his sooty face, and put on his Sabbath-day clothes, and looks as if he would gladly be merry, if any kind body would only teach him how! And there is Master Brackett, the old jailer, nodding and smiling at me. Why does he do so, mother?"

"He remembers thee a little babe, my child," answered Hester.

"He should not nod and smile at me, for all that,—the black, grim, ugly-eyed old man!" said Pearl. "He may nod at thee if he will; for thou art clad in gray, and wearest the scarlet letter. But, see, mother, how many faces of strange people, and Indians among them, and sailors! What have they all come to do here in the market-place?"

"They wait to see the procession pass," said Hester. "For the Governor and the magistrates are to go by, and the ministers, and all the great people and good people, with the music, and the soldiers marching before them."

"And will the minister be there?" asked Pearl. "And will he hold out both his hands to me, as when thou ledst me to him from the brook-side?"

"He will be there, child," answered her mother. "But he will not greet thee to-day; nor must thou greet him."

"What a strange, sad man is he!" said the child, as if speaking partly to herself. "In the dark night-time, he calls us to him, and holds thy hand and mine, as when we stood with him on the scaffold yonder! And in the deep forest, where only the old trees can hear, and the strip of sky see it, he talks with thee, sitting on a heap of moss! And he kisses my forehead, too, so that the little brook would hardly wash it off! But here in the sunny day, and among all the people, he knows us not; nor must we know him! A strange, sad man is he, with his hand always over his heart!"

"Be quiet, Pearl! Thou understandest not these things," said her mother. "Think not now of the minister, but look about thee, and see how cheery is every body's face to-day. The children have come from their schools, and the grown people from their workshops and their fields, on purpose to be happy. For, to-day, a new man* is beginning to rule over them; and so—as has been the custom of mankind ever since a nation was first gathered—they make merry and rejoice; as if a good and golden year were at length to pass over the poor old world!"

It was as Hester said, in regard to the unwonted jollity that brightened the faces of the people. Into this festal season of the year—as it already was, and continued to be during the greater part of two centuries—the Puritans compressed whatever mirth and public joy they deemed allowable to human infirmity; thereby so far dispelling the customary cloud, that, for the space of a single holiday, they appeared scarcely more grave than most other communities at a period of general affliction.

But we perhaps exaggerate the gray or sable tinge, which undoubtedly characterized the mood and manners of the age. The persons now in the market-place of Boston had not been born to an inheritance of Puritanic gloom. They were native Englishmen, whose fathers had lived in the sunny richness of the Elizabethan epoch; a time when the life of England, viewed as one great mass, would appear to have been as stately, magnificent, and joyous, as the world has ever witnessed. Had they followed their hereditary taste, the New England settlers would have illustrated all events of public importance by bonfires, banquets, pageantries, and processions. Nor would it have been impracticable, in the observance of majestic ceremonies, to combine mirthful recreation with solemnity, and give, as it were, a grotesque and brilliant embroidery to the great robe of state, which a nation, at such festivals, puts on. There was some shadow of an attempt of this kind in the mode of celebrating the day on which the political year of the colony commenced. The dim reflection of a remembered splendor, a colorless and manifold diluted repetition of what they had beheld in proud old London,— we will not say at a royal coronation, but at a Lord Mayor's show,—might be traced in the customs which our forefathers instituted, with reference to the annual installation of magistrates. The fathers and founders of the commonwealth—the statesman, the priest, and the soldier—deemed it a duty then to assume the outward state and majesty, which, in accordance with antique style, was looked upon as the proper garb of public or social eminence. All came forth, to move in procession before the people's eye, and thus impart a needed dignity to the simple framework of a government so newly constructed.

Then, too, the people were countenanced, if not encouraged, in relaxing the severe and close application to their various modes of rugged industry, which, at all other times, seemed of the same piece and material with their religion. Here, it is true, were none of the appliances which popular merriment would so readily have found in the England of Elizabeth's time, or that of James;—no rude shows of a theatrical kind; no minstrel with his harp and legendary ballad, nor gleeman, with an ape dancing to his music; no juggler, with his tricks of mimic witchcraft; no Merry Andrew,* to stir up the multitude with jests, perhaps hundreds of years old, but still effective, by their appeals to the very broadest sources of mirthful sympathy. All such professors of the several branches of jocularity would have been sternly repressed, not only by the rigid discipline of law, but by the general sentiment which gives law its vitality. Not the less, however, the great, honest face of the people smiled, grimly, perhaps, but widely too. Nor were sports wanting, such as the colonists had witnessed, and shared in, long ago, at the country fairs and on the village-greens of England; and which it was thought well to keep alive on this new soil, for the sake of the courage and manliness that were essential in them. Wrestling-matches, in the differing fashions of Cornwall and Devonshire, were seen here and there about the market-place; in one corner, there was a friendly bout at quarterstaff; and—what attracted most interest of all—on the platform of the pillory, already so noted in our pages, two masters of defence were commencing an exhibition with the buckler and broadsword. But, much to the disappointment of the crowd, this latter business was broken off by the interposition of the town beadle, who had no idea of permitting the majesty of the law to be violated by such an abuse of one of its consecrated places.

It may not be too much to affirm, on the whole, (the people being then in the first stages of joyless deportment, and the offspring of sires who had known how to be merry, in their day,) that they would compare favorably, in point of holiday keeping, with their descendants, even at so long an interval as ourselves. Their immediate posterity, the generation next to the early emigrants, wore the blackest shade of Puritanism, and so darkened the national visage with it, that all the subsequent years have not sufficed to clear it up. We have yet to learn again the forgotten art of gayety.

The picture of human life in the market-place, though its general tint was the sad gray, brown, or black of the English emigrants, was yet enlivened by some diversity of hue. A party of Indians—in their savage finery of curiously embroidered deer-skin robes, wampum-belts,* red and yellow ochre, and feathers, and armed with the bow and arrow and stone-headed spear—stood apart, with countenances of inflexible gravity, beyond what even the Puritan aspect could attain. Nor, wild as were these painted barbarians, were they the wildest feature of the scene. This distinction could more justly be claimed by some mariners,—a part of the crew of the vessel from the Spanish Main,—who had come ashore to see the humors of Election Day. They were rough-looking desperadoes, with sun-blackened faces, and an immensity of beard; their wide, short trousers were confined about the waist by belts, often clasped with a rough plate of gold, and sustaining always a long knife, and, in some instances, a sword. From beneath their broad-brimmed hats of palm-leaf, gleamed eyes which, even in good nature and merriment, had a kind of animal ferocity. They transgressed, without fear or scruple, the rules of behaviour that were binding on all others; smoking tobacco under the beadle's very nose, although each whiff would have cost a townsman a shilling; and quaffing, at their pleasure, draughts of wine or aqua-vitæ from pocket-flasks, which they freely tendered to the gaping crowd around them. It remarkably characterized the incomplete morality of the age, rigid as we call it, that a license was allowed the seafaring class, not merely for their freaks on shore, but for far more desperate deeds on their proper element. The sailor of that day would go near to be arraigned as a pirate in our own. There could be little doubt, for instance, that this very ship's crew, though no unfavorable specimens of the nautical brotherhood, had been guilty, as we should phrase it, of depredations on the Spanish commerce, such as would have perilled all their necks in a modern court of justice.

But the sea, in those old times, heaved, swelled, and foamed very much at its own will, or subject only to the tempestuous wind, with hardly any attempts at regulation by human law. The buccaneer on the wave might relinquish his calling, and become at once, if he chose, a man of probity and piety on land; nor, even in the full career of his reckless life, was he regarded as a personage with whom it was disreputable to traffic, or casually associate. Thus, the Puritan elders, in their black cloaks, starched bands, and steeple-crowned hats, smiled not unbenignantly at the clamor and rude deportment of these jolly seafaring men; and it excited neither surprise nor animadversion when so reputable a citizen as old Roger Chillingworth, the physician, was seen to enter the market-place, in close and familiar talk with the commander of the questionable vessel.

The latter was by far the most showy and gallant figure, so far as apparel went, anywhere to be seen among the multitude. He wore a profusion of ribbons on his garment, and gold lace on his hat, which was also encircled by a gold chain, and surmounted with a feather. There was a sword at his side, and a sword-cut on his forehead, which, by the arrangement of his hair, he seemed anxious rather to display than hide. A landsman could hardly have worn this garb and shown this face, and worn and shown them both with such a galliard*air, without undergoing stern question before a magistrate, and probably incurring fine or imprisonment, or perhaps an exhibition in the stocks. As regarded the shipmaster, however, all was looked upon as pertaining to the character, as to a fish his glistening scales.

After parting from the physician, the commander of the Bristol ship strolled idly through the market-place; until, happening to approach the spot where Hester Prynne was standing, he appeared to recognize, and did not hesitate to address her. As was usually the case wherever Hester stood, a small, vacant area—a sort of magic circle—had formed itself about her, into which, though the people were elbowing one another at a little distance, none ventured, or felt disposed to intrude. It was a forcible type of the moral solitude in which the scarlet letter enveloped its fated wearer; partly by her own reserve, and partly by the instinctive, though no longer so unkindly, withdrawal of her fellow-creatures. Now, if never before, it answered a good purpose, by enabling Hester and the seaman to speak together without risk of being overheard; and so changed was Hester Prynne's repute before the public, that the matron in town most eminent for rigid morality could not have held such intercourse with less result of scandal than herself.

"So, mistress," said the mariner, "I must bid the steward make ready one more berth than you bargained for! No fear of scurvy or ship-fever, this voyage! What with the ship's surgeon and this other doctor, our only danger will be from drug or pill; more by token, as there is a lot of apothecary's stuff aboard, which I traded for with a Spanish vessel."

"What mean you?" inquired Hester, startled more than she permitted to appear. "Have you another passenger?"

"Why, know you not," cried the shipmaster, "that this physician here—Chillingworth, he calls himself—is minded to try my cabin-fare with you? Ay, ay, you must have known it; for he tells me he is of your party, and a close friend to the gentleman you spoke of,—he that is in peril from these sour old Puritan rulers!"

"They know each other well, indeed," replied Hester, with a mien of calmness, though in the utmost consternation. "They have long dwelt together."

Nothing further passed between the mariner and Hester Prynne. But, at that instant, she beheld old Roger Chillingworth himself, standing in the remotest corner of the market-place, and smiling on her; a smile which—across the wide and bustling square, and through all the talk and laughter, and various thoughts, moods, and interests of the crowd— conveyed secret and fearful meaning.

XXII

THE PROCESSION

B EFORE Hester Prynne could call together her thoughts, and consider what was practicable to be done in this new and startling aspect of affairs, the sound of military music was heard approaching along a contiguous street. It denoted the advance of the procession of magistrates and citizens, on its way towards the meeting-house; where, in compliance with a custom thus early established, and ever since observed, the Reverend Mr. Dimmesdale was to deliver an Election Sermon.

Soon the head of the procession showed itself, with a slow and stately march, turning a corner, and making its way across the market-place. First came the music. It comprised a variety of instruments, perhaps imperfectly adapted to one another, and played with no great skill, but yet attaining the great object for which the harmony of drum and clarion addresses itself to the multitude,—that of imparting a higher and more heroic air to the scene of life that passes before the eye. Little Pearl at first clapped her hands, but then lost, for an instant, the restless agitation that had kept her in a continual effervescence throughout the morning; she gazed silently, and seemed to be borne upward, like a floating sea-bird, on the long heaves and swells of sound. But she was brought back to her former mood by the shimmer of the sunshine on the weapons and bright armour of the military company, which followed after the music, and formed the honorary escort of the procession. This body of soldiery—which still sustains a corporate existence,* and marches down from past ages with an ancient and honorable fame—was composed of no mercenary materials. Its ranks were filled with gentlemen, who felt the stirrings of martial impulse, and sought to establish a kind of College of Arms,* where, as in an association of Knights Templars,* they might learn the science, and, so far as peaceful exercise would teach them, the practices of war. The high estimation then placed upon the military character might be seen in the lofty port of each individual member of the company. Some of them, indeed, by their services in the Low Countries and on other fields of European warfare, had fairly won their title to assume the name and pomp of soldiership. The entire array, moreover, clad in burnished steel, and with plumage nodding over their bright morions,* had a brilliancy of effect which no modern display can aspire to equal.

And yet the men of civil eminence, who came immediately behind the military escort, were better worth a thoughtful observer's eye. Even in outward demeanour they showed a stamp of majesty that made the warrior's haughty stride look vulgar, if not absurd. It was an age when what we call talent had far less consideration than now, but the massive materials which produce stability and dignity of character a great deal more. The people possessed, by hereditary right, the quality of reverence; which, in their descendants, if it survive at all, exists in smaller proportion, and with a vastly diminished force in the selection and estimate of public men. The change may be for good or ill, and is partly, perhaps, for both. In that old day, the English settler on these rude shores, —having left king, nobles, and all degrees of awful rank behind, while still the faculty and necessity of reverence were strong in him,—bestowed it on the white hair and venerable brow of age; on long-tried integrity; on solid wisdom and sad-colored experience; on endowments of that grave and weighty order, which gives the idea of permanence, and comes under the general definition of respectability. These primitive states-men, therefore,—Bradstreet, Endicott, Dudley,* Bellingham, and their compeers,—who were elevated to power by the early choice of the people, seem to have been not often bril-liant, but distinguished by a ponderous sobriety, rather than activity of intellect. They had fortitude and self-reliance, and, in time of difficulty or peril, stood up for the welfare of the state like a line of cliffs against a tempestuous tide. The traits of character here indicated were well represented in the square cast of countenance and large physical development of the new colonial magistrates. So far as a demeanour of natural authority was concerned, the mother country need not have been ashamed to see these foremost men of an ac-tual democracy adopted into the House of Peers, or made the Privy Council of the sovereign.

Next in order to the magistrates came the young and eminently distinguished divine, from whose lips the religious discourse of the anniversary was expected. His was the pro-fession, at that era, in which intellectual ability displayed it-self far more than in political life; for—leaving a higher mo-tive out of the question—it offered inducements powerful enough, in the almost worshipping respect of the community, to win the most aspiring ambition into its service. Even po-litical power—as in the case of Increase Mather*—was within the grasp of a successful priest.

It was the observation of those who beheld him now, that never, since Mr. Dimmesdale first set his foot on the New England shore, had he exhibited such energy as was seen in the gait and air with which he kept his pace in the pro-cession. There was no feebleness of step, as at other times; his frame was not bent; nor did his hand rest ominously upon his heart. Yet, if the clergyman were rightly viewed, his

strength seemed not of the body. It might be spiritual, and
imparted to him by angelic ministrations. It might be the ex-
hilaration of that potent cordial, which is distilled only in
the furnace-glow of earnest and long-continued thought. Or,
perchance, his sensitive temperament was invigorated by the
loud and piercing music, that swelled heavenward, and up-
lifted him on its ascending wave. Nevertheless, so abstracted
was his look, it might be questioned whether Mr. Dimmesdale even heard the music. There was his body, moving onward, and with an unaccustomed force. But where was his
mind? Far and deep in its own region, busying itself, with
preternatural activity, to marshal a procession of stately
thoughts that were soon to issue thence; and so he saw nothing, heard nothing, knew nothing, of what was around him;
but the spiritual element took up the feeble frame, and carried it along, unconscious of the burden, and converting it
to spirit like itself. Men of uncommon intellect, who have
grown morbid, possess this occasional power of mighty effort,
into which they throw the life of many days, and then are
lifeless for as many more.

Hester Prynne, gazing stedfastly at the clergyman, felt a
dreary influence come over her, but wherefore or whence she
knew not; unless that he seemed so remote from her own
sphere, and utterly beyond her reach. One glance of recognition, she had imagined, must needs pass between them. She
thought of the dim forest, with its little dell of solitude, and
love, and anguish, and the mossy tree-trunk, where, sitting
hand in hand, they had mingled their sad and passionate talk
with the melancholy murmur of the brook. How deeply had
they known each other then! And was this the man? She
hardly knew him now! He, moving proudly past, enveloped,
as it were, in the rich music, with the procession of majestic
and venerable fathers; he, so unattainable in his worldly position, and still more so in that far vista of his unsympathizing
thoughts, through which she now beheld him! Her spirit sank

with the idea that all must have been a delusion, and that, vividly as she had dreamed it, there could be no real bond betwixt the clergyman and herself. And thus much of woman was there in Hester, that she could scarcely forgive him,— least of all now, when the heavy footstep of their approaching Fate might be heard, nearer, nearer, nearer!—for being able so completely to withdraw himself from their mutual world; while she groped darkly, and stretched forth her cold hands, and found him not.

Pearl either saw and responded to her mother's feelings, or herself felt the remoteness and intangibility that had fallen around the minister. While the procession passed, the child was uneasy, fluttering up and down, like a bird on the point of taking flight. When the whole had gone by, she looked up into Hester's face.

"Mother," said she, "was that the same minister that kissed me by the brook?"

"Hold thy peace, dear little Pearl!" whispered her mother. "We must not always talk in the market-place of what happens to us in the forest."

"I could not be sure that it was he; so strange he looked," continued the child. "Else I would have run to him, and bid him kiss me now, before all the people; even as he did yonder among the dark old trees. What would the minister have said, mother? Would he have clapped his hand over his heart, and scowled on me, and bid me begone?"

"What should he say, Pearl," answered Hester, "save that it was no time to kiss, and that kisses are not to be given in the market-place? Well for thee, foolish child, that thou didst not speak to him!"

Another shade of the same sentiment, in reference to Mr. Dimmesdale, was expressed by a person whose eccentricities —or insanity, as we should term it—led her to do what few of the townspeople would have ventured on; to begin a conversa-

tion with the wearer of the scarlet letter, in public. It was
Mistress Hibbins, who, arrayed in great magnificence, with a
triple ruff, a broidered stomacher,* a gown of rich velvet, and a
gold-headed cane, had come forth to see the procession. As
this ancient lady had the renown (which subsequently cost
her no less a price than her life) of being a principal actor in
all the works of necromancy that were continually going
forward, the crowd gave way before her, and seemed to fear
the touch of her garment, as if it carried the plague among its
gorgeous folds. Seen in conjunction with Hester Prynne,—
kindly as so many now felt towards the latter,—the dread inspired by Mistress Hibbins was doubled, and caused a general
movement from that part of the market-place in which the
two women stood.

"Now, what mortal imagination could conceive it!" whispered the old lady confidentially to Hester. "Yonder divine
man! That saint on earth, as the people uphold him to be,
and as—I must needs say—he really looks! Who, now, that
saw him pass in the procession, would think how little while
it is since he went forth out of his study,—chewing a Hebrew
text of Scripture in his mouth, I warrant,—to take an airing
in the forest! Aha! we know what that means, Hester Prynne!
But, truly, forsooth, I find it hard to believe him the same man.
Many a church-member saw I, walking behind the music, that
has danced in the same measure with me, when Somebody
was fiddler, and, it might be, an Indian powwow* or a Lap-
land wizard changing hands with us! That is but a trifle,
when a woman knows the world. But this minister! Couldst
thou surely tell, Hester, whether he was the same man that
encountered thee on the forest-path!"

"Madam, I know not of what you speak," answered Hester Prynne, feeling Mistress Hibbins to be of infirm mind;
yet strangely startled and awe-stricken by the confidence with
which she affirmed a personal connection between so many

persons (herself among them) and the Evil One. "It is not for me to talk lightly of a learned and pious minister of the Word, like the Reverend Mr. Dimmesdale!"

"Fie, woman, fie!" cried the old lady, shaking her finger at Hester. "Dost thou think I have been to the forest so many times, and have yet no skill to judge who else has been there? Yea; though no leaf of the wild garlands, which they wore while they danced, be left in their hair! I know thee, Hester; for I behold the token. We may all see it in the sunshine; and it glows like a red flame in the dark. Thou wearest it openly; so there need be no question about that. But this minister! Let me tell thee in thine ear! When the Black Man sees one of his own servants, signed and sealed, so shy of owning to the bond as is the Reverend Mr. Dimmesdale, he hath a way of ordering matters so that the mark shall be disclosed in open daylight to the eyes of all the world! What is it that the minister seeks to hide, with his hand always over his heart? Ha, Hester Prynne!"

"What is it, good Mistress Hibbins?" eagerly asked little Pearl. "Hast thou seen it?"

"No matter, darling!" responded Mistress Hibbins, making Pearl a profound reverence. "Thou thyself wilt see it, one time or another. They say, child, thou art of the lineage of the Prince of the Air! Wilt thou ride with me, some fine night, to see thy father? Then thou shalt know wherefore the minister keeps his hand over his heart!"

Laughing so shrilly that all the market-place could hear her, the weird old gentlewoman took her departure.

By this time the preliminary prayer had been offered in the meeting-house, and the accents of the Reverend Mr. Dimmesdale were heard commencing his discourse. An irresistible feeling kept Hester near the spot. As the sacred edifice was too much thronged to admit another auditor, she took up her position close beside the scaffold of the pillory. It was in sufficient proximity to bring the whole sermon to her ears, in the shape of an indistinct, but varied, murmur and flow of the minister's very peculiar voice.

This vocal organ was in itself a rich endowment; insomuch that a listener, comprehending nothing of the language in which the preacher spoke, might still have been swayed to and fro by the mere tone and cadence. Like all other music, it breathed passion and pathos, and emotions high or tender, in a tongue native to the human heart, wherever educated. Muffled as the sound was by its passage through the church-walls, Hester Prynne listened with such intentness, and sympathized so intimately, that the sermon had throughout a meaning for her, entirely apart from its indistinguishable words. These, perhaps, if more distinctly heard, might have been only a grosser medium, and have clogged the spiritual sense. Now she caught the low undertone, as of the wind sinking down to repose itself; then ascended with it, as it rose through progressive gradations of sweetness and power, until its volume seemed to envelop her with an atmosphere of awe and solemn grandeur. And yet, majestic as the voice sometimes became, there was for ever in it an essential character of plaintiveness. A loud or low expression of anguish,—the whisper, or the shriek, as it might be conceived, of suffering humanity, that touched a sensibility in every bosom! At times this deep strain of pathos was all that could be heard, and scarcely heard, sighing amid a desolate silence. But even when the minister's voice grew high and commanding,—when it gushed irrepressibly upward,—when it assumed its utmost breadth and power, so overfilling the church as to burst its way through the solid walls, and diffuse itself in the open air,—still, if the auditor listened intently, and for the purpose, he could detect the same cry of pain. What was it? The complaint of a human heart, sorrow-laden, perchance guilty, telling its secret, whether of guilt or sorrow, to the great heart of mankind; beseeching its sympathy or forgiveness,—at every moment,—in each accent,—and never in vain! It was this profound and continual undertone that gave the clergyman his most appropriate power.

During all this time Hester stood, statue-like, at the foot of the scaffold. If the minister's voice had not kept her there, there would nevertheless have been an inevitable magnetism in that spot, whence she dated the first hour of her life of ignominy. There was a sense within her,—too ill-defined to be made a thought, but weighing heavily on her mind,—that her whole orb of life, both before and after, was connected with this spot, as with the one point that gave it unity.

Little Pearl, meanwhile, had quitted her mother's side, and was playing at her own will about the market-place. She made the sombre crowd cheerful by her erratic and glistening ray; even as a bird of bright plumage illuminates a whole tree of dusky foliage by darting to and fro, half seen and half concealed, amid the twilight of the clustering leaves. She had an undulating, but, oftentimes, a sharp and irregular movement. It indicated the restless vivacity of her spirit, which to-day was doubly indefatigable in its tiptoe dance, because it was played upon and vibrated with her mother's disquietude. Whenever Pearl saw any thing to excite her ever active and wandering curiosity, she flew thitherward, and, as we might say, seized upon that man or thing as her own property, so far as she desired it; but without yielding the minutest degree of control over her motions in requital. The Puritans looked on, and, if they smiled, were none the less inclined to pronounce the child a demon offspring, from the indescribable charm of beauty and eccentricity that shone through her little figure, and sparkled with its activity. She ran and looked the wild Indian in the face; and he grew conscious of a nature wilder than his own. Thence, with native audacity, but still with a reserve as characteristic, she flew into the midst of a group of mariners, the swarthy-cheeked wild men of the ocean, as the Indians were of the land; and they gazed wonderingly and admiringly at Pearl, as if a flake of the sea-foam had taken the shape of a little maid, and were gifted with a soul of the sea-fire, that flashes beneath the prow in the night-time.

One of these seafaring men—the shipmaster, indeed, who had spoken to Hester Prynne—was so smitten with Pearl's aspect, that he attempted to lay hands upon her, with purpose to snatch a kiss. Finding it as impossible to touch her as to catch a humming-bird in the air, he took from his hat the gold chain that was twisted about it, and threw it to the child. Pearl immediately twined it around her neck and waist, with such happy skill, that, once seen there, it became a part of her, and it was difficult to imagine her without it.

"Thy mother is yonder woman with the scarlet letter," said the seaman. "Wilt thou carry her a message from me?"

"If the message pleases me I will," answered Pearl.

"Then tell her," rejoined he, "that I spake again with the black-a-visaged, hump-shouldered old doctor, and he engages to bring his friend, the gentleman she wots of, aboard with him. So let thy mother take no thought, save for herself and thee. Wilt thou tell her this, thou witch-baby?"

"Mistress Hibbins says my father is the Prince of the Air!" cried Pearl, with her naughty smile. "If thou callest me that ill name, I shall tell him of thee; and he will chase thy ship with a tempest!"*

Pursuing a zigzag course across the market-place, the child returned to her mother, and communicated what the mariner had said. Hester's strong, calm, stedfastly enduring spirit almost sank, at last, on beholding this dark and grim countenance of an inevitable doom, which—at the moment when a passage seemed to open for the minister and herself out of their labyrinth of misery—showed itself, with an unrelenting smile, right in the midst of their path.

With her mind harassed by the terrible perplexity in which the shipmaster's intelligence involved her, she was also subjected to another trial. There were many people present, from the country roundabout, who had often heard of the scarlet letter, and to whom it had been made terrific by a hundred false or exaggerated rumors, but who had never beheld it with their own bodily eyes. These, after exhausting other modes of amusement, now thronged about Hester Prynne with rude and boorish intrusiveness. Unscrupulous as it was, however, it could not bring them nearer than a circuit of several yards. At that distance they accordingly stood, fixed there by the centrifugal force of the repugnance which the mystic symbol inspired. The whole gang of sailors, likewise, observing the press of spectators, and learning the purport of the scarlet letter, came and thrust their sunburnt and desperado-looking faces into the ring. Even the Indians were affected by a sort of cold shadow of the white man's curiosity, and, gliding through the crowd, fastened their snake-like black eyes on Hester's bosom; conceiving, perhaps, that the wearer of this brilliantly embroidered badge must needs be a personage of high dignity among her people. Lastly, the inhabitants of the town (their own interest in this worn-out subject languidly reviving itself, by sympathy with what they saw others feel) lounged idly to the same quarter, and tormented Hester Prynne, perhaps more than all the rest, with their cool, well-acquainted gaze at her familiar shame. Hester saw and recognized the self-same faces of that group of matrons, who had awaited her forthcoming from the prison-door, seven years ago; all save one, the youngest and only compassionate among them, whose burial-robe she had since made. At the final hour, when she was so soon to fling aside the burning letter, it had strangely become the centre of more remark and excitement, and was thus made to sear her breast more painfully, than at any time since the first day she put it on.

While Hester stood in that magic circle of ignominy, where the cunning cruelty of her sentence seemed to have fixed her for ever, the admirable preacher was looking down from the sacred pulpit upon an audience, whose very inmost spirits had yielded to his control. The sainted minister in the church! The woman of the scarlet letter in the market-place! What imagination would have been irreverent enough to surmise that the same scorching stigma was on them both?

XXIII

THE REVELATION OF THE
SCARLET LETTER

THE eloquent voice, on which the souls of the listening audience had been borne aloft, as on the swelling waves of the sea, at length came to a pause. There was a momentary silence, profound as what should follow the utterance of oracles. Then ensued a murmur and half-hushed tumult; as if the auditors, released from the high spell that had transported them into the region of another's mind, were returning into themselves, with all their awe and wonder still heavy on them. In a moment more, the crowd began to gush forth from the doors of the church. Now that there was an end, they needed other breath, more fit to support the gross and earthly life into which they relapsed, than that atmosphere which the preacher had converted into words of flame, and had burdened with the rich fragrance of his thought.

In the open air their rapture broke into speech. The street and the market-place absolutely babbled, from side to side, with applauses of the minister. His hearers could not rest until they had told one another of what each knew better than he could tell or hear. According to their united testimony, never had man spoken in so wise, so high, and so holy a spirit, as he that spake this day; nor had inspiration ever breathed through mortal lips more evidently than it did through his.

Its influence could be seen, as it were, descending upon him, and possessing him, and continually lifting him out of the written discourse that lay before him, and filling him with ideas that must have been as marvellous to himself as to his audience. His subject, it appeared, had been the relation between the Deity and the communities of mankind, with a special reference to the New England which they were here planting in the wilderness. And, as he drew towards the close, a spirit as of prophecy had come upon him, constraining him to its purpose as mightily as the old prophets of Israel were constrained; only with this difference, that, whereas the Jewish seers had denounced judgments and ruin on their country, it was his mission to foretell a high and glorious destiny* for the newly gathered people of the Lord. But, throughout it all, and through the whole discourse, there had been a certain deep, sad undertone of pathos, which could not be interpreted otherwise than as the natural regret of one soon to pass away. Yes; their minister whom they so loved—and who so loved them all, that he could not depart heavenward without a sigh—had the foreboding of untimely death upon him, and would soon leave them in their tears! This idea of his transitory stay on earth gave the last emphasis to the effect which the preacher had produced; it was as if an angel, in his passage to the skies, had shaken his bright wings over the people for an instant,—at once a shadow and a splendor,—and had shed down a shower of golden truths upon them.

Thus, there had come to the Reverend Mr. Dimmesdale— as to most men, in their various spheres, though seldom recognized until they see it far behind them—an epoch of life more brilliant and full of triumph than any previous one, or than any which could hereafter be. He stood, at this moment, on the very proudest eminence of superiority, to which the gifts of intellect, rich lore, prevailing eloquence, and a reputation of whitest sanctity, could exalt a clergyman in New England's earliest days, when the professional character was of itself a lofty pedestal. Such was the position which the minister occupied, as he bowed his head forward on the cushions of the pulpit, at the close of his Election Sermon. Meanwhile, Hester Prynne was standing beside the scaffold of the pillory, with the scarlet letter still burning on her breast!

Now was heard again the clangor of the music, and the measured tramp of the military escort, issuing from the church-door. The procession was to be marshalled thence to the town-hall, where a solemn banquet would complete the ceremonies of the day.

Once more, therefore, the train of venerable and majestic fathers was seen moving through a broad pathway of the people, who drew back reverently, on either side, as the Governor and magistrates, the old and wise men, the holy ministers, and all that were eminent and renowned, advanced into the midst of them. When they were fairly in the market-place, their presence was greeted by a shout. This—though doubtless it might acquire additional force and volume from the childlike loyalty which the age awarded to its rulers—was felt to be an irrepressible outburst of the enthusiasm kindled in the auditors by that high strain of eloquence which was yet reverberating in their ears. Each felt the impulse in himself, and, in the same breath, caught it from his neighbour. Within the church, it had hardly been kept down; beneath the sky, it pealed upward to the zenith. There were human beings enough, and enough of highly wrought and symphonious feeling, to produce that more impressive sound than the organ-tones of the blast, or the thunder, or the roar of the sea; even that mighty swell of many voices, blended into one great voice by the universal impulse which makes likewise one vast heart out of the many. Never, from the soil of New England, had gone up such a shout! Never, on New England soil, had stood the man so honored by his mortal brethren as the preacher!

How fared it with him then? Were there not the brilliant

particles of a halo in the air about his head? So etherealized by spirit as he was, and so apotheosized by worshipping admirers, did his footsteps in the procession really tread upon the dust of earth?

As the ranks of military men and civil fathers moved onward, all eyes were turned towards the point where the minister was seen to approach among them. The shout died into a murmur, as one portion of the crowd after another obtained a glimpse of him. How feeble and pale he looked amid all his triumph! The energy—or say, rather, the inspiration which had held him up, until he should have delivered the sacred message that brought its own strength along with it from heaven—was withdrawn, now that it had so faithfully performed its office. The glow, which they had just before beheld burning on his cheek, was extinguished, like a flame that sinks down hopelessly among the late-decaying embers. It seemed hardly the face of a man alive, with such a deathlike hue; it was hardly a man with life in him, that tottered on his path so nervelessly, yet tottered, and did not fall!

One of his clerical brethren,—it was the venerable John Wilson,—observing the state in which Mr. Dimmesdale was left by the retiring wave of intellect and sensibility, stepped forward hastily to offer his support. The minister tremulously, but decidedly, repelled the old man's arm. He still walked onward, if that movement could be so described, which rather resembled the wavering effort of an infant, with its mother's arms in view, outstretched to tempt him forward. And now, almost imperceptible as were the latter steps of his progress, he had come opposite the well-remembered and weatherdarkened scaffold, where, long since, with all that dreary lapse of time between, Hester Prynne had encountered the world's ignominious stare. There stood Hester, holding little Pearl by the hand! And there was the scarlet letter on her breast! The minister here made a pause; although the music still played the stately and rejoicing march to which the procession

moved. It summoned him onward,—onward to the festival!
—but here he made a pause.

Bellingham, for the last few moments, had kept an anxious eye upon him. He now left his own place in the procession, and advanced to give assistance; judging from Mr. Dimmesdale's aspect that he must otherwise inevitably fall. But there was something in the latter's expression that warned back the magistrate, although a man not readily obeying the vague intimations that pass from one spirit to another. The crowd, meanwhile, looked on with awe and wonder. This earthly faintness was, in their view, only another phase of the minister's celestial strength; nor would it have seemed a miracle too high to be wrought for one so holy, had he ascended before their eyes, waxing dimmer and brighter, and fading at last into the light of heaven!

He turned towards the scaffold, and stretched forth his arms.

"Hester," said he, "come hither! Come, my little Pearl!"

It was a ghastly look with which he regarded them; but there was something at once tender and strangely triumphant in it. The child, with the bird-like motion which was one of her characteristics, flew to him, and clasped her arms about his knees. Hester Prynne—slowly, as if impelled by inevitable fate, and against her strongest will—likewise drew near, but paused before she reached him. At this instant old Roger Chillingworth thrust himself through the crowd,—or, perhaps, so dark, disturbed, and evil was his look, he rose up out of some nether region,—to snatch back his victim from what he sought to do! Be that as it might, the old man rushed forward and caught the minister by the arm.

"Madman, hold! What is your purpose?" whispered he. "Wave back that woman! Cast off this child! All shall be well! Do not blacken your fame, and perish in dishonor! I can yet save you! Would you bring infamy on your sacred profession?"

"Ha, tempter! Methinks thou art too late!" answered the

minister, encountering his eye, fearfully, but firmly. "Thy power is not what it was! With God's help, I shall escape thee now!"

He again extended his hand to the woman of the scarlet letter.

"Hester Prynne," cried he, with a piercing earnestness, "in the name of Him, so terrible and so merciful, who gives me grace, at this last moment, to do what—for my own heavy sin and miserable agony—I withheld myself from doing seven years ago, come hither now, and twine thy strength about me! Thy strength, Hester; but let it be guided by the will which God hath granted me! This wretched and wronged old man is opposing it with all his might!—with all his own might and the fiend's! Come, Hester, come! Support me up yonder scaffold!"

The crowd was in a tumult. The men of rank and dignity, who stood more immediately around the clergyman, were so taken by surprise, and so perplexed as to the purport of what they saw,—unable to receive the explanation which most readily presented itself, or to imagine any other,—that they remained silent and inactive spectators of the judgment which Providence seemed about to work. They beheld the minister, leaning on Hester's shoulder and supported by her arm around him, approach the scaffold, and ascend its steps; while still the little hand of the sin-born child was clasped in his. Old Roger Chillingworth followed, as one intimately con-nected with the drama of guilt and sorrow in which they had all been actors, and well entitled, therefore, to be present at its closing scene.

"Hadst thou sought the whole earth over," said he, looking darkly at the clergyman, "there was no one place so secret,—no high place nor lowly place, where thou couldst have es-caped me,—save on this very scaffold!"

"Thanks be to Him who hath led me hither!" answered the minister.

Yet he trembled, and turned to Hester with an expression of doubt and anxiety in his eyes, not the less evidently betrayed, that there was a feeble smile upon his lips.

"Is not this better," murmured he, "than what we dreamed of in the forest?"

"I know not! I know not!" she hurriedly replied. "Better? Yea; so we may both die, and little Pearl die with us!"

"For thee and Pearl, be it as God shall order," said the minister; "and God is merciful! Let me now do the will which he hath made plain before my sight. For, Hester, I am a dying man. So let me make haste to take my shame upon me."

Partly supported by Hester Prynne, and holding one hand of little Pearl's, the Reverend Mr. Dimmesdale turned to the dignified and venerable rulers; to the holy ministers, who were his brethren; to the people, whose great heart was thoroughly appalled, yet overflowing with tearful sympathy, as knowing that some deep life-matter—which, if full of sin, was full of anguish and repentance likewise—was now to be laid open to them. The sun, but little past its meridian, shone down upon the clergyman, and gave a distinctness to his figure, as he stood out from all the earth to put in his plea of guilty at the bar of Eternal Justice.

"People of New England!" cried he, with a voice that rose over them, high, solemn, and majestic,—yet had always a tremor through it, and sometimes a shriek, struggling up out of a fathomless depth of remorse and woe,—"ye, that have loved me!—ye, that have deemed me holy!—behold me here, the one sinner of the world! At last!—at last!—I stand upon the spot where, seven years since, I should have stood; here, with this woman, whose arm, more than the little strength wherewith I have crept hitherward, sustains me, at this dreadful moment, from grovelling down upon my face! Lo, the scarlet letter which Hester wears! Ye have all shuddered at it! Wherever her walk hath been,—wherever, so miserably burdened, she may have hoped to find repose,—it hath cast a lurid gleam of awe and horrible repugnance roundabout her. But there stood one in the midst of you, at whose brand of sin and infamy ye have not shuddered!"

It seemed, at this point, as if the minister must leave the remainder of his secret undisclosed. But he fought back the bodily weakness,—and, still more, the faintness of heart,— that was striving for the mastery with him. He threw off all assistance, and stepped passionately forward a pace before the woman and the child.

"It was on him!" he continued, with a kind of fierceness; so determined was he to speak out the whole. "God's eye beheld it! The angels were for ever pointing at it! The Devil knew it well, and fretted it continually with the touch of his burning finger! But he hid it cunningly from men, and walked among you with the mien of a spirit, mournful, because so pure in a sinful world!—and sad, because he missed his heavenly kindred! Now, at the death-hour, he stands up before you! He bids you look again at Hester's scarlet letter! He tells you, that, with all its mysterious horror,* it is but the shadow of what he bears on his own breast, and that even this, his own red stigma, is no more than the type of what has seared his inmost heart! Stand any here that question God's judgment on a sinner? Behold! Behold a dreadful witness of it!"

With a convulsive motion he tore away the ministerial band from before his breast. It was revealed! But it were irreverent to describe that revelation. For an instant the gaze of the horror-stricken multitude was concentred on the ghastly miracle; while the minister stood with a flush of triumph in his face, as one who, in the crisis of acutest pain, had won a victory. Then, down he sank upon the scaffold! Hester partly raised him, and supported his head against her bosom. Old Roger Chillingworth knelt down beside him, with a blank, dull countenance, out of which the life seemed to have departed.

"Thou hast escaped me!" he repeated more than once. "Thou hast escaped me!"

"May God forgive thee!" said the minister. "Thou, too, hast deeply sinned!"

He withdrew his dying eyes from the old man, and fixed them on the woman and the child.

"My little Pearl," said he feebly,—and there was a sweet and gentle smile over his face, as of a spirit sinking into deep repose; nay, now that the burden was removed, it seemed almost as if he would be sportive with the child,—"dear little Pearl, wilt thou kiss me now? Thou wouldst not yonder, in the forest! But now thou wilt?"

Pearl kissed his lips. A spell was broken. The great scene of grief, in which the wild infant bore a part, had developed all her sympathies; and as her tears fell upon her father's cheek, they were the pledge that she would grow up amid human joy and sorrow, nor for ever do battle with the world, but be a woman in it. Towards her mother, too, Pearl's errand as a messenger of anguish was all fulfilled.

"Hester," said the clergyman, "farewell!"

"Shall we not meet again?" whispered she, bending her face down close to his. "Shall we not spend our immortal life together? Surely, surely, we have ransomed one another, with all this woe! Thou lookest far into eternity, with those bright dying eyes! Then tell me what thou seest?"

"Hush, Hester, hush!" said he, with tremulous solemnity. "The law we broke!—the sin here so awfully revealed!—let these alone be in thy thoughts! I fear! I fear! It may be, that, when we forgot our God,—when we violated our reverence each for the other's soul,—it was thenceforth vain to hope that we could meet hereafter, in an everlasting and pure reunion. God knows; and He is merciful! He hath proved his mercy, most of all, in my afflictions. By giving me this burning torture to bear upon my breast! By sending yonder dark and terrible old man, to keep the torture always at red-heat!

By bringing me hither, to die this death of triumphant ignominy before the people! Had either of these agonies been
wanting, I had been lost for ever! Praised be his name! His
will be done! Farewell!"

That final word came forth with the minister's expiring
breath. The multitude, silent till then, broke out in a strange,
deep voice of awe and wonder, which could not as yet find
utterance, save in this murmur that rolled so heavily after the
departed spirit.

XXIV

CONCLUSION

AFTER many days, when time sufficed for the people to arrange their thoughts in reference to the foregoing scene, there was more than one account of what had been witnessed on the scaffold.

Most of the spectators testified to having seen, on the breast of the unhappy minister, a SCARLET LETTER—the very semblance of that worn by Hester Prynne—imprinted in the flesh. As regarded its origin, there were various explanations, all of which must necessarily have been conjectural. Some affirmed that the Reverend Mr. Dimmesdale, on the very day when Hester Prynne first wore her ignominious badge, had begun a course of penance,—which he afterwards, in so many futile methods, followed out,—by inflicting a hideous torture on himself. Others contended that the stigma had not been produced until a long time subsequent, when old Roger Chillingworth, being a potent necromancer, had caused it to appear, through the agency of magic and poisonous drugs. Others, again,—and those best able to appreciate the minister's peculiar sensibility, and the wonderful operation of his spirit upon the body,—whispered their belief, that the awful symbol was the effect of the ever active tooth of remorse, gnawing from the inmost heart outwardly, and at last manifesting Heaven's dreadful judgment by the visible presence of the letter. The reader may choose among these theories. We have thrown all the light we could acquire upon the portent, and would gladly, now that it has done its office, erase its deep print out of our own brain; where long meditation has fixed it in very undesirable distinctness.

It is singular, nevertheless, that certain persons, who were spectators of the whole scene, and professed never once to have removed their eyes from the Reverend Mr. Dimmesdale, denied that there was any mark whatever on his breast, more than on a new-born infant's. Neither, by their report, had his dying words acknowledged, nor even remotely implied, any, the slightest connection, on his part, with the guilt for which Hester Prynne had so long worn the scarlet letter. According to these highly respectable witnesses, the minister, conscious that he was dying,—conscious, also, that the reverence of the multitude placed him already among saints and angels,—had desired, by yielding up his breath in the arms of that fallen woman, to express to the world how utterly nugatory is the choicest of man's own righteousness. After exhausting life in his efforts for mankind's spiritual good, he had made the manner of his death a parable, in order to impress on his admirers the mighty and mournful lesson, that, in the view of Infinite Purity, we are sinners all alike. It was to teach them, that the holiest among us has but attained so far above his fellows as to discern more clearly the Mercy which looks down, and repudiate more utterly the phantom of human merit, which would look aspiringly upward. Without disputing a truth so momentous, we must be allowed to consider this version of Mr. Dimmesdale's story as only an instance of that stubborn fidelity with which a man's friends—and especially a clergyman's—will sometimes uphold his character; when proofs, clear as the mid-day sunshine on the scarlet letter, establish him a false and sin-stained creature of the dust.

The authority which we have chiefly followed—a manuscript of old date, drawn up from the verbal testimony of individuals, some of whom had known Hester Prynne, while others had heard the tale from contemporary witnesses—fully confirms the view taken in the foregoing pages. Among many morals which press upon us from the poor minister's miserable experience, we put only this into a sentence:—"Be true! Be true! Be true! Show freely to the world, if not your worst, yet some trait whereby the worst may be inferred!"

Nothing was more remarkable than the change which took place, almost immediately after Mr. Dimmesdale's death, in the appearance and demeanour of the old man known as Roger Chillingworth. All his strength and energy—all his vital and intellectual force—seemed at once to desert him; insomuch that he positively withered up, shrivelled away, and almost vanished from mortal sight, like an uprooted weed that lies wilting in the sun. This unhappy man had made the very principle of his life to consist in the pursuit and systematic exercise of revenge; and when, by its completest triumph and consummation, that evil principle was left with no further material to support it,—when, in short, there was no more devil's work on earth for him to do, it only remained for the unhumanized mortal to betake himself whither his Master would find him tasks enough, and pay him his wages duly. But, to all these shadowy beings, so long our near acquaintances,—as well Roger Chillingworth as his companions,—we would fain be merciful. It is a curious subject of observation and inquiry, whether hatred and love be not the same thing at bottom. Each, in its utmost development, supposes a high degree of intimacy and heart-knowledge; each renders one individual dependent for the food of his affections and spiritual life upon another; each leaves the passionate lover, or the no less passionate hater, forlorn and desolate by the withdrawal of his object. Philosophically considered, therefore, the two passions seem essentially the same, except that one happens to be seen in a celestial radiance, and the other in a dusky and lurid glow. In the spiritual world, the old physician and the minister—mutual victims as they have been—may, unawares, have found their earthly stock of hatred and antipathy transmuted into golden love.

Leaving this discussion apart, we have a matter of business to communicate to the reader. At old Roger Chillingworth's decease (which took place within the year), and by his last will and testament, of which Governor Bellingham and the Reverend Mr. Wilson were executors, he bequeathed a very considerable amount of property, both here and in England, to little Pearl, the daughter of Hester Prynne.

So Pearl—the elf-child,—the demon offspring, as some people, up to that epoch, persisted in considering her—became the richest heiress of her day, in the New World. Not improbably, this circumstance wrought a very material change in the public estimation; and, had the mother and child remained here, little Pearl, at a marriageable period of life, might have mingled her wild blood with the lineage of the devoutest Puritan*among them all. But, in no long time after the physician's death, the wearer of the scarlet letter disappeared, and Pearl along with her. For many years, though a vague report would now and then find its way across the sea,—like a shapeless piece of driftwood tost ashore, with the initials of a name upon it,—yet no tidings of them unquestionably authentic were received. The story of the scarlet letter grew into a legend. Its spell, however, was still potent, and kept the scaffold awful where the poor minister had died, and likewise the cottage by the sea-shore, where Hester Prynne had dwelt. Near this latter spot, one afternoon, some children were at play, when they beheld a tall woman, in a gray robe, approach the cottage-door. In all those years it had never once been opened; but either she unlocked it, or the decaying wood and iron yielded to her hand, or she glided shadow-like through these impediments,—and, at all events, went in.

On the threshold she paused,—turned partly round,—for, perchance, the idea of entering, all alone, and all so changed, the home of so intense a former life, was more dreary and desolate than even she could bear. But her hesitation was only for an instant, though long enough to display a scarlet letter on her breast.

And Hester Prynne had returned, and taken up her long-forsaken shame. But where was little Pearl? If still alive, she must now have been in the flush and bloom of early womanhood. None knew—nor ever learned, with the fulness of perfect certainty—whether the elf-child had gone thus untimely to a maiden grave; or whether her wild, rich nature had been softened and subdued, and made capable of a woman's gentle happiness. But, through the remainder of Hester's life, there were indications that the recluse of the scarlet letter was the object of love and interest with some inhabitant of another land. Letters came, with armorial seals upon them, though of bearings unknown to English heraldry. In the cottage there were articles of comfort and luxury, such as Hester never cared to use, but which only wealth could have purchased, and affection have imagined for her. There were trifles, too, little ornaments, beautiful tokens of a continual remembrance, that must have been wrought by delicate fingers, at the impulse of a fond heart. And, once, Hester was seen embroidering a baby-garment, with such a lavish richness of golden fancy as would have raised a public tumult, had any infant, thus apparelled, been shown to our sombre-hued community.

In fine, the gossips of that day believed,—and Mr. Surveyor Pue, who made investigations a century later, believed, —and one of his recent successors in office, moreover, faithfully believes,—that Pearl was not only alive, but married, and happy, and mindful of her mother; and that she would most joyfully have entertained that sad and lonely mother at her fireside.

But there was a more real life for Hester Prynne, here, in New England, than in that unknown region where Pearl had found a home. Here had been her sin; here, her sorrow; and here was yet to be her penitence. She had returned, therefore, and resumed,—of her own free will, for not the sternest magistrate of that iron period would have imposed it,—resumed the symbol of which we have related so dark a tale. Never afterwards did it quit her bosom. But, in the lapse of the toilsome, thoughtful, and self-devoted years that made up Hester's life, the scarlet letter ceased to be a stigma which attracted the world's scorn and bitterness, and became a type of something to be sorrowed over, and looked upon with awe, yet with reverence too. And, as Hester Prynne had no selfish ends, nor lived in any measure for her own profit and enjoyment, people brought all their sorrows and perplexities, and besought her counsel, as one who had herself gone through a mighty trouble. Women, more especially,—in the continually recurring trials of wounded, wasted, wronged, misplaced, or erring and sinful passion,—or with the dreary burden of a heart unyielded, because unvalued and unsought, —came to Hester's cottage, demanding why they were so wretched, and what the remedy! Hester comforted and counselled them, as best she might. She assured them, too, of her firm belief, that, at some brighter period, when the world should have grown ripe for it, in Heaven's own time, a new truth would be revealed, in order to establish the whole relation between man and woman on a surer ground of mutual happiness. Earlier in life, Hester had vainly imagined that she herself might be the destined prophetess, but had long since recognized the impossibility that any mission of divine and mysterious truth should be confided to a woman stained with sin, bowed down with shame, or even burdened with a life-long sorrow. The angel and apostle of the coming revelation must be a woman, indeed, but lofty, pure, and beautiful; and wise, moreover, not through dusky grief, but the ethereal medium of joy; and showing how sacred love should make us happy, by the truest test of a life successful to such an end!

So said Hester Prynne, and glanced her sad eyes downward at the scarlet letter. And, after many, many years, a new grave was delved, near an old and sunken one, in that burial-ground beside which King's Chapel has since been built. It was near that old and sunken grave, yet with a space between, as if the dust of the two sleepers had no right to mingle. Yet one tombstone served for both. All around, there were monuments carved with armorial bearings; and on this simple slab of slate—as the curious investigator may still discern, and perplex himself with the purport—there appeared the semblance of an engraved escutcheon. It bore a device, a herald's wording of which might serve for a motto and brief description of our now concluded legend; so sombre is it, and relieved only by one ever-glowing point of light gloomier than the shadow:—

"On a field, sable, the letter A, gules."*

THE END.

EXPLANATORY NOTES

CE: *The Centenary Edition of the Works of Nathaniel Hawthorne*, ed, William Charvat, *et al.* (Columbus: Ohio State University Press, 1962–).

1 *community*: the community immediately around Hawthorne in 1850 was that of Salem, Massachusetts, where the 'excitement' took the form of an attack, in the *Salem Register* (a Whig newspaper), on his 'heartless, utterly inexcusable and calumnious caricature' of the old gentlemen who worked in the Custom House. *The Scarlet Letter* was published on 16 March. On 19 March the Salem *Gazette*, a Democratic paper, printed a favourable review of the book. The attack in the *Register* came on 21 March. In it, the author was also accused of a 'venomous, malignant, and unaccountable assault' on the permanent Inspector (see below, note to p. 16 for further details). The *Register* returned to the attack on 25 March, when it printed censures of the Custom-House sketch from Boston and New York papers. The relevant articles are reprinted in Frazer Clark (1970).

2 *Kindlier spirit*: given the destructiveness of his portrait of the permanent Inspector, Hawthorne's comment here is surely disingenuous.

3 *first time*: this, in fact, resulted in the essay 'The Old Manse', subtitled 'The Author Makes the Reader Acquainted with His Abode', with which Hawthorne had introduced a collection of his stories and sketches called *Mosses from an old Manse*, published in two volumes in 1846.

Clerk of this Parish: the 'Memoirs of P. P.' formed one of the 'Memoirs of Martinus Scriblerus'—satirical sketches by members of the Scriblerus Club. Formed in 1713, the club included Arbuthnot, Gay, Pope, and Swift. Attribution of individual works is problematic, though Arbuthnot's biographers do not credit him with the 'Memoir of P. P.'. The bookseller's notice stated that Gay helped with this sketch. Hawthorne would have found the Scriblerus Papers in the *Works* of Alexander Pope, in which they were included in the 1741 Warburton edition. Hawthorne withdrew all ten volumes of the 1808 edition from

265

the Salem Athenaeum in 1828 (see Kesslring, 1949). 'Memoirs of P. P.' was a satire on the self-important *Bishop Burnet's History of His Own Time*, 6 vols., 1724–53. The clerk confuses the banal with the profound, for his idea of Church reform is whipping out stray dogs. 'P. P.' shares something with Arthur Dimmesdale, however, for he has begotten a child on a woman to whom he is not married. He decides not to betray the fathers of illegitimate children in the parish because, as he says, 'I also have sinned'.

4 *behind its veil*: compare CE, x 32–3, 'The Old Manse', when the speaker 'veiled his face'.

make up my volume: when Hawthorne sent the manuscript of 'The Custom-House' and all but the last three chapters of *The Scarlet Letter* to James T. Fields (his prospective publisher) on 15 January 1850, he proposed as the title 'Old-Time Legends; together with *sketches, experimental and ideal*' (see CE, XVI, 306). Fields responded with the suggestion that the romance should be published with the autobiographical introduction but with no other tales or sketches. Parker (1985) argues that Fields' own account of the matter, in which he claimed to have persuaded Hawthorne to lengthen what began as a short story into *The Scarlet Letter* (an account first published in the *Atlantic Monthly* in February 1871), is misleading since Hawthorne already had a sense of the final length of his romance when he sent the manuscript to Fields. According to Parker, there never was a 'short version' of *The Scarlet Letter*; only the last three chapters of the book were added after the decision to publish it without other tales and sketches.

King Derby: Elias Hasket Derby (1739–99), was a merchant and shipowner whose *Grand Turk* was the first New England ship to reach Canton. The voyage began in 1785. Derby developed trade links with India and Russia as well as China. See Phillips, *Salem and the Indies* (1947).

6 *last war with England*: the 'War of 1812' was declared in June of that year. A peace treaty was signed in December 1814. General Jackson's famous victory over the British at New Orleans took place *after* the signing of the treaty.

sends adventures: it was common practice for young men starting out on a commercial career by working in shipping houses to invest some of their money in privately financed trading ventures.

protection: passport, or any form of pass that makes it possible to travel safely.

7 *receipt of custom*: an allusion to Matthew 9: 9. Jesus called Matthew to follow him when the latter was 'sitting at the receipt of custom'.

slop-sellers: clothiers. 'Slops' were articles of clothing and bedding sold to sailors on board ship.

Wapping: the ancient dockside area of London. Here used figuratively for any dockside area.

8 *Loco-foco*: the term derived from the 'locofoco' matches used to enable an 1835 meeting of New York Democrats to continue after a prankster had turned out the lamps. Originally a term of derogation applied to radical Democrats, it was later used by the Whigs to refer to (and disparage) all members of the Democratic party. Hawthorne was in fact accused of 'locofoco' activity by the Salem Whigs in a letter they sent to the Treasury Department in Washington and made public in the Boston *Atlas* on 16 June 1849. See Hoeltje (1954) and Nissenbaum (1978).

Gallows Hill: the probable site of the hangings in the Salem Witchcraft episode in 1692.

New Guinea: the part of Salem in which immigrants from Southern Europe first began to settle.

of my name: Major William Hathorne (1607–81) came to Massachusetts in 1630 and soon became an important figure in the public life of the colony. See Loggins (1951).

9 *that first ancestor*: Hawthorne's account of family here focuses entirely on the paternal line, totally ignoring the Manning family from which his mother was descended, although Elizabeth Manning Hawthorne obviously played a more important part in her son's life than did the father who died when the boy was still a child of four years. Baym (1982) sees an implied connection between Hester Prynne's harsh treatment at the hands of the Puritan Fathers and Elizabeth Manning's unsympathetic reception by the Hathornes. Since her first child (a daughter) was born only seven months after her marriage, she may well have been made to feel some disgrace by her respectable in-laws. To Baym, the biographical significance of *The Scarlet Letter* is that it is a story about a mother told by a writer who has just lost his own mother.

their histories: the Quaker history from which Hawthorne derived his information about the persecution was William Sewel's *History of the Rise, Increase, and Progress of the Christian People Called Quakers* (1722). Sewel tells of the cruelty of William Hawthorne (the usual spelling in the eighteenth as in the seventeenth century was Hathorne), who was a 'fierce persecutor' of the sect. It was his warrant that led to the brutal whipping of Ann Coleman, who nearly died under the scourge.

His son: John Hathorne (1641–1717), did not in fact serve as a trial judge when the 'witches' of Salem were brought to trial in 1692, but he did conduct the initial hearings which resulted in the commitment of many of the accused. For his career, see Loggins (1951).

10 *fiddler*: the Puritan contempt for entertainers, which extended to art and artists, was one theme of Hawthorne's story, 'The Maypole of Merry Mount' (1836).

11 *The spell survives*: as many commentators have noted, the narrator's account of the mysterious attraction and irrational pull of Salem anticipates the force that Boston exerts on Hester Prynne.

12 *Old Manse*: the Hawthornes left the Old Manse, Concord, in October 1845, having spent the first years of their marriage there.

President's commission: James K. Polk (1795–1849) was the Democratic President when Hawthorne was appointed Surveyor. The commission—dated 3 April 1846—appointed him for four years, but he was removed from office after only three.

General Miller: General James F. Miller (1776–1851), who had achieved fame in the War of 1812, had been Collector for twenty-one years when Hawthorne took office.

13 *Whigs*: the name given to the party that opposed the Democrats from the early 1830s until the formation of the Republican Party in the 1850s.

political services: this statement is disingenuous, as Nissenbaum (1978 and 1984) has shown. For details, see above, 'Introduction' p. xxxvii.

14 *Boreas*: god of the north wind.

16 *permanent Inspector*: this was William Lee, who had been appointed in 1814 and was nearly eighty years old when 'The

Custom-House' was published. Hawthorne's insult to the old man was given extra prominence when the sketch of the Inspector was given advance publication in the *Literary World*. See Turner (1980) for the identification and for details. The anger of Lee's family was so intense that one relative threatened to horsewhip Hawthorne.

19 *elder Adams*: John Adams (1735–1826), president from 1797 to 1801, was the father of John Quincy Adams (1767–1848), president from 1825 to 1829.

20 *Western territory*: General Miller had been Governor of Arkansas Territory 1819–25.

21 *Ticonderoga*: a fort at the foot of Lake Champlain, in New York State, which was captured from the French by the British in 1759 and by the Americans, under Ethan Allen and Benedict Arnold, in 1775.

22 *Chippewa or Fort Erie*: the British were defeated at the Battle of Chippewa, 5 July 1814, when the Americans crossed into Canada. The Americans subsequently occupied Fort Erie for some months before withdrawing across the border.

23 *"I'll try, Sir!"*: words traditionally supposed to have been spoken by Miller when ordered to take the British battery at Lundy's Lane, Ontario, near Niagara Falls, on 25 July 1814, in the War of 1812. In the event, Miller's 21st US Infantry Regiment did succeed in storming the battery. As Ledbetter (1987) points out, the motto 'I'll try, Sir!' was inscribed on a flag flown on the barge in which Miller travelled to Arkansas when taking up his appointment there.

24 *man of business*: this was Zachariah Burchmore (1809–94), whose friendship with Hawthorne endured until the latter's death, and who was himself politically active in Democratic party politics while working in the Custom House. He too, was dismissed from the service by the Whig administration. See Nissenbaum (1978) and Turner (1980).

25 *Brook Farm*: this was the name of an idealistic communitarian experiment, founded by George Ripley—a former Unitarian minister—in 1841 and situated at West Roxbury, nine miles from Boston. Hawthorne joined the commune in April 1841, hoping to bring Sophia there after their marriage, but he left after a few months, unconvinced that physical and mental labour could be fruitfully combined (as Ripley had hoped to demon-

strate) and inhibited in his creative writing by the demands of communal life.

Emerson's: Ralph Waldo Emerson (1803–82) had proved himself to be one of the most original minds of his generation in lectures he had given in the 1830s, and in his *Nature* (1836), which had made him the chief spokesman for the ideas associated with New England Transcendentalism. Though not a Transcendentalist, Hawthorne had expressed his admiration for Emerson's mind in 'The Old Manse' introduction to *Mosses* (1846).

Assabeth: the Assabet river joins the Sudbury River to form the Concord River in Concord town, Massachusetts. While living in Concord (1842–5) Hawthorne often went boating on it with the two friends next mentioned.

Ellery Channing: William Ellery Channing (1818–1901), a poet of some talent and little discipline, nephew of William Ellery Channing (1780–1842) the great Unitarian preacher. A friend of Thoreau's and frequent companion on his excursions, Channing later became Thoreau's biographer.

Thoreau: Henry David Thoreau (1817–62) lived in Concord for almost all his life and was influenced by Emerson's thinking from 1836 on. He was famous—locally—for his profound interest in Indian culture and Indian relics in the Concord area; an interest which was given expression in his first book *A Week on the Concord and Merrimack Rivers* (1849) and in *Walden* (1854). In his notebooks Hawthorne comments on Thoreau's uncanny knowledge of the Indian past and of nature.

Hillard's: George Stillman Hillard (1808–79) was a Boston lawyer whose literary interests combined with personal friendship to lead him to give practical help to Hawthorne. Though a Whig, Hillard used his influence in an attempt to keep his friend in office in the Salem Custom House. When Hawthorne was dismissed, Hillard collected financial contributions from other friends and acquaintances to help the impecunious writer support himself and his family. In his legal career, Hillard was a protégé of Judge Story, a leading spokesman for the conservative interpretation of the law (see Thomas, 1987). Hillard's literary activities included numerous contributions to the *North American Review*, an edition of Spenser's works, and a biography of Captain John Smith.

Longfellow's hearth-stone: Henry Wadsworth Longfellow (1807–

82) was a contemporary of Hawthorne's at Bowdoin College, Maine. In 1837 Longfellow reviewed *Twice-told Tales* enthusiastically in the prestigious *North American Review* and thus helped the hitherto obscure author to achieve a national reputation. The two writers maintained a friendship (mainly by letter) from then on. From 1843 his hearth was at Craigie House in Cambridge, Massachusetts, where he lived in grand style, while fulfilling his tasks as Professor of Modern Languages at Harvard.

Alcott: Amos Bronson Alcott (1799–1888) was perhaps the most idealistic and certainly the least practical of the Transcendentalists. He lived in Concord while Hawthorne was there, after having founded an experimental school in Boston. He then (June 1843) founded a Utopian community at Harvard Village, Massachusetts ('Fruitlands'), which collapsed in January 1844.

26 *of little moment*: Hawthorne here exaggerates his lack of literary interests while at the Custom House. He abandoned writing for only eighteen months and resumed entering his thoughts in his journals by June 1847. By December 1848, he had completed 'The Unpardonable Sin' ('Ethan Brand') and offered it to Elizabeth Peabody for her *Aesthetic Papers* (1849). When this tale proved unsuitable, he submitted the sketch 'Main-Street' which he had written between early 1848 and October 1849. See J. Donald Crowley, 'Historical Commentary', *The Snow-Image*, CE, XI, 379–81.

Burns or of Cháucer: Robert Burns (1759–96) was appointed officer in the excise at Dumfries in 1791. Geoffrey Chaucer (c. 1343–1400) was made Controller of the Customs in the Port of London in 1374.

27 *anatto*: a yellowish-red dye obtained from the pulp of the Central American annatto (or annata) tree.

28 *musty papers*: compare 'The Old Manse', where the narrator refers to another set of papers in which there is no life—the piles of old sermons and theological works amassed by a former inhabitant of the Manse, the Revd Ripley.

Billy Gray: William Gray (1750–1825) was a very successful Salem merchant who owned a whole fleet of ships. He was one of the first New England merchants to trade with India, China, and Russia. Gray became Lieutenant-Governor of Massachusetts.

Simon Forrester: Simon Forrester (1748–1823) was born in Cork. He met Captain Daniel Hathorne in Liverpool and came to Salem with him in 1767, marrying Captain Hathorne's daughter Rachel in 1776. Forrester was a successful privateer in the War of Independence and continued to prosper after it. At his death, his estate was valued at over $900,000. See Phillips, *Salem and the Indies*.

29 *flight from Boston*: when besieged by Washington in 1776, the British troops under General Howe had evacuated Boston and moved to Halifax, Nova Scotia.

Protectorate: Oliver Cromwell ruled as Lord Protector from 1653 to 1658. His son Richard was Lord Protector until 1660.

'Change: the Boston Merchant's Exchange.

Governor Shirley: William Shirley (1694–1771) was Royal Governor of Massachusetts from 1741 to 1749 and from 1753 to 1756.

30 *Jonathan Pue*: in Joseph B. Felt's *Annals of Salem* (1827) which was one of Hawthorne's major sources of information on local history, he would have read that Pue's assumption of office took place in 1752. Felt gives the date of Pue's death as 24 March 1760.

"MAIN STREET": Hawthorne's sketch 'Main-Street' had been published in Elizabeth Palmer Peabody's *Aesthetic Papers* in 1849. It was not republished with *The Scarlet Letter* in 1850, although that was clearly part of Hawthorne's original plan (see above, note to p. 4), but was included in *The Snow-Image* (1852). The sketch would have made an excellent introduction to the story of Hester Prynne.

31 *Essex Historical Society*: founded in 1821, this society merged with the Essex County Natural History Society in 1848 to form the Essex Institute. Essex County, Massachusetts, contains the town of Salem.

33 *lucubrations*: products of earnest or laboured study, hence pedantic literary compositions.

37 *veteran shipmaster*: this was Captain Stephen Burchmore, brother of Zachariah, the 'man of business'. See Turner (1980).

39 *dig gold in California*: the California gold rush had begun in 1849 with the discovery of gold at Sutter's Fort, Sacramento.

its truth: see Nissenbaum (1978; 1984) and see above Introduction, p. xxxvii.

40 *General Taylor*: Zachary Taylor (1784–1850) was elected president on the Whig party ticket in 1848 and took office in 1849.

guillotine: in a cartoon that appeared in the *Boston Post* on 11 June 1849 Hawthorne's dismissal from office was treated as a decapitation. A letter to the editor on the following day stated, apropos of Hawthorne's dismissal, that 'the head of the poet and the scholar is stricken off to gratify and reward some greedy partisan'. Turner (1980) regards these allusions in the *Post* as the source of Hawthorne's reference here. The guillotining metaphor was not used only with reference to Hawthorne. In the Democratic press the dismissal of Democrats from office when the Whig administration took over in 1849 was generally treated as revolutionary. See Reynolds (1985).

take the offices: under the American spoils system, which was often supposed to have begun in General Jackson's presidency (1829–36) but which had in fact started under Presidents Adams and Jefferson, a political party filled government civil service posts with its own supporters when it came to power. The Whig administration that took over in 1841 instituted wholesale removals of Democrats from office, but in his 1848 presidential campaign Zachary Taylor had promised that he would remain aloof from such party-political procedures if he was elected. The Salem Whigs, however, had no intention of renouncing their powers of patronage and quickly used them to unseat Democratic appointees. See Hoeltje (1954) and Nissenbaum (1984).

the first that fell!: Hawthorne was removed from office on 8 June 1849.

42 *as an enemy*: for the enmity of the Whigs, see above, note to p. 8. Hawthorne identified Charles W. Upham, minister of the First Church, Salem, as a leader of the movement to displace him.

my affair: Hawthorne's dismissal became something of a *cause célèbre*. It was given prominent coverage in newspapers beyond the boundaries of Massachusetts. His cause was taken up by William Cullen Bryant in the *New York Evening Post*. See Hoeltje (1954) and Nissenbaum (1978; 1984).

43 *Irving's Headless Horseman*: a figure in Washington Irving's story 'The Legend of Sleepy Hollow', which was included in his *Sketch-Book* (1819–20).

quitted the Old Manse: see above, note to p. 12.

45 THE TOWN-PUMP: Hawthorne's sketch 'A Rill from the Town-Pump', which gives impressions of Salem, had been published in the *New-England Magazine* in 1835 and collected in *Twice-told Tales* in 1837.

47 *Cornhill*: now Washington Street, Boston.

Isaac Johnson's lot: Isaac Johnson (1601–30) died within months of his arrival in New England, after taking part in the move from Charlestown to Shawmut, as the future Boston was then named.

King's Chapel: this was the first Episcopalian church in New England. According to Snow's *History of Boston* it was built in 1688. There could be an allusion to sectarian intolerance in the reference, since the chapel was built in the face of opposition from some Congregationalists, who argued that Episcopalianism was what they had come to Massachusetts to avoid.

fifteen or twenty years: Boston was settled in 1630, so this takes us to 1645 or 1650. However, historical allusion sets the date of the opening of the story as 1642, see above, Introduction, p. ix.

indications of age: according to Caleb Snow's *History of Boston*, a house of correction was ordered at a meeting of the General Court on 8 May 1632.

48 *wild rose-bush*: an item in the *Salem Gazette* in 1843, which contrasted the iron door of the prison with roses, may have been Hawthorne's source for his reference. See Bush (1984).

Ann Hutchinson: Ann(e) Hutchinson (1591–1643) emigrated to New England in 1634, following the Revd John Cotton when he was silenced by Archbishop Laud. While living in Alford, England, she had also admired John Wheelwright's preaching of the Covenant of Grace before he, too, was silenced and left for Massachusetts. Ann had also become interested in the doctrines of the 'familists' who preached not only the 'impeccability of all believers' but also that 'the law is fulfilled in love'. Among the familists, women could preach as commonly as men. When she began to interpret the scriptures and hold public meetings in Massachusetts, Mrs Hutchinson had an enthusiastic following in Boston, but she offended the ministers of the Church and was banished in 1638. She first moved to Rhode Island because religious dissent was tolerated there. Then, in 1642, she and her family moved to what is now Pelham Bay, New York, an area then under Dutch control. There she and all her family except one daughter were massacred by the Indians. In his sketch 'Mrs Hutchinson' (1830) Hawthorne had stressed the danger she had posed to a colony in which public safety was incompatible with religious freedom.

49 *Antinomian*: see Introduction, p. xv. The Antinomians' rejection of instutional authority has led Battis (1962) to the conclusion that they stood for the unqualified power of the individual.

Quaker: an anachronism. The first Quakers to enter Massachusetts did so in 1656. Whipping was one of the milder forms of punishment they faced. Some were hanged in 1659. Hawthorne's early story about their persecution—'The Gentle Boy'—was first published in *The Token* in 1832 and collected in *Twice-told Tales* (1837).

Mistress Hibbins: Ann Hibbins was the widow of one of the principal merchants of Boston. According to Snow's *History of Boston*, after her husband suffered losses her turbulent and quarrelsome character led her into such disfavour that she was tried for witchcraft in 1655, condemned and hanged in 1656.

50 *man-like Elizabeth*: Queen Elizabeth I reigned from 1558 to 1603.

51 *Hester Prynne*: the biblical Hester, kinswoman of Mordecai, was the consort of King Ahasuerus of Persia (486–465 BC). She used her influence to save her fellow countrymen from massacre by Haman, the Persian Grand Vizier, in the year 473. See, Book of Esther 9: 24–6. Bercovitch (1975) points out that the biblical Esther was a homiletic *exemplum* of sorrow, duty, and love, as well as a *figura* of the Virgin Mary.

Prynne: William Prynne (1600–69) was called to the bar in 1628, having attended Oriel College, Oxford, and Lincoln's Inn. Sentenced to ear-cropping, a huge fine, and imprisonment in 1634 for slander against the king and queen, Prynne continued to challenge the authority of the bishops, thus involving himself in a second trial before the court of the Star Chamber in 1637, when his sentence was even more severe. (See Introduction, pp. vii–ix.) No believer in religious toleration, he called on parliament to suppress all anti-Calvinist works and to force all the clergy to subscribe to the Synod of Dort, whose Five Points embodied the least compromising Calvinist dogma.

When his enemies had been defeated in the Civil War, Prynne proved a relentless persecutor, in particular of Archbishop Laud, whom he hounded to death. As intolerant of religious independents as he was of the episcopacy, Prynne campaigned to get parliament to crush the sectaries. When a Member of Parliament himself, he championed parliament against the army, in 1647 and 1648, and was later imprisoned for pamphleteering against the Commonwealth.

gossips: originally a 'gossip' was a person who had spiritual affinity with another and acted as a sponsor in baptism (from God-sibbe: relative in God).

52 *Scripture and the statute-book*: the relevant scripture is Leviticus 20: 10: 'If a man commits adultery with the wife of his neighbour, both the adulterer and the adulteress shall be put to death.' The death penalty for adultery was on the statute book in Massachusetts from 1641, when Nathaniel Ward drew up the 'Body of Liberties'. In his *Journal*, Governor Winthrop referred to the execution of Mary Latham and James Britton for this crime in 1644.

53 *SCARLET LETTER*: in his notebooks, in 1844 or 1845, Hawthorne had written: 'The life of a woman, who, by the old colony law, was condemned always to wear the letter A, sewed on her garments in token of having committed adultery' (CE, VIII, 254). The Old Colony was Plymouth, not Massachusetts, and—historically—this was a punishment of the 1690s, not of the 1640s. (see Boewe, 1960).

Earlier, in his story 'Endicott and the Red Cross', published in the *Salem Gazette* in 1837 and in *The Token* in 1838 before being included in *Twice-told Tales* in 1842, Hawthorne wrote of a beautiful young woman of Salem who had been condemned to wear the letter 'A' on the breast of her gown. This young offender had embroidered the letter so brilliantly that it could be taken to mean 'Admirable' rather than 'Adulteress'. The tale is set in the year 1634.

55 *scaffold*: in the Boston of 1642 a scaffold would have been used only for executions, not for public humiliation, as Reynolds (1985) points out.

56 *image of Divine Maternity*: Moers (1984) takes this allusion as evidence of Hawthorne's fascination with Roman Catholicism—an interest that links him with those aesthetes who opposed

Victorian values. For the view that Hester's association with Mary represents the 'older, richer, iconic world' to the Puritans whose logical obsession has destroyed it, see Gervais (1979). See Todd (1972) for a Jungian interpretation of Hester's significance as the Magna Mater.

57 *Western wilderness*: though the Great Migration had brought over thousands of settlers to New England in the years 1630–40, by 1642 they had made little impression on the vast wilderness that stretched to the west of their coastal towns.

58 *a Continental city*: this will be identified as Amsterdam on p. 62. Some nonconformists left England to escape the authority of the bishops in 1608 and settled at Amsterdam or Leyden before leaving Europe to set up model communities in the New World.

62 *Daniel*: much of the Book of Daniel is concerned with the prophet's powers of interpretation. It was he who interpreted the writing that appeared on the wall at the feast of Belshazzar: 'You have been weighed in the balances and found wanting' (Daniel 5: 27).

63 *The penalty thereof is death*: see above, note to p. 52. Haskins (1960) points out that this was much more severe than the punishment imposed by the English archdecanal courts for this offence. They merely imposed small fines.

64 *Governor Bellingham*: Richard Bellingham (*c.*1592–1672) left England for Massachusetts in 1634. He was first elected governor in 1641. For the scandal that kept him out of office in 1642, see Introduction, pp. x–xi. He became governor again in 1654, having been assistant in the intervening years.

65 *famous John Wilson*: John Wilson (1591–1667) emigrated to Massachusetts in 1630 and became teacher at the First Church, Boston. His function, as distinct from that of the pastor, was to expound the scriptures. In the Antinomian controversy, he championed orthodoxy and was a stern opponent of Ann Hutchinson. In his *Magnalia Christi Americana* (1702), a Puritan history of Massachusetts and one of Hawthorne's sources, Cotton Mather celebrated Wilson for his orthodoxy and for his great zeal.

66 *speech of an angel*: 'angel' is a word whose significance shifts within the tale, as does the letter 'A'. Since Dimmesdale is an unconfessed adulterer, wearing a hidden 'A' on his breast, and since he will be associated with the Black Man by Pearl, the

uncompromising truth-teller (see below, p. 187), the fact that his speech affects the Puritan congregation thus must be an ironic comment on their moral system.

67 *thou deniest to him*: Dimmesdale's exhortation to Hester is convincingly described by Moers (1984) as self-serving and Jesuitical. He invites her to do what he makes it impossible for her to do and then blames her for not doing it.

70 *Master Brackett*: Hawthorne found the name of the historical Boston gaoler in Snow's *History of Boston*. See Ryskamp (1959).

71 *sagamores*: chiefs.

alchemy: through his alchemical interests, Chillingworth will be associated with Sir Kenelm Digby (see below, note to p. 121) whose sexual relations with Lady Venetia Stanley before she became his wife were scandalous. Hawthorne had used alchemy as a way of exploring the relationship between science, the occult, and sexuality in his story 'The Birthmark', first published in *The Pioneer* in 1843 and collected in *Mosses from an Old Manse* (1846). On alchemy in *the Scarlet Letter* see Van Leer (1985).

simples: medicines composed of only one constituent, especially of one herb-plant.

72 *Lethe nor Nepenthe*: Lethe, in Greek mythology, was a river in Hades whose waters caused forgetfulness. Nepenthe (Greek *ne penthe*: no grief) was a drug of oriental origin capable of banishing grief; it is mentioned in the *Odyssey*.

Paracelsus: a pseudonym of Theophrastus von Hohenheim (1493–1541), who was an astrologer, professor of physics and surgery at Basle University, and an alchemist.

74 *bale-fire*: funeral pyre (from Old Norse *bal*: great fire).

77 *the Black Man that haunts the forest*: the Puritan association of the forest with the devil and their identification of the Indians with the children of the devil was familiar to Hawthorne from his reading of Massachusetts history.

79 *alien from the law*: the Indians, being pagans, represent values remote from those of the Antinomian Christians who challenged orthodox Puritan beliefs in the 1630s, but the common ground is indifference to the law as formulated by Church and State.

83 *rich, voluptuous, Oriental*: in early nineteenth-century American fiction an association between passion and sensuality and the

orient was commonplace. Hester Prynne is one of several exotic, beautiful women in Hawthorne's fictions who are linked to the East. See McWilliams (1984) and Rahv (1941).

84 *the brow of Cain*: Genesis 4: 15, 'And the Lord put a mark on Cain, lest any who came upon him should kill him.'

86 *the hidden sin in other hearts*: in this supposed knowledge Hester is like the young Puritan in Hawthorne's 'Young Goodman Brown'.

89 *of great price*: Matthew 13: 45–6; a merchant sells all that he has to purchase the one pearl. Scholarly interpretation of Pearl's significance in the romance is voluminous. See Garlitz (1957) for a summary of the first hundred years of exegesis. Among the more interesting recent theories is Joel Porte's (1969). He argues that Pearl comes to stand for a romantic art that is based on the truth concerning the secret human passions; in other words, she represents the work in which she appears. The diversity of interpretations surely justifies Millicent Bell (1982) in saying that Pearl is an instance of the ambiguity of signs in the romance.

91 *amenable to rules*: being illegitimate—outside the law—Pearl is obliged to be outside society. She will later be associated with the wilderness (the forest) and its wild inhabitants, both human (the Indians) and animal.

93 *incapable . . . of human sorrow*: in its naturalness and spontaneity Pearl's wildness can be interpreted positively, yet the romance leaves no doubt that such freedom as Pearl experiences is also a lack. She cannot truly be a human being until she feels sorrow, for the capacity to feel sadness is an essential characteristic of humanity. For an earlier treatment of this theme see 'The Maypole of Merry Mount' in *Twice-told Tales*.

An *imp of evil, emblem . . . of sin*: to the Puritans Pearl is a sign—she is intelligible in their system of signification, just as her mother is. Pearl is to them the child of the devil (literally an imp) and thus does not deserve human status. When we are told (p. 98) that Pearl gesticulates like a little imp, we must presume that it is Hester who thinks her so, but—though Hester doubts Pearl's humanity—to her the child is wonderful and mysterious, as well as frightening. It is to Hester, presumably, that the child's furious cries against the Puritan children sound like 'a witch's anathemas' (p. 94), but the narrative is elusive here and does not indicate clearly who is supposed to be thinking.

EXPLANATORY NOTES

94 *scourging Quakers*: another anachronism. See above, note to p. 49.

99 *demon offspring*: like the Puritan view of Pearl as an 'imp of evil', this makes Dimmesdale the devil, though the townspeople cannot be aware of any such implication in their version of Pearl's paternity.

101 *selectmen*: in seventeenth-century New England the term was used for officers elected annually to manage local affairs. In Boston, they took over the burden of town government between town meetings.

property in a pig: see Introduction, p. xiv. The modification of the legislative framework that resulted was a division into two houses in 1644; the assistants sat as a senate, while the deputies constituted an independent house from then on, where before there had been only one chamber in the assembly. Hawthorne's sources included Winthrop's *Journal*, vol. 2, pp. 64–6; 116–20, where the governor recorded his anti-democratic views and appealed to Old Testment authority against democratic forces, and Snow's *History of Boston*, which notes that Keayne was an extortioner who had been fined for selling foreign goods at exorbitant profit.

102 *endowed with life!*: compare 'emblem . . . of sin' on p. 93 above. The New England Puritan imagination makes the sinner and the fruit of the sin into signs, or emblems, of that sin, but the 'life' of both escapes the signification imposed on it.

104 *seven years' slave*: free-born Englishmen who could not afford the cost of the ocean voyage yet wished to emigrate to the New World commonly indentured themselves to the wealthy men who paid their passages. Winthrop (JHNE, I, 104) refers to one indentured servant who said he would rather be in hell than serve his master, and to another who hanged himself out of misery (JHNE, I, 175).

105 *Chronicles of England*: Holinshed's *Chronicles of England, Scotland and Ireland* (1577).

106 *Pequod war*: the Pequod tribe inhabited south-east Connecticut when the English began to settle in New England. More warlike than their neighbours the Narrangansetts, they began to attack the settlers in 1633. The conflict ended four years later when a combined force of Englishmen from the Connecticut, Massachusetts, and Plymouth colonies slaughtered the Indians—men,

280

women, and children—in their fort on the Mystic River in Connecticut. See Introduction, pp. xiv–xv.

Bacon, Coke, Noye, and Finch: Sir Francis Bacon (1561–1626) was a man of affairs as well as a philosopher and writer. He was admitted to the bar in 1582 and made attorney-general in 1613. He was a bitter rival of Sir Edward Coke (1552–1634), who was called to the bar in 1578 and won the race with Bacon for the attorney-generalship in 1593, having been speaker of the House of Commons in 1592–3. Active in the trials of Essex and Southampton in 1600, and vindictive in his treatment of Raleigh in the 1603 trial that led to Raleigh's execution, Coke resisted King James I's claims for the royal prerogative, deciding against the king's power to create laws by proclamation. As Chief justice of common pleas in 1606, he also defended the secular courts against the attacks of Archbishop Bancroft, who had the support of King James. By 1615 Coke had published ten volumes of reports on the cases he had handled. Sir William Noye or Noy (1577–1634) was called to the bar in 1602 and made attorney-general in 1631. Zealous in his prosecution of William Prynne in the Star Chamber trial in 1634, Noye put all his legal skills at the service of King Charles I, earning the hatred of the people for his writ of ship money and his soap monopoly law. Sir John Finch (1584–1660), called to the bar in 1611, was chief justice of common pleas in 1637, when Prynne was censured. He, too, supported the crown in the ship money case. See Introduction, p. vii, for Finch's role in the Prynne trial and sentencing.

107 *Reverend Mr. Blackstone*: as Hawthorne knew from Snow's *History of Boston*, Blackstone was the first Englishman to settle at Shawmut, later Boston, and thus had title to the whole peninsula. Snow describes him as an Episcopalian, but also a nonconformist who left Massachusetts to settle in Rhode Island because he did not like the rule of the 'Lord Bretheren' any more than that of the 'Lord Bishops' in England. The legend of Blackstone's riding a bull can be found in the same source.

eldritch: from 'elf', via the Early Modern English 'elrich', meaning 'weird, ghastly, eerie'.

108 *John Wilson*: see above note to p. 65.

109 *old King James's time*: James I ruled England from 1603 to 1629.

Lord of Misrule: to the Puritans, the Lord of Misrule—a mock prince whose authority or rule extended through the Christmas

holidays—was guilty of encouraging all kinds of devilry and
scabrous conduct. Hawthorne had read Puritan denunciations of
this character in Joseph Strutt's *Sports and Pastimes of the People
of England* (1801). To Bellingham, Pearl not only looks like a
child of that lord, she is a product of mis-rule—of law-
breaking—of a sinful act.

110 *her of Babylon*: Revelation 17: 3–5: 'I saw a woman sitting on a
scarlet beast which was full of blasphemous names, and it had
seven heads and ten horns. The woman was arrayed in purple
and scarlet, and bedecked with-gold and jewels and pearls,
holding in her hand a golden cup full of abominations and the
impurities of her fornication; and on her forehead was written a
name of mystery: "Babylon the great, mother of harlots and of
earth's abominations".'

112 *New England Primer*: in England the *Primer* had been a prayer
book and devotional manual for the use of the laity long before
the Reformation. The earliest known edition of the *New
England Primer*, which combined traditional hornbook material
(alphabet and syllabarium) with traditional primer material
(Lord's Prayer, Creed, Decalogue, and Catechism), came from
the press of Benjamin Harris of Boston in 1690. It used rhyming
couplets as learning aids, among them: 'In Adam's Fall/We
sinned all'. The *Primer* sold in immense quantities and was
frequently revised and reprinted.

Westminster Catechism: in 1647 the Westminster Assembly of
Divines, which was appointed by the Long Parliament in 1643,
published the Shorter and Longer Catechisms. These embodied
clear statements of Calvinist doctrine. Ratified by Parliament in
1648, the Catechisms were subsequently adopted by the
Presbyterians and Congregationalists.

wild roses: another link between Hester and Ann Hutchinson
and between Pearl and the 'wild' forces that resist the law.

depravity: the total depravity of the natural man since the Fall
was one of the Five Articles of the Synod of Dort (1618–19),
which summarized Ur-Calvinist belief. This doctrine was
reaffirmed in the Westminster Catechism.

destiny: another of the Five Articles was that the depraved soul
was destined to eternal torment unless redeemed by God's grace,
acting through the intercession of Christ.

115 *tithing-men*: the English 'tithing' was a rural division of about

ten householders and their families. By the seventeenth century, the tithing-man was a parish peace officer or petty constable. In New England the word came to mean an elected officer of a township responsible for public order.

116 *witchcraft*: Mr Wilson's remark is here unsolemn—even jocular— but the rumoured appearance of the 'actual' witch and her supposed invitation to Hester to attend a witches' sabbath indicate quite clearly that a semi-serious comment on a little girl can become deadly when applied to an ugly old woman. Pearl, too, is in danger, since her 'airy' high spirits can all-too-easily be interpreted as diabolic possession. Women, of course, were particularly vulnerable to such superstitions.

119 *materialized*: the danger that medical 'science' might lead to a degradation of the spiritual, and its subordination to the physical, came home to Hawthorne in the nineteenth-century pseudo-science of mesmerism. Alchemy was the science that seemed to Hawthorne to have confused the realms of matter and spirit in earlier times. See Van Leer (1985).

Elixir of Life: this was a theme with which Hawthorne had already dealt in his story 'Dr Heidegger's Experiment' (1837). He was to devote his last years to unsuccessful attempts to complete romances on this subject.

121 *Sir Kenelm Digby*: (1603–65) was a natural scientist (he discovered that oxygen was necessary for plant life), astrologer, alchemist, philosopher, and author whose *Private Memoirs* (published in 1827) Hawthorne had read. As Reid (1966) points out, Hawthorne drew on his knowledge of Digby's life in his story 'The Birthmark' (1843). Associating Chillingworth with Digby could be a way of signalling something disreputable about the physician. In political terms, Digby was associated with the king and opposed to the parliamentary forces.

122 *New Jerusalem*: Revelation 21: 2, 'And I saw the holy city, new Jerusalem, coming down out of heaven from God.'

123 *freedom of ideas*: though the nature of the ideas is not specified, the fact that the freedom is not available to Puritan ministers suggests that Chillingworth may be speculating about spiritual matters and that he may share the 'freedom of speculation' that would put his wife in danger if it were discovered. Arac (1985) takes Chillingworth's interest in such ideas as a sign of the general loss of conviction in Puritan values.

126 *King's Chapel*: see above, note to p. 47.

Gobelin looms: the Gobelin family made tapestry in their Paris works from the fifteenth century on. The rich and highly coloured cloths they produced were the finest in Europe.

David and Bathsheba: King David desired Bathsheba, wife of Uriah the Hittite. He seduced her and deliberately sent Uriah to his death in battle so that he could have Bathsheba. See 2 Samuel 11.

Nathan the Prophet: sent to David by the Lord, who was displeased with the king's conduct, Nathan trapped David into condemning himself by telling him a parable of a rich man's avarice. Irwin (1980) sees the tapestry as a hieroglyphic of the central action of *The Scarlet Letter*, evoking the moral doubleness of being both adulterer and denouncer of adultery. Bronstein (1987) also makes the tapestry the key to the novel, which she interprets as a parable that trapped the antebellum American reader into a position analogous to King David's.

the lore of Rabbis: in his learning Dimmesdale resembles John Cotton, the minister over whom Ann Hutchinson apparently exercised some influence before the Antinomian crisis came to a head. In that crisis, Cotton distanced himself from Ann's views. The possibility that Hawthorne intends to suggest an analogy between Dimmesdale's relationship with Hester and Cotton's with Ann is discussed by Colacurcio (1972).

127 *Sir Thomas Overbury's murder*: Overbury (1581–1613) offended Frances Howard, Countess of Essex, by opposing her marriage to his friend and patron Robert Carr, Earl of Rochester. Knowing that Frances was already cuckolding her husband Essex by having an affair with Rochester, Overbury warned the latter against marrying his own whore. In revenge, Frances plotted Overbury's death by poison. The poisoning took place while Overbury was a prisoner in the Tower of London. Frances engaged the services of Ann Turner, a loose woman of unsavoury reputation, whom she had previously employed to help win Carr's affections with magic charms. When the plot was discovered, Ann Turner and her accomplices were tried and hanged. Frances (now married to Carr) was disgraced and exiled from court. The trial revealed the corruption of court life in James I's reign. Hawthorne read the story in the *Harleian Miscellany* (1808) and the *Loseley Manuscripts*, ed. A. J. Kempe

(1835), both of which he borowed in 1849 (see Kesselring, 1949). For a detailed account of the affair, and an elaborate—if unconvincing—theory that it provides the key to *The Scarlet Letter*, see Reid (1955).

Doctor Forman: Forman (1552–1611) was a sinister quack doctor who lived in Lambeth and had contacts at court. Ann Turner applied to him for help with love potions to win Robert Carr's affections for Frances Howard and for charms to make Frances' husband Essex impotent so that she could obtain a divorce and marry Carr. At the murder trial in 1615 letters implicating Forman—who had since died—in the love plot were adduced as evidence. In the *Loseley Manuscripts*, where the sordid story is told at length, Forman is said to have been 'a reputed wizard'.

129 *Bunyan's awful door-way*: in *Pilgrim's Progress* (1678) this was a doorway that opened on a byway to hell. The shepherds told Pilgrim that hypocrites and traitors to God passed through it.

131 *Holy Writ*: the text is James 5: 16, 'Therefore confess your sins to one another . . . that you may be healed.' Dimmesdale's interpretation of it is obviously self-interested.

132 *God's glory and man's welfare*: Dimmesdale's attempt to justify his failure to confess his sin is one that could carry no conviction to a devout, seventeenth-century New England Puritan, for—as Baughman (1967) convincingly argues—public confession of sin was considered of paramount importance. Winthrop recorded fourteen such confessions, four of them for adultery. Moreover, to officiate at the communion service with so grave a sin unconfessed, as Dimmesdale must have done, would be to ensure damnation.

134 *Black Man*: this was a common appellation for the Devil in the seventeenth century. Hawthorne would have found it in Cotton Mather's account of the 1692 Salem witch trials—his *Wonders of the Invisible World* (1693)—and in his *Magnalia Christi Americana* (1702).

138 *black-letter*: a typeface characterized by heavy black letters resembling those of early printed works. Also called Gothic.

140 *magician's wand*: the earlier reference to his acquaintance with Dr Forman has indicated what sort of magic Chillingworth is likely to be capable of. Reid (1955) sees parallels between the mental torture of Dimmesdale and the physical sufferings of Overbury while he was being poisoned in the Tower.

141 *Pentecost*: see Acts 2: 1–4: 'When the day of Pentecost had come, they were all together in one place. And suddenly a sound came from heaven like the rush of a mighty wind, and it filled all the house where they were sitting. And there appeared to them tongues as of fire . . . And they were all filled with the Holy Spirit and began to speak in other tongues, as the Spirit gave them utterance.' The Christian festival occurs on the seventh Sunday after Easter. The word Pentecost derives from the Greek *pentekonta* (fifty) and was first applied to the Jewish festival that occurred on the fiftieth day after the first day of Passover.

142 *the heart's native language*: the paradoxical implication is that the heavenly Tongue of Flame is given only to those who have sinned and can thus speak in the language of (fallen) nature. For a useful discussion of the connection between sin and art in Hawthorne, see Porte (1969).

Tongue of Flame: though the narrator seems to suppose that the power to speak thus was rare among the fathers of the Puritan Church in New England, historically the New England ministers regarded this quality as essential. See Van Leer (1985).

143 *the sanctity of Enoch*: Genesis 5: 24: 'Enoch walked with God; and he was not; for God took him.' The idea here is that this patriarch was translated to heaven without tasting death because of his perfect fellowship with God.

149 *the noise of witches*: the narrator assures us that Dimmesdale's shriek was mistaken for the witches' cries, but the association has nevertheless been made and will be reinforced by the link between Dimmesdale and the Black Man when Pearl asks her question in the forest (p. 187 below).

150 *Governor Winthrop*: the governor actually died on 26 March 1649. Born in 1588, Winthrop was educated at Cambridge, England, admitted to Gray's Inn in 1613 and to the Inner Temple in 1628. He sailed to the New World on the *Arbella* in 1630, having been elected governor before the ship sailed once it had been decided to take the charter to Massachusetts. He was re-elected in 1631, 1632, and 1633. His career, as recorded in his *Journal*, provided Hawthorne with an eminent example of the fusion of civil and religious concerns. It also illustrated the resistance of the early leaders of the colony to the democratizing forces within Massachusetts. In his *Magnalia*, Cotton Mather treated Winthrop as a model magistrate and as the leader of an

enterprise analogous to that of the Israelites when they returned to their promised land. To Mather, Winthrop was the American Nehemiah. See Bercovitch (1975).

Geneva cloak: a black cloak worn by ministers of the Calvinist faith and thus associated with Geneva, Calvin's city.

158 *portent*: the actual portent (a meteor) occurred at the death of John Cotton in 1652. In his *History of Boston*, Snow refers to 'strange and alarming signs' that appeared in the heavens when Cotton died.

161 *it meant Able*: see Sanderlin (1975) for the theory that Hester's power to transform the meaning of the letter undermines the Puritan sense of the identity of symbols and beliefs.

163 *the cross on a nun's bosom*: the comparison connects with the earlier association between Hester and the Virgin Mary to suggest a critique of evangelical Victorian values, according to Moers (1984).

165 *prophetess*: Kearns (1965) notes that the term 'prophetess' was frequently applied to Margaret Fuller by her contemporaries. For Fuller's relationship to Hester, and for seventeenth-century references to Mrs Hutchinson as 'prophetess', see Introduction, pp. xvi, xxvi–xxviii.

174 *a dark necessity*: Chillingworth's 'old faith' was, of course, Calvinism. At its centre was the doctrine of predestination.

176 *deadly nightshade, dogwood, henbane*: each of these plants was associated with witchcraft; each produced a poison or narcotic which supposedly had magical powers. On the connection between poisoning and witchcraft, see below, note to p. 221.

178 *horn-book*: a single sheet of parchment inscribed with the alphabet and covered with transparent horn.

180 *appointed mission*: in hovering about the enigma, Pearl is not only questioning the meaning of the 'A' her mother wears (and thus the relationship between womanhood and sexuality) but also probing the connection between Hester's public disgrace and Arthur's private torment. According to Bloom (1986), Pearl represents an anarchic influx of power and knowledge that derives from Emersonian Orphism and Gnosticism; her credo is that of Emerson's 'Self-Reliance': ' "What have I to do with the sacredness of traditions, if I live wholly from within?" '

183 *Apostle Eliot*: John Eliot (1604–90) was educated at Cambridge,

England, and emigrated to Massachusetts in 1630. He became teacher (minister) at Roxbury, where he stayed for sixty years. In 1646 he began to preach to the Indians at Dorchester Mills. The following year he preached to them in their own tongue at Nonantum. In 1661 he completed a translation of the New Testament into the Indian language, and in 1663 of the Old Testament. He also settled towns for 'praying Indians'. In Mather's *Magnalia*, Eliot is credited with raising 'those [Indians] that had hitherto lived like wild beasts in the wilderness' to 'the elevation of our holy religion'. Hawthorne had included an article on Eliot in the *American Magazine of Useful and Entertaining Knowledge* in 1836, when he was its editor.

the primeval forest: throughout *The Scarlet Letter* the forest represents pre-Christian values and is, consequently, beyond the pale of Puritan law. Hester's association with the wilderness therefore links her with paganism. Compare 'Main-Street', where the first inhabitants of the area that will become Salem are Indians, and the first to be visualized by the narrator is 'a majestic and queenly woman . . . the great Squaw Sachem'.

184 *the scrofula*: a tuberculosis condition of the lymphatic glands, characterized by enlargement, suppurating abscesses, and cheeselike degeneration.

185 *carries a book*: in his *Magnalia*, Mather wrote of a book which devotees were required to sign 'in token of their consenting to be listed in the Service of the Devil'.

his mark: Hester's outburst implicates Dimmesdale, and even associates him with the Black Man.

193 *why should we not speak it?*: the implied reticence—a reluctance to probe the depths of Hester's feelings—can only be understood in terms of the pretence of narratorial disengagement or aloofness from the tale that is being told.

197 *a magnetic power*: magnetism was a new and partly mysterious phenomenon in the 1840s. It served as a metaphor for occult and irrational psychic forces. Compare Captain Ahab's magnetic power over his crew in Melville's *Moby-Dick*, ch. 36, 'The Quarter-Deck'.

iron men: Hester Prynne is here using a metaphor that Hawthorne had used more than once to convey his sense of the inflexible (and ruthless) creed of his forefathers. In 'Main-Street'

he referred to the faith itself as an 'iron' cage. In 'The Maypole of
Merry Mount' John Endicott—the archetypal Puritan—is
described as an iron man.

198 *apostle of the red men*: Dimmesdale is returning from a vist to the
Apostle Eliot when Hester intercepts him. The narrator makes it
clear that Dimmesdale is not an independent spirit—he needs
the support of institutional faith—but the passionate side to his
character (as noted by Chillingworth) links him with the Indians,
who were considered incapable of any restraint by white
Americans of Hawthorne's generation. Compare p. 199, for the
association of Hester's intellectual freedom with the wild Indian.

201 *lawless region*: the words imply that the 'natural' is lawless and—
unless redeemed—depraved. Here, then, the narrator speaks as a
Puritan who sees all Nature as fallen. Elsewhere, the narrator
hints at the possibility that there are laws of the spirit that lie
beyond the bounds (and the comprehension) of the orthodox
Puritans.

205 *dryad*: wood nymph.

206 *dear old England*: on the opposition between Old and New
England in *The Scarlet Letter*, see Newberry (1987) who treats
this as a major thematic antithesis in the romance.

207 *living hieroglyphic*: though 'hieroglyphic' may mean 'any symbol
or character having an obscure or hidden meaning', the word's
etymology, from the Greek *hieros* (sacred) and *glyphein* (to
carve), links Pearl with holy mysteries. On the significance of
hieroglyphics as a theme in Hawthorne, and in American
Romantic writing generally, see Irwin (1980).

209 *her bright wild eyes*: like the animal analogues, the phrase
associates Pearl with the pre-Christian wilderness.

215 *hesitate to reveal*: another example of delicacy on the part of the
narrator (compare p. 193) and another invitation to respond to
him as a character in his own story.

Election Sermon: a sermon preached on the inauguration day of
the governor, who was chosen annually by the freemen of
Massachusetts. Election Day was determined by Easter, coming
fifty days after it. On the significance of the parallel between
Election Day and Whitsuntide for Hawthorne, see Newberry
(1977). The tradition lasted until 1684, when the charter of the
colony was suspended by Charles II. By the terms of the new

charter, issued in 1691, the governor was appointed by the monarch.

216 *thrust himself through*: see Crews (1966) for the sexual resonances of the verbs used to describe Dimmesdale's action.

220 *buckramed*: buckram was a coarse fabric sized with glue used for stiffening garments and used in bookbinding.

221 *Ann Turner*: this infamous woman was instrumental in the murder of Overbury in 1613 (see above, note to p. 127). She used a former servant of hers, one Richard Weston, to provide poison, which was fed to Overbury while he was in the Tower. Commenting on the Overbury affair in his *Letters on Demonology and Witchcraft* (1830), Sir Walter Scott noted the association between sorcery and poisoners and commented that the word for witch in Hebrew (chasaph) could also mean poison. Ann invented and made fashionable the use of a yellow starch on cuffs and ruffs. When condemned for the murder of Overbury she was sentenced by Lord Chief Justice Coke to be hanged in her own yellow ruff and cuffs.

224 *New Jerusalem*: Newberry (1987) takes Chillingworth's comment to refer to the fifth monarchy promised in the Book of Daniel (and thus to the Civil War in England and the overthrow of King Charles I) rather than to the Puritan kingdom in the New World.

the King's own mint-mark: another reminder, according to Newberry, of the revolutionary times in which Hester's story is set and of the fate of the king in 1649.

229 *a new man*: in fact, the governor elected in 1649 was not 'new'; he was John Endicott, who had served as governor before. See below, note to p. 238.

231 *Merry Andrew*: as Hawthorne knew from reading Strutt's *Sports and Pastimes of the People of England* (1801), in the England of James II this figure was an inseparable companion of the mountebank (a seller of medicines) and acted as his fool, engaging him in dialogue.

232 *wampum-belts*: *wampum* beads, or shells, were made into belts or necklaces and used as currency by the North American Indians.

234 *galliard*: a quick and lively dance in triple time.

237 *a corporate existence*: in Snow's *History of Boston*, the story of the oldest military establishment in the United States is told. This

was formed in 1638 as the 'Military Company of Massachusetts' and recognized by the General Court as the 'Artillery Company' in 1657. Its full title in Hawthorne's day was the Ancient and Honorable Artillery Company of Massachusetts.

College of Arms: founded in England in 1460, this institution was responsible for the records of the titles of those entitled to armorial bearings.

Knights Templars: an order of crusaders that flourished in the thirteenth century but was suppressed by the Pope in 1312. Newberry (1977) finds irony in the analogy, since the knights were described as cruel and usurping in Sir Walter Scott's *Ivanhoe* (1820), where Hawthorne had read of them. The association would, then, hardly be flattering to Puritan military men.

morions: helmets.

238 *Bradstreet*: Simon Bradstreet (1603–97) sailed to New England in 1630. He was secretary to the colony for the next six years and played a prominent role in the life of Massachusetts thereafter, being elected Commissioner (with William Hathorne) of the New England federation in 1644 and Governor of Massachusetts from 1679 to 1686 and from 1689 to 1692. In contrast to Dudley and Endicott, he was a moderate in matters of belief.

Endicott: John Endicott, or Endecott (c. 1589–1665) was one of the six 'religious persons' who bought a patent for territory on the Bay from the Plymouth Council in 1628. He was named among the incorporators when the charter was granted in 1629. Endicott sailed to Massachusetts in 1628 and settled at Naumkeag (later named Salem), serving as governor until Winthrop arrived in 1630 and again in 1644, 1649, 1651–3, and 1655–64. Hawthorne's ambivalent attitude to this stern and bigoted, yet dedicated, Puritan can be seen in his 'Mrs Hutchinson' (1830), 'The Maypole of Merry Mount' (1836), and 'Endicott and the Red Cross' (1837).

Dudley: Thomas Dudley (1576–1653) sailed to Massachusetts on the *Arbella* in 1630. He was elected governor in 1634, 1640, 1645, and 1650. More severe in his rule than Governor Winthrop, he clashed with the latter on some issues, but was equally opposed to the spread of democratic government.

Increase Mather: Increase Mather (1639–1723) was one of the most distinguished of the early New England Puritan ministers,

both as a scholar and as a man of affairs. He became teacher of the
Second Church, Boston, in 1664, and had published more than
twenty-five books by 1683. Two years later became President of
Harvard College, and remained in office until 1701. In 1688 he
was sent to the English court to petition on behalf of the
Congregational churches in Massachusetts and in 1689 negotiated
a new charter for the colony. Though primarily a theologian, he
maintained a lifelong open-mindedness towards science. In the
1692 witchcraft trials at Salem, he was one of the ministers who
warned against reliance on spectral evidence. He was the father
of Cotton Mather, author of the *Magnalia*.

241 *stomacher*: an ornamental covering for the chest worn by women
under the lacing of the bodice.

powwow: medicine man, sorcerer, or priest.

242 *Prince of the Air*: compare Ephesians 2: 2, 'prince of the power of
the air, the spirit that is now at work in the sons of disobedience'.

245 *tempest*: compare *Macbeth*, I. iii. 24–5: 'Though his bark cannot
be lost,/Yet it shall be tempest-tost'. The witch plans to use her
power over the winds to revenge a supposed insult.

249 *glorious destiny*: as M. D. Bell (1971) points out, Dimmesdale's
sermon flatters its New England audience in ways that make it
closer to the speeches of nineteenth-century orators (such as
Webster) than to the sermons preached by seventeenth-century
Puritans. See Introduction, p. xli.

255 *mysterious horror*: Young (1984, p. 144) argues that the only
mystery about the scarlet letter 'A' is why Hawthorne (and hence
his fictional New Englanders) found it revolting. In Young's
view, the 'diabolical letter—sin, crime—lies just underneath the
surface'; it is the *incest* (imagined or actual) with his beautiful
sister Elizabeth that had haunted Hawthorne's unmarried years
of seclusion in Salem. When Nathaniel discovered that ancestors
of his on the Manning side of the family had been accused,
convicted, and punished on charges of incest in 1681, he must
have experienced a shock of recognition, according to Young.
Hawthorne, we know, was familiar with the Quarterly Court
Records of what became Essex County, Massachusetts. The
Records contained the evidence of family servants on which the
culprits were convicted of incest. They also contained the
punishment, which included—for the Manning sisters—sitting

EXPLANATORY NOTES

in public with a paper on their heads stating 'This is for whorish carriage with my naturall Brother'.

261 *devoutest Puritan*: a clear indication, surely, that the narrator believes that money can conquer the superstitious belief in witchcraft. We might note, in contrast, that Mistress Hibbins was condemned as a witch after the loss of her wealth.

264 GULES: red, as used in heraldry. As Brant (1958–9) points out, a possible source is Marvell's 'The Unfortunate Lover' which ends:

> though
> Forced to live in Storms and Wars:
> Yet dying leaves a Perfume here,
> And Musick within every Ear:
> And he in Story only rules,
> In a Field *Sable*, a Lover *Gules*.

293

SELECT BIBLIOGRAPHY

AL   American Literature
AQ   American Quarterly
ATQ   American Transcendental Quarterly
ESQ   Emerson Society Quarterly
EIHC   Essex Institute Historical Collections
ELH   Journal of English Literary History
NHR   Nathaniel Hawthorne Review
NEQ   New England Quarterly
NCF   Nineteenth-Century Fiction
PMLA   Publications of the Modern Language Association
TSLL   Texas Studies in Literature and Language

Abel, Darrel, 'Hawthorne's Hester', *College English*, 13 (1952), 303–9.
——, 'Hawthorne's Dimmesdale: Fugitive from Wrath', NCF, 11 (1956), 81–105.
——, 'Giving Lustre to Gray Shadows: Hawthorne's Potent Art', AL, 41 (1970), 373–88.
Arac, Jonathan, 'Reading the Letter', *Diacritics*, 9 (1979), 42–52.
——, 'The Politics of *The Scarlet Letter*' in *Ideology and Classic American Literature*, ed. Jehlen (1986).
Barnett, Louise, K., 'Speech and Society in *The Scarlet Letter*', ESQ, 29 (1983), 16–24.
Battis, Emery, *Saints and Sectaries: Anne Hutchinson and the Antinomian Controversy in the Massachusetts Bay Colony* (Chapel Hill, 1962).
Baughman, Ernest W., 'Public Confession and *The Scarlet Letter*', NEQ, 40 (1967), 532–50.
Bayer, John G., 'Narrative Techniques and the Oral Tradition in *The Scarlet Letter*', AL, 52 (1980), 250–64.
Baym, Nina, 'Passion and Authority in *The Scarlet Letter*', NEQ, 43 (1970), 209–30.
——, 'Hawthorne's Women: The Tyranny of Social Myths', *Centennial Review*, 15 (1971), 250–72.
——, 'The Romantic *Malgré Lui*: Hawthorne in the Custom House', ESQ, 19 (1973), 14–25.
——, *The Shape of Hawthorne's Career* (Ithaca and London, 1976).

294

——, 'Hawthorne and His Mother', AL, 54 (1982), 1–27.

——, 'Thwarted Nature: Hawthorne as Feminist', in Fleischman, (ed.), *American Novelists Revisited* (1982).

——, Introduction to *The Scarlet Letter* ed. Baym (Harmondsworth, 1983).

Bell, Michael D., *Hawthorne and the Historical Romance of New England* (Princeton, N.J., 1971).

——, *The Development of American Romance: The Sacrifice of Relation* (Chicago and London, 1980).

——, 'Arts of Deception: Hawthorne, "Romance" and *The Scarlet Letter*', in *New Essays*, ed. Colacurcio (1985).

Bell, Millicent, *Hawthorne's View of the Artist* (New York, 1962).

——, 'The Obliquity of Signs: *The Scarlet Letter*', *Massachusetts Review*, 23 (1982), 9–26.

Bensick, Carol, 'His Folly, Her Weakness: Demystified Adultery in *The Scarlet Letter*', in *New Essays*, ed. Colacurcio (1985).

Bercovitch, Sacvan, *The Puritan Origins of the American Self* (New Haven and London, 1975).

Bloom, Harold, Introduction to *Nathaniel Hawthorne's 'The Scarlet Letter'*, ed. Bloom (New York, New Haven and Philadelphia, 1986).

Boewe, Charles and Murphy, M. G., 'Hester Prynne in History', AL, 32 (1960–1), 202–4.

Brant, Robert L., 'Hawthorne and Marvell', AL, 30 (1958–9), 366.

Breen, T. H., *The Character of the Good Ruler: A Study of Puritan Political Ideas in New England, 1630–1730* (New Haven, 1970).

Brodhead, Richard H., *Hawthorne, Melville and the Novel* (Chicago, 1976).

——, *The School of Hawthorne* (New York and Oxford, 1986).

Bronstein, Zelda, 'The Parabolic Ploys of *The Scarlet Letter*', AQ, 39, No. 2 (1987), 193–210.

Brumm, Ursula, *American Thought and Religious Typology* (New Brunswick, 1970).

——, 'Hawthorne's "The Custom-House" and the Problem of Point of View in His Fiction', *Anglia*, 93 (1975), 391–412.

Bryson, Norman, 'Hawthorne's Illegible Letter' in *Nathaniel Hawthorne's 'The Scarlet Letter'*, ed. Bloom (1986).

Bush, Sargent, Jr., 'Hester's Prison Rose: An English Antecedent in the Salem *Gazette*', NEQ, 57 (19874), 255–63.

Capper, Charles, 'Margaret Fuller as Cultural Reformer: the Conversations in Boston', AQ, 39 (1987), 509–28.

Carpenter, Frederic I., 'Scarlet A Minus', *College English*, 5 (1944), 173–80.

Charvat, William, Introduction to *The Scarlet Letter*, Centenary Edition of the *Works of Nathaniel Hawthorne*, vol 1 (Ohio State University Press, 1962).

Clark, C. E. Frazer, Jr., 'Posthumous Papers of a Decapitated Surveyor: *The Scarlet Letter* in the Salem Press', *Studies in The Novel*, 2 (1970), 395–419.

Cohen, B. Bernard (ed.), *The Recognition of Nathaniel Hawthorne. Selected Criticism Since 1828* (Ann Arbor, Michigan, 1969).

Colacurcio, Michael J., 'Footsteps of Ann Hutchinson: The Context of *The Scarlet Letter*', ELH, 39 (1972), 459–94.

——, 'Introduction: The Spirit and the Sign', *New Essays on 'The Scarlet Letter'*, ed. M. J. Colacurcio (Cambridge, 1985).

——, ' "The Woman's Own Choice": Sex, Metaphor, and the Puritan "Sources" of *The Scarlet Letter*', in *New Essays* (1985).

Cottom, Daniel, 'Hawthorne versus Hester: The Ghostly Dialectic of Romance in *The Scarlet Letter*', TSLL, 24 (1982), 47–67.

Cox, James M., '*The Scarlet Letter*: Through The Old Manse and the Custom House', *Virginia Quarterly Review*, 51 (1975), 432–47.

Crews, Frederick C., *The Sins of the Fathers: Hawthorne's Psychological Themes* (New York, 1966).

Cronin, Morton, 'Hawthorne on Romantic Love and the Status of Women', PMLA, 69 (1954), 89–98.

Crowley, J. Donald (ed.), *Hawthorne: The Critical Heritage* (London, 1970).

Davidson, Edward H., 'The Question of History in *The Scarlet Letter*', ESQ, 25 (1961), 2–3.

——, 'Dimmesdale's Fall', NEQ, 36 (1963), 358–70 (rptd in *Twentieth-Century Interpretations*, ed. Gerber, 1968).

Desalvo, Louise, *Nathaniel Hawthorne* (Brighton, Sussex, 1987).

Derrick, Scott, 'Prometheus Ashamed: *The Scarlet Letter* and the Masculinity of Art', in *Nathaniel Hawthorne's 'The Scarlet Letter'*, ed. Bloom (1986).

Doubleday, Neal Frank, 'Hawthorne's Hester and Feminism', PMLA, 54 (1939), 825–8.

Eakin, Paul J., 'Hawthorne's Imagination and the Structure of "The Custom-House" ', AL, 43 (1971–2), 346–58.

Eisinger, Chester, 'Pearl and the Puritan Heritage', *College English*, 12 (1951), 323–9.

Erlich, Gloria C., *Family Themes and Hawthorne's Fiction: The Tenacious Web* (New Brunswick, N.J., 1984).

Faber, Eli, 'Puritan Criminals: the Economic, Social, and Intellectual Background to Crime in Seventeenth-century Massachusetts', *Perspectives in American History*, 11 (1977–8), 84–144.

Feidelson, Charles Jr., '*The Scarlet Letter*', in *Hawthorne Centenary Essays*, ed. Pearce (1964).

Felt, Joseph B., *The Annals of Salem from its First Settlement* (Salem, Mass, 1827).

Fleischmann, Fritz (ed.), *American Novelists Revisited: Essays in Femininist Criticism* (Boston, 1982).

Foster, Dennis, 'The Embroidered Sin: Confessional Evasion in *The Scarlet Letter*', *Criticism*, 25 (1983), 141–63.

Foucault, Michel, *Discipline and Punish. The Birth of the Prison*, tr. A. Sheridan (London, 1977).

—— , 'What is an Author?' in *Textual Strategies. Perspectives in Post-Structuralist Criticism*, ed. J. V. Harari (Ithaca, N.Y., 1979).

Franzosa, John, ' "The Custom-House", *The Scarlet Letter* and Hawthorne's Separation from Salem', ESQ, 24 (1978), 57–71.

Freed, Richard C., 'Hawthorne's Reflexive Imagination: *The Scarlet Letter* as Compositional Allegory', ATQ, 56 (1985), 31–54.

Fryer, Judith, *The Faces of Eve: Women in the Nineteenth-century American Novel* (New York, 1976).

Fuller, Margaret, 'The Great Lawsuit: Man *versus* Men: Woman *versus* Women', *Dial*, IV (1843), 1–47.

—— , *Woman in the Nineteenth Century* (1845; rptd New York, 1971).

Garlitz, Barbara, 'Pearl: 1850–1955', PMLA, 72 (1957), 689–99.

Gerber, John C., 'Form and Content in *The Scarlet Letter*, NEQ, 17 (1944), 25–55.

—— (ed.), *Twentieth-Century Interpretations of 'The Scarlet Letter'* (Englewood Cliffs, N.J., 1968).

Gervais, Ronald, J., 'A Papist Among the Puritans: Icon and Logos in *The Scarlet Letter*', ESQ, 25, No. 1 (1979), 11–16.

Greenwood, Douglas, 'The Heraldic Device in *The Scarlet Letter*: Hawthorne's Symbolical Use of the Past', AL, 46 (1974), 207–10.

Gross, Seymour L., ' "Solitude, and Love, and Anguish": The Tragic Design of *The Scarlet Letter*', *CLA Journal*, 3 (1960) 154–65.

Hansen, Elaine T., 'Ambiguity and the Narrator in the *The Scarlet Letter*', *Journal of Narrative Technique*, 5, No. 3 (1975), 147–63.

Hart, John E., '*The Scarlet Letter*—One Hundred Years After', NEQ, 23 (1950), 381–95.

Haskins, George Lee, *Law and Authority in Early Massachusetts: A Study in Tradition and Design* (New York, 1960).

Hawthorne, Julian, *Nathaniel Hawthorne and His Wife* (2 vols., Boston, 1884).

Herzog, Kristin, *Women, Ethnics, and Exotics. Images of Power in Mid-Nineteenth-Century American Fiction* (Knoxville, 1983).

Hildreth, Richard, *History of the United States of America from the Discovery of the Continent to the Organization of Government under the Federal Constitution, 1497–1789, Vol. 1, 1497–1688* (New York, 1849).

Hill, Christopher, *Century of Revolution* (London, 1961, 1964).

Hoeltje, Hubert H., 'The Writing of *The Scarlet Letter*', NEQ, 27 (1954), 326–46.

——, *Inward Sky. The Mind and Heart of Nathaniel Hawthorne* (Durham, N.C. 1962).

Horwitz, Morton J., *The Transformation of American Law, 1780–1860* (Cambridge, Mass., 1977).

Irwin, John T., *American Hieroglyphics. The Symbol of the Egyptian Hieroglyphics in the American Renaissance* (New Haven and London, 1980).

Isani, Mukhtar Ali, 'Hawthorne and the Branding of William Prynne', NEQ, 45 (1972), 182–95.

Jehlen, Myra, *American Incarnation: The Individual, the Nation and the Continent* (Cambridge, Mass., 1986).

Jehlen, M., and Bercovitch S. (eds.), *Ideology and Classic American Literature* (Cambridge, Mass., 1986).

Johnson, Edward, *Wonder-Working Providence of Sion's Saviour, 1628–1651*, ed. J. Franklin James (New York, 1959).

Kaul, A. N. (ed.), *Hawthorne: A Collection of Critical Essays* (Englewood, Cliffs, NJ, 1966).

Kearns, Francis E., 'Margaret Fuller as a Model for Hester Prynne', *Jahrbuch fur Amerikastudien*, 10 (1965), 191–7.

Kesselring, Marion L., *Hawthorne's Reading: 1828–1850* (New York, 1949).

Kibbey, Ann, *The Interpretation of Material Shapes in Puritanism. A Study of Rhetoric, Prejudice, and Violence* (Cambridge, Mass., 1986).

Lamartine, Alphonse Marie Louis de, *History of the Girondists*, tr. H. T. Ryde (3 vols., London, 1847).

Lang, Amy Schrager, *Prophetic Woman, Anne Hutchinson and the Problem of Dissent in the Literature of New England* (Berkeley, Los Angeles and London, 1987).

Ledbetter, Carl Jr., 'General James Miller: Hawthorne's Hero as Territorial Governor of Arkansas', NHR, 13, No. 1 (Spring 1987), 9–12.

Lee, A. Robert, ' "Like a Dream Behind Me". Hawthorne's "The Custom-House" and *The Scarlet Letter*', in *Nathaniel Hawthorne: New Critical Essays*, ed. Lee (London and Totowa, N.J., 1982).

—— (ed.), *The Nineteenth-century American Short Story* (London and Totowa, N.J., 1985).

Leverenz, David, 'Mrs Hawthorne's Headache: Reading *The Scarlet Letter*', NCF, 37 (1982–3), 552–75.

Levin, Harry, Introduction to *The Scarlet Letter*, ed. Levin (Boston, 1960).

Loggins, Vernon, *The Hawthornes: The Story of Seven Generations of an American Family* (New York, 1951; 1968).

McCall, Dan, 'The Design of Hawthorne's Custom-House', NCF, 21 (1967), 349–58.

McElroy, John H., 'The Conventionality of *The Scarlet Letter*', in *Melville and Hawthorne in the Berkshires: A Symposium*, ed. Murray (1968).

McNamara, Anne M., ' "The Character of Flame": The Function of Pearl in *The Scarlet Letter*', AL, 27 (1956), 537–53.

McShane, Frank, 'The House of the Dead: Hawthorne's Custom House and *The Scarlet Letter*', NEQ, 35 (1962), 93–101.

McWilliams, John P. Jr., *Hawthorne, Melville, and the American Character: A Looking-Glass Business* (Cambridge, 1984).

Male, Roy R., *Hawthorne's Tragic Vision* (Austin, Texas, 1957).

——, 'Hawthorne's Literal Figures', in *Ruined Eden of the Present*, ed. Thompson (1981).

Manierre, William R., 'The Role of Sympathy in *The Scarlet Letter*', TSLL, 13 (1971), 497–507.

Martin, Terence, *Nathaniel Hawthorne* (New York, 1965).

——, 'Dimmesdale's Ultimate Sermon', *Arizona Quarterly*, 27 (1971), 230–40.

Mizruchi, Susan L., *The Power of Historical Knowledge: Narrating the Past in Hawthorne, James and Dreiser* (Princeton, 1988).

Moers, Ellen, '*The Scarlet Letter*: A Political Reading', *Prospects*, 9 (1984), 49–70.

Murray, Henry A. (ed.), *Melville and Hawthorne in the Berkshires: A Symposium* (Kent, Ohio, 1968).

Newberry, Frederick, 'Tradition and Disinheritance in *The Scarlet Letter*', ESQ, 23, No. 1 (1977), 1–26.

——, *Hawthorne's Divided Loyalties: England and America in His Works* (Rutherford, N.J., London and Toronto, 1987).

Nissenbaum, Stephen, 'The Firing of Nathaniel Hawthorne', EIHC, 114 (1978), 57–86.

——, Introduction to *The Scarlet Letter and Selected Writings*, ed. Nissenbaum (New York, 1984).

Parker, Hershel, 'The Germ Theory of *The Scarlet Letter*', NHR, 11, No. 1 (Spring 1985), 11–13.

Pattison, Joseph C., 'Point of View in Hawthorne', PMLA, 82 (1967), 363–9.

Pearce, Roy H. (ed.), *Hawthorne Centenary Essays* (Columbus, Ohio, 1964).

Phillips, James Duncan, *Salem and the Indies: The Story of the Great Commercial Era of the City* (Cambridge, Mass., 1947).

Porte, Joel, *The Romance in America: Studies in Cooper, Poe, Hawthorne, Melville and James* (Middletown, Conn., 1969).

Ragussis, Michael, 'Family Discourse and Fiction in *The Scarlet Letter*', ELH, 49 (1982), 863–88.

Rahv, Philip, 'The Dark Lady of Salem', *Partisan Review*, 8 (1941), 362–81.

Reid, Alfred S., *The Yellow Ruff and the Scarlet Letter: a Source of Hawthorne's Novel* (Gainesville, Florida, 1955).

—— (ed.), *Sir Thomas Overbury's Vision (1616) by Richard Niccols and Other English Sources of Nathaniel Hawthorne's "The Scarlet Letter"* (Gainesville, Florida, 1957).

——, 'Hawthorne's Humanism: "The Birthmark" and Sir Kenelm Digby', AL, 38 (1966), 337–51.

Reynolds, Larry J., '*The Scarlet Letter* and Revolutions Abroad', AL, 57 (1985), 44–67.

——, *European Revolutions and the American Literary Renaissance* (Cambridge, 1988).

Rowe, Joyce, A., *Equivocal Endings in Classic American Novels* (Cambridge, 1988).

Ryskamp, Charles, 'The New England Sources of *The Scarlet Letter*', AL, 31 (1959), 257–72.

Said, Edward W., *Beginnings: Intention and Method* (Baltimore and London, 1975).

Sandeen, Ernest, '*The Scarlet Letter* as a Love Story', PMLA, 77 (1962), 425–35.

Sanderlin, Reed, 'Hawthorne's *Scarlet Letter*: A Study of the Meaning of Meaning', *Southern Humanities Review*, 9 (1975), 145–57.

Schneider, Herbert W., *The Puritan Mind* (Ann Arbor, Michigan, 1930, 1958).

Smith, Allan G. L., *Eve Tempted. Writing and Sexuality in Hawthorne's Fiction* (London and Totowa, N.J., 1983).

——, 'The Elaborated Sign of *The Scarlet Letter*, ATQ, NS 1, No. 1 (1987), 69–82.

Snow, Caleb, H., *History of Boston* (Boston, 1824, 1828).

Stoever, William B., 'A *Faire and Easie Way to Heaven*': *Covenant Theology and Antinomianism in Early Massachusetts* (Middletown, Conn., 1978).

Stouck, David, 'The Surveyor of the Custom-House: A Narrator for *The Scarlet Letter*', *Centennial Review*, 15 (1971), 309–29.

Sundquist, Eric J., *Home as Found: Authority and Genealogy in Nineteenth-century American Literature* (Baltimore, 1979).

Swann, Charles, 'Hester and the Second Coming: a Note on the Conclusion to *The Scarlet Letter*', *Journal of American Studies*, 21, No. 2 (1987), 264–8.

Thomas, Brook, *Cross-examinations of Law and Literature: Cooper, Hawthorne, Stowe and Melville* (Cambridge, 1987).

Thompson, G. W., and Lokke, Virgil L. (eds.), *Ruined Eden of the Present: Hawthorne, Melville and Poe* (West Lafayette, Indiana, 1981).

Timms, David, 'Authorship and Authoritarianism in Hawthorne's Tales', in Lee (ed.), *The Nineteenth-century American Short Story* (1985).

Todd, Robert E., 'The Magna Mater Archetype in *The Scarlet Letter*', NEQ, 45 (1972), 421–9.

Turner, Arlin, *Nathaniel Hawthorne: a Biography* (New York, 1980).
—— (ed.), *The Merrill Studies in 'The Scarlet Letter'* (Columbus, Ohio, 1970).

Van Deusen, Marshall, 'Narrative Tone in "The Custom-House" and *The Scarlet Letter*', NCF, 21 (1966), 61–71.

Van Leer, David, 'Hester's Labyrinth: Transcendental Rhetoric in Puritan Boston', in *New Essays*, ed. Colacurcio (1985).

Walsh, Thomas F., 'Dimmesdale's Election Sermon', ESQ, OS 44 (1966), 64–6.

Walter, James, 'The Letter and the Spirit in Hawthorne's Allegory of American Experience', ESQ, 32, No. 1 (1986), 36–54.

Warren, Austin, Introduction to *The Scarlet Letter* (New York, 1947; revised and reprinted, 1963).
——, '*The Scarlet Letter*: A Literary Exercise in Moral Theology', *Southern Review*, NS 1 (1965), 22-45.

Wentersdorf, Karl P., 'The Element of Witchcraft in *The Scarlet Letter*', *Folklore*, 83 (Summer 1972), 132–53.

West, Harry C., 'Hawthorne's Editorial Pose', AL, 44 (1972), 208–21.

SELECT BIBLIOGRAPHY

Whelan, Robert E. Jr., 'Hester Prynne's Little Pearl: Sacred and Profane Love', AL, 39 (1968), 488–505.

Willett, Maurita, 'The Letter A, Gules, and the Black Bubble', in *Melville and Hawthorne in the Berkshires*, ed. Murray (1968).

Young, Philip, *Hawthorne's Secret: an Un-Told Tale* (Boston, 1984).

Ziff, Larzer, 'The Ethical Dimension of "The Custom House" ', *Modern Language Notes*, 73 (1958), 338–44.

——, 'The Artist and Puritanism' in *Hawthorne Centenary Essays*, ed. Pearce (1964).

——, 'The Elaborated Sign of *The Scarlet Letter*, ATQ, NS 1, No. 1 (1987), 69–82.

Snow, Caleb, H., *History of Boston* (Boston, 1824, 1828).

Stoever, William B., *'A Faire and Easie Way to Heaven': Covenant Theology and Antinomianism in Early Massachusetts* (Middletown, Conn., 1978).

Stouck, David, 'The Surveyor of the Custom-House: A Narrator for *The Scarlet Letter*', *Centennial Review*, 15 (1971), 309–29.

Sundquist, Eric J., *Home as Found: Authority and Genealogy in Nineteenth-century American Literature* (Baltimore, 1979).

Swann, Charles, 'Hester and the Second Coming: a Note on the Conclusion to *The Scarlet Letter*', *Journal of American Studies*, 21, No. 2 (1987), 264–8.

Thomas, Brook, *Cross-examinations of Law and Literature: Cooper, Hawthorne, Stowe and Melville* (Cambridge, 1987).

Thompson, G. W., and Lokke, Virgil L. (eds.), *Ruined Eden of the Present: Hawthorne, Melville and Poe* (West Lafayette, Indiana, 1981).

Timms, David, 'Authorship and Authoritarianism in Hawthorne's Tales', in Lee (ed.), *The Nineteenth-century American Short Story* (1985).

Todd, Robert E., 'The Magna Mater Archetype in *The Scarlet Letter*', NEQ, 45 (1972), 421–9.

Turner, Arlin, *Nathaniel Hawthorne: a Biography* (New York, 1980).

—— (ed.), *The Merrill Studies in 'The Scarlet Letter'* (Columbus, Ohio, 1970).

Van Deusen, Marshall, 'Narrative Tone in "The Custom-House" and *The Scarlet Letter*', NCF, 21 (1966), 61–71.

Van Leer, David, 'Hester's Labyrinth: Transcendental Rhetoric in Puritan Boston', in *New Essays*, ed. Colacurcio (1985).

Walsh, Thomas F., 'Dimmesdale's Election Sermon', ESQ, OS 44 (1966), 64–6.

Walter, James, 'The Letter and the Spirit in Hawthorne's Allegory of American Experience', ESQ, 32, No. 1 (1986), 36–54.

Warren, Austin, Introduction to *The Scarlet Letter* (New York, 1947; revised and reprinted, 1963).

——, *'The Scarlet Letter*: A Literary Exercise in Moral Theology', *Southern Review*, NS 1 (1965), 22-45.

Wentersdorf, Karl P., 'The Element of Witchcraft in *The Scarlet Letter*', *Folklore*, 83 (Summer 1972), 132–53.

West, Harry C., 'Hawthorne's Editorial Pose', AL, 44 (1972), 208–21.

SELECT BIBLIOGRAPHY

Whelan, Robert E. Jr., 'Hester Prynne's Little Pearl: Sacred and Profane Love', AL, 39 (1968), 488–505.

Willett, Maurita, 'The Letter A, Gules, and the Black Bubble', in *Melville and Hawthorne in the Berkshires*, ed. Murray (1968).

Young, Philip, *Hawthorne's Secret: an Un-Told Tale* (Boston, 1984).

Ziff, Larzer, 'The Ethical Dimension of "The Custom House" ', *Modern Language Notes*, 73 (1958), 338–44.

——, 'The Artist and Puritanism' in *Hawthorne Centenary Essays*, ed. Pearce (1964).